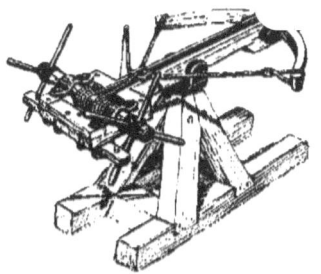

The Queen's Return

A Hidden Shaman Novel

Gary Wedlund

Loconeal Publishing
Amherst, OH

The Queen's Return

A Hidden Shaman Novel

Copyright © 2013 by Gary Wedlund
Cover Art © 2014 mizueyes777
Edited by Barbara Taft Verducci

Loconeal Publishing can bring authors to your live event. Loconeal books may be ordered through booksellers or by contacting:
www.loconeal.com
216-772-8380

Published by Loconeal Publishing, LLC
Printed in the United States of America

First Loconeal Publishing edition: 2014

ISBN 978-1-940466-04-0 (Paperback)

Hidden Shaman

The Shaman Within
Search for the Queen
The Queen's Return

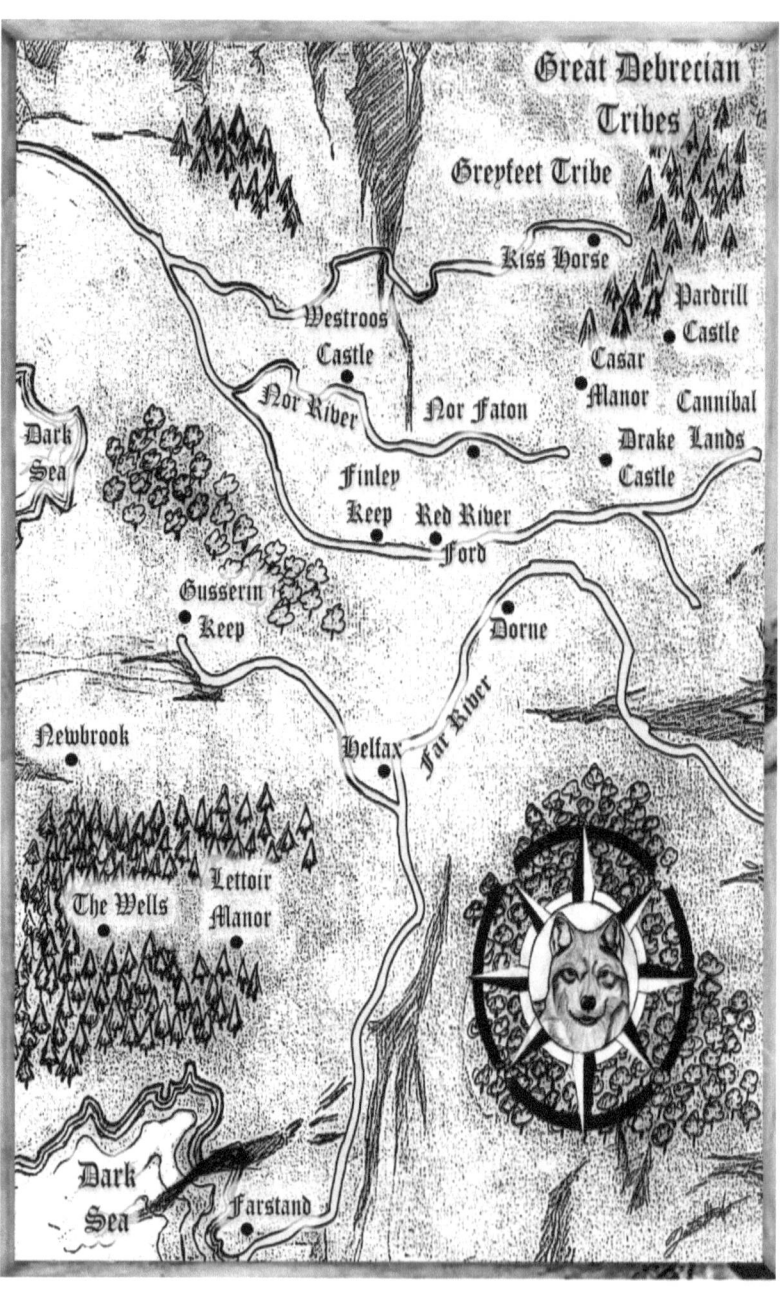

Great Debrecian
Tribes

Greyfeet Tribe

Kiss Horse

Westroos
Castle

Nor River

Nor Faton

Pardrill
Castle

Casar
Manor

Cannibal

Drake Lands
Castle

Dark
Sea

Finley
Keep

Red River
Ford

Gusserin
Keep

Dorne

Newbrook

Helfax

Far River

The Wells

Lettoir
Manor

Dark
Sea

Farstand

Table of Contents

Chapter One

I woke to a burlap bag smothering my head. The world had become rotten onions, blindness and chill buckets of rain. Every breath seemed a drowning. I'd even peed my britches, though the continual shower killed the warmth.

The wagon lumbered into every ditch and over every rock on earth. The driver couldn't have possibly been trying to avoid anything short of a tree. I could only thank him for the wet cloth under me. He apparently didn't want the goods beaten entirely to death before he delivered them to their next hell.

There was no slack in the knots holding my hands behind, only more rope binding my wrists to the small of my back. This seemed trivial compared to sucking in the next lungful of wet air, which came better when I aimed my lips toward where the bag was loosely tied near my neck.

After one of my coughing spells, the wagon rattles and axle squeaks ended. I barely discerned the clink of tack buckles. A horse whinnied, as if bucking. I tried to speak to the animal by using the talent for such in my head, but his wee mind was preoccupied with the early spring weather.

The rain came on heavy, smacking across leaves and puddles in a blur. Bandages muffled my ears as I strained for details beyond the roar.

A person climbed into the wagon, which earned him a kick from my two bound legs. He groaned but stepped right back in, only this time with several others who made the tailgate sag under their weight. I cringed, awaiting the boot that seemed certain to meet my ribs. Over the years, few were unfamiliar with the delightful experience of breaking.

A hand clutched the fabric near my chest. After a while, it withdrew without any of the expected groping. The hand came back and this time I felt it around my neck. It too didn't seem interested in taking advantage of the fact that I cherished my virginity. The hand left me in peace after only a feel, seemingly in regards to my health.

Several muffled voices sounded distressed, but that was all I gathered because of the stuffing over my ears. Everyone left the wagon, and the journey resumed, only this time with another blanket over my neck. The blanket became wet and as cold as everything else, not even allowing my neck the temporary dry respite. The wagon moved faster, finding all the rest of the ruts and rocks in the world that it had previously missed. My body jumped around the boards so violently that I considered using the boost to help me bounce over the sidewalls.

I imagined the anxiety of those on horses around me. Having captured the shaman warlord who'd murdered the duke, they undoubtedly were unsettled to learn I was catching my death of lung illness. Alive, they could present me and let my bewitched mouth serve as witness to my identity. My death left room for doubt.

Well, I couldn't fault them much for their overly cautious sack and bindings either, for indeed I'd become known as a fairly decent curse hag, and I was also keen with knots.

Perhaps they thought it possible for me to suck their souls out of their bodies with a long glance from the pond-shade eyes under my witch-flamed locks. I didn't think I could, but then again I'd never tried and became sorely tempted to see if such an idea was possible, should they ever remove the sack that was killing me one misty breath at a time.

I hoped they were taking me directly to the King of Farstand. The Baron of Helfax wasn't apt to hang or torch or even quarter me nicely, given I'd burned his city to the ground and stolen his baby daughter only a month back. By contrast, I'd only killed King Falstaff's brother.

Not that the baron had any use for a daughter. But then again, like any possession of a man living in Farstand, its value increased astrologically the moment it was removed from his control.

The wagon stopped, interrupting my thoughts, which was good because my head ached from the floorboards' beating.

Several came in and groped each arm and leg. They gently lifted, and with unexpected good order, reminding me of the time the Goddess had found it humorous to levitate me in front of the White Shirts, my most hated enemies.

I closed my useless eyes and prayed for her to see my thoughts and hear my words. I said through bound and cracked lips, "Lift me up, my Goddess, so I may float above the clouds and escape both the cold rain and my captors."

The Goddess's voice came as a whispering giggle, but in my condition it seemed louder than most other times.

I started to rise. Four pairs of hands raked, grasping to hold me down. Soon they struggled from below, apparently finding it hard to hold on at all. That's when I felt a new rope around my ankles. Other ropes joined the first one, even as the last of the hands fell below me, out of reach.

I floated like an upright statue, but I didn't sense rising very far, for the ropes soon pulled mightily. No doubt they'd tied the other ends to their horses, or perhaps even to the wagon.

As they reeled me in, the Goddess laughed in earnest. The gods are full of humor, seemingly always at my expense. I should have been choking out a laugh as well, given the preposterous nature of my attempted escape. To be sure, I was lucky nobody had shot me with an arrow as I'd floated about.

When they had me back in their grips, I reconsidered escaping. There seemed something to this yet. "Tis the Goddess's will," I said.

Some of the hands on my arms and legs trembled then; more-so, I felt, upon hearing my muffled words. It struck me that they were as afraid of this enterprise as I; and here I laid, ill and at their mercy.

There came no sound of porch planks before they carried me into a room. The rain and wind stilled. A smell of wood-smoke pressed enough to sense through the onions, as did the lesser patter of rain beating on a thatched roof.

They stood me upright. Hands fussed at my wet clothing. I could barely steady myself, for my illness had taken me beyond good control.

.

When the rags proved difficult to unravel, the cold backs of steel knives met my flesh, cutting the cloth away instead of unbinding my ropes. Soon I knelt on my knees from weakness; that well before they whittled me down to only the onion sack.

Judging from rustling sounds, I surmised that the peasants were collecting a few goods before hurrying through the door and into the cold, rainy night.

Just as that settled, the fire in the fireplace grew in intensity, a good feeling, though by then I sagged over my knees. My stomach churned. I fought the urge to retch into the sack covering my face.

Someone came from behind and sat me in a chair. I expected to be bound to it, but they left me there naked while some unknown preparations were made. This took time, so I sat in silence, trying as best I could to control my coughing and to listen for signs of what I was up against.

After a time, they helped me into a halved barrel. The water around my ankles felt warmer than expected. Several hands steadied me while others scrubbed my body with soap. Some fingers were rough while others were surprisingly gentle.

When every part had been touched by these strangers, they hurried me out of the barrel and dried my body with a cloth. I fell onto a soft cot, face down. New ropes spun around my wrists. The old ones were removed. My wrists felt no longer bound together, but had been given leeway with two feet of slack, the length of which remained behind, though I imagined it easy to slip the rope in front, given some inattention from my captors.

They untied my feet and a blanket settled above. Nothing could be more cruel. Such comfort wasn't in keeping with the notion of torment, which I'd come to think of as a thing to cherish while in bondage and in need of ample motivation for an escape.

Since I remained close to the floor, I counted the footfalls, estimating no less than a half dozen enemy. One by one, they left the room, told by the lessening of footfalls and the opening and closing of the outside door.

Then there remained only one person with me, and that one's feet fell light on the flooring. I considered the odds of overpowering such a tiny guard, even though I remained blind and ill and slightly bound. That last part I took up promptly: I eased the rope down as low as I could get it, seemingly as part of rolling over on my cot, and in the process, slipped each foot through so the rope came just that quickly to my front.

I twisted a knot in the middle of the roping. The blanket wiggled over me, mostly hiding my new weapon. It seemed best to wait until my prey grew close enough to whip or garrote. Then I'd be about the business of figuring out how to slip past the rest of the men who'd left their prisoner so poorly attended.

When the person came close, I felt hands on the ropes at my neck, untying the cursed sack. All the better. I coiled, tense as a bow string.

After the sack was lifted away, the inrush of air sent my lungs into a long spell of coughing that weakened me even further. That delay allowed my vision to focus. There stood a peasant. I wasn't beyond killing a peasant, should the chore prove necessary, but I wasn't willing to do so without more consideration than I'd first planned.

Instead, I stared at her. She must have thought my big eyes pathetic, for her hand came down with a cloth and washed away much of the onion oil coating my burning head. The woman even hugged me to her bosom. She took the same rag and dipped it into a bowl of warm water. She cleaned my hair as best she could without a proper soaking.

Long ago I'd learned I had one inescapable flaw. I couldn't kill kindness, and was often put at awe by the rare and beautiful magic of it. It was as if she was the charmer, and I the snake. I thought, perhaps she isn't with my captors at all, but is simply the woman who lives in the cottage, left to tend me while the others ravage the neighbors? In such a case, we are both captives. *I might do better to treat her as an ally and probe her for information?*

"Who—" I started to ask, but was quickly overcome by more coughing, this time leaving myself with too little air to continue with the enquiry.

"Ya be still now. We have healin' to do, now they've come near to killed ya," the woman said.

She was a middling-aged lady of nearly two score. Her hair was brown and long, as were her eyes, brown and drooping long like an old hunting dog, filled with thoughts long settled. Her hair was combed, but otherwise unadorned. The dress she wore felt like thick wool. It was also dark brown and fell all the way to her ankles.

She arose. Her hem had been soaked almost to the knees. Over by the fireplace hung a coat of groundhog furs and a broad travel hat, both still dripping. No, not the house's peasant, she was part of the party who'd captured me.

Such observations took a great deal more time than normal as a result of the spinning world. By the time I'd fully thought these things out, the woman pressed a small bowl of tea to my lips.

I was hesitant to drink, remembering that the last memory before waking had been the sipping of tea around a table in a boarding room not far from Sir Lacellor's castle. We'd spent most of that day in negotiations with the rebel lord.

How long ago was that? I guessed it had been two days, judging from the late hour. My mind felt numb and body full of cramps.

The green tea tasted of bitter walnuts, just like most poisons. If they'd wanted me dead, though, none of this bother would have mattered, so I drank it until the tiny fish at the bottom of the bowl touched my lips.

Taking the bowl back, the woman plucked the fish out and squeezed off the last of its bloody oil before tossing the fish into the fire and refilling my bowl. She told me to have another.

I hesitated, knowing the bloodied tea wasn't likely to stay down, but the woman said, "Black walnuts and fish oil, you're tastin'; that salty li'l fish be my clan's secret for wet lungs. Jarred right outa the big sea. Never known a fish ta drown, even in all that water, though I hear they sometimes jump right onto the land, making themselves a gift, spite of no talent for our air. Took Little Man Jaren all of two seasons ta go all that way for some special things. Drink, girl, lest ya offend his offering and his spirit draws afoul."

I'd also used black walnuts in green tea, but had never given thought to how good fish were at surviving wet lungs, so I managed as many sips as I could, though the coughs and illness prevented me from finishing.

I whispered, "You're a witch, aren't you."

"Yes. These came and took me two weeks past. They said, 'Give us the best with the spells,' but instead I come. My daughter cannot be spared from the babes, so t'was me who stood up."

I braced myself for a long wait, for it is always useless to kill a person of peace. I said, "Well then, you are as much their prisoner as I."

She answered, "I suppose, though they be seein' some special thing in ya' ta' go to this trouble. Me, I do duty and be done with this here. My duty be no easier by way ya' saying so much and not resting as the Goddess wills ya'. All the teas and oils in the world, doing no good for a cantankerous woman."

I rested back, as bid, but whispered, "They'll be killing you too . . . soon as they're done with you. Soon as they find a good pole . . . to spit and burn you on . . . or a drowning pit to do the testing. Or, even a tree . . . that says hanging all over . . . the way one . . . of its big long limbs looks just right."

She answered, "It be a fever speakin', child. Lay back and no more words afightin'." The wet rag was laid across my forehead, cooling me, for I'd shook off the chill and was now nothing more than a limp body of heat.

The woman kept dipping the rag in the water, cooling my head and singing to me. The words were in an old tongue, older than I'd ever learned, which was old indeed. I only recognized parts of a few sayings and not enough to know what she meant other than the words had spells woven within. None were as strong as the spells the Goddess had taught me, but the woman was unrelenting.

Her song sent me into waking dreams so deep that even with others walking around in the room and with my eyes wide open, I was disinclined to see them as more than shadows, or even to stir from the work of healing. Odd how there'd been others in the room and my mind had not been able to focus on any details.

* * * * *

As my thoughts emerged from slumber, so too did my lungs from the sickness. I took a deep breath, finding I could do so without too much difficulty.

A plume of steam blew out of a teapot that hung over the fire. The steam whistled away, unattended, because the witch who'd mended me so well was over by the door propping an axe up against the handle. The door shook from someone on the outside kicking at it.

I cleared my throat.

She spoke first: "Shush, child. Be on back to ya' sleepin'. This be none of your concern." She rammed her shoulder against the door with all of her might and set a latch that had only been half engaged.

Of course, everything was my concern. "Who are you keeping out?" The words were mere scrapes.

"Just a loony girl. She come inta camp and is all trouble. Somehow they no tie her up and lower 'er in a dry well or give 'er some poppy, like I figure fitting for a whirlwind up ta' trouble," the woman said.

Staggering over, I sat down at the base of the door and lent my weight. It didn't seem I could go wrong by befriending the good witch. After all, she'd nearly healed me and was the only friend I had at the moment. As far as I was concerned, keeping everyone out was a good idea. Given another night of rest, I'd undoubtedly find a weapon among the cabin's rubble (the axe tempted) and maybe even enough strength to fight both of us out of our fix.

It was then that I noticed I no longer had any ropes binding me at all. The witch had put a short gown over my body. Even my smell was decent, mostly mint leaf.

Whoever was out there banging on the door was strong, and strangely lacking in grunts, given the amount of energy going into the chore. Surely it wasn't my captors, for I remembered they'd been many, and I didn't think the door strong enough to outlast more than two or three good sized men. Finally, the door stopped shaking. I sat low enough to the floor to hear the person on the other side of the door step back. That person sat down hard with a rustle of clothing and leather.

After the ruckus settled a while, I asked the witch, "What happened to the men who brought me here?"

"Ain't no such," she answered, clearly trying to put me at ease. Then she felt my head and looked into the pupils of my eyes like they were telling stories. "You seem to have fit up nice, child." Done with looking, she pulled me up and walked me back to the bed. I let her; best they think me a cripple, instead of mostly healed. The Goddess's hand was always upon me, and thus my healings were often quite sudden, as were the depths of my ills.

That ploy worked nicely because after giving me some soup and tea, the woman went to sleep on a cot she dragged by the door. I had the impression it was the first sleep the old woman had managed since we'd gotten there. As soon as she leaned back, her breathing slowed and she slept too deeply even for snoring.

I owed the witch a good deal, but on the other hand, I couldn't much pay her back as a captive, so I decided I had to get away if I was to be of any use to anyone.

It was just starting to brighten up outside, I noticed through the smoky glass window that was good for no more than a wee touch of light. Such wasn't the best light for avoiding my enemy, but I couldn't be choosy, so I bundled a bag of food and clothing, and stuffed my bare feet into my stiff but dry boots, only lacing the bottom few hooks.

Best yet, a knife, not good for much more than poking potatoes, sat by the fireplace. I stuck it between my teeth then climbed up into the thatch bracing.

I didn't have much strength. Once up there, I dangled by my legs with my tunic dropped well over my head, but the pause allowed my head to stop rolling the room around. Every so often my dizziness cleared enough to let me muscle up and swipe a few of the thatch bindings in two. Then I just poked myself up between some roof braces and into the thatch. I wiggled outside, looking at the sun wink at me through the tree limbs that came right up to the back side of the cottage.

Some of the little buds had already sprouted into yellow leaves. It was like a new day in all sorts of ways. Birds chirped out love songs to one another, filling me with joy. Some of them noticed me and raced out of the close trees in a swarm, startling me as much as I'd startled them.

My satchel came through, and then the rest of me. I stayed low so nobody close to the cottage could look up and see. I wormed my way across the roof some, stopping to rest in places because of the strain of the climb. There was a gap in the trees out back and I was surprised to see several other cottages blowing smoke into the sweet morning air. All the streams of smoke carried a smell of breakfast. Three cottages in back accounted for something of a small hamlet of their own, with gardens, chicken houses and at least one pigpen.

Out a little beyond the last house, several strings of horses were corralled by roping around a few trees, done the way a company of professional scouts might do it. There were several of these corrals because of the many horses. I counted three score animals, far more than I'd expected. They were no plow ponies either, but strong mounts made for long running, which made sense because sixty horses were too many for even a whole city full of rich farmers. Most small villages were good for only one or two, if any.

There were guards out there as well; a tiny plume of smoke told me that. Fire is a luxury for any soldier put to guarding horses. They weren't afraid of any enemy apt to surround them in the night.

Taking a peek over the cottage ridge filled in the rest of the story. There, in the grassy circle around which the main hamlet sat, a full score of tents were set up. The tents were not tall, but low and big enough for three or four. They were of a strange design, mostly circular. Off to the side were several more horses, fully saddled and sufficient to put a good squad onto mounts in a matter of seconds.

A fire pit was shared by every three or four tents. Women sat at several. Almost as soon as I realized they were Debrecians, I also saw one of the horses was my own black stallion. There, just beside the stallion stood Ella, the horse I'd gifted to my sister, Batya. My stomach flopped, instantly relieved that I'd not become the captive of the vile King of Farstand, but I was also wary of the way the Debrecians had chosen to make their introduction. They were not happy with me.

Right on the heels of recognizing the horses, a tapping came from a tree behind me. I startled and looked up to nearly the top of a big pine where there appeared a Debrecian scout sitting on some sticks wedged between a few stout limbs. She wore several branches of leaves on her body, as well. I'd missed her entirely while scouting the back of the house. She didn't have any weapons, other than a staff, but she smiled down at me and used the staff to tap steadily on the trunk. The signal filled me with dread, causing my stomach to drop.

When I looked back over to the tents, every one of the women by the fires glared right up at me. Worse, the tents were emptying their Debrecian warriors. In half a minute, the whole yard buzzed full of them, some clothed, and others in the process, even as they walked in my direction or ran to surround the cottage where I perched like a pigeon.

Coming over closer to the edge, I found my mute bodyguard, Angel, standing before the doorway. She was the only person on the ground who wasn't looking up. Instead, she faced the oncoming crowd. Two long knives were fisted in her hands. Ah yes, the crazy woman—how had I not managed to guess who had been beating down the door?

There were two courses of action. I could run, leap off the back of the cottage, and chase down one of the horses while on two broken legs. On the other hand, I could see what could be made of the inevitable confrontation without embarrassing myself with an act of cowardly futility. I didn't think it possible to run more than a couple strides without running out of breath anyway, so there really weren't two choices.

At the moment, I was most concerned for Angel. She seemed apt to get herself killed defending me, even if I was on a horse running away and even if she had to jump onto the pointy ends of sixty Debrecian short swords in order to get her knives within range of someone she didn't like. Probably every Debrecian warrior alive had more skill than Angel, but there is a certain hidden value to lunacy.

"Hold on, Angel. These are my sisters."

She startled when she found me up on the roof. I dropped my boots over the edge and, once sufficiently lower by hanging from my hands, fell to the ground. My bodyguard helped me up while my feet still buzzed from the impact. Then she went right back to standing in front of me so nobody could come too close.

Three of them were silly enough to wander within a dozen feet of her knives. One had her sword out, and it was she who said, "You are our prisoner! No escape! Go back in!"

She obviously was a blunt person, probably with a great number of skills, none of them diplomatic. The way she talked to me from the other side of my bodyguard felt unhealthy though, so I put my hand on Angel's shoulder and stepped a little closer.

The Debrecian leader was a tall woman, perhaps ten years older than me, blonde and blue of eyes, mirroring the look of nearly half the women around her. Every last one of them was fair by Farstand standards. In fact, I'd never seen so much paleness, only colored by years lived under the sun. Five coins dangled from her necklace, a sign of a woman either of great power or great responsibility.

"I'm sorry, but I've been stowed up in the cabin a mite longer than I'm used to. Thought I'd try for a walk. Perhaps you'd like to accompany me?"

"You will go into the house, breeder. The witch will tend you until I say we go!" the tall woman answered.

Such warriors were unlikely to listen to me, for I leaned half on my bodyguard's shoulder from weakness. I stepped up another step and said, "I may be half dead on my feet, girl, but there's an end to how much of an insult I'll bear. Lend me a sword and we'll both find out who's the breeder among us!"

That's when the second woman stepped up and clamped a hand on the other's arm. She was a person I knew. The peg on her leg looked new though. Discounting my mother, the Queen, and the crone who'd been my teacher (also a great Debrecian warlord and like my mother, dead except for within my soul), this woman was the first Debrecian woman I'd ever met. The meeting had been mostly just me meeting her, for we'd been in a dark prison where I'd cut her festering leg off and dragged her to a horse. I had the night eyes of a wolf, and so she'd not seen my face up close, though I knew hers as healed from a mighty grimace.

"Murder is not honorable, Kirsta," the one-legged woman said. "Remember our talk when we agreed to stop the carelessness and let the witch tend her illness. If you kill this breeder, the council will not smile upon it. We will have failed our mission." She turned her eyes toward the tall Debrecian, Kirsta, who snorted in reply, as if it had been she who'd been insulted.

The third woman didn't step forward, but instead held closer to the army of women behind the taller two. Batya said in a voice still young, "Kirsta, either Angel or I will kill you if she is harmed. But that is not likely. My Queen is a shaman warlord, the first among us in a fight and close to the Goddess."

"Now you tempt me to slay the imposter and displease my council. Be quiet, small girl. I have listened to enough and have twice commanded you to silence." Kirsta had actually turned her face while saying those rude things to my sister. I couldn't imagine a more dangerous thing, for Batya had grown into a mighty warrior in only half a year, surely blessed in war by the Goddess herself. As well, nobody sane ever turned their face from me or my bodyguard, Angel, in the heat of a disagreement.

I had to take charge, or I'd lose Kirsta before I knew her worth. "Nobody will fight. Instead, I will peacefully accompany you to our council, though I had hoped to finish my treaty with Sir Lacellor before this mission. As to that, I would thank you to send word back to the great lord and to my people there, so they will not be troubled by my sudden disappearance. Now that we have relieved our concerns, I hope you will settle down and make this more pleasant."

"Silence! Your words have no bite in my ears. I have paid witness to your lies!" Kirsta spat on the ground in front of me. "Queen!" Her sneer roused agreement among most of the women behind her.

"Did you not see the levitation?" My sister asked.

"The work of Sho. She serves the man God. I saw her in his army."

"Not true," my sister said. "We both fought the forces of Farstand. Her heart is with us and the Goddess."

"You are little. One more word and I shall take your tongue!" Kirsta said. Others came up close to Batya, as if threatening that her tongue could be taken without a fight.

I said, "Will you take the tongue of the Queen's warlord before her Queen has even spoken to her council? Who are you to do such a thing?"

"She is a child, and you are an imposter!"

"And, you would test one who has twice been tested by the Goddess?" I asked. "It is you who are the child. Should I ask her, the Goddess will send you back to the womb just to prove it. Yet, I shall not tempt the Goddess with such a small favor. Do not tempt my sister either. Let her come sit with me instead."

"I know her kin. She's not your sister, breeding woman."

"We share an ancestral soul." I shook my head. "How does one share a soul and not be a sister?"

The woman without a leg intervened. "Swear on your sister's life that you shall come with us peacefully."

"Though I took your leg and you may hate me for it, I saw your honor even in the darkness of the pit, my child. I ask: Do you not already owe me a life?"

She shook and stilled, but then she composed herself enough to say, "It was not you. That was a smaller woman."

Still, in her eyes I saw she didn't believe her own words. "Such doesn't matter. All that matters is that I saw both a curious woman worth saving and a woman with honor who was among the first who inspired me to grow." After a pause, I added, "I have already sworn to come in peace. A queen needs not swear on the lives of her friends, for I've already sent far too many of them to their graves."

The woman with one good leg replied, "Then you will rest with your sister while we make ready."

Surprisingly, even the contrite Kirsta heeded her words. And, though I could have used two days of leisure, we mounted after one day's rest and were on the move.

Chapter Two

Here was a woman of fifteen, three years younger than I, a good marrying age. Already she commanded my borderland army of South Women. She stood no taller than my chin, and though a great archer, was not nearly my equal with a sword. I'd known her only a short time; we'd been raised in different lands, and she'd been sent to spy on me. Still, I loved her like a sister, almost from the moment I'd seen her.

She rode my first horse, a gift I'd given her after she'd stolen it and after having known her for only a few days. The sword she carried into battle was my own, a rare and magical gift that my soul had given her while I laid on my funeral bed. As to my soul, she'd taken that as well—or at least the angry one that had invaded me upon the death of my teacher.

When I looked at her as we rode north, drawing closer to the Debrecian tribes, I saw plainly on her face that it had been she who'd slipped the drug in my ale on the night of my capture.

We didn't speak of it. I knew this for the best. The guilt that clearly gnawed at her was doing far more than any scolding I was likely to impart. After all, harsh words go only as far as the ears. Guilt races around in the stomach, courses through a person's veins, and even alters the beating of a heart.

Batya would give her life for me; more now than ever.

I heard what she thought: All of my people and the council of my tribe over here—over there my Queen and sister.

They would have lied to her, saying no harm could possibly come to me. They would have said a queen's place was with her tribe, even though it was clear most of them did not imagine it even remotely possible that I was that person. Yes, Batya was young, and she would learn from this, but not by the lashing of my tongue; rather, by the witness of this trial we shared.

And, of course, the guilt which was best left festering—until I saw fit to lift it with rebuke.

As proof of her guilt, there was Angel. She was still both present and alive. I couldn't imagine strangers taking me without Angel diving on them with her knives. No, someone had told Angel of the necessity for patience, and bargained with her as I'd been taken. That person had told her she could come along as assurance I'd come to no harm. I couldn't imagine how Batya had managed that, but she had, or else someone would have died. And, not just the mute peasant lunatic who never left my side. After all, there is a great deal of blood in a body, and much can be done before it's all fully drained, which was the best way to think of my bodyguard's talent.

Batya had spoken about these borders between the lands of Lacellor and those of the first tribes. There were some creeks, but no mighty river. Rolling hills of grass marked the first of the lands, and within them were no people at all. "They've gone to other pastures," Batya said. We crossed lands that took us all of a day to traverse without a sign of huts or distant cooking fires. We'd taken an unmarked route. It was as if we were the first travelers crossing a vast rolling plain fit only for grazing deer.

Days later, a sea of women materialized in front of our line of travel. There must have been four or five hundred women, all on horses, all armed with bows and spears. They were the most beautiful army I had ever seen.

Some seemed children, those bearing only knives and short bows. They parted just before us, silently watching our passage as we waded through two abreast. I felt every eye on me, as if they sensed I was the true stranger. None spoke. The curiosity in their eyes sparkled.

I had Angel to my right and Batya to my left. We were in the middle of our three score warriors. The witch rode just behind us, near some of the older warriors.

I asked my sister who these women around us were.

"They're a southern tribe of Greyfeet," she said. "Horse thieves, mostly. We pay them in goats and forgive their trespasses into our fields, hoping to keep the peace between us in these troubling times. They pay us retribution in horses or golden trinkets without any asking where they came by the coin. As well, they breed with whatever is at hand." It was clear Batya did not much like the Greyfeet, and breeding habits had more to do with it than wandering horses or stealing gold from the lands down under.

Further observation showed me that most of the Greyfeet weren't blonde, nor fair of skin, which accounted, I assumed, for the way our tribes viewed them. Nonetheless, they appeared fiercely comfortable on their horses, weapons a single movement away from hands. They were better warriors than mine on the southern borderlands, and by a good measure.

We were greatly outnumbered, and yet our women showed no outward signs of fear. I could smell though, and knew the smell of tension. There was little love here between these tribes of women warriors, though I had long learned that all the Debrecian tribes were at truce because of the threat from the King of Farstand across the small lands of Lacellor.

On an impulse I said, "We will stop here for the night and rest."

Upon hearing this, Batya made to speak, but then realized it had been her Queen who'd spoken, not her sister. I dismounted, causing the women behind to have to stop as well.

We were still in the midst of the parted Greyfeet tribe, but well up on a broad hill. Such a place made for a good view and comfortable place to bed, but was totally indefensible because of the gentle nature of the slope. We were at the mercy of the Greyfeet, and thus was just what I had in mind as I pulled my pack from my horse and helped Batya take our tent down from the back of Ella.

Some of the Greyfeet had to move their horses to make way for the first pegs.

Our women remained mounted, looking at one another in confusion. When they saw my glare, several slid off their horses and started pulling their packs down as well. I marked the faces of those few who were quick to comply with my unspoken command.

A great clamor of hooves told of the arrival of Kirsta from the front ranks. By that time, Batya and Angel had the corners of our tent staked and set to putting in the poles. Behind us, three other tents were in the process of being unrolled.

Kirsta arrived. "What is this!" Her horse's hooves stopped nearly on me.

I said just as forcefully, "You'll have my people pitch their tents here. We are under the protection of our friends, the Greyfeet."

She turned a circle with her horse, but then spun once again for the front, but not before giving me her most hateful face. A command to make camp was sent back through the ranks. This surprised some of the women still sitting on their horses, but Batya stepped beside me after setting the poles and whispered, "Kirsta hates Greyfeet. Even so, she cannot so obviously insult this many of them while so straddled."

I smiled at her and sat down on a large rock, intentionally avoiding any of the labor, while remaining in full view of all the warriors.

The witch came over and handed me some cold tea after squeezing another fish dry over it and saying some chants that were so timid they barely interrupted the soft sway of the afternoon breeze.

"This isn't the sort for sleeping, I hope," I told her, mostly to let her know I'd figured out who among us had the skills for such potions.

"It be for the illness, me Queen. Same as afore, only with somethin' ta' aid fever."

"Ah, green tea and black walnut for the lungs; as well, willow for the sweats. We will have to compare recipes someday." I took a sip without bothering to smell it first. This seemed to surprise the witch, though it brought a little smile to her lips.

In the meantime, the Greyfeet backed off, probably because of some command passed among them by quiet word of mouth. They camped to either side of our line of tents, some score paces distant. Several stood on the edge of their camp, watching. I didn't sense that any of them had been overtly posted, meaning their captain labored at showing no offense.

These were good signs, and so I went into the tent to rest and sent Batya ahead to bring back the woman with only one leg. She arrived quickly, and not alone, for Kirsta came with her and was eager to complain.

Kirsta, who had donned her best leather and even chain, did all the talking for a while, letting me know I'd put them all in grave peril and had no authority to do so. She particularly impressed upon me that the council wouldn't see this as favorable, given my poor judgment, and thus it would be her honor to personally execute me for the crime of impersonating the great queen of her tribe, upon their judgment. I listened to her intently until she ran out of things to say.

When she finished, she turned to leave, and that's when I nodded to Angel, who stepped between Kirsta who'd gone outside, and the woman with one leg who was not so quick to go.

I asked, "I sent for you, not Kirsta, who has much to learn about good manners before her Queen. What is your name, child?"

"Salonia. And, both Kirsta and I are ten years your senior." Her words seemed harsh, but the song of her voice more cautious.

I locked eyes with hers. "Salonia, you will meet with the Greyfeet and tell them I wish to speak with their Queen."

She looked away. "This cannot be done. Their Queen is sacred. It will be taken as a grave insult."

"Angel." I waved my hand to my bodyguard. She stepped away from the entrance of my tent. "It will be done, and you will do it." I picked up my cup of tea and sipped at it, dismissively.

When Salonia left, my sister shook her head. "She'll not do it. If we send a breeder to speak before the Queen of the Greyfeet, the insult will be unforgivable; assuming she is here at all."

"I am no breeder." I nearly laughed. And a year earlier I would have—hysterically.

"This I know," Batya said, "but Salonia does not; nor do the Greyfeet. They have seen enough to know we have many views in this matter."

"My question is: What has Salonia noticed? Imagine the dilemma in her mind, sister. If I am her Queen, and she disobeys me on such an important matter . . . ."

Batya hit the tent flap. "She stands by Kirsta."

"Yes, last I saw, but will this always be so? Salonia does not fear Kirsta. Besides, I'll need to know how far Salonia bends. In either case, all I need do is wait; which is much easier than assaulting some keep's walls while standing under a rain of arrows. If this Greyfeet Queen doesn't send for me, I shall send you to ask an audience."

"I do not much like Greyfeet," Batya said. I knew it was deeper than that because she showed absolutely no emotion.

Enough time passed to allow us to go outside and watch the sun go down. Here on the open plains, the sun threw a kiss goodnight with bright streaks of red and orange. Then when it fell, the whole horizon was purple with the tops of tents and heads of horses as company. It seemed the stars came out even before the sun left, and when the sun quit entirely, there were far more of them than in any southern sky.

Two common warriors of the Greyfeet tribe came through the screen of tents and walked up to mine. One bowed her head politely. "Our Queen calls for the one named Abi. She will attend her at our Queen's evening feast."

I noticed she'd not asked for our Queen, but I had not expected it. I stood. "I'll bring only two, bearing feast knives, as my attendants."

The women nodded their approval.

Batya started to put her sword aside and find her best vest. I turned to her and said, "Go find Salonia once more and tell her the Queen of the Greyfeet has requested she attend me in her tent. As well, I shall be taking Angel.

"I should go, Abi," my sister said.

"No. I'll not bring my shaman as my guard. If she is a true queen, she'll know your soul better than these other women and take it as a sign of my distrust."

When Salonia arrived, we walked into the sea of Greyfeet tents. Every eye among them lingered on us as we passed. I feared the reaction of my bodyguard, who was dressed nearly as raggedly as I, and without an inch of leather or chain. When I looked into her soul, Angel was not in the least bit tense or fearful. It seemed she almost always gloated with the prospects of attending her Queen at a challenging encounter. This was a sure sign that the Goddess smiled on our enterprise, for none among us was more a child of the spirits than my lunatic.

Salonia, on the other hand, moved as rigidly as a stick, her eyes always forward and her hand resting close to the knife in her belt. She walked closer to me than even Angel. I wished to stop and tap on her freshly adorned tunic and ask if she was truly afraid for her Queen, but of course such would require a commitment that I felt sure hadn't yet made the trip all of the way up to her mouth.

Instead, I whispered to both, "When we enter the tent, you should come to each side of me and show their Queen some respect by briefly bowing."

Salonia snorted, but Angel glowed with enthusiasm, practicing her bows with little nods toward every warrior nearby. It was a big contrast from when I'd first met her and she'd spat on everybody within sight.

I went into the well-guarded tent first and sat on the largest of many-colored cushions. Unlike all the more modest tents that I'd peeked into during our walk, the Queen's tent had several great rugs on the floor and even some small tables that held many scented candles. There blazed a small fire on the floor, the little smoke crawling up to the hole in the middle of the tent's roof.

My guards bowed then sat down at my sides.

The woman opposite said, "You are welcome to my tent, Abi of the Great Northern Tribes."

I said, "I thank you for your hospitality. When I saw that you had come to greet us, I was beyond joy and eager to seek out your thoughts, great shaman, blessed healer and warlord of the Greyfeet."

"You are mistaken, warrior Abi," the woman before me said. She was a woman of forty, with wise eyes ten years older still, and she sat adorned in a great black and yellow gown. Hanging around her neck were seven golden coins, all highly polished on a wire necklace, also of gold.

I smiled at her politely. "I am not mistaken." I turned my pillow so I faced the similarly aged woman sitting two warriors to her right. I told the woman, "Your shaman has been most gracious, for the captain of my own guard can only see far enough to call me breeder."

"I suspect your captain is better in the craft of warfare," the Queen said. She was possibly the most modestly dressed among them. Her tunic consisted of grey goat hair, though her short britches and skirt were pitch black wool. She nodded at me then reached into the top of her tunic, from which she pulled a wire necklace of ten golden coins. When she stood, the two women beside her shifted over, giving her the seat before me.

"I am sorry, child. I was told you were likely an imposter. A test was needed. Now I see you have some magic. I am Risha." She was surprisingly clear spoken.

"What else do you see, Risha, Queen of the Greyfeet?"

She pointed to Angel. "There is small magic in this one."

She pointed at Salonia. "This one is not your shaman."

Then she pointed at me. "Your soul is many; both Queen and shaman, as well as others, perchance. Such is not the way of our tribes. I have never seen such a sharing of gifts within one vessel."

"Our Goddess speaks to us," There was no question in my heart.

She found my reply insufficient, I could tell, but nodded politely. The old Queen clapped her hands, and two of the four surrounding her went out of the tent, returning with two trays. Short strips of goat were coated with a red spice. On the second tray sat onions and some kind of radish. Clearly they intended to see what became of us as we drank too much of their ale.

I turned to Angel. "Angel, would you please go back and have the witch prepare some green tea with walnut. I fear my lungs have not yet fully healed, and I wish to share the witch's gift of health with the great Queen."

I said to the shaman: "We have a witch with us who has a talent for healthy teas."

Both the Queen and her shaman nodded politely, as did the rest, a half second behind them.

Angel stood and ran out of the tent like she was a little girl who'd been asked to go outside and play with the neighbor's dog. Apparently the Goddess had emptied my bodyguard's head of all thoughts of danger.

"That is a strange woman. South dark and not of the north. Tell me how you came by her?" the Queen asked.

"She was a vile peasant breeder of no worth until I healed her soul. Her father sold her to me, though we later robbed him of his payment, for any woman sold by her father is not fairly bargained. I have a thousand such warriors in the border lands between Farstand and Lacellor, and though they claim no blood of the great Debrecian tribes, they are all angels given to us by the Goddess."

"Are you their Queen? Perhaps these are the people for whom you have been made Queen, and are not also the Queen of the north?"

I smiled. "Perhaps. Thus far the Northern Tribes have not earned my service. Yet, my mother was Queen Mayran, and upon her death both she and the Goddess were most insistent that I should trouble myself with the north."

I looked over at Salonia with a challenge in my eyes. She looked away, taking the opportunity to pick over some goat.

Queen Risha said, "Yes, I think few in the north see you as Queen."

"It doesn't matter."

"How is that so?" the shaman of the Greyfeet interrupted.

"The Goddess wills; fickle though she be. I have never known her to make a thing simple."

Queen Risha said, "Ah yes. That would be the women."

Several nodded, as if in short prayer.

That conversation seemed to settle the Queen, so we bent to eating the fiery food, costing me the chore of drinking two tankards of head-strong ale. I'd never managed to do well with spirits and was relieved to see Angel, who promptly filled my next tankard with bitter tea. The Greyfeet sipped at the tea I offered with trepidation, not through fear of poison, given I drank it heartily, but probably because it was awful.

I had to say, "I'm sorry, but I fear our tea is best for those with bad lungs. The old witch squeezes fish oil into it, small ones from the sea; a trick I'd not known until I saw her doing it. When you come to the north, I shall find something more pleasant." I bid Angel to give the rest of it to their shaman, who took it and surprised me by smiling and setting the tea aside gently, as if a great prize. Shamans are, after all, both healers and warlords, both in equal measure so as to maintain the balance that restores their magic.

"There is trouble to the north," the shaman said.

The Queen quickly added, "We are at truce. Your traders are gifted passage through our lands, but we are not . . . enjoyed among our sisters to the north."

"Tell me how you see these troubles?" I asked.

She thought some then asked, "What would the Queen of the north do if one came to you saying, 'A goat has gone missing, and I saw Greyfeet near my holding.'?"

"She might say, let us buy five good horses for the price of a hundred goats, and if one goat should go missing on the road to the south, such is fate and the will of the Goddess."

"Then I shall remember to always trade for a hundred and one goats," the Queen said.

I laughed. "How many goats has your army slaughtered this night? None here know the count, and yet we share this tent and are not troubled by it."

"The Goddess provides," the Queen said as she filled her tankard with more of the wicked ale.

* * * * *

When we rode away from the Greyfeet, none of the women surrounding my little group of four were the same ones as had been riding around us previously. I noted that some of the faces were those who'd been first to dismount the day before. As well, Salonia was the leader of these few, often coming back to check on their welfare and discipline. She didn't come to me and make a formal apology for doubting my gifts, but I was no longer troubled by her leanings.

We passed other small groups of warriors and hunting parties, not of the Northern Tribes. They remained well to our flanks, always watching with interest. Some word had taken wing, and from the few birds had come murders of crows.

Two days after leaving the Greyfeet, we entered the lands of the Northern Tribes. Both men and women on horses raced up and greeted various women in our party. I was curious to see how the men were treated, but each sex was regarded with the same joy and the men wore weapons as proudly as the women when among these out-riding parties. Sometimes warriors left our group entirely to go with their kin. Others joined us at the same time, such that when we rode into a group of hills that hid a river seam, we were more than when we'd started.

I rode down into a sea of cottages, pens for vast herds of animals and small vegetable farms that stitched for miles along both sides of the vast valley. In a land of tents, it felt strange to see houses braced against forests and farmland again. I had begun to think of the Debrecians as a purely nomadic race. This is true only in parts.

There was no city at first. Instead, some orderliness compelled the people here to keep their houses spaced far enough apart to make room for pastures and fields. When I gave it some thought, I realized that the fertile valley was too valuable to waste on a big city of stone walls.

Then, after traveling for a good length through the many plots, a field of tents appeared. These colorful, round tents were each squat, but wide enough to house a small family. Some were taller and open on one side, showing well-tended horses resting out of the weather. These tents appeared fifty wide and twice that deep along both sides of the roadway. We headed for the center of this strange town in the midst of the more permanent cottages and fields of prosperity.

All along our route, every man, woman and child among them seemed outside their tents, some pointing at us as we passed.

Batya took on the sober look of a deeply troubled warrior, more than I'd have thought right, given this was her home.

The witch appeared as if she wanted to flee, for witches are solitary by nature.

Angel, who could not have been mistaken for anything other than the greatest of strangers among us, smiled continually. She remained my clue to the disposition of the goddess.

The rest of our Debrecians waved, sometimes yelling greetings, even if they didn't know the person they were addressing; to them it was a homecoming and promise of rest and loved ones.

As we moved to some sort of center, the spaces between the tents widened, as did the size of the tents. Finally, we entered a large circle of grass surrounded by a dozen of the largest and most multicolored tents in the whole city of fabric. There were many benches for the working of cloth and leather, including kilns and places for social sittings by the coals. Over on one side of the great circle stood two stout poles, one of which had a man of wood belted to it. He'd suffered hundreds of slash marks across his upper torso, probably from busy swords. Right through the center of the circle of grass was a run to the dummy. It showed a deep rut of mud, churned up from the iron shoes of a thousand mounted passes at the staked-out targets.

I looked to one tent, noticing a statue of a lady in front of its main flaps. The statue was much the same as the wooden man, only better carved, permanently affixed and the same size as we women. An artist had painted it in the Goddess's likeness, fully clothed in a fresh woolen gown. Someone had thought to pick and give her a floral crown.

I said, "Ah, my Goddess. It would have surprised me to have not found you here."

I rode right up to within a few horse lengths.

From there I looked down at her likeness. "All this confusing mess is your doing, my Goddess."

I added, "Forgive my complaint." It seemed important that good things come from such a complex beginning to my life. Had my mother died for nothing? It was she who'd sent me in her stead, for she'd been the Queen, and I'd been no more than the daughter who'd been too late in her rescue.

Thus is how the Goddess often speaks—through thoughts full of guilt and worry.

It seemed the Goddess looked up at me, and her face hinted a warm, motherly smile. It might have been my imagination, or the shifting light as so many of our horses filtered between the tents, disappearing. Warriors were finding more appropriate places to house their mounts, rather than soil the grass in the midst of the great tents.

But I lingered, not knowing what was expected of me next.

I dismounted to more formally greet her with a kiss. There I knelt and lingered at the feet of the Goddess, touching the humble wooden texture of her legs, feeling the love the carver had given to the chore. It was only wood, I knew, but wasn't wood one of the greatest blessings given to us by the world she'd mothered?

When I came back to my senses, I turned, seeing the vast area empty of both horses and warriors. Even Angel was gone, telling me the turn of events was indeed sacred. As well, not a single person emerged from any of the great tents, even though all their main tent openings were aimed toward the center of the field.

Batya's teacher's sword had been left, stuck in the ground. I walked over and pulled it out, feeling how lovely it fit my hands, as if the craftsman had fashioned it solely for the pleasure of my grip.

Someone screamed a deathly wail.

I turned in time to witness a tall Debrecian warrior run out of one of the tents. Her small breasts were bare, but her skirt and leggings were thickly leathered. Red and white mud had been streaked across her face and body. The woman stood taller than I, allowing her to look perfectly at ease with the long sword that she flayed the air with while glaring in my direction. I felt familiar with many of her sword forms, having learned mine from the best I'd ever seen, the old and dead shaman who'd first given me the sword I held in my hands.

Then, having given fair warning, she came running. The woman intended to slay me with her sword, I realized, for nothing could have been more obvious. Thus, I lifted my sword up and just before she arrived, took several steps in her direction.

Our swords crossed, spitting a spark and a screech of metal on metal. I had her at a disadvantage, having killed so many and so recently, and also having had the foresight to have taken a few steps in her direction, ruining her timing entirely. After all, I was no wooden dummy, strapped to a pole.

Thus, when the swords next met, I leaned low enough to brace her and kick her aside. That made my next two moves simple parries, against which no one has ever matched my art. Reluctantly, for we'd not yet been formally introduced, I had to cut this perfectly toned warrior just above the belt and a little to the side so she'd still be able to sleep on one arm the next few nights without too much torment. While first pained, I nicked the guard, sending her weapon to the ground.

The woman completely changed her demeanor and fell to her face, near to weeping. I, on the other hand, had fallen into the spirit of my training with the guards of Lettoir, where minor hurts were thought of as part of the routine. I told her, "Aw, to be sure, it was just a cut. Take your sword and go about your business."

The woman looked up with fear in her eyes, as if my patient words had done worse than murder. She grabbed her mighty sword and, while bent over her wound, fled between the tents nearly as quickly as she'd arrived.

No sooner had she done that then a second warrior emerged from another tent, telling me this might be a very long and tiring afternoon, for there were at least a dozen tents facing the grounds.

This one was not as tall, but better dressed, with leather covering the whole of her body except for her arms and the parts of the legs nearest the knees. Her whole face had been painted red and her hair was browner than most here. In her hands she held a well-carved spear with a metal tip. Such was a nasty weapon. I'd come to respect the way a properly wielded spear could compromise the most skilled warrior. I preferred a good long weapon in a cavalry charge, even though I often lost mine after sticking the first person.

I had no armor, nor did I bear a shield. This caused some fretting within my soul.

At a distance, and against a lone soldier, the weapon was useless. Closer up, against a sword, it was equally without value. My dread was that she'd toss it after coming within a few short feet. Against that there was no good defense, save a shield.

When she came at me, yelling as had the first woman, I ran to the side, reaching the protection of the wooden man before she could come close enough to throw her weapon.

She came around the dummy, poking, but I ducked to the other side. When she jabbed at the other side, she drew too close to the dummy. I grabbed the end of her spear just beyond the steel tip. My sword chipped the spear nearer her forward hand. This caused both of her hands to retreat on the spear. After that, I dropped my sword and put two hands on her spear. We were equals.

While falling back, I tossed her over with my feet. She rolled as far away and to the side as possible, no doubt hoping to yank the spear free with the weight of her body. It was a good move, but I never stopped crawling, right up until we were face to face. There I butted her head with my own which had been hit enough times before to have grown another plate of bone.

We clamored to our feet, still wrestling for the same weapon. She seemed a master with the spear, but I knew no equal with the staff, and thus had the advantage of good balance and footwork thereafter. Around the tenth time I kicked her, she fell to the ground weaponless and also looking far too miserable to kill. By then I had the spear, and liked it too much to give it back. I said, "Go on. Run between the tents and join your sister."

She did just that and a mite quicker than the speedy way she'd attacked me in the first place.

I kept my new spear and picked my sword up as well. Back in the center of the grass I waited, certain that such things always came in threes and maybe never ended at all.

Another woman came out of the tent behind the Goddess.

She was shorter than me and about my age. The woman approached while entirely naked, save for a whole body of ash paint. Her hair was not blonde like most of these women, but white as snow, nearly matching the paint all over her body. As well, her eyes matched the color of the sky, blue, though nearly as light as her hair. Her hands held nothing but air.

I knew her at once, for I could see her soul. She was no shaman, but she knew some magic, and thought herself the same as one. This was a mistake, probably caused by a score of years without a proper queen or shaman against which she might compare.

There was no need to wait for her to scream or come running at me. As well, I knew she wouldn't do so, for magic can be wielded from a field away. Instead, I surprised her with my own little chant.

I whispered, letting the wind from behind me carry my will to her ears:

> "I gift you with courage.
> I gift you with a warrior's art.
> I give you the skill of blood.

I lend you my warrior's heart.
Your soul be ever changed to only this.
Gifts of a sister's soul.
What you once were, no more.
Go train to the bow and make this so,
Such is the will of the Goddess."

She stepped forward and tried to curse me with her own riddle. The poem was a vile thing, and no child's play, for the greater the curse, the mightier the damage to the strength of the witch or shaman who'd uttered it. With her mite magic, the curse might well have killed her, had I not done her the favor of stealing magic from her entirely. I felt sorry for her, for she had no queen to guide her, ending up with this angry mistake before having even met me.

I staked my weapons in the middle of the field and walked toward her, unarmed. Terror came to her eyes when she discovered that her spell had proven impotent and mere words. When I got to her, I embraced her with both arms. She trembled and fought against my grasp, but I wouldn't let her go. After some time, she grew to understand I meant her no harm and settled.

Standing back so she could see my face, I told her, "I have taken your magic as my own, child. You were not meant for the troubles of a shaman, don't you know. In its place, I've given you the greater joy of a mighty warrior. This is no small duty, but will soon ease your heart, for it's the gift to which you've been born. Now it's time for you to make your way between the tents and join your sisters."

She looked around with uncertainty twitching on her face then slowly backed away. The warrior within yielded, and with a different look of great shame, she ran between the tents.

I shouted with a mighty voice: "I have killed the whole world. Is that not enough? Well, I say it is not! There is more to a queen than fighting and death! I will forgive you these petty trials, all of which pale by comparison to the true ones the Goddess has sent me through, but if you do not cease this blasphemy, I shall ride away and leave you forever without a queen and, as well, a proper shaman soul will no longer visit your lands! Do not think about it long, for any good queen is made both of patience and the lack thereof!"

The ambassador and prophetess, Beckli Kahnsa, emerged from her tent. The woman was magnificent. She stood taller than most, with a fountain of golden hair. She was fully adorned in a great gown of wool and goat hair that had been dyed many broad striped and earthy colors. At her breasts, her necklace displayed medallions of gold and about her wrists were a dozen rings of silver.

She said, "Last I saw you, child, the Goddess had blinded my sight to the gift of a new shaman. *Then* she saw fit to deny us the presence of your magic for much of three seasons. What has she made of you now, and how can it be that she has found room for both a shaman warlord and a queen in only one body; and it so young, as well a stranger to our tents?"

I bowed my head politely to the woman from whom I'd learned that there was more to the world than my one tiny life. "Has the Goddess also forgotten to tell you she has seen fit to give you a new shaman in my stead?"

She answered, "No, my child. She has only seen fit to show visions of the terrible things surrounding your coming. These visions are silent, so I might bear them. Do you not know the Goddess only speaks to queens?" She sighed. "But, enough of this. Come, let us dine in my tent. It is time to call for better wisdom from the council than what we have witnessed in this field."

Chapter Three

Beckli Kahnsa, the great prophetess and diplomat of the Northern Tribes, led the way into her tent where I sat. She introduced me to her young daughter and son, Kahnsajin and Erkeo.

"The children were told to remain with their fathers until morning, but as you can see, each has earned a scolding. You must think me impolite," Beckli Kahnsa said as she uncovered several dishes. One was baked fowl, and another consisted of beans with red spices. Beckli set a little of each on a square wooden plate and handed it to me before serving the same to herself. The abundant and well-displayed food suggested she assumed my survival.

Next, she uncorked a bottle and poured me a red drink that smelled of grapes. I'd heard of wine and tasted a little in a drinking house I'd once raided, but thought little of the beverage.

I took a sip, surprised when I found it considerably better than the sort I'd tasted previously. The great woman waited for me to sample the bird, which I did, for fowl was always one of my favorites, and then she ate some of her own. It was all very formal, we two sitting cross-legged and the two children well in the corner of the round tent where the walls met the canvas of the surrounding ceiling. The older son carved on a hand-sized soapstone with a small knife, seemingly in his own artisan world, while the girl, at best twelve, and reminding me of Batya, save for blonder hair, watched from over a pillow. Her blue eyes were as huge as those on my horse.

Here I sat in the presence of the middle-aged woman I'd always thought worthy of patterning my life after. She ate with me in the strictest formality. It was as if she thought me a stranger. How could that be? Then it occurred to me that, for her, we were just that. At the baron's court, she'd not even seen me, and it struck me that if she had, she might have marked me as the Queen then and there, saving us all a good deal of trouble. No doubt it had been the Goddess who'd shaded my mind and compelled me to hide so thoroughly behind a fat noble woman's skirts so I might be put to further tribulations.

Then in the battle, the mighty woman had fought the baron's brother, no doubt slightly preoccupied and not troubled by the presence of what she must have then seen as the lesser player on that field of four. Her only glimpse of the true me had lasted a short few seconds before the dead duke's knights chased her off. She'd been in fear for her life. So, other than visions of some terrible future, the woman knew me for all of five seconds, and here she'd been a mighty statue of all that was right in my head since the moment I'd first laid eyes on her. I had to find a way to set her at ease. It was then that I recalled her last words to me, seemingly a redundant question.

I said, "Would it be rude of me to ask if your children could also dine with us? I'd so much like to meet them."

This startled her. I suppose I'd breached some protocol, for there was great uncertainty in her eyes. Her words were almost fearful when she obeyed my desire and asked her children to join us. The girl leapt to the occasion, but the boy came with nearly as much hesitation as I'd sensed from his mother.

I took the liberty of picking up two wooden plates and portioned out a goodly part of the meal for each of the children. Having done that, everyone seemed terribly ill at ease once again, probably because I'd taken leave to serve them.

I had to say something. "If I seem rude, I apologize. You see, I don't know our customs. Further, I am yet a virgin, and have not enjoyed the pleasure of children, save in camp with the southern women. There I have found them a blessing and cheer to my warriors."

"I have many reports of these women." She nodded.

I sighed. "To be honest, the prospect of bearing children frightens me. My father was unkind, making my childhood miserable. I'm now betrothed to a great knight, Sir Daren Drake. It is the same man I fought, and with whom you made your appeal to the duke. He would enjoy a son. As well, he is certainly troubled at the moment, considering my sudden departure."

"Are you really the Queen? Some say it's a lie and we'll have to fight you." The words tumbled out of the mouth of the daughter, Kahnsajin. Oh yes, she was certainly a handful of straightforwardness. A bundle of—well a bundle.

"Kahnsajin! You will return to your father, at once!" her mother scolded. Her face was far redder than the loudness of her voice implied.

"But they do say it! I like her. She can be my Queen, and then you won't have to kill her!" the girl said as she jumped up and stepped back from the setting of food that was so beautifully displayed on the floor. I noticed she carried a handful of honey cakes, even as she retreated.

"I'll take her, mother," the son, Erkeo, said. Ah yes, I thought, the proper one, and from the shift in Beckli Kahnsa's eyes, I could tell, the favored of the two. So, I thought, they did love their sons, and seemingly their men as well, for apparently Beckli Kahnsa had fathered her children with two of them and they were all the more different for it.

Just that quickly, the children left and the room became less joyful.

I have to say that I favored the girl. Such brutal honesty is rare in the world, and even though I could attribute much of it to youth, I determined I'd not be the source of its erosion. I said, perhaps a bit too forcefully, "Beckli Kahnsa! Do you not know that I love your children? I think that if the council should prove as honest and enlightened and as full of the joy of life as your daughter, then there shall be no end to my pleasure."

"One must learn to not always be honest, nor rude to guests," she advised me.

I don't know why the notion had such power over me, but it was a crushing thought that reminded me of how so much of my childhood had been entombed in layers and layers of lies. Just to escape it and certain death, I'd had to wrap myself in yet another lie that denied my own self. I was the very spawn of deception. I had a tear in my eye when I yielded the smaller point. "It is always good to be kind when one can afford the luxury."

Upon that, Beckli Kahnsa sat staring at me with new interest. After a short while she said, "I have small magic compared to a queen or shaman, but I can see something ancient in you that I had not at first imagined. All I saw before in my visions were terrible omens of war and death, so I was reluctant to acknowledge what the Goddess has brought us. Many of us will not survive your rule, I fear. And yet, you speak of truth and kindness as if they are your greatest treasures." She took a moment to drink.

I sighed.

"I knew your mother like a sister. Why did she not come, and why did our shaman not rescue her?"

"The Goddess had a plan." I knew this to be true, but had never come to like it.

"I see. You know, your mother also had the rare gift of saying things that gave me pause. Abi, child of the Goddess, I have no doubt that you are as you claim. Like my difficult daughter, I declare you my Queen without hesitation. The only question is this: Can we survive you? Will there be nothing but death, in spite of your wisdom?"

I said, "I will give you my answer, but not here. What I have to say, I shall say before the whole council." After that we ate the rest of our meal in silence.

* * * * *

We left the tent of the prophetess. The great circle of grass inside the ring of large tents was once again clear of all inhabitants, to include the spear and sword I'd planted in the middle. We passed one tent, and the shaman's, and then entered the third. Four middle-aged to elderly women, in thick and colorful ceremonial gowns, sat around a fire.

Beckli Kahnsa told the woman sitting just opposite the fire to get up and move to a different place.

There was a great gasp from all four of the women, and an even greater reluctance to get up from the old lady sitting opposite the fire.

She implored Beckli with her eyes, but to no avail, and thus relented, slowly finding another blanket to sit on. I was led to her place, and there I sat, feeling very much the stranger. I'd never seen four more troubled faces, all of them glancing at me, but lingering more longingly on Beckli. It was as if they hoped she'd made a big mistake and was soon going to correct it.

When it looked as if all was settled, Beckli Kahnsa sat down as well, completing my council of five.

There I sat in the Queen's place.

A young woman came in, her eyes steadily looking at me, though the front of her face remained aimed at the pitcher and tumblers she filled. When we all had a drink, she retired from the tent. Prior to the flap closing, I saw her feet break into a run. The whole camp was certain to know something, and quite soon, I realized.

I noticed an empty blanket, that to my right.

I decided to start the conversation: "You are all my senior. I respect your wisdom, and promise to always listen to your council. You are the people. You bear their souls. In the south, I also have made a council. Even in my lacking presence, I do not overly trouble myself with the well-being of my people, for my council is wise and bears the burden of their needs. For twenty years you have ruled this land with your wisdom, and though you have lacked a queen and a shaman, you have prospered."

"And if we do not accept you?" the elderly woman to my left asked. She'd just been asked to move to a different blanket.

I said, "Then the Goddess will find a new people, for I am already Queen in the heart of the people in the south, and the Goddess has already found it in her heart to love them."

There was an even greater gasp than the one breathed when I'd taken my seat.

A second woman said, "If we seem hard, it is the duty of the council to be so. Further, you are new to us, and we only have the words of our scouts and prophetess that you are the woman you profess to be."

This was curious. "And what word have you from your scouts?"

A third woman said, "That you are mighty in battle. That you command breeders to do your bidding, and that they have grown better with their horses over time. They even say you have grown comfortable with the men of the south."

"Have you no men? Were you not breeders before the Goddess blessed you? Who was the first Queen among you, and how is her memory regarded when she and her warriors were yet young in tradition?" I asked.

"This is not the point," a fourth woman told me. "If you are to be our Queen, why did you trouble yourself with these breeders and male warriors? Why did you not come to us as soon as your mother told you of her soul and gift? As well, who sent you on your trial, if not this council?"

I looked at the fourth woman steadily. "When my mother was one month dead and her corpse rotting behind the baron's dungeon walls, her voice still echoed in their pit of hell. It said I'd long been your Queen, and that was the first I knew of it.

"At first, I was only looking for the Queen, not even knowing she was my mother. I did not know the ancient Queen's soul also dwelled within me. This was the test the Goddess gave us. She blinded me from the truth, giving me the trial of seeking out the Queen's wisdom, knowing it more valuable than the person blessed with it."

"The required quest," the woman to my right whispered.

"Yes, and out of it came a Queen, for the Queen is more than me or a birthright, nor is the duty found by slaying enemies. It is what comes to a person when she has seen the world at its worst and found space within her heart to lend an act of mercy."

Beckli's eyes shifted to the side, reflectively. "This is great wisdom."

"Let me be clear: A year before this day, I was not ready to be a queen. A year before now, I didn't even know I was a Debrecian and was short a season from finishing my unwitting trial as a shaman."

There seemed some hesitation on the part of some with the council, so I asked, "How do you think a warrior of the tribes comes to become a queen?"

The fourth woman said quickly, "It is by both blood and a test set before her, sent by her council."

I said, "I do not think so. I know a woman who once told me that her council had not sent her on a great quest. And yet, she is now a fierce shaman.

"Upon the completion of my test as Queen, the Goddess moved me to see my duty. So, some might say a queen and her shaman are made by the Goddess, and it is she who makes the quest."

The woman then said, "It is, of course, also the will of the Goddess." The others around the fire nodded.

So then I added, "But I don't think it is only by blood, trial or even the will of the gods. This brings me to a new revelation. I think that mostly a queen is the one who has suffered so she may more clearly serve her people. A Queen is a queen simply because to look upon her, nothing can be plainer in their sight."

The old woman to my left said, "I can find no wrong in that."

A second woman agreed: "It seems the Goddess has sent you."

I didn't wait for all of them to accept me with at least a nod of approval. "I will have to spend some time with each of you and learn about the troubles you endure in your duties. As you know, I am powerless without your guidance and know nothing about the people for whom good leadership is more important than my title."

We drank our tea a while in relative silence, for I'd grown tired from my trip and wished to savor one large victory before going on to other problems.

Soon, the girl who'd been serving us returned and refilled our cups, looking even more startled than before when she noticed I remained in the Queen's place and none of those around me had the look of contesting women. In the place of that seemed more fear than relief on the faces of the elders. The girl left, once again running off before the curtain could fully close. She'd not done nearly as well as before at hiding her incredible determination to spread the gossip.

"Beckli Kahnsa," I began, "is concerned about visions she has had regarding great violence that portends my return. Have you heard her omens?"

Several of them said yes, and their faces remained grave.

"When she spoke of this to me, I decided to bring it before the council instead of giving my thoughts on the matter in private. This is not a minor concern, for I wish no ill upon our people. What are your opinions on the matter?"

One was defensive: "We have great respect for the prophecies of this woman." She nodded to Beckli, who sat quietly.

I said, "Such is not debated, for we all respect her words and know her visions are true. If she portends calamity, calamity it shall be. What I am asking about is your opinions on what should be done?"

This was no small question. I could almost see their heads working, saying within: Just one moment ago I'd thought this no large problem, for surely the girl was not our Queen and could be easily killed for the insult of her claim. Now, however, what truly can be done in the face of this prophecy? To kill our true Queen is to spit on the face of the Goddess.

I wished to relieve them of their tension. "There are three possibilities. One is to await our fate and trust to the wisdom of the Goddess. Second is to seek out our courses and change future actions by even better works. Neither of these seem good options, for we always are subject to the will of the Goddess, and if our hearts are true, we continually seek courses in our lives that yield the greater result for us all."

It was Beckli Kahnsa herself who asked, "And the third course, my Queen?"

"I have unfinished business in the south," I said. "I was abducted and have found new needs through the course of this journey. I shall return to the south for a short time in order to fulfill these duties. I will require a company of good women. When presented, they will help me hasten our negotiations before the good knights who question my authority as your Queen."

"And how does this resolve the issue of my visions?" Beckli asked.

"Upon this journey I shall ask the Goddess to send you a new vision in my absence. I shall say to her, 'What is the future of the tribes if I remain apart?' I shall tell her, 'You must show Beckli Kahnsa this world, so the council can judge which tragedy is best for our people.'

"You see, I have been to Farstand and know their minds. The

King will not abide the rebellion of Sir Lacellor. Once Lacellor is conquered, he will kneel to this King and be forced to ally his armies against us. All in the south will then be our enemies. Perhaps this knowledge is why the Goddess saw fit to raise me among them?"

Beckli nodded. The others shifted nervously and spoke a comment or two among themselves a moment.

"No doubt I bring great tribulation to our warriors," I said. "What I question is if my absence will bring less trouble than my guidance. We must see both possibilities in order to see our course."

The old woman who'd sat on my blanket asked, "What if it is found that we are better off without you?"

Several of the women in the circle moaned, as if she'd asked something horribly rude and unthinkable.

"Then I shall be your Queen, but trouble you no more, just as my mother did not trouble you for a score years. Surely that will alter the course of our history."

Beckli Kahnsa said, "This you must ask with a mighty voice. The Goddess must see the wisdom of a clear and certain answer."

Another said, "And she must give this vision soon, for as we wait, our hearts are full of dread."

All those around the circle nodded with grave certainty.

That business was done, and so there was even more time spent in silent contemplation.

I asked, "You say you had some scouts watching my progress. But, did you not send one more scout?"

Beckli Kahnsa said, "There was one, but she was too young, and as you know, fell into your hands."

The third woman explained, "She was sent to observe you, and was discovered."

"Ah," I said, as if this was news to me. "What do you suppose is to become of her?"

"She is shamed, but will be given more training and returned to her duty," the third woman said.

"Well then, there seems to be a problem." I furrowed my brow. "You see, the Goddess has seen fit to not only bless her with the soul of her shaman grandmother, but also to give her my sword, which also once rested in the hands of a great shaman warrior."

"This can't be so," the fourth woman said.

Others added:

"She is too small for the duty."

"Too young as well."

"The girl has no meat and will never be any use with a sword."

"She was discovered; already proven not up to the duty."

"We did not send her on a shaman quest."

I pretended innocence when I said, "The Goddess herself gave her both the soul and the sword. It was a moment of great magic that lingered through the night like a whispering fog."

"Could it be some other duty the Goddess intends for her?" the woman on my right asked.

Beckli Kahnsa seemed surprised to recall, "I've seen her in my visions; at the head of our warriors in this bloody war. I thought her only too eager to meet the swords of our enemies. Might it have been something else?"

I was through pretending: "None of your scouts did their duty as well as she. None of them watched me as closely. Do you not know that she was the first to see me as her Queen, even when she didn't know me as one, nor why she followed my every commandment. The woman led my armies into all my victories and has even grown wise in the prudence of war; one of the warlord's greatest lessons.

"Her skills in healing are not inconsiderable. As well, countless times she has stood between me and death, and when I commanded her to step aside so I might fight my own battle against a high lord, she would not relent, saying only that when unleashed on the enemy, she may disobey me in favor of her duties. I ask, in what way is she not worthy, and in what way is she not like a shaman to you?"

"What of her trial?" Beckli Kahnsa asked.

I said, "Do you not know you sent many scouts on this trial and only one came back with the soul of the Shaman of the Northern Tribes; the same that has been lost for a score years?"

I looked over to the empty space by my right hand and said, "Next council, you will find her and bring her to this blanket, for she is far too young and will greatly benefit from the wisdom of your advice."

* * * * *

When we stepped outside, a thousand warriors stood in the vast grass filling the space between the tents. Not a word passed between them as I emerged under the escort of Beckli Kahnsa. The warriors stood silent, eyes full of both questions and wonder as I was led past the tent of the shaman once again. We stopped at the tent between the shaman's and Beckli's. There she bid me enter the tent set aside for the Queen.

Before I went in, I said within earshot of half the warriors, "I'll rest until morning. At first light, bring me the three who thought it wise to test me in battle before my people and against the will of the Goddess. As well, I will need the attendance of Salonia and Kirsta. Kirsta is a woman who has much to learn about courtesy, so see to it that she has a lesson in it before she arrives."

"As you say," Beckli said, though I could tell she was displeased to see the vengeful side of my tongue and had many things she wished to tell me about the circumstances.

I noted this, forcefully saying, "Would you have me coddle women such as these? We are warriors, not children!"

"Yes, my Queen," she said. For the first time, I noticed more humility on her face than was comely on the great woman.

"Good. I also wish to have my shaman find her tent. Both the witch and Angel will sleep there once they have tended to our horses and provisions. They are low-born women, but blessed by the Goddess who is wise regarding these things."

The eyes close to us appeared more and more worried the more they heard my voice issuing commands to the great prophetess.

The discomfort was as I'd hoped, and so I added, "If you choose to also attend, I'll not be displeased. Bring your daughter as well, for I have seen small magic in the child and wish to show her the difference between the fine and pretty stories of a queen and those things that are needful."

Regarding this, she was too troubled even to answer, and so I took my leave and discovered the incredible comfort within the tent of a queen.

Chapter Four

"Are you really the Queen now?" little Kahnsajin squealed as she sat in the circle of women, all of whom wore repentant faces and knew better than to say anything until I'd spoken first and given them my much-dreaded judgment.

As expected, Beckli Kahnsa appeared mortified. She'd sat behind her daughter, obviously uncertain where she should sit within my council of rebuke.

"I am. How this remains depends largely on the visions of your mother, Kahnsajin."

She glanced at her mother then turned her attention back to me. I could see her pride in her mother, in spite of the hard look her mother had given her in return. The other warriors I'd called cast startled faces, perhaps because I'd spoken to the outspoken girl and even called her by name.

I told Kahnsajin, "May I ask you a favor? You see, my bodyguard, Angel, is a blessed woman, kissed by the Goddess as much as you, but she has little skill as a warrior beyond a spear and her knives. I thought you might be willing to help her learn some lessons, perhaps with a better spear or bow. I must warn you, she is mute and needs one such as you who can speak to her with an abounding spirit instead of words. She is also no good at too many lessons at once, but if you treat her like a little sister and give her only one small and patient task per day, I'm sure she'll surprise you with her diligence."

The girl looked over her shoulder and asked, "Can I, mother?"

Beckli's body sighed. "Well of course. You will still have your own duties, but it is good to share your lessons with a friend."

Angel, who guarded beside the flap, also beamed. In many ways she was as childlike as the wild soul of Beckli Kahnsa's beautifully forthright daughter.

"Go along now. These lingering matters are not as interesting. And, be sure to come and breakfast with me each morning, so you can keep me apace of each small step of progress."

"Yes!" the girl shouted as she jumped up. "Come on, Angel. I have lots I want to show you . . ." The girl paused, as if considering her words carefully, adding, "and we'll find something little to start with." She went to the tent flap and grabbed the woman's hand whereupon they disappeared with good flourish. Beckli Kahnsa's demeanor lightened noticeably.

"What sense is this woman as a guard if she has to learn so slowly and from a child?" Kirsta asked.

I gave her a stern look. "Is it protocol here to speak before the Queen has spoken?"

This rebuke had a chilling effect on all the faces, as was my intention. "I am your Queen, and thus the voice of the Goddess. All of you have stood between the Goddess and her will. Should I ask her what she thinks of this? Would you tempt her by demanding that she give me an answer? If not, then I will ask that you stay your tongues until I've spoken and given you my rebuke in her stead, which you should take as a kindness, regardless of my ruling."

All of Kirsta's confidence faded instantly to that of a mouse. I noticed Beckli Kahnsa was also giving the woman a stern eye, and that Kirsta's eye fidgeted from Beckli's face to mine.

It suddenly seemed possible for us to sit in the tent for the whole day without the distraction of an imposing comment.

"I am going south. The council has come to this wise decision. Batya will remain with our tribe, learning healing from the witch and the shaman's book of magic. She must store up the blessings of healing, for troubling times are upon us. Since my shaman will have to remain, I will need new leaders to return south with me in her stead; women who are fearless, though perhaps not so foolish as before, once under the guidance of a queen.

"Khulan, you will go to my sister's tent and ask for healing. Tomorrow you will find ten strong women suitable for leather armor and good with bows, spears and swords."

The tall and proud Debrecian was older than the other warriors, and showed it by bowing her head with great dignity. "As you say."

"Hulan, have you learned the arts of the bow?" I asked the young woman who'd thought herself a shaman.

"No, my Queen. I am shamed, having taken the wrong course for my life, and have been slow in asking my sisters for forgiveness."

"There is no time for shame," I said, "and I don't know what good it does us. You are destined to lead a company of archers, and I have no patience with delays. Choose ten women with strong bow skills. Pick women who are good teachers. They can practice for their duties in the south by teaching you on the way."

This seemed to startle her, so I added, "You were never a shaman. Find a useful skill. Let me suggest leadership, for your duties as shaman must have taught you something of the talent. Now we are through with pity, and you must do as I say."

"Yes," she said, and yet I still sensed uncertainty.

"Consider this: If ten good archers and one weak archer fall upon a foe, is it not better to have eleven good archers?"

"Yes, of course," she said.

"That is how you are thinking," I said.

She sagged.

I held up my left hand. "Over here, eleven good archers fall upon an enemy, but are poorly led." I held up my right hand. "Ten good archers fall upon the same foe, but are better led by one who knows her limits and who now knows the Goddess's will." I put my hands to my sides. "Which is more useful?"

She started to answer, but I put both palms up, stilling her tongue before going on to the next woman in my circle.

"Chotan will find ten who are best with spears."

"Yes, my Queen." Chotan seemed pleased with the assignment. Spears were not favored, I'd observed. Most preferred bows. Perhaps her brown hair instilled in her a desire to embrace other differences? If so, I'd make use of it.

"Salonia. You will have to go tell Queen Risha that I need ten of her archers. In return, we'll give them twenty of our warriors from the south to train and return to us after one month so they may teach others."

Salonia looked at me questioningly, and asked, "What do we give them in return for these gifts?"

"Tell the Greyfeet that we will obviously have no secrets between us if we work together. If this doesn't impress her, tell her Queen Abi is asking in order to return her favor of hospitality."

"How is this a returned favor?" Salonia asked.

I laughed. "Don't you know that more friendships are born from asking favors than from giving them? Have we already forgotten the lesson of Kahnsajin? Didn't I ask her a favor? Wasn't she pleased? Ask this of the Greyfeet Queen. When you join us on the march to the south, I will have need of your services as my chief of scouts."

Then I looked at Kirsta, who was quiet and determined to await my words, though it was clear enough that she did not love me.

I lowered an eyebrow in thought. "You, I will need to lead our best raiders, for my shaman must stay and learn from the council. The women of the south need a woman who is hard headed and too mean for her own good. Bring with you, a score of like-minded women."

Never had I seen a woman more surprised, nor so uncertain if she'd been insulted.

"If you choose, you may bring your families. The south needs leaders, not visitors who only want to show off in front of breeders. Pick your people carefully, for some may choose to make this new settlement their new homes."

"What about men?" Chotan asked.

I said, "I don't know much about men. If any are good at smithing or other trades, we will find wise uses for them."

"Some among us have fathers for our children, and have family with men we favor. We might ask them to come along; those who are willing," Kirsta said.

"Do you mean marriage?" I asked.

The women around the circle laughed, some more bashfully than others.

Chotan asked, "Why?"

Beckli Kahnsa spoke up: "The southern custom of marriage is

foreign to us, though some of us couple for life, and so some of us are not so different. Particularly as we age, we tend to merge our households, and grandparents also help us raise our children. Still, once a woman has a child with a man, they are bound to share in the responsibility of the child. This is not the same as being bound to the man and never looking at another."

Chotan smiled. "I'll never be stuck with just one man to please me. Besides, how would I keep him from spooning my sisters when I'm gone?"

Khulan interrupted, "Better to ask, how can we keep them all from you? Jamukho is too over-worked with his carpentry and keeping track of my lone son and your three daughters, Chotan. If you give him another, he'll be forced to give it to some other man with less work. Already you are mother to four whelps, and three to my Jamukho, before any are grown enough to help, seems hardly fair to my son. Best you learn the life of a breeder and stay on a farm."

"Bah!"

"Bah yourself. We are both thankful to Jamukho's mother and father for their long coupling and common tents. If you keep it up, we'll be forced to declare you a breeder and his helper, taking your horse out from under you so you may do more of the raising and serve as grandmother before your time."

"Ah, Jamukho would have neither of us for long!" Chotan shouted.

"That's not the point! You must stop breeding so many babies to be raised all at once by the same man! Soon he'll think he owns you, ruining you both and confusing my son." She scowled.

"Khulan! Chotan! You are in the Queen's tent!" Beckli Kahnsa shouted.

Of course I had to agree, but deep down inside I was fascinated. How would I keep Sir Drake in a tent with my babies? I smiled at the preposterous thought, which only added to the confused looks from the women studying their new Queen.

* * * * *

Lacellor didn't enjoy the honor of fifty Debrecian warriors

passing through the gates of his mighty castle. Nor, did he witness the passage of a hundred families, over five hundred people, complete with their wagons loaded well above the sidewalls with all of their possessions and skills. Though a negligible fraction of my people, every trade of the Debrecians migrated, a nomadic wealth of skills regarding which the tribes had no rival. All of this equaled only a tiny portion of my people, those who were willing to lend support and the extended families of fifty warriors.

These, as well as our herds, to include nearly two thousand horses, half of them fit for light warriors, passed several miles to the northeast from where I neared Norfaton. I'd sent them around on far roads, hoping to avoid undue royal distractions and speed them on their way. In the south they were needed to help establish the new community and add to the training of my women on the border. Lacellor would learn of them after they'd passed, certainly, but at the time of my arrival near his gates, he'd not yet been informed. To him they'd undoubtedly look like poor refugees from some northern squabble; to me they were beyond value.

Instead, his guards only saw my small contingent at the outskirts of his city of Norfaton. Angel and Beckli Kahnsa's daughter were the only ones in my party. Kahnsajin had pleaded with her mother that she was due her first outing as a young warrior in training. No better outing could be imagined than one with her new Queen. The answer from Beckli Kahnsa was an emphatic no, which only brought more misery to Kahnsajin's mother. She had no peace until she relented, by then agreeing she'd perhaps be better off without the child. This emotion was fleeting as well, for the look in her eyes upon our departure was tormenting even for me to watch. Kahnsajin seemed oblivious to it and only smiled back at her mother, thanking her, blowing kisses to the great prophetess, and promising her trophies from the mysterious south. I noticed the rest of the elders lending comfort to the mother, but also seemingly content with seeing the anxious Kahnsajin gone.

At the edge of the great rebel's city, a lesser knight spotted me and fled toward the castle with the news of our arrival. By the time we got within several houses of the castle, the soldiers in front of the businesses beside the road milled around, looking a little too wary. Then, at the entrance to the castle, I found the gates closed at the gatehouse and the drawbridge beyond in the last moments of being raised.

The only person who didn't shun us stood before the gatehouse. She wore the ragged grey dress of a servant, including an enormous, off-white apron. The whole front of it appeared white with flour, matching the whiteness of the woman's face, which I knew to actually be a little browner than normal for these climes, matching her hair. At her side, two horses waited. One had a small cart attached to him. The cart was filled with all her belongings, which had grown some in the short time the former maid had spent in the castle as both my ambassador and friend to Lady Lettoir.

A little to the side, two members of some minor merchant's family sat on a pile of belongings that had been dumped, telling me Lady Minari had just finished a rather quick transaction for the purchase of the cart and one of the horses. No doubt the master of the load would be back soon with a better horse and a bigger cart.

I knew at once that Sir Lacellor's heart had hardened toward me, and he'd come to some decision regarding a new tactic in striking a firmer position and showing me his displeasure. He'd always shown his annoyance regarding both my offer of conditional alliance and insistence upon a good measure of independence. The lands my women in the south occupied had been his, though abandoned because of the many raids from Farstand knights. It had been my view that our occupation of it served his interests, regardless.

It was, in fact, a welcomed message that he'd so poignantly delivered. After so much tedious negotiation, it was good to at least have an answer.

I asked Minari for the details after she'd mounted and had some time to ease in beside me on the way south from the castle moat. She took her time formulating some thoughts and untying the apron, which I did not slight her. The lady looked bedraggled, and her spirit partially crushed, telling of a long political struggle with the knights in my absence.

Kahnsajin glanced at her with the most curiosity. She asked, "Did you used to be a maid? Do they have so many rooms in their castles that they need people to always clean them and never do anything else? Can we go back and see inside?"

Minari's face showed no patience for it. "Another sister or is she a cousin to Angel?"

"She is neither," I told her, introducing the daughter of Beckli Kahnsa.

This introduction eased Lady Minari some. She nodded to the girl. "Well, they do have some big houses that are endlessly in need of someone to clean them. Perhaps I'll fall back on that profession after this. As for the castle, they appear to have closed the door to us. Sir Lacellor is tired of hearing Abi's long-winded speeches."

"Huh. I didn't know I spoke so much," I told nobody in particular.

Minari said, "It might only seem long. Still, I am tired of speaking to these men for you, and have a good desire to spend the trip in silence."

"As long as you tell me what is around the next corner before we are past it." I studied the woman.

"The great knight has decided he doesn't have to worry about you," she answered, "given you are clearly an idiot and not the Queen. He fears that coddling you has weakened his position with the Debrecians to the north."

"Big mistake, both in his logic and his read of the situation before him. Should I go back and correct him, or let him learn from his error?"

She looked at Kahnsajin again, and I could see the wheels going around in Minari's head, contemplating the meaning of my return with the daughter of a great and much-honored Debrecian leader. The former maid said, "Let him stew. He gave me no end to trouble, and even threatened to fend me out to some old noble woman's household. This was after I made it clear that I wasn't interested in marrying one of his cousins. His ideas seemingly abounded for my better use."

"I shook my head.

"Only the protests of Lady Lettoir, or I mean, Lady Finley now, kept him from putting me into sackcloth as junior maid in the cellars.

She convinced him to let me just linger in the castle until word came from the north, either way. Then she left with her new husband."

"I'm sorry I missed our lady's wedding," I said.

Minari nodded then went on: "A few days back, when they were sure you'd died, I was put in the hands of the cooking staff. I've learned how to roll every kind of bread imaginable."

"My chamberlain and diplomat, subject to the head of cooks?"

"And, now an expert at baking—I should open a shop. As to the head cook, more like her understudy's lackey. My stiff hands will always and evermore smell of bread starter." She sighed. "Not that I am beyond chores, as you know, but I think we all understand the meaning was an insult, not to me, but to your memory."

"I think you are right. We should leave him to stew and let him find our relative values on his own."

"Yes; my thinking exactly. Then, of course, you showed up, and you see how quickly I managed to cross the drawbridge, even before word came down to lift it entirely. It's embarrassing seeing so many grown men afraid of even talking to you. I've had enough of the place, and even if you're not the Queen, how does that change what remains to be done in the south? This whole negotiation has been a waste of time."

"Not entirely," I said. "You see, they've dug themselves a hole. All will become clear, once it has been filled in, and thus I've come upon one of my better ideas, and a solution to what has been troubling me for some time."

Kahnsajin's eyes shifted from one of us to the other, taking in every ounce of our conversation with a level of intensity I'd never imagined possible in a twelve year old. She asked, "Are you going to go back and fight them for saying you're not the Queen and for being so rude to your maid diplomat?"

I smiled at the girl. "No, of course not. They are our allies against the evil lords across the river. Sir Lacellor simply hasn't come to appreciate our contribution yet."

"So he's like a big hole then?" the child asked.

"Yes. Like an empty place waiting to be filled with understanding. Think, Kahnsajin. Are there not great holes in your mind, eager to be filled and leading to so many excellent questions? She nodded.

"Well, Sir Lacellor is like a very young child who has not come as far as you have." I said. "He is not eager to see things before they fall on him while standing in a hole. Nonetheless, they shall."

The girl smiled, obviously pleased to hear she was miles ahead of the great rebel knight in understanding simple things like keeping things from falling on her.

Lady Minari saw the young girl's satisfied expression and said to me, "You terrify me, still. I don't know why I care for you and your causes so much, given your carelessness with wee minds."

"Oh, I'm not so hard. I mean the man no harm, though I imagine we have more surprises from him soon and directly before us."

"It isn't Sir Lacellor I'm concerned about. The child, Abi; she's impressionable."

I looked at Kahnsajin, who was clearly about to say she wasn't impressionable, I could tell. Instead, I beat her to it: "She's on her first ride away from home and in the company of warriors. What should I teach her? That the world is lovely; that everyone she meets wants to tuck her in at night and brush her hair in the morning? Surely you've grown beyond that, and no longer see the world through the eyes of a maid who is content and at peace with a world that dares not invade the sanctity of her mistress's doorsteps."

She thought about it a while. "Fine then, but don't speak to the child in riddles. Tell her what you think, so she will know and not have to guess."

I realized she was right, and so I told the girl, "The great rebel knight, Sir Lacellor, fights against our common enemy, King Falstaff, who is farther to the south, across the great river. We have taken over some of Lord Lacellor's land on the border. We need it for the protection of our women, who have joined us after lives of persecution under the evil King. There, we train women as warriors. These warriors are not as good as us Debrecians, but they are learning and fierce to win their freedom. It is the duty of us strong women to help them."

Kahnsajin pressed her lips together determinedly and nodded.

"Sir Lacellor imagines we should be his subjects. He would be delighted to set some knight above us, so we will slowly lose our freedom through the domination of new men who cannot help but want to rule over us because of habits in the south that make this seem right to them. When they are done, we'll again be weak and no use to either him or ourselves."

She looked at me thoughtfully.

"As the daughter of a great ambassador, you know these things can be complicated. We need the rebel knight and he needs us in this war against the mighty neighbors to our south. But, I ask, what good does it do us if we win our freedom from Farstand, and lose it to another lord?"

"That isn't fair at all." Kahnsajin's face grew twisted in concentration, as if imitating her learned mother.

"Have I told her right?" I asked Minari.

"Better," she answered.

I continued, "We don't hate Sir Lacellor, nor should we hate men, for they are beautiful to women. Yet, it's important that we not trust any man fully, even if his heart is pure, for he shall have sons and they more sons, and one of them will not remember us kindly. We need to make it clear that we are not the footstools of some future king, nor are our lands to be passed to sons when there are good older daughters in line to inherit. So you see it's clear that Sir Lacellor has done us a mighty favor by shunning us."

"Abi! There you go again, confusing the child! Such is not clear at all!" Minari shouted.

But, over to my left, Kahnsajin appeared satisfied, as if she had come to the same conclusion as me and had much to think about in the meantime. And even farther to my left, Angel seemed also content as we moved by the Goddess's will, beyond the city walls of Norfaton.

Chapter Five

The lands between mine to the south and Lacellor's city of Norfaton belonged to the knight, Sir Finley. He had taken a new wife, our own much loved Lady Lettoir, and so I sent Lady Minari ahead to the knight's keep and manor, hoping to invite the new Lady Finley to the south. Minari promptly returned, rebuffed at the gates. I noticed no slacking numbers of Finley guards on the road either, instantly wondering if they were friendly to our cause.

These lands of my South Women abutted the Redwater, to include the only good ford to Farstand. War had flattened it into no-man's land until we'd settled, doing the knights loyal to Sir Lacellor a favor, though they continually acted as if they could not comprehend it.

Kirsta and Salonia met us several miles north of the ford. "Trouble at the ford," Salonia said. "We've found land for our families to the east. Better to settle there."

"Those would be Sir Drake's lands," I recalled.

"And Sir Finley's. Near enough to the border to still be mostly abandoned, though with good farming fields and passable trails."

"And of little strategic value. A few of my women have an encampment, securing our east there. Is this near?"

Salonia nodded, telling me it was the same place. She stared at me, clearly hoping for approval. Would our ten thousand offend the Duke, father of the man I hoped to marry?

"It protects our industry," Salonia advised.

"Yes. One might hope to establish industry in places removed from the enemy's first attention," I thought out loud while nodding toward my chief of scouts.

I turned to other matters. In spite of his kindness in marrying my good friend, Lady Lettoir, Sir Finley might prove more difficult than Sir Drake. It seemed as if I could smell him personally occupying my main settlement at the ford.

"Minari, go to Sir Drake and inform him of our new settlement. Kirsta, organize the tribes in this new place. Salonia, I have use for Hulan's archers and the Greyfeet."

A few minutes later and before these three departed, Hulan emerged from the woods, alongside her ten. A Greyfeet leader named Hara accompanied her. The new woman had another ten archers who hesitated near the edge of the woods. The Greyfeet Queen had sent me ten around the age of sixteen, save perhaps Hara, who seemed a year older. I sensed a great deal of magic within her. I suspected she was a daughter to their shaman. It was no small thing that her Queen had given this young woman to my care.

I had them all dress in more local styles, lest a Finley man pass this strange assembly.

"Hara," I said, "I have promised your Queen we will have no secrets between us. She has graciously given us the gift of you and your archers."

Salonia and Hulan nodded agreeably.

I added, "The Greyfeet are our sisters, just as the women in the south are our poorest sisters. It's clear to me that Queen Risha has sent us dark-haired women, thinking it helpful in dealing with the southern women. This doesn't matter. You can see the Goddess has chosen a Queen with red hair, in between our colors. We will bind all of our forces in a single color, disregarding kin. We are bound by the will of the Goddess. You will have to learn to trust your lives to Hara and her young archers."

This time when they nodded, it seemed with harder thoughts.

"Good. Now, Sir Finley, also an ally, is only a small distance to the south. I suspect he sees himself the heir to our Southern Women. I'm not sure how he'll receive us. I'll have to ask him to clarify his intentions. No doubt he will disappoint me."

Salonia laughed as if the whole picture had shown itself to her. This laughter brought smiles to Hulan's and Hara's faces as well.

I continued, "Yes. I am going to ride right up to him. When he tells me something stupid, I'll have to either pretend it's a good idea or try to convince him otherwise with kind words and patience and all of the other fine tricks a queen needs to learn in the passage of her tests."

"He'll refuse you." Hara grinned and nodded.

Ah yes, I thought, that little squint also contained delight at the prospect of violence, a sign of the shaman within her.

"He'll refuse everything I ask. What is interesting is his refusals will serve my interests. I know how to deal with Sir Lacellor's stubborn mood, for it only clarifies the Goddess's will."

* * * * *

By the next day, I rode with only the brown-haired Kahnsajin on the road south, already passing several northward traveling carts pulled by ponies. More than once, a wheelwright, fletcher or smelter nodded at me as we passed, always with a knowing smile on their faces, as if delighted to be out of the way of some impending trouble. Occasionally I stopped to speak to them and ask about their welfare, for they were my people. I found them most polite and appreciative of my attention.

Kahnsajin endlessly questioned them about the contents of their wagons, and in particular their tools of trade. Between these occasional wagons, I had to tell her that my life would soon depend upon her silence, regardless of what next happened.

She said, "I was only asking the craftsmen—"

"Some of the nobles will be able to see everything about us by your simplest word, or even by the leanings of your accent."

"Oh, I won't tell them anything."

"This is what I know. You are a girl who is used to being answered by breeders, which is not common for children of low station in these parts. You are intelligent and educated, which is rare and certainly not likely for a peasant. Your accent says you hail from the north, and are Debrecian. Those closest to the gods, once they look at you carefully, may even see magic within you, and a destiny that is unbecoming to the men of the south, though it is beautiful to the Queen. They will find out the rest by tormenting you in front of me, forcing me to confess everything we know so they will stop it."

"Oh." She said nothing more for the whole remainder of the trip as she contemplated the consequences of the smallest thing.

After a while I told her, "A leader knows that more is often said without speaking than with a mouth full of words. Not always, but sometimes. By your silence, you've shown me another side to your beauty as a young warrior."

The smile on her face was one that told me she'd come to understand this was our little secret, and most of all, that the lesson was big in her mind.

Sir Finley's men became increasingly less friendly as we neared the settlement. Once near the outskirts, a man even turned and ran south. My flaming hair was tied with a ribbon at the top of my hair, allowing it to scatter like a fountain, a purely Debrecian fashion. I rode my black horse and dressed in the short skirt and baggy britches of a Debrecian warrior. The sword across my back marked me as rare as a virgin in a drinking house.

Kahnsajin spit when the one guard ran away south. I'd recently disguised her as my young servant in a coarse dress. We'd left her bow among the archers.

By noon we entered the main settlement that my southern women had spent most of a year making ready for both industry and war. A few remaining tradesmen busied themselves here, churning out goods for a battle. Some of the new cottages and outbuildings lay boarded up, telling of a recent exodus. Many of those in retreat I'd met on the road.

We passed a half-finished mound of dirt surrounded by pikes. To the south, spiked embankments braced for the defense of archers. These reached a few feet into the river. The ford would prove useful to King Falstaff's main forces, though my raiders had denied him the ability to scout it. I felt sure he imagined it defended by only a few weak women in shallow trenches, which was how I knew he regarded us.

This war seemed predestined to come here just after planting season, a month at best, or maybe as soon as tomorrow.

Up ahead a tall house stood in the midst of construction. Clearly,

Sir Finley had wasted the efforts of many of my new carpenters while I'd been gone. If I was the invader, I'd burn it just for spite.

He stepped out of the portion already finished. Lady Finley emerged behind her man. As I approached, four more knights on horses trotted up from the surrounding settlement, as did several mounted archers of lesser blood. None of my women rode mounts. I noticed several companies of them practicing in distant fields, all afoot and learning crude long pikes under the guidance of some male sergeants.

"Good day to you, Sir Finley," I called.

He stepped forward. "Good morning to you, Lady Abi. I see you have avoided the wrath of the Debrecians. My wife told me you were most resourceful and liable to come back to us only scolded, but I did not believe her."

"Yes, the lady knows me well. So, having thought my return impossible, you've seen fit to build me a house and add your knights to the command of Sergeants Sasha and Hadarm, as well as under the leadership of Lady Marci, whom I last put in charge?"

"Ah well. Do not fear for your sergeants and council member. I've put them to good use, and of course, Sergeant Hadarm is a good man at arms. I have allowed him to retain his rank," Sir Finley said. This meant, of course, that the women had not.

The four knights urged their horses closer, making it clear that they'd discussed me and decided to put me in some kind of loose custody. I looked over at Kahnsajin and gave her a small smile, hoping to relieve her tension and let her know things were not as bad as they seemed.

I said to Sir Finley, "I see. Then there is no reason for me to kill your knights, who seem overly wary, but not nearly enough to save their lives should I be intelligent enough to feel insulted. Perhaps there is an enemy close that has them tense?"

Sir Finley raised his hand. "We should not fight, Abi. I have no desire to harm you. After all, I am good friends with Sir Drake, who intends to make a lady of you. As well, your efforts toward fortifying this ford have convinced even the great knight, Sir Lacellor, that you are simply misguided, not lacking resource. You have proved loyalty to our cause and are perhaps even useful, once settled."

He was right, bloodshed served nobody's interest. I unfastened my sword, and handed the weapon and sheath to Kahnsajin. I pointed to a distant man, knowing him to be Sergeant Hadarm.

"Girl. Take my sword to Sergeant Hadarm, and tell him my full intentions." I was pleased to see Kahnsajin obey me without comment and ride off with my weapon. The men paid her no mind at all.

"And that would be?" Sir Finley asked.

I glanced at Lady Finley's knight and laughed. "To be your guest. And to be as much of a pain in your backside as possible." Upon saying that, I looked at the lady behind him. She grimaced, knowing me too well.

One of the knights came closer, the back of his hand ready to strike. Before he could, Sir Finley commanded, "Sir Carling! Leave her. If she'd have said anything less, it would have rung dishonest. No point in us lying to one another. Besides, Sir Drake will have all of our heads if you were to blemish her face."

"Good for you, Sir Finley—chivalry. Why are you here?" I dismounted. One of the knights grabbed the reins and promptly led the black stallion away.

"We are here to defend the ford, and to make better use of the resources you have collected in this place," Sir Finley said.

"My women ahorse, you mean?" I drew closer.

"We'll have better use for the horses and have learned from your example, putting a few peasant men on a score or so already, as you can see by my new archers. We honor you by experimenting with the new tactic."

"My women?" I asked as we made our way into the house.

"Some are out practicing with pikes, as you've seen. It keeps them busy. My wife insisted that some be kept as peasant soldiers. Their ranks include your Sasha and Marci, both of whom are solid enough, though this Marci is burdened with a child, it seems, and does little but tend her squad's camp, most days. I have relented in many such ways, against my better instincts, so do not press me, Abi."

"I would not think of altering your course."

"Yes. Well, I've put most of the rest of them to the chore of adding to the battlements near the river. A few of the others will soon be on their way to my own lands. There they'll find good men or duties in the town adjoining my keep. I intend to given them letters of worth, and each woman who leaves is to be paid a silver to tide her over. I will see to their welfare and am not unjust."

He thought small. I didn't bother to tell him that Marci's child was the Baron of Helfax's kidnapped daughter.

I stepped forward and shook my finger in his face. "Sir Finley, surely you know this is an offense. You've seen them fight. Even half trained, they're not so bad as to warrant these demotions, nor are they worth much with pikes and afoot. The King will see a few hundred light footmen and laugh!"

Lady Finley stepped back a half step. "Abi! Do not be so overly wrought!"

"Do not fret, good lady. I have no intention of murdering your husband."

The remainder of the knights also entered the house. Sir Finley turned to the one who'd nearly backhanded me. "You see. The woman is honest and has already gotten a good start on making a pain in the ass out of herself. She spoke that way before Sir Lacellor as well, winning herself little grace, but somehow she's managed to cobble Sir Drake with the very same tongue, proving the gods exist."

Sir Carling snorted. "I can see it. Women should be more quiet. Perhaps we'd do well to take her knife and bind her until she settles."

I'd had enough of Sir Carling. "Sir Finley, please tell this man that if he touches me I will kill him and feed his privates to the pigs. Then tell him I am content to let you defend the ford for me. When you are through telling him that, tell him you have the good sense to send your wife all the way back to Sir Lacellor's castle for safekeeping, or perhaps to Sir Drake's castle, which is farther to the side of their likely advance. As well, I hope you have the good sense to stay away from the fighting here, thus not making a widow of her twice."

I left them there, speechless. I approached the fireplace and studied the gruel pot, finding it ample and worth cleaning a bowl out for. While I ate, they looked at me as if I was a crooked picture, but they eventually got on with their other business which was mostly talking nonsense and sending people out to see to the business of the camp.

It seemed they didn't have much for me to do at all, except be quiet and stay put. In minutes, I came to understand the place of a woman, imagining a life of this boredom, plus of course, much more work.

Lady Finley finally got up enough courage to sit with me on some flagstones piled up by the fireplace because the room next door where they went was still being built. She said, "I'm sorry for all of this, Abi."

"Don't let it bother you, Lady Finley. I know you have to do as your husband says."

"What could I—"

"It's because you're a noble, and the blood in you sings to lick his feet and shrink your brain to the size of an acorn the moment he tickles you in the right place," I finished.

"I am not all that! Honestly, Abi. We all thought you were dead. What did you think Sir Lacellor would do? He was ill-content leaving you the lands from the beginning. Since they adjoin our own, he gave this thankless chore of defending the ford to my husband. It isn't as if these men mean to do ill, nor are they virgins at the art of war. As you've well seen, they've beaten the King of Farstand every time, so far."

I nodded to her, vacantly.

"Tell me."

I just kept on nodding.

"For your Goddess's sake. Tell me."

"Fine then. Here's what will soon happen. When the King's men cross the ford, they'll see two hundred women holding pikes, a few hundred more quickly assembled peasant men as well, perhaps. He will see some horribly trained serf soldiers on horses and a handful of knights, including your husband. After he is through laughing at all this, he'll march over us like we are straw dummies, good for a little practice, seeing we are in one place and easily had.

"First, a light rain of arrows. Then the blocks meet." I touched fist to fist. "Women are no good for that. Farstand will butcher these souls to the last. The enemy will be heartened for the next battle. You'll be a widow. My women will have perished or been taken for slaves." I shook my head. "I never intended to hold this ford beyond killing a few of the enemy under a shower of arrows before our retreat."

"Well, my husband is a great knight. He will not be so easily defeated."

"He is a great knight. That is not enough."

* * * * *

Every so often, Lady Finley came by, wanting to engage me in idle chatter or to have me help her knit by holding her yarn. This was supposedly great fun for some women, but I was not in the mood. At least she knew me well enough to not press when I was fretting inside. The day passed into the first signs of dusk without me bothering Sir Finley and his knights, which I'm sure Sir Finley found quite curious; noted by many glances in my direction. This was particularly true when a scout came in with reports, and the knights all huddled over a map, speaking of new sightings of troops near the new duke's castle, two hard days distant. Sir Finley knew me well enough to know that such a tempting discussion was not easy for me to avoid; which is exactly what I did, for there was no report that could have been good, regardless, and my ears were better than any man imagined.

Surprising them even further, I cleaned up with some water and went directly to sleep at the first sign of darkness, curling up on a cot in a convenient corner even before any of the knights had left the lady's house. Lady Finley offered me a cot in an upper room, but I was not in the mood to accept any hospitality beyond the front room and the crudest of accommodations, which I knew to be the best way to show her my displeasure. I wasn't permanently angry with Lady Finley, but it didn't suit me to see her so completely cowed. I had always thought better of her than a herd animal.

In the wee hours of night, everyone in the room cleared, some to upper chambers, some to the sides, most outside to other tents and cottages. It didn't startle me to find a sergeant sitting on a stool by the door. A good spear rested in his hand and a long knife shone at his belt. He eyed me suspiciously. I stood and went to the door where he blocked me.

"I'll not want to pee in the lady's parlor, Sergeant."

"There's a bucket, wench." He waved toward it.

"Wench? Even Sir Finley has the courtesy to call me, Lady, though I confess Lady is not my true title and I don't feel much like a lady at the moment."

He didn't offer an apology.

"I will do my business in the woods, and you are not enough to stop me, though you may accompany me far enough to see that I remain your captive."

"You are meant to stay inside. I was instructed to tell you that you are Sir Finley's guest, not his captive."

"Oh, I see. Well, that would make his instructions to you wrong on two scores then. Perhaps you would do better to make up your own mind on these matters, as it seems you have already figured out the riddle regarding my captivity."

My speech didn't seem to impress him, for the man's eyes appeared dull. I wouldn't have such a man as my sergeant, for I preferred sergeants who disagreed with me in ways that made sense.

Thus I spoke a small spell and put him to sleep before I leaned him on his stool and walked outside. One man in the wee of the night had never been a problem for me. Unfortunately, there were four more soldiers just outside the door. I had no desire to murder them, which I'd always found easier than talking.

"The sergeant has asked you men to see me to the privy." This proved confusing enough. I smelled the obvious direction and went directly to the chore. Once done, I went right back into the house and lay down. The sergeant woke up. He did circles by the door. Finally, he strode in my direction, seemingly both shocked and relieved to find me in the dark corner.

Going back to sleep, I woke up a few hours later. A new sergeant was by the door. This one was thinner and less alert. I got up, put my boots on, and found some bread and cheese which I wrapped in a cloth and stuffed into my shirt pocket.

"Going somewhere?" the sergeant asked.

"Ah yes, Sergeant. I've much to do this morning, and will need to be off well before the nobles awake."

He started to laugh, but then fell asleep when I prayed my chant and twirled my finger into the air, finishing the spell with the magical words, "Tpunwvw Own."

I really liked his spear. He'd carved rings around it and polished it with oils. Instead of stealing it, however, I propped it up beside him and leaned him on the stool, taking only his long knife. It was also handsomely carved and polished about the handle and over half as long as a sword. As well, I took his cloak which matched the fashionable orange colors of Sir Finley's house.

When I stepped out, only one of the four soldiers remained awake, making it easier to put the last one to bed with my chant. One of the men wore a bow and some arrows which I also took, given it had probably been taken off one of my own archers when they'd given her one of their useless pikes.

Four good horses occupied the house's shed, including my own, and so, being of a mind to reclaim much that had been stolen from us, I took my time and saddled them all before leading the string out toward the east road.

Our main settlement spread out for several miles, including many new longhouses, workshops, practice yards, fenced meadows full of livestock, as well as horse sheds. All of this was quiet. The guards lay about, tied up and mostly dragged out of view by my archers, making it quieter still.

I got halfway through the portion of the road that ran through our reclaimed eastern fields before I met Sergeant Hadarm, Angel and Kahnsajin. They came out of the wood line where Sergeant Hadarm later told me they'd recognized my horse. He was also impressed by my plodding manner which suggested I was nothing unusual, always a good stealth-trick.

Kahnsajin rode straight up and handed over my sword like a well-trained squire.

A couple of other men were with them. Sergeant Hadarm made introductions, "You know Niko. His fellow is also steady. They mean to come along, if you give them your word that you'll protect them from any charges of mutiny, should Sir Finley make a stink of it, Abi."

Niko beamed, causing me to recall that he'd once proposed to me. Like me, he was a Farstand traitor; a former guard who'd served with the Baron of Helfax. I gave him a friendly smile.

Then I glanced over at the other one. "You look as tightly wound as Niko. How long have you served?"

"Five years as a guard. I was with Sir Drake's men at Helfax, though I hail from the lands of Sir Finley. Name is Kreger, Lady Abi." He was a stout man. He rode his horse up closer and nodded respectfully.

I admired the sacrifice Sir Drake's new peasant cavalry had made in Helfax. "Well then, the three of you are now sergeants in my company. That is, assuming Sergeant Hadarm wishes to also come along instead of staying with Lady Lettoir."

"I would love to help protect Lady Finley." Sergeant Hadarm shook his head. "I suspect my only chance of saving her is tactics beyond the foolishness of Sir Finley. For that I yield to you."

"So, you rightly see something grand afoot," I said.

"We have a lot to do if your crazy plan is going to work. There's a start on it. I don't know where you got those nine new archers of yours, but they've proven most efficient. They have set up way stations and are most organized. People are already on the march east."

While Sergeant Hadarm filled me in, Hara and her archers came from between the dark shadows of two horse sheds. Hara arrived in our midst almost like magic. It was Hulan's archers that Sergeant Hadarm had originally referred to, but now Hara joined their ranks. He halted his report, clearly startled to see eleven more emerge so silently from the dark creases of our settlement.

I greeted them gladly, and gave Kahnsajin the bow I'd stolen, putting the girl in their care. Hara showed a small smile, clearly pleased to learn she was being trusted with the care of Beckli Kahnsa's daughter, but Kahnsajin was beyond ecstatic when given the stout longbow and set among eleven archers, even if they weren't from her own tribe. The longbow appeared awkward while shot from a horse, but she seemed to hardly care.

All the pastures beyond us to the east had been emptied. Livestock wandered the road eastward, prodded by walking women with sticks. The sergeants scattered out, immediately tending to a host of matters even farther east.

As we returned toward the west, under escort of the Greyfeet and Angel, we left the remaining pastures of livestock for Sir Finley. We left a deepening trail of his guards bound in the tents and barracks. Liberated women were tasked with taking all they could find that was suitable for cavalry. Others, farther to the west and having been told by Salonia's scouts about the expanding conspiracy, found their way past us, lucky to bring only their bodies.

It gladdened my heart to see my women tossing the pikes aside and taking up short spears and bows. Even children and lame women migrated, often bearing loads of arrows, cloth and other needful wares. Their support proved critical to our cause as industry and motivation.

Men who'd been a part of us prior to Sir Finley joined the migration. Most of those were valuable craftsmen. Two days earlier we'd put women north. There they still redirected retreating workers east to Sir Drake's border.

Everyone skirted clear of the center of the holding before finding the eastern road, giving the center of the settlement and the male soldier camps a peaceful morning, complete with the early chirping of songbirds. The air felt crisp. Roosters crowed out the coming new day like they always did. Cows mooed, begging to be milked. Goats ran to the fence closest to the first passing person, hoping for a handout. Sheep took their first lazy mouthful of grass and kept right on growing our next winter's cloaks. Sir Finley would need some animals for his men, but otherwise, the crossing he defended would once again become no-man's land, and the less we left the enemy the better.

When I arrived back at the house, Sir Finley seemed busy organizing a search party for me. It wasn't an inconsiderable posse, consisting of a half score archers, some knights and of course, Sir Finley himself.

This was too much of a temptation, so I waited a few score yards short of mingling with his units. It was still half dark, though I saw very well in the gloom compared to most and thought their torches unnecessary.

"Sir Finley!"

They all turned my way.

"I've come back to thank you for your hospitality, as well as to apologize for mistakenly thinking you meant to keep me captive."

He rode up with Sir Carling and some others. "Ah, so you've not gone far. My wife misses you and has scolded me for my rudeness. Come into our house and we'll have breakfast. As well, I can see you have assembled some of your women as escort. Leave them to the sergeant on duty, and they'll be treated well. In time, I'll not even begrudge you a small guard of women, perhaps for when you are returned to Sir Drake, which may be as soon as end week. He may come himself, and escort you to his keep. This is on my honor. I'll send word, if you like."

"I'm sorry, but I have other things more pressing."

Just then, several men came running in from the west, shouting that a score of women had deserted in the night and had taken good weapons, saddles and the best of the unit's horses. Little did they know the extent, for we'd worked these desertions steadily west.

Sir Finley looked at me, and then at the women behind me again. He possibly thought the Greyfeet were the same women. He shouted for the men to be still.

All of this was too much diplomacy for Sir Carling, whom I took as a man unused to being made to wait by women. He charged at my horse without even bothering to pull his sword. I suppose he thought he'd just terrorize me, grab my reins, and be the hero of the moment.

Angel rode forward, saving me from killing him, for my sword quickly escaped my back and found my hands. My bodyguard blocked him with her horse. She grabbed the halter on his mount with both arms and her chest. The likes of her fierce hold had probably never been seen before, nor since. Then she slowly drew forth a knife and deeply slashed the animal's neck from ear to ear.

It was a rather startling and brutal idea, driving home a point that all of my talking had not yet managed. The cut was huge. Blood spurted from the horse's neck in buckets, causing him to rear, squealing into the clear morning sky. After half rising, the horse fell over dead, pinning the knight's leg under his belly. The knight screamed with rage and pain. Several of Sir Finley's archers ran to his aid.

None of the other men approached us. I looked around, seeing that Hara had twelve bows notched and aimed at Sir Finley and his company. Even Kahnsajin looked steady, though she didn't have a curve-backed bow, and thus her bow was more than her own height and only half as powerful as the others.

Any good soldier could see that these twelve Debrecians had been born with their weapons.

Sir Finley also knew that if he killed me he'd have to answer to Sir Drake.

"I grieve the loss of an innocent horse, Sir Finley."

"Such is not chivalrous, Lady Abi," the knight declared.

"Better a horse than your man. It was a near thing. My bodyguard isn't used to letting hostility so near me. Let me also introduce you to the Greyfeet. They are hand-picked by my very close friend, Queen Risha, of the Debrecian Greyfeet and led by a princess of shaman blood, Hara. She is destined to be a mighty warlord and kill hundreds of her enemies. I have determined that both bodies of Debrecian tribes shall enjoy eternally harmony. I advise that you understand this lesson."

His eyes lit up, and I saw that all the men remained tense, some pulling on their reins, causing a horse or two to back up.

"Now, you'll leave me and my women alone so I can complete their training. Stay and greet the King's men here at the ford, if you think it is wise. This should also make Sir Lacellor happy. In the meantime, let me husband my own army in peace, for you shall soon have need of our help and thank the day I took them from you."

I left him under the watchful screen of my archers. These few Greyfeet stood guard over the western end of the eastern road for the whole morning, allowing my army of women to march halfway to the border of Sir Drake before night.

When we made our first camp only half a day from the lands of Sir Drake, Kahnsajin found her tongue again, yielding me little sleep as she told me all about her time as an archer with the Greyfeet and thanking me endlessly for her first full-sized bow.

Chapter Six

Two weeks later, four hundred warriors had swelled to two thousand, over half coming from the lands of the King. My sergeants, Sasha and Hadarm, had been doing the work of captains before rudeness interrupted their work in the form of Sir Finley. Now they did the work of generals.

I counted less than a month before war, and what I'd thought enough in cadre had become too little. Half my women had no training at all.

We only had enough good horses for my best seven hundred warriors. The planting appeared late. Our first chore became lending some of the stockier horses, of which we had over a thousand, to the plowmen so we could raise enough food to feed my new city of tents and sticks in the midst of Sir Drake's peasants. Hundreds of warriors helped the farmers, saving my best and least for training.

Almost immediately, the Debrecians became the new standard. There could be no greater pretend enemy than a squad of Debrecian scouts.

Across a field, Hulan's warriors mingled with two South Women squads. In the field itself, other women wrestled with horses and a plow; the planting had grown desperate.

Hulan had made a new curve-back bow, having discarded her learner in favor of a more powerful version.

A pole held a straw man wearing a breastplate. One of Hulan's archers showed her how to slowly bring her bow down as she drew. Thus timed, the target entered her sights as the strain of the weapon became highest.

Hulan drew the bow down, aiming it at the breastplate which was thirty paces away. I started to tell her that breastplates cost a smith a full week's labor. Marking one up with dents seemed a shame.

The arrow loosed at the bottom of her draw, ending its flight in a loud bang. To my dismay, the arrow penetrated the plate.

I startled everybody by making my way through the crowd. Convinced that I must have seen a glancing miss, I went over to the breastplate. The arrow had gone halfway through a good thickness of copper.

Hulan stammered, "I'm sorry. We found it in the raid pile. I thought it useless. None of us will ever wear it. It's too heavy for our horses." She paused before adding, "But, we should have asked before putting a hole in it."

"That wasn't good thinking at all then, was it. You'll have to do better. We could have sold this in Lacellor's city for two mounts."

"I'll steal four enemy horses, making it right," Hulan said.

I clapped Hulan on the back. "Don't worry about it. Just remember we cannot afford to be wasteful. Our resources are short, and anything of value means lives. Don't you know that when we burnt Helfax it was by my command and not a rash act."

"No, I didn't know that." Hulan imagined herself nearly a shaman and therefore one of the wise women of our tribes.

I walked her back to where the others waited. "Do me a favor. Put another hole in it?"

"You want me to put another hole in it?"

"Ah yes, and your whole squad as well. Come, all of you. Let's see if we can put eleven holes in it."

Their faces grew uncertain, but the crowd had gathered since my arrival. A hundred women shouted encouragement.

The straw man and his breastplate danced and rattled. Two arrows glanced past. Three dented the metal and fell broken in front of the target. Six stuck.

We all went over to look at the damage. I turned to Hulan. "Is this what you expected?"

The woman put fingers to her lips. "Hum."

"Yes indeed. Keep the breastplate, and after some study, let me know why only half the arrows passed through while others only marked the metal. The power of your bows, shot close enough and at a square angle, might change everything in a battle against knights."

* * * * *

Within the next week, Minari, Marci, Kirsta and I endlessly busied ourselves finding cleared lands upon which we trained, settled, and farmed. In spite of her rough edges, and initial hesitancy toward me, I quickly found that Kirsta was a good choice as a leader for the combined Debrecians. Together with Chotan, they organized two competing units. When not together, these Debrecians acted as trainers and adversaries to squads of South Women. Each Debrecian took command of a score during maneuvers. Niko and Kreger did the same, giving us four advanced-training units.

I remember one maneuver in particular. Kirsta appeared on the offense and charged Chotan's hundred with just under a hundred mounted women. They formed a double line. Kirsta's women came on, soon shifting to wedges two deep, clearly intent upon dividing Chotan's horses.

At nearly the last moment, Chotan obliged, splitting her unit for Kirsta by pulling back at the center and turning both flanks of Kirsta's army inward. The side of a horse is not nearly as frightening as the front of it. Chotan brought her archers up and forward, pretending a flight of arrows at their broadsides. Given that most of Kirsta's archers were mixed in and farther from the new front, I judged Chotan's pretend shots twice those returned by Kirsta.

Wheeling around to the left and meeting half of Chotan's forces caused Kirsta to lose much of her order when some of her women didn't respond as quickly as the others, but it was the only counter-maneuver that made any sense. It at least allowed her forces to meet the enemy better than horse to horse. This change in plans, in fact, hadn't been ordered by a single commander, but by training and through the quick action of each squad leader, for the pound of horse hooves on the practice field deafens and the cloud of dust in the center of the field makes it impossible to see very far.

Chotan quickly altered her plans as well, falling upon the enemy's rear with half her forces, the ones Kirsta had turned from.

I learned a great deal from that exercise, to include that one should never assume an enemy inclined to sit still and let a warlord do whatever she pleased, even if the idea was sound. As well, it was important for each company and squad to have good leaders who knew what to do when all the plans went out the cottage door.

In Kirsta's case, they relied on good leaders in the field. In Chotan's case, the half of her force left unattended looked for a new signal, and all of them saw it when it came, responding to the change without a moment's pause.

Chotan was declared the winner by the three judges who were unanimous in their decision, though I left impressed by both leaders. Kirsta had deployed trained people in the front, and once they'd broken through Chotan's forces, they'd disengaged in good order. Kirsta had also set a screening force of a few reserves. Thus her people withdrew without new losses. In fact, they'd probably survived intact enough to try a second charge, had the exercise allowed it.

Of course, none of these women had actually been hurt, so there came a petty squabble when the judges told Kirsta that she'd lost as many as thirty of her warriors. That happened because of her haste to break through Chotan's lines and not become trapped by the other half of Chotan's army bearing down on her rear. Chotan had only lost ten. I had to agree, but Kirsta showed signs of a proud woman.

"The strength of our horses was enough to kill more than ten!" Kirsta screamed as she ran up to one of my judges.

Chotan slipped off her mount and held out a skin of wine.

Kirsta scowled.

"You beat me yesterday," the calmer warrior said.

"Ahh!" Kirsta grabbed the wine from Chotan's hand, as if stealing it.

Chotan laughed.

"Tomorrow I will beat you so soundly you will weep."

"If you do not fall off your horse."

This went on a while until Kirsta decided to laugh. It seemed forced, but it was just her way.

I rode away with Chotan to see some of her new inventions.

She pointed out Jamukho and the son they shared. The boy was eight or nine, and yet he already did a good job of sanding the rough edges off a tall stack of boards that had been cut to similar dimensions. He stopped his work the moment he spied his mother then ran up to her horse and leapt right up over the rump, hugging her back while she reached around and rumpled his hair.

Beside him scampered two of Jamukho's daughters, I assumed by Hulan. They helped their grandparents spin sinew and hemp into what looked like bow string, though the string seemed a few times thicker.

Some of my South Women worked with them, helping saw boards into even lengths. Everyone labored, though not without chatter and a little singing. Even the occasional view of those lying about and playing had a pleasing effect on me as I rode by. Over on the ground I noticed some learning letters made of block. These people were all about wood, but they were not made of it.

"So this is what a good family is like," I said under my breath, recalling my own miserable childhood.

Chotan looked over at me. She introduced her son and the man who raised him. Jamukho was not the most handsome man in camp, but the steady nature of his polite hello told me he had a good deal of appeal.

"I am glad you have come, my Queen. You will like this." We walked toward a row of short carts. Each was supported by a pair of wheels larger than the beds they bore.

Jamukho showed a sparkle in his eyes when he spoke. It struck me that these Debrecians were not at all like the people of the south. Down there, any person of station was regarded with fear and suspicion. Speaking to southern nobility brought pains of dread disallowing any warm feelings between the classes.

We walked on. "Your family seems content. How do you manage so many small children?"

"Ah! They are no trouble." Jamukho said. "If they get to be a pain, I send them to their grandmother. She has a gift for old war stories and a mighty hug, both of which delight them, but she also has a wooden stick. I think the worst part is that they can't stand it when she pulls it out and tells them she might have to use it someday. It's not the stick. It's the thought that she won't love them as much while hitting them with it. In the end, she makes them sit by themselves until they settle, which is maybe worse than the stick."

I thought that his story might have been the most incredible one I'd ever heard. I couldn't imagine my father sending me to the crone for discipline, or him only showing me some thin little stick and saying, "Now I might have to use this someday. Now, go sit down for a minute."

Once we drew close to the cart, however, I completely forgot the story of his wonderful family. Jamukho lifted some metal braces. He bolted the body of a new machine onto the cart and restored the bracing. Once the slotted machine was secure, he yanked a crank on it ten good thrusts, tensing a thick bow string one snapping tooth at a time. He loaded the center slot with a spear.

"I found some old plans for this. When Chotan told me you'd put her in charge of spears and inventions, I thought it might be worth putting one and two together. It took some tinkering, but I've now put my family to the chore of making more from this modification. I have thoroughly tested this one and I have become convinced of their possibilities. Two can be affixed to every cart."

"It's a ballista," I suddenly recalled from my readings.

"So, it is not a new invention?" he asked.

"New enough to us. I've only read of them in ancient texts of the Vini. I'd imagined ever seeing one. You've not invented a new weapon, Master Jamukho, but you have brought one back from the dead, and from the look of this one, given it new life."

"Well enough. As long as the enemy doesn't have one."

"How far does it shoot?"

He smiled then laughed, as he turned the weapon around. Chotan's face grew a smile, clearly as eager as him. She helped him turn the cart so it pointed out into a long and recently planted field. Once they'd settled the legs of the cart into the dirt, Jamukho nodded to Chotan, whose smile broadened, seeing that he intended to give her the honor. She pulled a handle. The spear took off with all the force of a catapult. It sailed right across the field and across the next one as well, landing in the woods a quarter mile away.

"I can send you more women to help," I said. "We'll need twenty of these, Master Carpenter."

"No need for the extra women, unless you send them to the smiths who make our spear heads. I imagine these things eat up spears, and they need a special kind, shorter with a front-heavy balance. As for the machines, I've set up a way of making all the parts first then spending a couple days putting them together. In fifteen days you'll have no more of these on hand, but in twenty days I'll have your twenty. That's how we intend to make them faster, by building similar parts until they're all finished at once. You have my word on twenty in as many days."

"Well, I'll send you three more helpers anyway and have Chotan come by on occasion to keep me up to date on the work. You'll still need time to play with your children, so make good use of the help. I'll not have your family worked so hard that we all lose sight of why we are fighting this war."

Both Chotan and Jamukho smiled, and though I didn't ask them what so pleased them, I suspected Chotan was no longer worried that Jamukho and Hulan would be making any more babies in the very near future.

* * * * *

Salonia was not so happy when she rode up to tell me her scouts had intercepted four knights coming into the camp from the north road. She'd tracked them from an inn they'd left just before dawn, which was in a small town five miles to the north. I had Salonia send me Khulan. (Khulan had the stoutest women among us, all armed with spears and swords). We set out to greet these knights before they discovered the secrets within our camp.

The knights halted in the road before us, looking much like the knights of Sir Finley, only shinier. I could not imagine them having ridden their horses the full previous day while bearing so much frill and armor. Their horses looked tired already, though I noticed that each led a spare. Perhaps the knights had packed their armor until the inn.

I had no trouble recognizing two of the men, for I'd met several of Sir Drake's knights during the raid on Helfax.

The knight wearing the prettiest armor said, "I am Sir Esaudrin, here at the bequest of Sir Daren Drake. He has sent us as an honor escort for Lady Abi. He wishes that all who see us note the special circumstance of her ladyship."

His eyes remained on Khulan who was a solid warrior and clearly the leader of her ten. The two who knew me blushed because of his mistake, as did Khulan. She glanced my way.

I rode forward. "I am Lady Abi."

"Ah. I should have known, but thought you too lovely for our young master." These polite words accompanied a rude gaze at my bosom. I'd dressed in a long, tan tunic, dark brown skirt and baggy britches tucked into my knee-high boots. Other than the length of britches, this was standard for a Debrecian, and increasingly so for the women of the south as well, but his eyes lingered upon my bosom anyway. After that, he fell to studying my hips, as if measuring me for children.

Then he regained his mind. "He told me to read this salutation, my lady."

He unfurled a scroll. "Dear Lady Abi, holder of my heart. I have had word from Sir Finley and suspect that he has not treated you as kindly as he should. Do not fault him, for he is overly proud and sees your contribution as temporary. No doubt, he thought he was doing you a favor. I have sent him a message telling him otherwise. He and Sir Lacellor thought it likely that you had not survived your captivity at the hands of the Debrecians. Well, even though I tasked men to scouring the lands, I have seen the Goddess's hands upon you and did not doubt your return. Please accept my most honorable escort, and bring those with whom you share confidence, as I invited you to my father's castle. He and my mother would be pleased to meet you. Last, I must say, I am more pleased than any other. It is signed, Sir Daren Drake; your beloved knight."

"Tell me, fair knight; why has Sir Drake not come to me himself?"

"It seems that neither Sir Lacellor, nor Sir Finley, informed us of your arrival. Only upon the arrival of your envoys, requesting the use of our lands, did he become aware of your exact whereabouts. The man opened his cellars, you should know, upon hearing of your safe arrival within his borders and nearly upon his hearth's steps. Still, he has committed to training and exercises, and thus awaited your visit while teaching sword and horse sense ceaselessly. When neither you nor further word came, he grew increasingly anxious, sending me with these messages of welcome. To be honest, my lady, the man works twenty hours a day, knowing the closeness of the King's next invasion, for he is not only the champion of Sir Lacellor, but will soon be called upon to defend the lands of his own father. He has nightmares; visions of his parents suffering under the King's siege."

I nodded, knowing the feeling.

* * * * *

The best I owned was the same skirt and tunic under my council robe. The robe had been dyed with large, vertical stripes of brown, yellow and red, marking me as a Debrecian Queen, though it was not nearly as fancy as the dress on the lowest serving maid in a high lord's keep. I'd not worn the gown since leaving my council's tent in the north, knowing I still awaited the judgment of Beckli Kahnsa's prophecies, but it felt necessary to wear it on such an official visit as this one to the home of my fiancé's parents.

I put my sword across my back and affixed my knife sheath onto a belt. That helped me feel a little more comfortable in the large wool robe.

When I emerged from my tent, all the women gathered around and dismounted their horses. Even those afoot fell to a knee. This was the first reaction of all the Debrecians. Every woman around them saw it, doing the same.

It was the first time I'd felt like a Queen among these South Women, and it felt a wee bit uncomfortable, so I had to say something. "I'll be away for a short time. Rise and go about your many good duties. In my absence, listen to Marci on matters of the camp and to Kirsta on matters of war and to Sergeant Hadarm on matters of training, and most of all, to your hearts on matters relating to the Goddess and the health of your families."

This they took as a blessing, rising and going about their duties cheerfully, though they still watched my every move as I straddled the horse whose reins were held by Kahnsajin. She presented a quiet and respectful countenance, as if about to explode with a million words the moment she uncorked. When I'd first told her about the trip, she'd simply screamed the word, "Castle!" That apparently tided her over long enough for me to dress. Needless to say, I could not leave her behind. Besides, who would speak for Angel if I split them apart?

Seeing all of this respect from my people, the four knights showed upraised eyebrows. They no longer spent long moments looking at my breasts, though some still measured my hips for children.

Chapter Seven

My hometown consisted of a barn, a drinking parlor and some houses, all at the edge of the mountains where thieves and murderers prospered. My father had never liked seeing me there, so I'd only gone on a few occasions. People thought me strange in my hometown as well, for I was a headstrong, gangly and red-haired wench when young, clearly the spawn of some bad seed and most probably a witch. A few of the men, I am sure, were well aware that my mother had been a Debrecian, captured in a war. She'd been horribly crippled, tamed to the leash of my father's cabin. I knew far too little of this until too late.

I did not like towns much.

"How fast can you pee and get back in the metal britches?" Kahnsajin's voice carried from the rear.

On other occasions, I'd hid myself from prying eyes or been openly scorned. Never will I forget being paraded through towns at the end of a rope, battered by rocks and whatever else was handy and could be spared. Even while traveling to the south and escorted by my Debrecian warriors, the many had looked upon us from a fair distance and with great mistrust.

Well, I traveled north again, looked upon in yet a third say.

"Do castles drip like the rocks in caves?"

Riding northward toward Drake's castle, we passed through several more towns within the lands of Sir Drake. First among us came two of the knights in their finest armor. Then Sergeant Sasha and Khulan rode side by side, taking the time to grow familiar with one another's ideas of tactics, camp gossip and home-life.

"How do you scratch an itch in there?"

Two of Sasha's archers rode behind those in front. I came next, escorted by Sir Esaudrin. Also in my party were Minari, Angel, a fourth knight and of course Kahnsajin who spent much of her time pestering whatever knight whose turn it was to travel beside her.

"How do your people move around if all the houses are wood and stuck in one place?"

"I can sneak up when you have your metal hat on!"

"If you fall down, can you get back up?"

"Bet I can run my horse around yours three times before we finish racing to that yonder tree!"

"Here! See if you can shoot my bow with steel fingers and without snagging the string on a plate!"

"Trade my bow for your sword! I can make another bow. Trilan's teaching me how to make a curve-back; she's with Hara and knows everything about how to make the best bows in the whole wide world, and sometimes out of nothing but what she finds off a tree and a dead animal while out hunting."

Last rode the rest of our women guards, two stout Debrecians of heavier arms. They were at a perfect distance to hear every word Kahnsajin said as she persisted in finding the answers to everything known and a few things never meant to be. More than once I heard a snicker from way back there among the last two.

It was an entirely different experience riding into these towns under the honor escort of some of Sir Drake's finest knights. People came out of their houses to watch and showed us polite faces.

Children raced and stood beside the road, gawking up, guessing who each and every person was and how we ranked among ourselves or in what way we fought against the enemies of the land. The gossips stopped talking altogether as we entered the center of town. They gave us their full attention, hence feeding their stories for the next decade or two.

The trip had started in the morning. Thus we had several occasions to stop and water our horses and even enter roadside parlors. There we ate hot food served on tables and on both wooden and glazed plates. The serving wenches curtsied and presented the food while employing stiff postures and stilted words, as if unsure of what pleased the high-born.

People looked at me the most, for it was quickly apparent that even the knights bowed slightly my way while speaking. I don't imagine that my Queen's gown appeared obviously noble to the peasants either. Yet they could not remain completely ignorant of the way the men acted, nor of my escort of Debrecian bodyguards.

I made every effort to be polite in return, giving greetings to all we passed. As well, even though the knights insisted that it was our noble's due, we paid in full for their goods and services. If I was to be a wife to their lord's son, word would more quickly spread by the peasants' mouths than any others.

An hour before nightfall we rode through a peasant town, and up to the moat that circled a steep hill. Four towers arose on each corner of a handsome keep with a pitched wooden roof that showed a hand higher than the stone walls.

We had arrived at the small castle of Sir Drake's father and mother. It struck me that I'd neglected my fiancé to a fault. It wasn't until we were at the gates, and the drawbridge lowered, that apprehension crushed me. The chains rattled and the great wheel squeaked, sounding like something between my soul and my bones, both suddenly under siege and falling as heavily as the great bridge.

It soon settled, and the gates yawned. Kahnsajin sat quiet in her saddle, though my shaman ears heard her heart racing. Her eyes were so wide that I doubted she missed a single detail of her first view of a castle entry. Never had I imagined a child so excited. It was impossible to not love her, for her strength was all the strength I could muster. Angel rode beside her, giving the knights some peace. My bodyguard smiled and appeared pleased to see the castle. She usually did not like any place other than our tents.

Minari and two of the knights raced ahead, eager to make some kind of announcement to our hosts.

The sun had almost faded, lending a red glow and deep shadows to the punctuating yellow lights of a hundred torches. The place was overly lit; as if adorned with the word anticipation. The lights and gaping gates on the other side of the moat represented every glow and depth of anticipation and fear within me.

My horse's hooves struck the wooden bridge, echoing across the lonely watery moat and cold castle walls; tapping into vacant stillness, the sounds of strangers.

What was I getting myself into? My hands trembled! My stomach strained in knots worse than before any battle. Sweat beaded along my forehead and dripped like rain across my face.

How was I to manage this? I already had two nations to manage, not to mention coddling allies of varied disposition. Both of my peoples had needs and were soon to be plunged into a war with an enemy several times their numbers. Had not the actions of Sir Lacellor and Sir Finley shown me what became of anything left unattended even for a few days? *I have no time for this! Surely it is not practical! Where will we live? Among what people, and who will be in charge of who, or even what lands? What am I thinking? How can I even dare think myself capable of managing a husband?*

I looked over at Kahnsajin and asked myself: *Or children?* Could I bear them into battle? Could I leave them at home? And where was that?

My horse moved me forward, along with the others, as if my mind had no rule whatsoever over the matter of my own fate. I'd become ice in my saddle. A thought of turning my horse and launching us into the moat went fleeting through my head.

My horse moved me to the other side of the castle walls. There appeared a vast mid-grounds stretching to either side. After several yards, the flagstone roadway stopped at the entrance to an enormous keep. Pretty brown stones braced the entry. Comely drapes masked the arrow slits. People were assembled on steps that were broad and four high and thus capable of giving a good impression for noble greetings.

I could not ride up to the steps, for my soul felt crushing. Instead, I stopped my horse, dismounted, and knelt in the middle of the road. I lifted my eyes to the heavens, and through the hesitant movement of horses, saw the pattern of the early stars above. They changed into the likeness of the Goddess's face. She had no end to her means of showing herself.

"Tell me what you see before us, for as great as you have blessed them, my eyes cannot see the sense of it!"

The stars spoke. "The world." The Goddess once again left me a message of irritating ambiguity.

I screamed with all my voice, "The world? The world, you say? How big is this world that you should place it upon my back!?"

"Not all that I lay across your back shall be without pleasure."

"While I do not doubt you, my Goddess, I am endlessly reminded of those things weighing my back. They cannot be witnessed by the senses. Tell me more, and while doing so, visit a good dream upon Beckli Kahnsa, for much remains unfinished."

"Child! Do you not wish to speak to me better? Can you not say, holy is the mother, or blessed is the Goddess and tremble under my sight just a little?"

"Surely all of that, should we ever have the time for it." My body shook.

She laughed. "You are my delight. I shall send a dream to your prophetess. And, you shall get up out of the dirt. Go greet this man whose heart is breaking."

"And so, what do I make of this breaking heart that is before me, and what sort of agreement should be made regarding the responsibilities assailing the lives of both me and this man?" But, upon asking, I noticed the stars were no longer aligned in her image, but only tiny dots of fire arranged as nonsensically as before.

When I awoke from my loud prayers and self-absorbed trance, I expected to witness all the people looking at me as if I'd lost my mind. Instead, I saw only the backs of nine women. They'd formed a ring around me, lending as much privacy as possible. The horses were absent. I noticed through the women's legs that they were being taken to a distant stable by some boys bearing lanterns. The knights were assembled with the onlooking and curious crowd of nobles that filled the steps and landing before the inner keep gateway.

I came to my feet, somewhat embarrassed about my screaming. Kahnsajin turned and quickly assumed the squire's task of brushing my clothing free of dirt and debris. Minari started on my hair, brushing it with an ivory brush before braiding several strands above my ears and then together behind my head, lending some kind of order to it.

Still guarding the edge of our circle with the others, Angel looked troubled and fidgety, but not in a violent way. It was more like she was concerned for my state of mind and eager to let it be known that our business in the middle of the road was serious and not to be looked upon as a sign of weakness. It always amazed me how easily I read Angel's moods, not to mention the seemingly unpredictable nature of her awareness of some situations that confronted her. Most thought her crazy and deficient, but when it came to matters of the spirits, Angel was a lighthouse.

I sensed a quiet awareness from the Debrecians, for the presence of the Goddess's spirit lingered as thick as soup.

I asked them to turn my way. "The Goddess has placed the world upon our backs. Thus I must go greet this man. Yet, know I am only one woman and will need the help of all your kind faces, if only for my nerves."

Of course, they did not know what to say to this, but there was no doubting the devotion I saw in all their eyes. I asked Minari to introduce me to the mother and father of Sir Daren Drake. They were only a few paces away and still waiting patiently, though much mumbling came from within their ranks.

A rather startled group of faces met me ten steps farther and at the base of the steps. Fortunately, Sir Daren Drake was the first to speak after Minari's simple but eloquent introduction: "May I present Lady Abi."

"My beloved. I am relieved that you have arrived safely." He bowed, took my hand, and kissed it under the Goddess's stars.

This man, I thought, is the most dangerous thing I have ever met in my entire life. I knew this because he caused me to forget all my apprehensions, to include the world that weighed my shoulders. I'd become a warrior without a shield. I stood as if a woman disrobed. Not a person in the whole yard existed but the man before me who'd twice called me a murderess and traitor to my face. I'd let him live so that he might someday bow before me like this and call me his beloved.

Chapter Eight

"We know so little about your blood," Lady Drake said. "Daren's
. . . vague on the subject. All we've heard is ridiculous gossip that you
proclaim yourself a Queen. What gains us, an alliance with your
family? For that matter where, pray, is this family?"

"She has made her own way as a well-regarded warrior who has
gained a considerable following," Daren said.

I squeezed his hand under the table.

The father stared at me as if I was his worst nightmare. That came
between sizing up the purse of my lips, the taper of my neck and the
swell of my breasts.

They'd given me an hour for cleaning and rest, as well as to select
from among a half-dozen dresses that someone had seen fit to hang
in my room. So, sitting there in the plainest one—and without even a
knife for company—I felt unprepared. How was I to compete with a
woman so used to the tedious gossip of court? When it came to
matters of high-blood, I was an utter disaster.

When I felt at my worst, I always lost my senses: "I am a bastard.
But, of course, such cannot be true, for some man must have raped
my mother, lest I'd not woken up in our cabin and also be here. Then
again, there are no bastards, only wandering parents."

I did not proceed. Daren's eyes widened when his mother's
mouth startled to move. He quickly interrupted, "What she means to
say is—"

"But of course I am exactly as I seem," I interrupted. "When a
child, my best days were when my father was out murdering and
thieving and thus leaving me and my mother alone to plot against him.
I would murder him now and steal his soul, if I had the time."

I doubt anyone breathed.

"I poached from Lady Lettoir's forests. At night I ran with wolves. For clothing, I had one piece of cloth, and endlessly mended it until indecent. My teacher was an old witch who sinned against our King daily. She would have hanged had they known what she taught me. We prayed to strange gods, cast spells, and learned how to ferment rebellion.

"I was made from dirt, lived in dirt, and have eaten dirt when hungry enough. Lady Drake, the dirt of the world was my teacher, and so now the dirt of the world is my domain."

"My word." She covered her mouth with a fancy cloth bearing hours of stitching.

"Oh, do not faint," I said. "It is not my will that makes the land mine, Lady Drake. The Goddess has proclaimed it. Perhaps she is right. After all, any peasant can stand on a hill, look down her arm and hold the next mountain in her hand. I only dare to draw my hand back and take what has been given."

Daren had gone stiff, as had his father. It looked to me as if Lady Drake might soon get up and leave the room entirely, assuming she did not keel over dead from redness.

Kahnsajin shook her head and sighed. I glanced over at her, hoping she would not say anything that might embarrass us. Well . . . perhaps not embarrass us more than I already had.

I realized I'd stood and sat back down. For the moment, I came to my senses and took a bite of the warm rye bread. It was delicious.

Over by the door, Angel stood at loose attention, showing no expression other than thought. She lingered beside a serving maid who was having a hard time pretending to show a face of utter ignorance, which I knew was preferred by those in power whenever they chanced a glance at the servants. Down the table, Minari sat stone-mortified, probably wondering if any of her hard diplomacy would ever bear fruit.

Completing our table, Sir Esaudrin tried to sit comfortable beside Khulan. His eyes were saucers of surprise and hers were saucers of wonder. Khulan and Kahnsajin knew for whom I spoke, taking my words quite seriously, even when the words were only about my miserable childhood. Did these nobles not understand that it was not where a woman came from that mattered, but rather what it had made of her?

After an embarrassing pause, I said, "Look at Khulan, and you will see the truth that goes unspoken among these meaningless questions and answers."

The parents glanced at the tough Debrecian, but I knew they only saw a hard woman in woodsman clothing and did not even discern that the Debrecian's belief in me was power itself.

"It was that Zosh priest whom I will never forgive!" Daren's mother said. "Zosh is old. He is probably dead; assuming such a blessing can be had among the heavens."

When her husband did not comment, the woman went on. "He told our Daren he would marry late and should spend his time solely in the arts of war. Well, now that he has become Captain of Sir Lacellor's knights, what have we in return?"

"It is a high honor," Daren said. "I will soon be needed."

Her husband said, "Dear—"

"Adalina was a perfect match. Sir and Lady Pardrill are too old to bear more sons. That left poor Adalina. The families of Drake, Pardrill and Lacellor would be solidly linked, I told these men of mine, but . . . that priest! Gods, I hate the day he came and told my sixteen year old son to turn Adalina's offer away and keep playing on his horse. Now . . . now my son is a score and seven, and thinks he needs to settle for a peasant bride who makes false claims and cannot even find her proper place in a good peasant house; thinking herself one of the boys!"

"What you see is only the surface, mother. Give it time."

"You can do better than this woman," the elderly Sir Drake said "As even she has said; she is barely a decent peasant."

"Who knows not her tongue," finished his wife.

Kahnsajin jumped half out of her chair, and shouted, "You can't talk to her that way. Don't you know—"

I held my palm her way. "If this Lady Adalina had married Daren, how many more men might come to the aid of Sir Lacellor?"

"Hardly the point," Lady Drake said.

While glancing at her husband, I said, "I have four hundred

warriors on good horses. Many times that will be ready in short order. These four hundred are bloodied and well-armed, but most importantly, well led, for I have found good leaders and charged them to mentor others in the subtle arts of war. We will be a great deal of trouble to the King. I know, for I was trained by a great warlord, masquerading as a witch, but one nonetheless."

The older Sir Drake peered at me. "I have heard of your squatters on our lands. I put up with this in the interest of peace in this castle, and of course, insist that it's temporary. As for women on horses . . . ." His shaking head and expression said the rest.

I had heard this before. I stood. "Insult me all you like, but do not insult my women! They will either be given, or *take,* all the room they need to live good lives. Not even this family will stop it."

"Abi, please; sit." Daren stood beside me and held my arm.

Kahnsajin took that pause as her opportunity. "Don't you know that Abi is our Queen too? If she wants, she can bring as many warriors as she wants to fight for you if you're nice to her! And, we've got lots more land than here and can fight as good as any old knight in a steel can!"

I sat down again, hoping to calm her and let her know she couldn't shout in a room and have anybody actually listen to her.

"I have decided. You are a philandering peasant and may not marry our son." The older Sir Drake stared at me again, seemingly expecting me to swoon and beg, or even better, storm out.

"I think this has all been too hasty," the younger Sir Drake tried. I felt his hand loosen somewhat on my arm.

"Good. Then it is settled. I will not disrespect the parents of my fiancé." I reached for more of the excellent food, finding half a pheasant.

"You have heard what my husband has decided? Do you understand that our hospitality is no longer extended? You are free to leave the room," the woman across from me said.

She had probably expected more of a fight, but I'd already gone onward in my head. "Of course I heard you, my Lady. I can't say it is unexpected, for I am notoriously terrible before courts of nobles. It seems I can speak before any audience, but the moment I am before nobles, I forget my manners, grow haughty, and am soon dismissed. Someday, perhaps, you will teach me how to do better."

"Young lady, we will do no such thing. You and your rabble are dismissed. You may stay the night, but my husband's knights will have you out of this castle by the first of dawn."

"As it should be. We have much to do; all of us." I picked up a good portion of lamb and bread and piled it up on the useless cloth made only for cleaning my mouth. After all, Angel had been asked to stand through the entire dinner without a scrap. Even my other guards had been fed at a good table among Sir Drake's men.

"I'm terribly sorry," Daren Drake said, and one look over at him told me he truly felt that way. He kissed my cheek.

"Do not despair, beloved," I said. "If you do not mind terribly, we shall wait to be married until after your parents change their minds."

"Never!" the mother declared.

"Oh, most surely. The Goddess has spoken on the matter of our marriage, and she is always right, oft to my lament. As for Zosh, I do not know him, but he seems an insightful old God to me; perhaps wise in his old age. He must dislike Sho as much as I do, and it is a good thing Sho is slow to pick up on certain mysteries. Anyway, Zosh has clearly allied himself to the Goddess in this matter, given your news. Such is too apparent to be a mere coincidence. Do you not see the plot that brings your son and me together, befitting their sense of humor and godly tricks? All of this is quite clear, once you come to understand how the gods work their magic."

"You are mad and have bewitched my son with your talk of gods and low-brow magic," the woman yelled.

I folded the cloth over the food and stood to leave with it. As I departed, I thought to say that the Debrecian way was to bed the man and let the marriage take care of itself in the form of wee ones. Of course, I could not flaunt the Debrecians at these people without a good prophecy from Beckli Kahnsa, in spite of Kahnsajin's flickering eyebrows and endless hints that I should show some proof that I was indeed the great Debrecian Queen.

Perhaps I should have done a parlor trick, and lit a candle with a chant? I thought: Let them think I am only a woman of the south, and my alliance with the Debrecians a mere fantasy. It is better to show them what I am willing to risk today than what I hold as reserve against the King's might.

I turned at the door. "We differ on these matters of the heart, but in regards to war we must be allies, Lord Drake. The King will soon be at the steps of this castle. Your knights will come to my call, and my women will defend your lands in ways you have yet to envision."

"My wife has spoken. I doubt an alliance is possible," the elderly noble said.

"That is not the right answer, Lord Drake. We will have no time for hesitation. Think clearly on this matter. Ask yourself what you have to lose, should Sir Finley fail to defend the ford with a few hundred peasants holding pikes and with a score of overconfident knights."

He thought for a moment, ignoring the looks from his wife who seemed intent upon persuading him that an alliance with my women was a terrible idea. It was going to be horribly difficult having that woman as my mother in law.

"She will have those in my band, if not all our knights," his son said. "On the field of battle, there are few as clever. I know none other who rides with a God."

Daren's mother sighed heatedly, obviously disliking that sort of talk from her son.

To his credit, her husband nodded, though with great reluctance.

"Good. Now listen. When I send my messengers, do precisely as they say. My prophetess has told me this will be a terrible and bloody war. We will not have time for foolishness, for I will not ask if the need is not pressing. If you do not accept me as a Lady, do not make the mistake of thinking of me as a cowering peasant who is ignorant in matters of battle. I have seen visions of a thousand men dying before my blade. That prophecy is well written and yet to be fulfilled."

Daren looked at me, then his parents, then back at me, his expression uncertain. Only his glossy eyes tattled on the sorrow inside.

I gave him a smile and left them to their displeasure.

* * * * *

At dawn, my fiancé watched from across the court. He had a half score knights with him, all in chain and travel clothing. My fiancé intended to ride to Norfaton, summoned by the little rebel King. He meant to leave moments after my departure.

Daren's father stood close to his son, stern faced. The man's arms were crossed. Our last horse had not even cleared the bridge before the portcullis in the gatehouse beyond crashed down and his men manned the moat bridge's wheel.

"Their knights will not come," I told Minari, Khulan and Kahnsajin, who rode with me. Angel and our other five scouts, worked both ahead and behind.

"You may have made an enemy," Minari said.

I looked over at Minari, a woman who had come a long way in my company since the day she'd been the meek housemaid of Lady Lettoir. Sometimes I hated the things she said to me, mostly because she was right.

"Lady Minari, next time I go before the nobles to speak, bind my hands behind me, and put fetters on my ankles and a scarf across my mouth. Then I shall say my peace."

She laughed once, breaking the iron face she'd aimed toward me since the evening meal. "That might keep you from saying something loony."

"Ah, it is not that. It's that a bound and harmless woman seems the only type a nobleman and noblewoman admire. I was not loony, but honest and forthright. It is clear to me that such is completely unexpected and totally under-appreciated. I was much better as a speaker when sixteen and ignorant. Then I bowed and uttered one lie after the other, not even knowing it."

She was not content to take my lesson: "Well then, Abi, you now know the difference between a Queen and a diplomat. Maybe someday they will see you as a Queen and make allowance for your loony penchant for honesty. As for me, my job is made much more difficult by your insistence that I not bring you before them bound, fettered and properly gagged, as you so well noted on your own and without my help."

Khulan found that amusing, but surprisingly, Kahnsajin took offense. "You can't talk to the Queen like that!"

Minari shrugged. "I believe it is my job to speak to the Queen any way I feel is honest and constructive. I'll save my cowering and lying for the knights and nobles I have to go before while representing her. You, above all the rest, should know this. Isn't your mother a great diplomat?"

Just then, Yellow Eyes made his appearance, which was unfortunate, for I'd just gotten the impression that Minari had rendered Kahnsajin speechless with her answer, and I was denied the amusement of seeing how long it lasted.

Yellow Eyes strolled right in among our horses, sending them scurrying in a number of directions, including into the ditches on the right side of the road.

He was laughing inside, always fond of the way horses made a fuss over him, usually even for several days after making his acquaintance. I had to agree with him: Horses were like large knights; the bigger they came, the smaller their brains.

Over by the left side of the road, an old and mangy bitch poked her head out of the bushes where she impolitely displayed her teeth. A streak of brown ran through her grey coat, giving her an almost sickly cast of yellow.

"Where have you been, Yellow Eyes?" I asked when the horses settled some.

"Chasing after you, all the way north and then all the way south. I'd appreciate it if you stayed put for a little while," he told me in my head.

Yellow Eyes had his way of complaining that really wasn't a complaint at all, but rather a statement of fact, as if it really didn't matter much either way, since it was over with, but was just something a little bit on his mind. Knowing this made getting to the next point of a conversation easy. "Who is your friend?"

"Oh, that is Slow Leg. She is the one who made me too slow to catch up to you, and she's useless at hunting. I nip at her, but she won't leave me alone."

He went over to the bushes, and bared his teeth at the bitch. After a nudge, she scrambled out of the cover and onto the road. The wolf came showing teeth again, but with her tail between her legs and a pretty ugly limp from a bad back leg. The leg had lost most of its fur. When I dismounted she nipped at me, making a mighty show.

Yellow Eyes couldn't possibly have run across a meaner, uglier, thinner, sicker, older and more useless bitch if he'd sorted through every pack from Farstand to the Debrecian borders. She'd clearly been cast out, and I could count at least five reasons why.

I reached up on my horse and unpacked my staff. Then I set myself to the chore of beating the mean bitch senseless. One more blow to the head was all it would take, I determined when she passed out in the middle of the road and closed her eyes, barely breathing. Yellow Eyes was right; she was slow, and, in spite of all the snarling, hadn't even put up much of a fight.

"For gods' sake, Abi! That's cruel! Leave the poor animal alone!" Minari screamed. She had a kind streak, mostly toward whatever was suffering under my spite. The rest of the women were shuffling their horses away, seemingly embarrassed and pretending to not notice what I was doing.

I knelt in the dirt, and picked the unconscious wolf up, setting her on a fallen tree. Then I called my warriors around. For the first time, I noticed timidity in Kahnsajin's eyes. She'd finally seen something in me that she did not idolize.

I had their attention. "This wolf is what will soon be the lands of Lacellor. In my visions I see this land beaten and near death. Much of it will be their own doing, for their ways of thinking are old and they are barely limping. To our eyes, much that we see is not right."

I knelt, raised my hands to the heavens, and said the same chant I'd said over Reba, my first horse who'd been a broken nag. She'd become the favorite horse of my shaman, Batya, because of a blessing of youth and vigor given to her by the Goddess.

I said all the proper words and spun my fingers into the air. "Tpunwvw Own!"

The wolf woke up, and seeing all the attention, leapt to the ground. She ran a good ten strides down the road before glancing back. She tilted her head, as if wondering why she no longer had the desire to attack and bite me for what I'd done to her.

Kahnsajin spoke with slow words of wonder, "She's beautiful. How did you do it?"

"I did not do it. The Goddess wants you to know what is before us. It is a vision for your contemplation. We will have our portion of Farstand, after we have suffered enough." My warriors no longer glanced about as if they did not want to bear witness.

"My Queen," Khulan said, "I will follow you and your wolves to the ends of the world and beyond. There my soul will be blessed even in death and return a shaman. I have heard enough of questions these past two days, and I have come to know what it means to see the return of a queen."

Khulan was a woman of few words, and so both Debrecian and Southern Women listened carefully to her oath.

The wolf was only paying attention to herself. She snarled once, liked the sound of her own voice then sniffed at her backside. The sickly brown stripe was a deeper brown, rendering the streak pretty in a way. I could even smell a lovely new spirit about her. She trotted around in a circle, spry as a fox in spring, obviously in love with the look of herself. It struck me that much of her ugliness and mean spirit before had stemmed from self-loathing.

Yellow Eyes walked up to her and sniffed her tail. He said, "That's a good trick."

"I think you two should go off hunting for a while," I said.

"We are pack," he said to me. He showed me his fun face; the one with his tongue hanging out and his legs planted stiff at a wee angle in front. His bitch looked at me too, seemingly curious to know why the male showed a human so much attention. Without further word, Yellow Eyes raced off into the woods. Slow Leg looked from him to me in two fleeting glances, but Yellow Eyes wasn't even completely off the road before she went racing after, and with her new good body, catching up.

* * * * *

We were only halfway home and the morning sun nudged only half up when one of Salonia's scouts, along with one woman from the south, whom she mentored, came riding hard from the direction of Sir Drake's castle. "Nine knights in mail have ridden from the castle, and are making fast time in this direction. They bear swords, three longbows and spears; made light for travel, though ready for battle. I do not like the look of it."

I tried to imagine what they wanted. Salonia was the best and her report ominous, but why would the Drakes want to meet me in combat instead of just ignore my presence?

When we saw them coming over the last hill, I had us deployed in a battle stance. My archers were well to the sides and Minari had custody of Kahnsajin to our rear. The scouts vanished in the woods where they'd be ready to swell our numbers and hit a flank. Together, including Kahnsajin, we had seven bows, five of them curve-backs and all of my archers were experts.

One of Sergeant Sasha's women took on the role of negotiator. She met them at a fair distance. They stopped in front of her. Two of their knights moved forward until they braced her. Without warning, they stabbed her in the back and gut with their spears, a clear breach of all rules of chivalry.

I was horrified, seeing one of my women mercilessly murdered by men who should have been allies; kin and knights from the house of my very own fiancé. My first instinct was to ride my horse forward, and even without thinking, my sword found my hand. All the other women had the same thought, and so we were several strides at a measured trot before I decided to raise my hand and stop to give the situation thought.

The woman I'd sent fell from her horse. These knights, strong as they might have imagined themselves, were destined to die, for we were far mightier than their wee minds imagined. I had highly skilled warriors in my guard. And yet, what good would come of it? Would I make enemies of the men of little King Lacellor, as well as I'd made enemies of the King of Farstand?

Across from us, a good sixty paces away, the knights must have thought we'd stopped out of fear and might even run. I had us wait.

When they were a good thirty horse away, I raised my hands. "Let the goddess send heat. Let her burn them with shame." I waved my hands forward and said the benediction: "Tpunwvw Own!"

Numbness washed over my fingers. I found myself leaning to one side of my horse. Still, the spell that I'd cast showed good results, causing the first four knights to scream and lose the spears they'd raised in readiness. Even before the spears hit the ground, the wooden shafts smoked. Their iron vests became hot enough to cause their linen to smolder. They feverishly worked at the buckles of their armor. Their horses came to a standstill.

Light headed, but determined, I spoke the words of a second and more familiar spell, asking the Goddess to make them all very tired.

I felt another wave of exhaustion consume me.

The knights' horses slowed. My women remained in their places. I rode to one side of the knights and took on the first of a string of them. I was not alone as I'd wanted, but well to the front, and after some small trouble with a few spears and swords, was able to shove several men off their horses.

"Kill none. I want them captive," I commanded.

Knights fell like lumps at the smallest kick or prod from our weapons, until only horses stood on the roadway.

I had some of my women gather the drowsy horses. Others separated the prisoners from their weapons, removed their armor (all of which I considered forfeit to us, regardless of any further judgment). We tied their hands behind their backs.

My warriors finished this while I got down from my horse and found a soft portion of grass. There I passed out from the strain of using too much magic.

When I awoke it was well past noon. Two good blankets were under me. They'd leaned a tarp for shade. Minari and the others sat close. They looked comfortable, eating a good meal over a fire. Two scouts appeared to be out. Over in a clearing, all the knights remained tied up, and their horses were missing. I saw the back of one woman, off in the distance, leading many new horses south. Those horses bore backs loaded with light armor and some good new weapons.

I fixated on the wrapped body of the murdered woman. She

sagged across the back of her own horse. The horse waited by the creek with some others, eating grass and drinking water. I could touch his mind and tell that the animal felt confusion and sorrow. He suspected his mistress was no longer with him, and he did not like the thought of it very much.

I did not like the thought of it at all and sat up with the help of Angel and Kahnsajin.

When I got up on my rear, I could see across the road where the other women sat, and noticed eight unexpected captives near them. Their hands had also been bound behind. These were not knights, but rather, Sir Daren Drake's professional peasants. He'd used my example and made a small cavalry force out of them, some time back. I knew six of their faces. Some were the same men who had taken the lead while forcing the gates at Helfax. They were good men, loyal to Sir Daren Drake, and I loved them for their small skill and unflinching bravery.

I asked, "What are those men here for?"

"Ah, they came riding in after the knights. They said they'd only speak to you." Khulan appeared relieved to see me awake.

I nodded, and made to get up. Angel and Kahnsajin had to help me. The world was still spinning around, telling me to sit back down, which of course I could not do.

"It was all that I could do to keep us from killing them all." Khulan added, "We were not raised to take kindly to any man who kills one of our sisters."

Sasha scowled. "We suspect they were sent to murder you."

I nodded again. It impressed me that Khulan had referenced the dead southern woman when she'd said the words, 'one of our sisters'.

"Lady Abi," shouted one of the men on the other side. Some gave him a stern look, but I walked over with the help of Angel and Kahnsajin under each arm.

"We were sent by Sir Esaudrin to warn you. He is a good friend to Sir Daren Drake who rode off for duties with Sir Lacellor just after you left the castle and thus did not see these nine knights leave in haste. Sir Esaudrin, however, took note. He is honor bound to the lord of the castle, but also good friends to the younger lord, and so he thought to send us to warn you which was the best he could do without breaking his oath and his absence falling under notice. I thank our lord that you are unharmed. The lady of Drake castle wishes you dead. I may be speaking out of turn. My master, Sir Esaudrin, begs that you not take offense and that you understand the complicated nature of . . . well . . ."

The man before me was a peasant. "I understand. Sir Esaudrin imagines that Daren Drake does not wish to offend the high lord and lady of the castle, nor does Sir Esaudrin imagine that Daren wants his fiancé dead." Then I asked, "And when you were to come upon the knights before you came upon me, what did you hope to say, for surely you'd have come upon them before our party, had you been faster?"

He looked both confused and tired, but after a while he shook his head. "It is a wretched thing to be only a peasant and sent on an errand certain to offend so many in power."

I looked into his soul, finding it honest, and I nodded. "That is the right answer. Come, Khulan. Help Angel and Kahnsajin untie these men. They are without fault and have come to us with good intentions. I think we shall keep them a good long while, for here is yet another excellent thing that the nobles of these lands do not value."

I addressed the men: "In time, I will speak to the Drakes and see your honor restored, if not increased. But, for now, you must stay with our people and help us fight Farstand."

I sent the peasant soldiers south with Minari. The rest of us marched the knights back toward their castle, using the rest of the daylight and much of the night before we found ourselves a good place to camp.

When morning came, I rode through the small town alone. Yellow Eyes and Slow Leg had finished their honeymoon, and caught up, one to each side of my horse.

As well, I led the horse bearing the body of our dead warrior. She'd been wrapped in a bundle of light-brown linen. Both the dead woman and my angry wolves made quite an impression upon the innocent inhabitants of the village. None in the town spoke, apparently seeing this as a nobleman's game and not likely to gain them much if they interfered. As for permanent warriors, the castle had been nearly stripped; Daren's going west, and many of the others chasing after us. None seemed in the streets. Others, of course, would be in the fiefs, making ready to come and engage the war.

"Sir Drake! You need to apologize for murdering one of my warriors!" I yelled.

The older Sir Drake stood on a battlement, the far edge of a bowshot's distance. "You aren't in a position to demand anything. You are squatting on my lands and are holding more horses and weapons than half the landed lords north of the great river. These should be put to better use in the hands of men. Stand aside and I shall send some knights to take charge, as is only right. If you leave, never to return, all will be right."

"That was a missed chance to beg my forgiveness, Lord Drake. Now I must ask which of those two men on that distant hill is childless, and which has an excuse of wee ones, so he might be spared?" I pointed over at a hill.

Several of my warriors walked over the crest with two of Sir Drake's knights. The men straddled horses. Both men faced the back of the animals and had their hands tied behind. Above the men dangled two ropes from a tree. These were quickly affixed around their necks.

He yelled down, "You wouldn't dare. Killing a knight of this land is an act of treason. You are on my lands, and my word is law. I demand their immediate release!"

"Sir Drake, consider it a blessing that I do not hang all nine of your knights for this foolishness. I will soon be wedded to your son. As well, we must be allies in this upcoming war. Otherwise, I would not be so kind."

"I am the law, and I will empty this castle of warriors if you as much as harm one of my men." He paced about on the rampart.

"Your men are few this day and slow ahorse. My women are ready and well-schooled in war. The slaughter of your men is not worth it, and so I will not war against you. Equally, you are no fool. You sought to murder me with small losses and little effort, thinking it costing you nothing. Now you will see that my women are not easy prey, nor can you easily kill us, for the Goddess has her hand upon her servants."

He made a fist at me.

"Now ser, tell me which man I should send to the gods for the sin of murder."

"Neither!" He spat into the moat.

His wife appeared by his side. She too scowled at me, though I could see her fretting and wringing her hands for her husband's benefit. She screeched, "It is that foul peasant woman who has bewitched my son. Go and rid me of her!"

It pleased me to ignore my future mother in law. "Then it shall be the oldest of the two." I waved my left hand toward my women.

At first nothing painful happened, as the woman holding the horses unfastened the rope from around the right-most man's neck. She led him away. When the one man was alone, a rider rode across the front side of the hill. She stood in her stirrups and took aim with her bow. The shot rose up the slope a good five yards and flew thirty yards in total. It was shot from a swift horse, but the arrow struck the man nearly in the center of his chest. I'd never seen anyone do such skillful archery in all of my time among the nobles, for the gallop of a horse is not even remotely steady, particularly on a sloping hill.

The condemned knight jumped, and the horse, having been kicked by his rider's own heel, walked out from under. Though well hit, the man was not dead. His legs flailed the air. He fought both the pain of the arrow and the loss of his air.

A woman screamed. Shouts of rage rang from the battlements. I heard cogs in the great gates clank as it started lifting. Someone rattled chains, meaning the drawbridge was nearly lowered.

Thus warned, I turned, leading my dead warrior away and through the center of the town at a fair gallop. Some dogs in a pack growled, but their leader was sent yelping by one good nip from the freshly energetic bitch, Slow Leg. Peasants watched the hanging knight. Others kept round eyes of fascination on my wolves. They lined the doorways, but remained loath to interfere.

Up on the tall hill, a second archer rode. She shot the hanging man a second time. This too came from a racing horse and from a warrior standing in her stirrups.

This proceeded quickly until it was Kahnsajin's turn. She rode near the man, but stopped. The young woman took careful aim with her bow. I could almost see her hesitation, for killing a man is nothing to be taken lightly, regardless of the warrior's age or anger.

Her shot struck the dead man just above the knee. I felt certain that Lady and Sir Drake knew that it was the same young woman they'd dined with who'd made that shot. Minari would have objected, but this girl was a Debrecian. It was an insult to her pride to not let her take her vengeance against such an obvious insult to her people.

When the archers finished, up came Angel, Sergeant Sasha and Khulan's warriors. They charged the corpse in a line, hacking with swords upon his neck or body as they rode by.

Khulan came last. She charged. Standing in her stirrups, the great warrior took both hands to her mighty sword. As she swept past, her whole body came around. She screamed loud enough to be heard in Farstand. The woman separated the knight's neck from his body in one vicious stroke.

Both parts fell. The head rolled farther down the slope, finally resting in a clump of tall grass two dozen yards lower. The noose spun in the air like a butterfly.

All of this occurred in the plain view of all those in the valley and on the ramparts of Sir Drake's castle which had filled with servants and fancy ladies. Some of them I'd met the night before while dressed and disguised as a gentle and kindly woman of noble purity.

When it was done, we rode past the last of the knights. They sat in the middle of the road, mostly in small-cloths. Their hands were still bound behind. Their faces were a mixture of pain, humiliation and anger.

The anger vanished when I rode by with the corpse of my warrior behind me and the bared fangs of my wolves to the fore. "You owe me your lives for the death of this woman," I said. "Never forget it, lest I decide it's time to collect what's due her beautiful soul."

Chapter Nine

"Farstand intends to march their left flank too close to the woods." Kirsta stood in her stirrups. Her head moved like a hawk's, seemingly seeing everything near the ford at once. "We've a full company in there. I should have them harass the flank."

"No, I think not." I occasionally raised my spyglass.

"My Queen! Do you not see? Most of their knights are near the center, tied up with Sir Finley's knights as soon as they start, or at least they must remain and be wary of his force, lest they lose the maneuverability of the road. Two passes from two score of our women could put two hundred arrows into the center of their right block, well over the front shields. Forty or fifty men are sure to die in a minute, and I can guarantee no losses, for we'd pass beyond their reach. Should their knights pursue, they'd be swallowed up by our curve-backs along the east road."

"That is good thinking, but I do not wish it." Clearly she was correct. The road was bordered by an open field and when they came, they'd be exposed, as she'd stated.

"And, if they don't pressure us, we can do it again; all day long if they are pigheaded. At the least, we will force some of their knights away from Sir Finley," she continued.

Kirsta had come to love me, but not without some reservations, for she did not yet trust me as a warlord overseeing such a majestic battle. Conversely, she knew that her instincts were as good as instincts came on the matters of war. Without a doubt, her idea was a good one. It just did not fit my vision.

After all, what were a few dead Farstand peasants, compared to the five thousand that were crossing the ford. To be more accurate, only a thousand were actually across, or nearly so, while four thousand converged from the other side of the bank, waiting for the roads to clear. The King's generals knew Sir Finley's five hundred peasants and two score knights were no more bother than gnats to such a large force. They could even afford great losses and not be stopped.

"Why?"

"I don't want them knowing us."

I turned my horse and brought us down the back side of the hill. Angel and Kahnsajin remained with us as we rode down the back slope. Soon we found the north road. I had a squad of South Women, as well as messengers waiting.

We rode past the increasing bustle of war. The sights and smells of it crackled all around. Bonfires raged. Messengers raced from the lines to the captains. A wagon bearing baskets of arrows struck a large rock and nearly toppled as it rushed toward the front. Some peasants were being fitted with pikes and crude short swords. A soldier handed them shields made of brittle and nearly useless bark shavings, sending them to the front with only a pose showing them how to hold their weapons. This he managed in the time it took us to ride past. He hustled these same men straight over a rise, certainly to their deaths.

Sir Carling limped out of the doomed house when Kirsta and I arrived. I gave the startled man a shove to get past when he became stuck over-thinking my arrival. I stumbled directly into Sir Finley's parlor.

"Good morning, Sir Finley."

He huddled over the map while speaking to two captains. The man took one look at Kirsta and me. He waved dismissively and returned to his map and instructions.

His map showed knights awaiting an advance so they could take advantage of a shield of archers positioned behind pike-guarded embankments. We'd worked making those even before Sir Finley intruded on my land. In order to defend that, he'd have to back his engaged block up a hundred yards along the roadway. His map showed his intentions of doing just that.

It was thus no surprise when he explained to his captains, "After tempting the enemy into an advance, I intend to back the foot onto the side of this good hillside. Make them know to do this slowly and in formation, upon hearing a horn's double blast. The King's knights are certain to flank that movement, bringing their knights right beside the largest embankment of archers. That is where I will meet his knights with ours, between the blocking force of pikes and our archers. In the seam, the King's horses have the worst range of maneuver and cannot bring all of their knights to bear."

Anything that spared his innocent peasant footmen a little bit longer, I saw as a blessing. As well, his knights would be supported when they hit the King's knights, though the odds were impossible, for the King had a hundred knights, and that counted only those currently available.

"A good plan, Sir Finley."

"What do you want?" he shouted.

"I've come to collect Lady Finley and escort her to a safe haven. We'll need transportation. A horse is fine. If not, I'll give her one."

"Would you also like an escort of a score or two of my best knights? Can you not see I am busy fighting a war!"

"That would be kind of you, but I have good escort and don't want to be slowed by lumbering warriors in heavy armor. So, do you want me to escort your wife or not?"

"Yes, yes, by all means, take her. It'll save me sending an escort. I need all I have. You've already taken all the good fighting women we were counting on."

"Good then. I'll only take a few wagons and the Lady then. As for foot, you'll likely lose them all, so what's the harm in saving the few who cross my path?"

One of the captains turned and glared. "Stay your mouth, wench. Those women could have saved a flank. We shall prevail, however, without your help. Leave us, as your lord requires."

How quickly I'd been demoted. The captain was young, however, so I made allowances for him probably having been born with veins full of rich, noble blood, crowding out any sense.

"Yes, of course."

Over by the stairs, Lady Finley supervised a couple men wrestling a huge trunk. "Ah, I see the lady has packed and is ready. Well then, we shall be off and leave you great lords to your masterful defeat."

"So, you actually think it is a poor plan, and have only come to hound me." Sir Finley stood from his map.

"Well, since you asked . . . ." I stepped up and gave the map a longer look. "Here and here are excellent places to put a dozen archers. You see the narrows in the trails. With archers there, they can't bear upon you with more than a few soldiers as you retreat. Yes . . . otherwise, your army will not escape to harass the King's men all the way to Lacellor's castle. You must already know you will be denied the road. You must also know you will do far more along the flanks . . . along this road, as they seek stores. There you will always win in uneven battles. Face to face the King's knights outweigh you."

"We have no use for retreat," the young knight said.

I spoke only to Sir Finley. "Do you intend to make a widow of Lady Finley? We have had our disagreements, ser, but I give you this advice, hoping to see you in your old age. Your battle plan is sound, but don't press it once the King's forces overcome. Plan your return, and battle where you can."

Sir Finley thought for a second. "Ah, off with you. The King's men are already across the river, and I've no time."

I stood back and watched the lady kiss her new husband goodbye, truly hoping she was not doing so for the last time. Several soldiers loaded the huge crate of clothing on a wagon. I took Lady Finley by the wrist and pulled her out of the house before she could send more men up the stairs for another one.

On the way out, I heard Sir Finley tell the young captain, "The witch is right. I want ten archers here and here. Make sure every sergeant and knight is informed that we don't intend to press this to the end. Once the tide turns, we will withdraw in good order through the narrow trails. Then, once reorganized, we'll give the King a hard time all the way up the north road."

* * * * *

The smells of war lingered behind an hour farther north. Otherwise, it remained on everybody's mind.

"Why didn't you attack the flanks?" Kirsta complained as we

rode north. "Now the enemy will cross without good losses. We've not even touched them. Surely, an extra hundred dead foot are not much to them, but it is a help. In time, such tactics might add up to a persuasive argument against this invasion."

I spotted another wagon heading south with provisions and directed Sergeant Sasha to send horses to waylay it. We added it to the nearly two score I'd already stolen from Sir Finley's effort. The truth of it was, even without seeing the battle, and only an hour out from the ford, I knew he'd already lost his little battle. If any of his army survived, it did so by taking to the side trails. They'd be too few and too scattered to even harass the road until reorganized. Any wagons going that direction were either stolen by me, which was good, or lost to the enemy, a waste.

Lady Finley did not like it, however, and scolded me endlessly for abandoning her husband at a time of great need. The furor increased as I stole obvious war supplies.

I had to ignore one more such scolding from my right while I addressed my chief warlord on the left. "The problem is I don't want the King to know he has to contend with us. His generals might learn something from it. Think on this, Kirsta: He has conquered Sir Finley, and now he thinks he can march right up to the gates of Lacellor's castle with impunity."

"Ah! That he can," she stated.

Lady Finley released a wail, knowing it as well.

I stopped and got down near a good spot for watering our horses. My warriors gathered around. "I've heard a lot of mumbling this morning. So I should tell you the first part of my plan. We'll empty the wagons of all but war supplies in the next village. Sergeant Sasha, this is your first chore."

"What of the Lady's goods?" Sasha asked.

"Those as well. We'll dump everything but food, arrows and those things useful. I am assuming that when the enemy comes through the town, all of these things will be forfeit to them. Let them waste wagon space bearing them back to their castles and keeps."

Lady Finley sighed, but she was not so silly as to complain.

"Kirsta! You'll ride ahead with a score of warriors, and command everybody in the next town to collect only the things they need to survive. Start them filling any carts they have. When these carts come, fill each with as much grain as is left in the silos. Make sure the peasants don't bring their fanciest chairs and cabinets, but instead a good bundle of seeds and what tools they need for their trades. When you see a start, move to the next town.

"As well, organize men to drive all the herds north. Any seed or animal that is left in the towns two hours after your arrival is to be burned or slaughtered."

Kirsta smiled for the first time since I'd known her. "Ah, now I see what you are up to."

"Yes, and don't forget the side roads. I want nothing left for the King's men as they march through. We'll harry all the peasants north and give them no time to complain—past Lacellor's city and his castle. We'll not trade one disaster for another. Prod any who complain and threaten to disobey. Also, try to not kill many peasants; it is supposedly impolite."

"They will complain, but we will be persuasive," Kirsta said.

"Good. When we get close to Lacellor's city, we'll have the local soldiers take over and free us for the next part of my plan. After all, these are the lands of Sir Finley between here and Sir Lacellor's castle, and his wife is agreeable to us. They are bound to obey her edicts."

"I am?" Lady Finley asked. "They are?" Her face changed from angry to sadness. "Yes, I suppose it must be done."

The woman was often too kind, but she was also no fool. If we didn't turn the villagers north, the King's army would do worse, and still no grain or livestock were likely to remain after their rape and pillage.

I cleared my throat. "When I was a soldier in the King's army, the only thing that kept us alive was poaching and stealing. We starved in our tents. I don't imagine they are any better in this regard, and I hope to take advantage of the lunacy. Leadership is more about keeping your army fed than winning battles. We hope their nobles are also made to go hungry, for it will be a new experience for them."

The women went straightway to their tasks. At first it took some goading to get the villagers moving. We had to start burning cottages first and asking later. But soon, the burdened peasants, trotting livestock and wagons full of grain, added their own persuasion to those along the path of the great migration.

We were relieved in our efforts by a growing number of town guards, though I had to leave several women behind to finish the burning of winter crops and what could not be carried, for the guards were all part of the communities. They were reluctant to put anything to the torch. The sky to the south of us slowly became thick with smoke.

A human storm rushed toward the castle of Sir Lacellor. Often we rode past villagers already in the process of picking up and moving. The biggest challenge was confronting angry peasants when we tossed their belonging into the ditches and forced them to carry goods more appropriate to the labor of survival.

What allowed us this work was the reluctance of the King's men to swiftly pursue us up the road without all sorts of self-imposed delays. As well, my scouts confirmed they had two hundred knights at hand by the third day. Even their footmen swelled, making the King's army the largest ever to invade northward. Such a force seemed capable of sweeping through the countryside with impunity. It was also cumbersome, and consumed far more time organizing and supplying then first envisioned.

I rode into Norfaton. Homeless peasants had already beaten us there and were camped on the hills surrounding the seat of power. Others were bold enough to find space in alleys and alongside streets. How they imagined that this helped them, I dared not guess. Anybody with a gram of warrior within could see they camped on the very next battlefield and delayed settling among decent fields.

The city's inhabitants were abuzz. Soldiers who'd normally hung around the drinking parlors and houses of pleasure ran about in groups, some one way and some the other, seemingly nonsensical.

This time the gates were open to me. The great grounds in front of the moat were filled with knights and no few footmen. I'd been announced by messengers. At the head of a double column of fifty armored men, Sir Daren Drake awaited.

In response, and due to no command of my own, my women fanned out. We were mounted four deep, filling the end of the last road leading to the open space. Since beginning the four day march, one which normally only took a good day or two, groups of my messengers had come and gone, giving my ranks a final count of sixty warriors when I finally approached Sir Lacellor's castle. Ten more lingered, busy burning the last village to our rear.

I rode forward with Lady Finley and Kahnsajin. Sir Drake watched alongside Sir Casar and Sir Lindie, good knights who'd once fallen under my command.

"Good day to you, Sirs." I imagined I looked a bit stiff and formal, though I did not feel it after four days of ugly work on the road to Lacellor. My dress was a war tunic, leather vest, loose britches, and the short wool skirt of a Debrecian warrior. I had my sword across my back, two knives in my belt, and a pair of spears tied across the rump of my horse. Road dust coated my face, other than where I had taken to wearing a bandana to hold my hair back. I also reeked of too long without a bath and too much time both sitting and holding onto leather. Everywhere mixed with the smell of smoke.

"Good day to you as well, my beloved." The tall and handsome man, Sir Daren Drake, added, "We have heard troubling things about the work of your army. I have been charged to ask: Are you a friend to my lord, or have you become his enemy, laying his lands to waste?"

He might have spoken more harshly. As Lacellor's Captain, it was his duty to be angry for all the burning. I gave a little smile. I wished I'd stopped at some house and made myself a little lovely, for I hoped to keep the affection of the man.

I shook my head. "Troubling things indeed. First, I must say that your mother has found a most convincing way of telling me she disapproves of me. She sent knights to murder me and ended up murdering one of my warriors. I will grieve that senseless loss for a long while."

Several in my command grunted similar sentiments.

"Did this woman not attack our men? A message has been sent, outlining an attack by several score of your women upon our knights who had been sent only to escort you to your settlement."

"I watched her murdered," I said. "She rode up to them in my stead, hoping to determine why they rode us down in so much haste and while seemingly armed for battle. There was no weapon in her hand when two of your knights rode close to either side. They murdered her with their spears while she continued her enquiry. Never have I seen such a cowardly act. My first impulse was to kill them all, but the wisdom of the Goddess overtook me. Still, as I've said, I will grieve this and not seek further vengeance, in the name of peace between our houses. I have hanged one of the men who did this, and granted mercy to the other. For this kindness I now must endure false witness."

He nodded and showed a grave face.

"It is done, save for the pain in my heart. It is my burden to feel for the women who die unjustly in this war, since it seems no man finds them worthy."

Sir Drake looked even more troubled than before, as did Sir Casar. Sir Drake asked, "Is this vengeance also why you have burned so many of Sir Finley's holdings?"

"I have only denied the King's men the pleasure of your fields and cattle. Either we move what we can, and burn the rest, or we feed him."

"Ah. This was how I saw it, but Sir Lacellor is not so convinced. He intended to feed his men on those lands as he moved south. Perhaps you should have asked him first."

"I might, should he ever leave the safety of his castle. Or, better yet, cease raising his drawbridge in response to the first sight of my messengers."

He smiled. "The man is convinced you are not a good ally. He says the Debrecians will not follow you. Your women in the south are not Debrecians and are only in the way of good order. It may even be true that your new liberal ways regarding the sexes raise a curse upon his kingdom.

"Ah, so it is a kingdom now, is it? Now I know the source of his increasing lack of sanity. Well then, go back into your castle and tell the little King this: My women shall deny the King of Farstand the food he needs for a long siege. Further, all the peasants in this city should be sent north with their grain and livestock. As well, I suggest that he leaves only a small force in his castle; only enough to convince the big King of the south that the little King of the north is at home and worth the time it takes the big King of the south to starve the little King of the north out of his keep. If there are few mouths inside, all the better. It will take longer to starve them than Lacellor's enemies can last."

Sir Drake lost his smile, knowing my words were meant to sound treasonous, and that my whole life had continually been on the edge of it. To his credit, he did not say it, for he also knew I'd sworn no oath to Sir Lacellor, and that my thoughts were always upon the arts of war and not the arts of fancy speaking and making high nobles comfortable.

"I shall speak to him for you," he said. "In my judgment, your strategy leaves my knights new room to maneuver and is sound, though the latter idea leaves this castle defenseless, should there be an early breach."

I turned my horse slightly toward Sir Casar and asked the big axe-man, "What says you, good knight. What will come of a breach, should the King exploit it with ten thousand on foot and two hundred armored knights?"

He started to answer, but Sir Lindie was first to reply: "As always, Lady Abi has done our thinking for us. Perhaps this time we will listen."

Sir Drake waved a hand in rebuke. "Such is up to Sir Lacellor. Now I must ask, having given this some thought: Tell me, Lady Abi, how do you truly stand among the Debrecians to the north? Have they rejected you entirely? Or, have you renounced the title of their Queen? If so, why do you travel with the daughter of Beckli Kahnsa who is well known to be high among their council? It also seems to me that some of these women behind you are not new to their horses, but have ridden them many years. Given you have spoken so little on the subject, I have grown curious."

"All is explained within a prophecy, Sir Drake. It seems I shall bring blood and death to my people. The question remains: What shall happen, should I not lead my Debrecians south into this battle? We do not wait upon the pleasure of Sir Lacellor, Sir Drake. Nor do we further question who is Queen of the great northern tribes. We only await a new prophecy, within which we shall see the wisdom of the Goddess, for she shall answer the question of what should happen to my people if I do not bring them to this war."

"Then I shall ask you one last question before I consult with Sir Lacellor in his castle. Why did you not tell my mother that you were a Queen and accepted by your people?"

I answered, "Because she needs to see me as a woman in love with her son. Until she understands why that is all that is important, she will not enjoy the pleasure of my company."

Chapter Ten

Several miles east of the Redwater Ford, we'd long-established a ferry. The King's men didn't know it existed because we guarded it closely.

While their scouts became entangled in the maze we'd made of our trails, we struck their camps near the ford with ease, always in the dead of night, concentrating on horses. Many newly trained women coveted even the enemy's nags. Horses made us flexible, the core of my strategy. Most of their horses were draft animals, of which they had plenty, and though slow, they were still both mountable and able to pull any spoils. At the very least, we still had a crop to bring in.

Sir Daren Drake waited with me at the ferry. We watched another four women blindfold their horses and board. Two men and two women pulled at the ferry ropes. Our Debrecian men gave good examples to those who joined. I worked by their side and often called them by name. On occasion, I made time to fetch their water. They, of course, did the same, and more often since I'd become their queen."

Soon halfway across the Redwater, I reflected upon the fact that many of my women had turned up pregnant. This we celebrated in order to avoid the usual stigma, for it was not easy being one of us, calling for many sacrifices.

I, however, remained a virgin in spite of a lovely night on a hillside with Sir Daren Drake. That had come the day after my arrival at Lacellor Castle, and three days back from when I overlooked the ferry crossing.

It seems that Sir Drake had spoken a bit too harshly with little King Lacellor regarding my titles and value. In return, he'd been cast out of the great rebel's castle and demoted back to nothing more than a knight in his father's household. My betrothed said Sir Lacellor only meant to scare some sense into him, but the sense had already been scared into him by me.

Sir Daren Drake was not just another knight in the eyes of his fellows either. As he left, so too did those from his household.

All the soldiers and knights who rode with him were not as eager to follow the whims of Sir Daren Drake's father and mother, instead abiding the wishes of the younger knight. Thus they lingered and spoke kindly to me. As well, several other well-placed knights followed the lead of Sir Drake. These men also trickled out and swelled Sir Drake's little knights of a score and a half.

They'd met me on a high hill that overlooked Norfaton. I'd been up there with my warriors, overlooking a road and forcing a thousand peasants to move farther north. Since I had no authority to do it, I was sure Sir Drake had come to stop me with his thirty knights, but instead he joined my forces, pleasing me more than any person might imagine.

So, we'd spent that first night under the stars on a blanket. There we explored the taste of one another's mouths, wondering who'd die first. Then we had to take some time for rest, for I'd never known such pleasure and grown dizzy. I lay back, but only pretended to sleep.

The only other man who'd kissed me like that had been Niko, and that had been in the line of duty. I'd had the mission in Helfax on my mind, at the time, allowing me to escape Niko's press. Not so with Sir Drake. The only thing that allowed me an escape from him was his own sense of chivalry. Finally, I thought, a good use for the word. None of the other times when I'd heard it uttered had I found the word practical. And, of course, practical is exactly what I mean by saying I was saved from the bliss of having boundless and beautiful sex with the man, for the word desire pulled me in the opposite direction from virtue.

Thus, after some rest, we ended up telling one another many excellent war stories. Even this was romantic, though I imagine we were uniquely disposed to see the subject in such light. It occurred to me that much of Sir Lacellor's genius in battle had actually been the tactics of the young Sir Daren Drake.

Sometime near dawn, we witnessed Sir Lacellor's knights exiting the castle. They rode south after mustering several hundred footmen. Just behind, and for the rest of the day, servants and skilled laborers worked at righting then moving a pair of small catapults.

"He hopes to stop the King's army where the road narrows, an hour out. Lacellor is distraught over the reluctance of many of his lords to give him all their knights. There are nine high lords. If each gave up all of their knights, Sir Lacellor might even outnumber the King's armor. As it stands, each lord wants to hold back at least half his strength to defend his own castle or keep."

"That is silly. If Lacellor loses, a score of knights at any given keep is useless."

Sir Drake nodded sadly.

"So, why did he let you and your men leave?"

"He thinks of us as his rear guard. I don't imagine he thought all of these men would follow me out of his castle when he dismissed me. After a good count of heads, Sir Lacellor might not be all that pleased to note that he now stands with only three score knights, half of them little more than squires."

"Will he retreat to the castle after this battle?" I asked.

Sir Drake nodded.

"I wanted him to leave only a handful and join me in striking the King's men along the supply lines," I said. "Under such pressure, the King's men might never muster a strong-enough assault on the castle. We could arrange it so we would always have an advantage, cutting them piecemeal. If he'd have met with me . . . ."

"How interesting. Another strange tactic. Sir Lacellor, however, can't imagine leaving his lands and castle to only a few defenders. He contends that a seat of power is power itself."

"A seat of power surrounded is the same as a seat of power lost, but it also freezes Farstand's men. He might lose it in a week, now. Then what will he have?"

We both watched a little longer. If he put all his worth into that castle, the whole kingdom would soon fall.

Once Sir Lacellor bowed, all the remaining knights in Lacellor's castle would become our enemy. Then, all of those hesitant lords to the north and west would be conquered one castle at a time, or more likely relent and bow as soon as word reached their ears.

Perhaps Sir Lacellor would lose his head—a small price for peace. Just as likely, Sir Drake would lose his. My fiancé had been a continual pain in the side of the King and all of his efforts in every battle to date. Most certainly, my women would be trapped on the border lands, enslaved, murdered, or worse. Then who would remain between the nobles and the tribes? Nobody. I needed my Debrecians, but could not force the Goddess's prophecy.

Yes, two days later at the ferry, my biggest wonder remained how long Sir Lacellor could hold out in his castle after his inevitable retreat. We watched the four warriors offload on the other side of the river. My scouts had informed me that the battle down the road from the castle had not yet begun, but was in the posturing stage. That was encouraging at least.

I looked over at Sir Drake then reached for his hand, giving it a squeeze. "Do you remember me once telling you that long ago four hundred men defeated over six thousand knights?"

"Such stories are grand, but do not help a sound man plan," he told me.

The ferry returned, this time taking on four of Sir Drake's peasant cavalry soldiers. These were some of the same men I'd admired at Helfax, and who'd also been captured by my women after the murder by the knights of Sir Drake's mother. They were the core of a new group of male cavalry that had been the love and charge of Sergeants Niko and Kreger. These were two companies each, and all of them were joining four hundred of my warriors across the river. The whole crossing had taken the ferrymen nearly two days of work, giving me nearly five hundred mounted demons on the Farstand side of the border. More would follow.

When these last four were halfway across, I told Sir Drake, "Still, you might like my story of the Mongs. With only a few more men than that, they conquered more land than any other force in history." I paused to let that sink in. "And, do you know what is most interesting about them?"

"Well, I cannot guess what is more interesting than that," the man said.

"Then I shall tell you, my good and beautiful knight." I leaned over close, cupped my lips and whispered toward his ear, "They could not keep it."

A little later the ferry came back. I stood in my stirrups, leaned over and kissed my knight goodbye. Then I rode my horse onto the large wooden raft where Kirsta, Angel and Kahnsajin preceded me. The ferry took us across to the vast lands of King Falstaff of Farstand.

All the way across, I worried for my knight, for his first chore was to take a hundred of Sir Finley's abandoned, but reassembled footmen, as well as his own thirty knights, and attack the ford, sweeping the critical, and hopefully lightly defended, northern link in the enemy's supply.

* * * * *

My chief of scouts, Salonia, said, "Young Duke Crestlin, heir of the man you are renowned for having defeated in battle, sits in his castle, barely a score of knights with him. The city of Dorne is empty of soldiers; it is no more than a way-station for men coming to the front. In his stead, a high knight from the King's own court has been sent to lead the offensive. A Sir Janis leads two barons and the rest against Sir Lacellor. The man we captured claims that Sir Janis, a close cousin to the King, is renowned for his gifts both on the battlefield and at court. They say he studies war and diplomacy with equal vigor, and has been trained by the High Council of Priest who resides well to the West in their strong city state. It seems they have a desire to see our little rebellion extinguished in the name of their God."

I had to ponder this report, for there was much in it that was cause for worry. In particular, I'd always counted on the incompetence of the nobles giving me an edge. In my readings, however, the old Gostics of the lands formerly known as Roan were not just good at fighting, but spectacular. Much that I knew about warfare had been gleaned from their histories.

Even more troubling was the report that this man, Sir Janis, was a master at diplomacy. More kingdoms have been altered through the trickery of diplomacy than the struggles of armies.

In the end, my head became so wrapped around her report that all I could say was, "I did not defeat the King's brother in battle. I murdered him in cold blood."

My head of scouts looked at me with a wide mixture of emotions playing across her face. She said, "Ah, but it sounds better the way I said it. Besides, if you murdered him, it must have been for a good reason."

"I suppose it might have been, but I cannot remember my old and petty complaints."

Just then, Kahnsajin rode up. "Did you see what Angel made me?" She held out a beautifully polished curve-back bow. I'd never even seen Angel shoot a bow, but it was obvious she had the talent for producing one. That, of course, made sense because Angel's talent was stumbling across weapons and giving them to anybody who needed one.

I took some time looking the bow over. It was several inches shorter than most of the ones carried by my warriors, and when I pulled the string back, I found it bent quite a bit easier than most. Angel had not only made Kahnsajin a good curve-back, but she'd made the draw light so the young girl could actually use it without breaking an arm.

"This is a really well made," I said. "If I had one, it would have to be just like this."

It was nice seeing Kahnsajin smile again. She'd been very quiet since the day she'd shot the hanging knight with her old and weaker longbow. Such somber thinking was proper, and I'd left her to it.

Angel also smiled toward the bow.

I nodded to Kahnsajin. "Now that you have a bow, your duty will be to keep the enemy off Angel. She keeps forgetting that she has a spear and sword and gets too close. Besides, any good Debrecian warrior knows the best tactic is to shoot at them then run away."

"Is that true? Is that a real tactic?"

"Well of course it is. If you run away, you can do it again sometime. And again and again. Else, they might get you, and you can only do it once. Part of what makes us so fierce is the terror of not knowing when we will return again and again until they give up and go home. This is particularly true if you're still young and small."

"Oh. I see. Hum. That makes a lot of sense, Queen Abi."

All of my cavalry was assembling, which was no tiny chore with five hundred warriors, all of them having slept and prepared while scattered out in the deepest woodland.

The time was ten days since Sir Finley's battle of the ford. None had seen any sign of Sir Finley since, though our people north had found and employed some of his footmen.

It was also the day after a scout had ridden in hard and told us of Sir Drake's victory at the ford. Less than a hundred enemy soldiers, mostly footmen, had been left to defend it, and so his victory had been both easy and complete. Both of us were hoping that none had escaped to tell Sir Janis of our little success, but I didn't imagine my fiancé holding the ford for very long without discovery. In fact, we'd planned on his withdraw to the east at the first sign of pressure. That way he'd bear no losses and be able to quickly hit the enemy at another weak spot.

We knew far less of the battle farther north between Sir Janis and Sir Lacellor. Outriders from both the King's men and Sir Lacellor had kept my observers away. All that I could say was Sir Lacellor was in organized retreat. If true, it was the best I could imagine from him, given that a pesky retreat delayed Sir Janis and implied that Sir Lacellor still had enough of a force to not call it a rout.

Still, that report was two days old, and I kept looking to the north, expecting to see the smoke from Lacellor's burning city, though it was too far away.

* * * * *

My women stayed off the road, but were continually ready at the forest's edge, eager to reinforce Niko's partial company. The male cavalry did their best to look like a host of Farstand scouts. They tended some horses in seemingly haphazard fashion. Several even pitched tents on the roadside grass, just to make us look more malingering. Two or three were also continually crossing the roadway, ensuring that any who came our way slowed.

Peasant travelers passed, as always, seeing only too many soldiers and knowing war was afoot. They scooted past as quickly as they could.

I had more experience at this than anybody else, so I'd slipped into male trousers and put my hair down into a warrior's tail, as opposed to my new Debrecian style where I kept it well up like a crown and secured by bandannas. It felt awkward wearing my sword at my hip. The tight britches and tunic of a peasant messenger also no longer suited me. Debrecian wear could never be mistaken for lady's wear, but it was ours and made properly loose for easy movement in battle. A layer of mud smeared across my face served to disguise my peach cheeks.

Two days ride away and nearer the ford, Khulan was starting the same duty alongside Kreger's company. Both movements were scheduled for dawn. She only had fifty warriors, but it was certain to be enough, assuming Sir Janis didn't fall into full retreat and run her over. That wasn't going to happen unless the Goddess started flicking the enemy around with her fingers.

Soon, a messenger arrived from the direction of the duke's castle. Some of the men moved their horses aside, showing only slight interest. They waved, letting him pass. Once he trotted beyond escape, an archer shot him off his horse. Then we stripped him of his message and clothing, the latter of which was promptly taken to a tub and scrubbed clean of the fresh blood. One of Niko's men was sent on his way north with a slightly altered message for Sir Janis.

The message going north read, 'Six score knights will soon arrive, along with a contingent of a thousand and four hundred footmen in groups. Leaving Crestlin Castle in four days.' Their discarded message had suggested half as many reinforcements and in half the time—I wanted him planning on what he'd never have, but also not suspicious too soon.

This happened two more times, once from the north. A messenger from Sir Janis had passed onto the road a day or two before Khulan would have blocked it, and apparently even before Sir Drake had taken the ford, making the messenger a malingerer. Sir Janis wrote that he was sure Sir Lacellor's forces would soon fold, and that the castle was as good as his within the week. I thought that optimistic, given that Sir Lacellor's castle was well built for a long siege, and that he'd enjoyed plenty of time to stock it with provisions.

Then at the end of the day, a hundred footmen marched down the roadway. Three knights in chainmail rode ponies in front of the soldiers. The knights enjoyed twice as many servants on horses. Each servant led two or three more horses, one warhorse for each noble and other ponies that were too good for pack. My mouth watered.

Our scout had warned us of this especially good prize, and so a hundred mounted women lined up three deep and across the road ahead. They anticipated the fight just around a dogleg. Most of the rest hid in the woods, though the cover was low, forcing them to hide on foot. Others tended their horses beyond a rise. These closer women bore spears and bows.

By the road, the six of us in Niko's group mounted our horses as Niko hailed the tall knight who led: "Good Ser! Might there be news you are willing to share with a common soldier?"

The tall knight was thick with muscles. A linen vest displayed a family crest. It overlaid a short vest of chainmail. He said, "Only that the last report calls us to the fight. The war appears to be going better than expected. We may arrive in time to secure the castle of a Sir Drake. He is one of the rebels to the east of the main traitor. Do you know a good road in that direction?"

"Ah yes. It is only a half mile beyond the ford, and a wide one it is, at least near its start. Sir Drake's castle, I've been told, is only two or three days ride beyond the river."

"Very good. We shall look for it."

"And Ser, I thank you for the good news. We hear little beyond those things pertaining to our duties."

"And, what might be that duty, young man?" a bald knight beside the tall one asked.

Niko hesitated before answering: "To do as we're told, such as here and now where we've been told to wait. When someone comes wandering down the road, we are supposed to look soldierly and ask questions, as well as step aside, good knight."

All forty of Niko's soldiers stood or sat mounted along the roadside to his left. I sat mounted third from his side, and we all were well attentive, as if making a good report of ourselves and ready for their review.

"I see. I have not been made aware of so many messengers. You also appear too well armed for runners. Who is your lord, for I wish to ask him about such a group. I hear there was no end to trouble when a similar body of peasants was so raised in the last great encounter." The tall knight shifted his horse's orientation directly toward Niko. The knight's two friends bracketed his sides. Behind him, his men marched past, most of them beyond the bulk of Niko's men by the time of the last question. I became nearly face to face with the bald knight.

They had insulted Niko. Our men fidgeted, seemingly not liking it much, but they did not break. How strange, I thought, for only a short time earlier in their lives, they'd have wallowed.

Niko stammered, "That would be Lord Eron Prescott of Olan, Baron of Helfax, Ser."

"Ah, that explains it," the tall knight said. "That's the same man who let peasant women burn his city." He chuckled, looked side to side at his companions. "He is also the baron who brought that she-witch to the front in the last battle, also disguised as a peasant knight. That bitch murdered the King's own brother. Shows what comes of coddling the peasantry and raising them to anything but a pike. Clearly your lord cannot control his women, much less his men."

"I'd loved to meet that sheath," the third knight said. "Far be it from me to mistake a man for a woman, and far be it from me to let peasants ride like true men. I'd have killed her just for mounting a horse, much less for being a witch."

Judging from the redness, Niko seemed about to burst. "We are ahorse, Ser, and are keen to do our duty . . . as free men."

"Free? Free of what? It is only that you are not women that spares you from our spanking." The bald knight smirked.

"What fool gives you the right to kill a woman," I said, "just for sitting on a horse?" I hoped many of my hidden women heard me.

All of the knights glared my way.

"Shut up, boy, lest I have my servant take you into the woods and beat you," the tall one said.

Behind them, all the footmen had finally passed. Only a single servant waited. He held the reins on a couple spare horses.

I unsheathed my sword. "That'll be hard to do with his head lying on the road! As well, it will be hard for you to ask him, with yours lying beside it."

Niko also pulled out his sword, but I stopped him with a shout. "No, Niko! Step aside and find someone else to kill. These three belong to me."

"You are the witch!" the bald knight screamed.

He went for his sword, but before he could get it out, I cut his hand at the wrist. One of the bones broke below my cut. I stabbed him under the chainmail. Before he fell, I stabbed him again in the same place, and twisted my sword. He toppled off the other side of his horse, helping me pull it out.

Niko, of course, did not listen. He busied himself with the knight on the far side of the leader. All of Niko's men rushed around us in an arch. That was good and showed fine training as they filled the south end of the road, blocking the footmen. Our men quickly reached for the enemy with their spears and swords.

The footmen panicked right away. I knew from experience that these were peasants fresh out of the fields. They turned in circles in the road. Some in the new rear ran. Those closer to us backpedaled from the rush of forty mounted men. Their footmen became a mob. Our attack became a slaughter.

Even farther north, a shower of arrows punctured thirty of the footmen. Nearly all of them were hit within a couple salvos. This shooting came from the fields and woods by the women who'd left their horses in the rear. The men in front started falling over bodies, desperate to get away from being trampled by horses and impaled by spears. Our cavalry hardly had need of their swords, for their target diminished in front of their hooves and often before the footmen could get their crude swords out.

A large contingent of mounted women came rushing around the bend, finding little work left. I heard some cursing their bad luck upon finding no more targets. Kirsta was particularly livid, screaming insults to everyone near because she'd played only a minor role. Next, some of the women in the woods retreated, returning on their horses. Thus, even the stragglers rushing into the weeds became trapped.

The third knight, who was fighting Niko, seemed winning, but he suddenly stiffened when an arrow found the small of his back. I noticed Kahnsajin with an empty bow. She paused, eyes round as coins, but only for a second. She quickly joined Angel in their search for other dangers.

Niko finished the man, taking good advantage of the knight's sudden stiffness.

The middle knight had a hard time making his way around the newly fallen riders and their horses. When he did, he came straight for me. Our swords clanged, and then again and again.

Finally, I backed off. "Good knight, I fear for our horses. Let us finish this afoot, sparing their flanks, for I covet your gelding and would have it as a prize."

"Then what is in it for me? Surely these bandits will not let me leave in peace when I slay you."

"Your life. Let it be known that if you kill me, you may go free with your horses. You may have my horse as well. He is a good prize, as you can see. I stole him from one of your high lords."

This must have seemed an excellent deal to him, so he dismounted. We walked to the middle of the road.

To the north, his men lay dead or dying. Over four hundred of my warriors lingered. Some were busy stripping his dead men of weapons and goods. Most of them remained on horses. Scouts raced over both horizons.

I pulled my warrior's tail apart, and quickly tied my hair up into a fountain. Angel handed me a rag, with which I cleaned my face of the dirt I'd caked on to hide my femininity. I put my sheath aside, no longer liking the balance of it at my waist.

Having had enough of my fussing, he came right at me. I had to sweep his first cut aside with a sidestep and a good two-handed deflection. The man knew the usual tricks, beating down with the first blow, taking a step with each swing as he came.

Once he'd gotten the sudden and brutal part of his training out of his system, he put one hand behind and swirled his sword around in a circle. That, I suppose, was intended to mesmerize me and scare me out of my wits because of his good arm strength. Instead, I saw it as an opening, for all I needed to do was slap his sword aside and nick his arm each time before he recovered.

He quickly became tired of that, deciding to go back to two hands. His sword came across, catching my blade. I leaned in as he did the same. Our hand guards braced. The tip of his blade continued to the side while I'd kept mine straight, driving the point of it right into his face.

He jumped back, and I let him.

The man's skills paled compared to my fiancé. Even in her worst moments, the crone could have beaten him. Fighting him was not art. I quickly grew bored, which is quite dangerous.

The cut had been to his cheek, right beside the nose, and it had been deep. The nobleman spit blood the next time he came at me. "Witch!"

I spun to my left, circling him as we fenced. Every so often he was slow to turn, taking another jab to the arm. When he lost more strength, our guards met. I poked him in the neck.

Once again, he'd been hit, three inches deep that time, but as luck would have it, I'd missed anything vital, which was amazing given the nature of the area I'd poked.

My sword circled next. He tapped at it, but I waited. He could barely see for the smeared blood across his face, arms and upper body. When he reached back with his off hand to rub it away, I snapped his sword aside, and continued to his chest before recovering and stopping his blade from doing the unkindness in turn. The strike had been just above the chain, and under the neckline. That bled nicely— a killing blow—though I thought it might take a minute.

He stumbled toward me.

I moved away.

The knight staggered to one knee. His sword fell from his bleeding hand.

Angel ran in and took it.

I leaned back.

"Foul woman! Finish me!" His words came weak.

I felt cranky; sometimes people just rub me the wrong way. I let him suffer and only looked at him. We all waited for his last moment. His body sagged deeper, but he glanced up with a sneer and a hateful gleam.

I said, "When you see Sho, tell him the Queen of the Debrecians killed you, and not some peaceful witch, nor even a lowly peasant who is used to bowing before men dressing and acting like peacocks. As well, tell him she is no longer surrounded by cowering breeders, but instead, free men and women who form an army of souls equal to any knight."

"Agh!" He coughed then sagged into a heap.

I grabbed his hair, pulling his head up out of the dirt. "And then have Sho pass this message down to the King: All days are numbered on this earth, including his own."

I don't think he heard me.

Chapter Eleven

While we fought, Minari recruited in the villages between the duke's castle and the ford. Those wishing to join us were sent across the ferry where they swelled new training groups.

While the King and Sir Lacellor depleted their armies, mine grew, some from my new lands and others from the enemies. We had a thousand trained warriors, all told, even before the new recruits, though a good third rode nags.

After eight days of fighting we learned that Sir Janis had retaken the ford. His messenger had been stopped by Khulan. She promptly sent the note on to me. Sir Drake had taken few losses in the retreat and had finally met up with Sir Finley, meaning that his forces were also becoming larger. I didn't imagine that Sir Finley was in good spirits, given his wife was in my custody and his castle either fallen or under siege. I doubted that Sir Finley could even get close enough to it to tell, given his castle sat barely off the road between the ford and Sir Lacellor's Norfaton. That was just about the center of the enemy forces.

No doubt, Sir Drake was more determined to set up blocking positions short of my south community and his father's castle to the east, as well as to harass Sir Janis's supply along the main road between the ford and Lacellor's castle. I didn't envy my fiancé's chore of managing Sir Finley under such circumstances.

As for Sir Lacellor, his scouts no longer hampered ours up north. Instead, Sir Janis's scouts harassed us. Marci and Sergeant Hadarm were hurriedly putting together new forces to complement the hundred women we'd left to defend the region. These were led by Chotan and Hara, for Hulan was with us, leading our archers. I had infinite trust in all these people, but knew we were thin. Our main force, with me, might find itself so far south that we'd rendered ourselves irrelevant whenever some great need presented itself.

Near the end of the eighth day across the river, some Debrecians managed through Sir Janis's lines, and after some good scouting, sent messages back, telling us that Sir Lacellor's castle was under siege and a quarter of Norfaton city burned. Every time I received a message like that I knew it was at least three days old, only making me worry more. I could have already been late for some enormous disaster that might take years to correct. Worse, if we went home by the ferry, it'd take two days to move our whole force. If we went by the ford, we'd be in for a fight; and it'd be no unsuspected ambush either, once they saw us approaching the river.

Where we stood, it seemed a mighty success. Yellow Eyes did not like the smell along several stretches of the road, but the buzzards feasted without reservation. We had to move ever closer to the duke's castle in order to prevent the enemy from becoming too suspicious through seeing so many of the grave-birds flying over the bodies that we'd dragged into the woods. Thus, the destruction took us increasingly south and ever farther from our own lines.

In all, we'd stopped an army of stragglers equal to a hundred wagons, fifty carts, three score knights, twice as many servants and messengers and over a thousand footmen. That was a good-sized army, in and of itself, equal to a siege on any two keeps. Our losses accounted for nearly a score who'd either died or become too wounded to fight on. Yet, considering, our losses were low because we repeatedly won. The enemy never moved their forces in groups over a hundred and were easily overwhelmed.

We were temporarily winning in Farstand because the enemy had no communications and didn't even know what plagued them. No supplies moved other than those diverted across our ferry, and we had enough new arms and horses to mount another hundred and make Marci and Sergeant Hadarm quite happy. I was, of course, assuming this, also knowing that not much made Sergeant Hadarm happy, save a good round of training drills and some ale.

This other thing; we were tired.

Then disaster struck.

It came in the form of one knight dressed in mail, a breastplate and a cursed wooden spear. He was a young man, a boy really, probably on his first trip to war. His chore seemed to be as sole minder for fifty peasant footmen, every last one of them years older than him. We fell on them with a pair of waves, one from the north road, and the second from the woods.

As soon as he realized the inevitability of the slaughter, which was well before we'd started, or even properly blocked the south road, he turned his pony around and raced straight down the middle of the roadway toward Duke Crestlin's castle. I was an observer, for we'd decided to test a company of newly arrived warriors, along with fresh squad leaders. They needed training and the enemy force was not strong, making it good practice. I watched the arrows fly past the fleeing knight, each missing him, seemingly by the width of a finger.

We'd moved quite a bit south, expanding the amount of road under our control. This meant the first outskirts of Dorne were just over a couple hills. There, the duke had several outposts within sight of one another.

We'd considered the possibility of a fleeing straggler. Upon the start of any ambush, two women were posted remotely, assigned to stop any straggler hoping to race home. On rare occasions this meant stopping a fleeing servant or escaping horse. However, this knight, though a coward, had also been well trained. Instead of going for his sword, he held fast to his spear and did not slow at all. As soon as my women came near enough for a certain throw, he tossed his spear through the lower body of a young South Woman.

Our second woman shot an arrow at his breastplate as he released his spear, but the arrow's angle was not good, causing it to harmlessly glance off. A second arrow was launched at his back, but it missed his speeding horse. The little battle had only lasted a few seconds.

Ten warriors raced past the archer and injured warrior, but the knight was on an incredibly good horse, the likes of which are rare. They returned empty handed, not having gotten close.

I'd never seen women as angry with themselves as were the warriors who'd let that knight get away. Then, as they straggled closer, one by one they noticed the speared woman and quieted.

Her horse had walked over by the brush. She was pinned to him by the way the spear had come so far through her lower body, and exited her hip. The spearhead had ended up well into the back of her animal. Only the last couple feet of the weapon remained in front of her.

I galloped to her side where I only managed to hold her up and ease the strain by bringing my horse close. On the other side, her horse had found a few trees convenient and used them to help keep steady.

More women arrived, but nobody could figure out how to get her off the weapon. We had axes that were useless.

I feared that the horse would collapse.

Slick blood made holding the warrior difficult. She was frightened out of her wits, sometimes slipping her hands along the spear. The blood kept her from a good purchase. Her eyes pleaded with me for relief, going back and forth from me to the wood. Every so often she screamed, but each scream tailed off in pants because of the pain. As the horse shifted less steadily, she screamed again with what sounded like the last of her strength. It was merciless.

I held her like she was my own daughter. What if she had been Batya, my sister, or the child I'd grown to love, Kahnsajin? No, she was only a poor woman from the south, but at the time I saw my sister and my child and someone whom I loved as much as anyone I'd ever known. I hugged her as best I could.

She slowly collapsed, more and more into my arms, but even there she struggled and screamed in a hoarse voice with her mouth pressed against my breast. Her breaths were short, driven, then quivering and always racing as wildly as her heart.

Other warriors came around once the killing of the peasant footmen stopped. All of our women wanted to help us, but nobody knew how to do it.

My head leaned over hers, as she sagged farther into my bosom. From above, I whispered into her ear, "This I promise you. You shall live. I will tell the Goddess to bring you to me, and to nobody else. She shall hear my prayers, for we are good friends. Do you hear me?"

She shuddered. It was the best she could manage, no longer able to yell, but I understood her.

"Good. It is a joyful day then, for this will not be the last time I hold you in my arms. Now my child, rest. I promise, when you wake, all will be better, for the Goddess is the divinity of women and birth." I spun a finger into the air and whispered the magical benediction of sleep, "Tpunwvw Own."

The woman went to sleep. It was not a moment too soon, for her horse quickly lost the use of his front legs. His chest crumbled forward. I held onto the woman's arm, but two other women afoot had to help me pull her off the spear. By the time we wrenched her loose, she was no longer breathing, but she was also no longer in pain.

I'd never taken those little deaths well.

I was tall and strong and had no difficulty putting the woman over the back of my horse. Someone brought a shovel from our pack animals, and so I took it as well before going into the woods to find a secluded place to bury her.

Others wanted to come, but I refused them.

It was Kirsta's duty to ask me her orders, for the escaped soldier was an immediate threat, likely to bring back his fellows.

"Do as you see fit, but don't do anything small, for the enemy is great and just over the next few hills. The time has come for us to say hello to them, face to face."

I could see that she wanted to ask me more, but I turned away. In my state, I could not lead.

* * * * *

My emotions wallowed deep in the pit of despair as I led my horse into the trees. The fact is I'd lost my way, so far from my home, wherever that might be, and knew that things were not going well up north. What was I to do? Could I really make a difference when the King could waste more warriors than I had on hand, just on this little road north, and had not even missed them until one cowardly knight changed even that wee blessing?

I'd only had one advantage: The men of Farstand thought less of me than appropriate. We'd been very careful to sustain that myth, including allowing nobody to escape our ambushes. We even went to the extreme of using our few and now precious male horsemen to lead many of the charges, just in case someone made his way back to a noble and reported the ambush. Now, a knight was surely telling the duke that a huge number of strong women were in the woods along the roadway, ambushing those sent to the main battlefield.

What kind of fruit might that bear? I knew, without a doubt, that the new, young duke was mustering the greatest force he could and was going to come at me in numbers. Since his castle remained the main assembly point, that might be a fair army. Equally troubling, when the next battle was done, the King of Farstand was going to know a great deal about us.

Yet, here was what I knew for sure: Without the help of the Debrecians, we were not strong enough for a bigger war. But then again, we were in a big war; who was I kidding.

And, in spite of our successes, and all of my ramblings about winning the road in ways meant to keep our losses low, we were losing the big war. The north was surely in shambles and close to crumbling.

* * * * *

My search for a clear spot with soft soil took several minutes. Digging a deep hole took far longer. I jumped into the pit and dragged the poor girl in with me so she'd not have to suffer the fall. She'd fallen enough.

I came out of the pit, holding her knife. I thought better of taking it, instead dropping it in beside her.

Yellow Eyes and Slow Leg sat on the eastern perimeter of the clearing, watching and wondering about the many new smells coming from the south and east. I smelled the oncoming enemy too, for I shared the nose of a wolf. As well, I had the eyes of a hawk, the ears of a fox, the duties of a Queen and the heart of a powerless and impoverished peasant girl. Only the last part of that mattered at the moment. When I put the dirt over her, it felt like I buried the better part of myself.

It was my fault. I'd killed her when I'd decided to let my least-experienced squads take the sole lead in what seemed to be an easy ambush. "A practice," I'd told them in my cockiest mood. Such foolishness!

We'd become too successful for our own good, killing most of our enemy with arrows before we even got close enough to be threatened by their pikes, spears and swords. Both our accuracy and our bow strength had improved nearly to that of the Debrecians. The difference between a weak bow shot and a masterful one is unimaginable. Given our growing strength, why would this one little raid be any different from the rest?

The assault had not been overly complicated by more than two lines of approach, reducing the risk of crossfire and confusion. Still, if I'd only put two more archers on that south road . . . .

The dirt fell over her.

It was a clear day and sound traveled. Somebody's sergeant barked out orders in the distance. It was a man's voice, though not Niko's. Horses were riding toward us, large ones; the kind that bite and are found under knights in heavy armor. At a distance, the clamor of swords, spears and pikes tapping on shields and armor told of men collecting in haste.

"My Goddess, give me the power to vanquish the duke's army.

Send the fiery wind of death before me.

And when it is done, and peace has come . . .

Send the soul of this warrior to my womb,

So something good might come of her suffering."

I looked up from where I knelt and saw the Goddess sitting on a cloud. She had a golden crown of leaves. Her hair appeared white, her dress pale flowers and her face, hands and feet the peachy color of life, unlike the ghostly white on the face of the woman I'd just buried.

I sternly gazed at the Goddess, cast my hands into the air, and shrieked.

She arose. For some reason, she was not in good spirits, which was unusual for her. I even saw her step back, as if afraid of me. It must have been something else though because how could she fear me? I was just an old maid of nearly nineteen, out in the woods alone, with only the wolves for company.

Still, I felt compelled to tell her, "Ah, do you not know that I love you and count you special among my friends?"

She said, "Is that what you call worship?"

"Oh, my Goddess, surely you are not so vain as to need endless babble. I trust we are beyond such nonsense in the midst of all this tragedy."

"And yet, should I trust you with the blessed gift of the passion's fire and magical wind. Do you know what you ask of me?"

"It is a saying. I need your attention, is all I ask. If you don't see my heart, then you've been away tending to the troubles of others too long. You should have paid attention to us on this border. Here, things are rapidly changing. This, of course, I understand, for no doubt there are endless travails for all women. The torment must span the whole world. But, my Goddess, do you not see the pressing and special nature of what we face?"

Her face mellowed some. She stepped to the front of the cloud. "So be it, child. I shall give you your desires, but only a little, for now, so I might see what you make of it before I give you full measure."

I was not sure what the Goddess was saying. She kissed her hand and blew the kiss my way. I'd seen lovers and family members do that to one another, though it had never happened to me before.

The wind kicked up. It was a terribly warm gust for spring.

Thinking and feeling more comforted, I didn't expect to find myself waking up between the feet and under the belly of my horse.

For some reason, he'd wandered over a few steps to where I'd passed out. Yellow Eyes was licking my face, and his girlfriend, Slow Leg, was telling him that she thought maybe I was dead and it might be a good time to go hunting and let the buzzards sort it out while they were gone. My horse didn't like the attention of the wolves, and stepped farther past me, missing me mostly, but not entirely, leaving a pinch bruise on my arm that later hurt for days.

When I got up, I staggered around a little like I'd had too much ale. Something strangely hot warmed the inside of me. I don't know what it was, but it was a little dragonish, like a million little fireflies coursing around in my veins. Oh no, not another crone spirit, come to possess me, I at first thought, but it felt a little different.

Somehow I found the top of my horse and from up there sensed the coursing inside of me mellow some.

Oh, what has the Goddess done to me now? I looked up. It would have surprised me if she'd still been there. Typical Goddess. Once again, she'd done something to me then left me without a clue.

I took inventory. I had a good knife in my belt and a great sword across my back. For a spear, I had the shovel with which I'd buried one young and innocent warrior.

For one breath, that was enough. Then it struck me that I didn't even know the name of the woman who'd died for me. I slid from sadness to outrage.

With a cold and furious spirit, I nudged my horse southeast. Two wolves, a horse and a Queen rode toward the increasing sounds of war.

Chapter Twelve

"Where is this new boy duke, pray tell?" I asked the enemy knight in front of me.

Hara, Angel and Kahnsajin parleyed by my side, a hundred yards in front of our lines. Four knights sat mounted before us. All of them were swallowed in silver and white armor. The one with a silver X on his breastplate was clearly a boy, and though richly armored, probably only barely able to hold his sword with one hand. At first I'd thought him the new duke, but instead had been informed by Sir Barker, who was by his side, that he was a baron and only loosely akin to the duke.

I'd grown fond of these little discussions the knights insisted upon before every major battle. They always proved fruitless, but it gave me time to gloat.

Kirsta was well behind us, up a small rise and just in front of a hundred and twenty mounted women. That company was her pride and joy. I had to appreciate how she'd managed to find the only good rise on the fields for her favorites.

They'd been there for most of an hour, awaiting the formality of allowing the duke's knights to assemble two decent blocks of footmen totaling three times our number. It simply would not be proper to charge down on them until they were good and ready to defeat us. Such was the silliness known as chivalry, and Kirsta had thought it interesting enough to watch it unfold before her eyes.

So too had I, knowing their true weaknesses, and seeing that they had only two score archers among their ranks. None of them had good bows and half were city peasants pressed to this singular duty. The other half appeared to be castle guards, as were two score of the other footmen, suggesting much about the depletion of better forces.

"The duke will not be troubled by women. He dines in his castle and has sent me in his stead," the boy in front of me said. His words jarred me away from my more important thoughts.

I turned my attention back to Sir Barker. "You are fated; always a minder to children, Sir Barker. This boy will not last, should I confront him afoot and bearing a hat pin."

"He will do, witch. I'll have you bowing before the honorable baron and our duke before the night has sat upon your army's corpses." He nodded his head to the side.

I looked back in the direction he'd indicated. Nearly two score knights on meaty horses came from the castle gates. As well, two score squires and another half score of peasant messengers. The last, bearing only spears, trailed in the wake of those nobly born. In all, these alone nearly matched Kirsta's lines.

In the last war, they'd done well to muster as many knights as I counted on that one field alone. The King must be taking this war seriously, I realized.

"I see. Four score knights, by my count. Very impressive, Sir Barker. How many of these are also children?"

"You will address the baron, not me, and with a civil tongue!" he commanded.

I nodded, and asked the boy, "Who is minding your playmate in the castle, Sir Baron, with all of these knights and castle guards in the field?"

"I see that it is unwise to parley with a witch."

"Then boy, why have you called us forth?"

He said, "Your army will meet mine in the middle of this field. I will give you ten minutes, after which time we shall attack, even if you don't." The boy carried a surprisingly manly voice, considering his age, which was only a little more than Kahnsajin's.

Beside me, Kahnsajin appeared all eyes, barely able to contain her excitement at being in the middle of such a gathering. Angel, however, licked her lips, obviously eager to kill someone. I feared she might leap upon the big knight just in front of her. He was mouthing kisses at her like a man eager to see her gates. The gates of hell were more likely to befall him, should they meet.

Thus, it surprised me when instead the Greyfeet warrior, Hara, rode forward a step. "You! Keep a good tongue when addressing the Queen of the Northern Tribes, lest you find it the only thing of use, next you meet a woman."

I laughed, perhaps more heartily than the occasion merited.

"What is the matter with these women?" the boy asked Captain Barker.

"They worship evil gods who elevate them all to royalty among the demons, knowing not the humble blessings of womanhood, as required by the all-knowing Sho," the White Knight said.

I had heard enough. "You have wasted our time with this. Next we meet, it shall be to the death." We turned to leave.

"Like the duke's father whom you murdered while unarmed?" the boy said, once I'd turned my back.

I turned back around a bit, and showed a smile. "Oh, he was armed, all right, though not well enough. Ask Sir Barker."

"Liar!" the boy knight said to my back.

On the way up the rise, I asked Kahnsajin, "Now, what have you learned?"

"Only questions. Like, what did Hara mean about the baron's tongue?"

I answered, "Never mind that. We were just peacocks, showing our feathers. Besides the feathers, what did you learn of your enemy?"

"They have boys for leaders. I am almost as old as that baron," she told me.

"No, Kahnsajin. Those boys will allow the men to do their fighting. Sir Barker is a better leader than any baron or duke. If the baron was older, then he'd do us the favor of getting in their way."

She pressed her lips and thought about the lesson.

I stopped beside Kirsta. "I am sorry for earlier. I took things harder than I should have and neglected our army."

"No, I think not. You are a Queen, and with such it is good to see a heart. It is also a compliment to trust me with your army," she said.

"Ah, I have always trusted you. Except, of course, to send you to capture someone and bring them to me whole. If not for a good witch, you'd have drowned me with that onion sack."

She laughed, which I'd never seen before. All sorts of rare things were happening around me. But, of course, war was one thing sure to alter moods.

"Tell me the logic of your plan?" she asked.

"They have most of their knights to the western side of their blocks, nearest us. Some are also on the far left. If we attack, they'll wait until we hit their footmen then immediately descend upon us with armor from the flanks. If we attack their flanks, they hope to whittle us down, letting the footmen assault us with long pikes when we have slowed and trusting to the armor of their knights for protection until we are dragged from our horses," I explained.

"Each is a good strategy for them," Kirsta said.

"Yes it is. Now, think on this. If you and one other warrior, bearing only swords, found two quick enemy scouts and one lumbering knight on the road, what would you do?"

She thought for a while. "We would coax the scouts away where we could kill them one on one. Once done with them, fall upon the lumbering giant as if mosquitoes."

"That is why I trust you with my army. The blocks of footmen are a lumbering giant. When they attack, we shall move forward only far enough to release one flight of arrows. Then we'll ride to the field on our right."

"And, if they don't follow?"

"They will follow," I assured her.

A score of our horses rode to our far right. The rest of us moved forward in two long lines of horses. We could see the enemy blocks stiffen. Several sergeants ran in front of their two blocks, sometimes grabbing a pike and screaming to the man behind it to hold it more steadily and with the butt ends in the dirt. Then, once we'd come close enough, the same sergeants yelled for them to raise their shields higher.

Once we came close, their archers, who were in back, shot a shower of arrows into the air. Some of us put our shields up high, wishing to catch them. Others cringed underneath. I was one of the older warriors who had a small shield, and thrust it in the direction of the flight. Oddly, the arrows seemed to hover in the air just then, as if hit by a small breeze that only blew a little above us. They fell harmlessly between our lines, though one or two came quite close to the front lines of the enemy block. It seemed that the wind was with us. This encouraged us all, allowing us to come up a little farther, which is always good for accuracy's sake.

Only the first few rows of footmen had shields, so we lofted our volley of arrows high into the middle of each block. As soon as the arrows were in the air, we turned to the right while still in formation and threaded in two files through the shield of our twenty flanking warriors.

Once we were a couple hundred paces away, our shielding force joined our ranks, and from our midst, a new shield of twenty set itself even farther to our right.

Some of the knights rolled out of formation, but were called back by a captain, perhaps Sir Barker. Instead, they marched the blocks forward then tried to wheel them to their left while in formation. They came out of that in a mess, but once the sergeants put them back into order, they marched them toward our new position.

Arrows flew, but each time I put up my shield, the wind seemed to push away, altering their flight.

We had ample room to maneuver. Our faux attack and realignment happened twice more before we riled a response from the boy baron. By that time, all we'd accomplished was putting three score footmen on the ground with arrows in them. This was not impressive, but if we did it until next dawn, we'd murder half their army.

So his white flag went up, as our hundred and twenty returned to the same hill we'd been on at the start. Only another hour of daylight remained to us when Angel, Kirsta and I met the four knights in between our lines. On the way down, I told Kirsta that I wanted her to speak for me because the last time nothing had been accomplished. I thought maybe it was because I didn't have the skill of speaking to nobles.

The boy baron started by saying, "I see you are indeed cowards and do not intend to meet my army like men."

Kirsta told them, "Send your knights, else meet us a thousand times along the road north. We are not fools and have no desire to become tied up among your breeding men."

This, of course, was a lie because we had no intention of wasting any more time on the road, now that we'd been discovered. Only a rear guard would remain, harassing forces intended to make them think we'd not moved so far north, joining the fight in Norfaton.

"This is not how it is done. You should meet us in battle, face to face, like men." The boy's face showed frustration and bewilderment.

"We are women. Now I've said that, so you can cut the snide insults, boy. Which of you is a man and can talk sense?" Kirsta asked.

None spoke up. To do so would have been an insult to the baron.

Kirsta finished it, "We're waiting for your knights. You have nearly sixty men on horses. You say you are good as any ten footmen and any five of us. Prove it or we'll ride off and you'll miss the chance you have long desired."

Not long after that, the knights, squires and messengers lined up opposite us. They were indeed impressive. Most held lances that were many feet longer than our spears. As well, we had modified most of our captured wooden shields, making them smaller and easier to carry, while they held large ones mostly hammered from metal. Some of those lances, however, I saw waver, confirming my suspicion that half of their knights were mere squires.

When the first horse took a step in our direction, Hara shot an arrow nearly straight up into the air. She anchored our left flank, and so the rest of our forces near the field had no trouble identifying her signal.

The knights were less than halfway to us before another hundred women came out of the woods near our left. Hulan led them from the front. From the way they charged, it was clear that she was tired of waiting the whole day in the woods.

Kirsta ignored our flanking force and signaled the women with us. More than half of our hundred and twenty bore curve-back bows. These archers nocked arrows. Kirsta dropped her arm and they fired into the breasts of the enemy horses.

Some of the horses had small breastplates. They were thin, but hitting them caused most of our arrows to deflect or stick harmlessly. Still, nearly a third of the horses took lucky hits through or around the breastplates. Not many horses fell, but a half dozen stumbling or slowing horses is enough to reap havoc upon the order of such a rank. Good gaps formed in the enemy's line.

We chose to not meet this charge and instead broke into two ranks of sixty each the moment the arrows were released. Each half of us raced to the rear. The two ranks grew farther apart, leaving a gap in the middle of the battlefield. We were still in rows and had not bothered with columns.

In our place, a hundred hidden women from the woods charged into the eastern half of the baron's knights. Some took them on the flank where they were not well defended and scattered thin because of their formation that was oriented to sweep my group in a wave. Ten brave men turned and formed a small wall against the onslaught, allowing the rest to chase our command group and evade this surprise.

The effect of this was to tie up that side of the remaining knights. There, those of our women with spears struggled to hold back the weighty knights while our archers shot into the knights as they wrestled with their lances, swords and shields.

The men fought well, and I saw over my shoulder that a good number of women fell from their horses.

A little over twenty of the enemy knights followed my group of sixty as we retreated toward the distant woods to the northwest. Since they did not relent, we continued into the trees.

Unlike us, the eastern half of our group turned back. They'd fallen under command of Hara since Kirsta was with me. Once they saw that the knights on that flank couldn't follow because of being hit by a hundred warriors, they returned to the fight. At close range, they riddled twenty bogged-down knights with arrows. Those knights had their shields mostly aimed toward the larger group of women assaulting them from the east. Hara's women had excellent shots because of the hill and misdirected shields. All of the messengers fell, swept from their horses. As well, our arrows pierced the armor of many of the knights. The effectiveness of powerful curve-backs, shot at close range, was something entirely new to them, as they found their armor nearly useless if hit flat and not at an angle.

With only one salvo, the knights were swamped because of

widened gaps and slow horses. Hulan's women, who'd been fighting the wall of ten lances, streamed through the many breaches and around the flanks. Once through, they roamed the field, even killing those who'd fallen from their stricken horses.

Finding itself a free unit, Hara rolled her line of three score women around, and walked her line of horses toward the footmen.

That's the last I saw of the battle for a while because we'd run ourselves too far into the woods. Once there, I spent most of my time helping Angel keep track of Kahnsajin. The young Debrecian was good on a horse, but sometimes tense. I didn't think she appreciated how much joy her young death would bring one of the enemy knights. To her credit, she was better on a horse than I was, once she dropped her shield—which was too heavy for her—and took the time to put her bow across her back. This allowed her to pick a path avoiding all the low branches.

We curved right and came out on the main road. Behind us, we heard the knights still following, though the snaps of branches and no small amount of swearing told me that their heavy horses and long lances were giving them fits. This trouble was at the core of my plan. From there, we raced straight back down the road and into the fields, only well to the east of the battle. I was desperate to see how things were going.

The first thing I saw was a field littered with standing horses, and fallen warriors. Then, over to the left of that, and closer to the first houses of Dorne, the blocks of over three hundred footmen no longer existed. In place of the organized units, less than three score men huddled in a circle. All of their too-few shields pointed outward. Bodies were everywhere around them, and no few under as well.

Behind these peasant soldiers, another several score were running for the protection of the houses. Hara and Hulan had split out most of our force into squads. Some imitated vultures, circling the huddle of men. Others hunted small groups of fleeing footmen like they were elk. This fighting seemed confusing, but had a certain order to it that I recognized.

The fleeing men were cut down with arrows shot at close quarters by women standing in their stirrups. Some were slashed by swords.

One man was struck by a spear, though most of our spears had been lost in the greater battle and had not yet been recovered. Only a few of the men made it all the way to the houses where Hara's squad leaders had the good war sense to leave them alone.

Only a small force of fifty women stood in formation, awaiting our return. These were a combination of women, though most were from Hulan's group.

I found Hulan again. She'd fallen to a knee, bloodied but alive and still holding the reins on her horse. A woman was stripping her chest bare. Another woman tended long gash wounds on both an arm and her back.

For the moment, the ever-active Greyfeet leader, Hara, was the only high commander on the field. She rushed over, upon seeing Hulan fall, and took charge of the fifty. These were guarding the battlefield against any unknown enemy force. I was once more convinced that Hara was a reliable leader and a gift to me from her Queen Risha, for we had long-since passed beyond the portion of the battle that had fallen under our plans. When I next saw Queen Risha, I resolved to sing praises to the Queen for her gift, hopefully before their council and talented shaman.

We joined the fifty. Together, and once again with a force of a hundred, we waited for Sir Barker and the boy baron.

Behind us, Hulan stood, though she seemed only strong enough to direct the decimation of the peasant footmen, and from the look of her wounds, not for long. I intended to put her in a bed as soon as things settled.

Our warriors finished chasing the last of the enemy soldiers into the houses. Most of those women returned and their presence added new arrows above and into the last few footmen who'd huddled in the small circle. Hulan set two teams of archers to the task of shooting from opposite sides and under command, so that the few shields proved less useful. Some from her group split off and started gathering war goods, as well as redistributing some spears to their fellows. Others collected arrows that had not broken.

The circle of peasant footmen was slowly becoming a mass grave. I saw some fall without even being hit. Those pulled bodies over them for protection. I knew they hoped for night and the cover allowing them to escape. It was coming on the heels of long shadows. Good for them if they succeeded. The peasants deserved my pity, having mostly been brought here under force by the nobles.

It was incredible how long it took the knights to emerge from the wooded edge of the north road. When they arrived, they came with only four of their long lances. Thinking back on it, how those four had managed to bring their twelve-foot lances through the dense forest was the real puzzle. Some had even lost their shields in the woods. These were no small losses, for it meant we could more easily approach and slaughter them with our spears and powerful arrows. For us, replacement shields abounded on the battlefield that we controlled.

I could tell that the setbacks on the field didn't sit well with the knights either, for they saw the same things we did and had just learned that their twenty were the last good unit standing. Leading them astray had been a huge success, allowing our main force to hit their friends while their armor was split. Now that it was together, less than half of it stood before us. These had been educated in our tactics. That was our biggest loss of the day, for I preferred them ignorant.

Farstand was not the only loser in that battle. Near the place where our women had met the knights' right flank, thirty women lay among the enemy dead. Even more women were down, though they were more scattered.

I gave command over to Kirsta, who clearly did not need my help. Together with Kahnsajin, I made my way to the women on the ground. Angel came as well, but she stopped halfway between the wounded and Kirsta's force. She remained ready with a spear and her knives, in case any enemy should come too close.

Kahnsajin collected some broken spears and arrows, with which I created a small fire with a short spell. With that I heated a knife and sealed the worst of the wounds on the closest woman. Kahnsajin poured spirits over the steaming injury. She no longer had to be told how to do it, though she still flinched at the screams. We'd been in battle for nine days, and she'd long ago learned her role in healing. Her efficiency freed me to ready a good bone needle. In spite of the horrible gash, the woman quit yelling and fainted straight away the moment she was pricked. Such was convenient, so I sewed quickly while she remained out of her wits.

Once done with the first woman, I left Kahnsajin to the binding while I went to the next.

To the southeast of us, the killing continued until there were no more footmen who were not either dead, fled, dying, or pretending to be dead.

When I looked up from the second woman, the knights up on the hill had endured an attack from Kirsta's archers. Several of their horses had fallen, leaving ten mounted. They wandered out of range. Their friends, now afoot, backed up as well. Among those afoot, I saw the great white armor of the baron and Sir Barker. The boy baron lay draped across the rump of another knight's horse. These men were desperate to move toward the castle road, but our women had gained control of all of Dorne's passes. This left them with no options. After some time watching, they retreated to the west.

Out that way was another road. It led to a distant Farstand keep of some minor noble whose name I'd not bothered to learn. I did know that it was two days distant, giving us at least four days before Sir Barker would return, and even then with probably only a few more knights.

A greater concern was who might be coincidentally coming down other roads and from other lands. Dorne's Crestlin Castle was, after all, a staging ground and the funnel for the whole war effort.

Looking back at the castle whose peaked turrets I could just make out over the houses, I saw a wisp of smoke curling into the sky. Above the tallest spire, the duke's flag had been stricken.

Good, Chotan and Sergeant Niko had found a way in. We'd all suspected that the duke might keep his gates open, allowing his knights and soldiers to come and go as they pleased during the battle. This is why we'd put all of Niko's men into the colors of Farstand messengers. The plan had put Chotan's hundred a minute behind him. She and her women were strong with spears and swords, and the best we had for the duty of taking dukes and castles.

As I finished mending the third woman, wagons arrived from the city. They were full of goods. I hailed the first one, finding it loaded with oar and two barrels of freshly made arrows. Blacksmith tools had been haphazardly scattered over top of the ore. Also among the goods were some chairs and bundles of linen. Sitting on a pillow on the top of the pile was a crying boy of perhaps five. Riding up front was a frightened girl of roughly ten. Her angry father was a muscular man, though not tall.

"What is your profession?" I asked him.

"Smith!"

"Good to see that you have joined us," I told him.

"Joined you, you say! With a knife at my back!" He shook the reins, causing the wagon to lurch forward under the power of two stout horses. His wagon disappeared over a hill on the north road.

Several other wagons passed me, all of them laden with needful goods and tools showing signs of skilled labor. Behind those came some wagons full of seed peas. Crestlin's city was emptying its larder.

One of Hulan's squad leaders rode up. She was a Debrecian from my tribe, and I asked, "How'd you manage to win over all of these tradesmen?"

"My Queen, the boy in the first wagon belongs to a family ten back. The smith's wife is boarding yet another wagon that is still being loaded. We've let them bring their families, but one is always a hostage, though riding with friends, so they know they are safe," she told me.

"And, if they choose to escape and go back, once they've recovered their missing member?" I saw it as a big possibility.

"We are setting torch to their homes and businesses, as you suggested, my Queen. Don't you remember? Anything useful for war is being taken or destroyed, by your command. Their life is at the settlements now. They've been made to know this."

The woman rode on at my nod, and so too did every wagon and draft horse in Farstand, seemingly. One after the other, they rode by. I was watching the rape of Dorne, and we were making hostages of the most skilled laborers among them. I wondered, what is the core of a city, if not its skilled labor, for the nobles did well to warm their own beds and were otherwise useless. Months might pass before the enemy reestablished these trades of war, and the supply was now severed between Farstand and the invaders in Norfaton.

It was a high half moon by the time I tended to all the women who might be saved. Other midwives had joined me. Even with all our skills in healing, thirty women counted from the whole of the battlefield were dead or dying.

By the time I finished tending the worst wounds, the wagons thinned to a trickle, ending in mostly carts. A hundred of my women were spread out along the roads, bearing torches and seeing to the night movement of goods and tradesmen toward the north. Less and less of us occupied the city while more of us took to the highway home.

Hara still held a force of fifty in the field, ready for any surprises. We were increasingly concerned about any force that might stumble across us in the duke's city because of poorly timed arrivals. None came, though this did not settle me, for their scouts could easily see our fires and sacking, and would also warn any travelers coming into the city region by any number of roads. In time, these forces would build to the point of wanting to test our lingering strength. Judging from the rate of travel we'd seen on the north road, building a decent force might take them several days, and most likely a good week, but we had no way of knowing. I felt us pressed too thin to send out any more scouts.

Over the house roofs, several fires gave an orange cast to the night sky. This included the castle which burned brighter than anything else. By morning it would certainly be no more than a shell of perfect walls and towers, all well blackened and missing floors, stairwells, roofs, treasures and all of the bones lying freshly dead within.

I had not hoped to burn the whole city, but it was only because of the lack of a good wind that it didn't burn entirely, for much of Duke Crestlin's city had been devoted to the skills and trades of war. The stronghold was close to the front, and the conflict had been long lasting, so the city both prospered and stood under threat, becoming too comfortable with both for its own good.

Many of the city's women were grieving their recently dead husbands and sons. They were not the sort of widows who were willing to go with us.

Still others, longer abandoned by the ways of Farstand, eagerly joined. Our warriors sorted through them, seeing only if they had ample bearing. Three squads totaling fifty women were set into formations. A third as many men comprised a small group eager to join Niko's forces. Those were marched past me. The guard left them a few yards beyond, without comment, for my healing grounds had become our assembly point.

It was the wee hours, and I felt exhausted, barely giving a glance toward them, much less getting up. Some were with children, hand in hand or clutched to their bosoms. They looked about, excited or terrified or both at once. An army is a terrifying thing. This is true even to its own members, and in particular, to its newest converts. Perhaps that is how it should be.

It was not a good place to greet new warriors, for I sat among rags full of blood and women whose souls had fled. Close, a stack of arms and legs rested beside a fire, a sharp, thin knife, a two-handed saw and a heavy war axe.

I was not through grieving a recent failure, for the last women I'd tended were the ones least likely to survive, and not one of them had. I'd chanted endless spells of healing. Magic is costly in strength, and I had not slept in two days, other than during my little tussle with the Goddess. Around me, other women loaded the last of our wounded onto five wagons. They did this without my help, for I doubted I could even get up the tailgate without assistance.

The new recruits waited. Some stooped. A few sat in the grass. One came over and told me, "Midwife, bring us some bread and water. Can't you see we are destined to be warriors and are hungry?"

An archer, upon hearing this, made to come over. The look on her face suggested she might kill the woman. I raised my hand, stopping her.

It pained me to get up, but I did. There was only a little bread in my saddlebags and we'd used all of the nearby water on the wounded. Thus I went from warrior to warrior, taking up a collection from the last of their provisions. I reasoned that we had plenty, just not right here and at this moment.

Several warriors rode away to get more water for our skins.

Others helped me carry the food, seeing that I was determined to do the young recruit's bidding.

I came to her with bloody arms full of bread, jerky and apples. When she did not step forward to take some, I set it on the grass before her.

She took a little of it, seemingly not entirely pleased for some reason that I was too tired to sort out. Others, as well, came forward, some grateful, more with small glances of scorn. Ah yes, I understood; they are warriors and I but a midwife whose hands had tainted their meal.

That old thinking only showed how little they knew of midwives and warriors, for any good warrior quickly came to love a midwife and would stand in the face of death to keep her whole. Farstand peasants, however, saw them as necessary evils, useful only upon the occasion of birth or illness. They were usually late coming or not called at all unless the child was breech. Midwives were also little better than witches in the eyes of the people of Farstand. They used them, and once done, often turned them in to the White Shirts who murdered them. That, of course, is pretty much where life began for me. The fact is, I'd come to know that the best of them were indeed witches, or nearly so, and they often did not know it.

Soon, all of the new women were fed, and so I went back to my spot on the grass and leaned back, using one of my fallen warriors as a headrest. The dead warrior might have been cold and lifeless, but she was ours, and thus resting with her was the only thing that seemed right to me at the time. I was saying goodbye to her and to all of those like her on that field. All of my warriors knew this, I suspected, for we'd come to understand one another during our time on the road.

"Oh, by the gods, what are you doing?" shrieked one of the new women, perhaps because she saw me resting among our dead.

"Quiet, you idiot!" One of my warriors had finally had enough and broke our spell of tolerance. I heard the new recruits being swiftly marched north, and with some strong insistence from the women who led them away. Some ways off, they stopped for a good scolding, making me wish I didn't have such good ears.

As for good ears, Yellow Eyes came, and lay down close. On the other side of him, Slow Leg planted herself. She said in her mind: *She's dead now; can't you smell? The last time she was only fooling.*

Yellow Eyes said: Hush, bitch. It's almost morning. Time for the pack to sleep.

Our pack drifted off while I held a warrior's stiff, frozen hand and watched the falling of the half moon that had wisps of black smoke, tinged orange, crawling across its face.

Chapter Thirteen

"Do you think your big horse can last as long as my rangy one if the creeks are all dried up and you have to go a long ways?"

There was a silent pause filled only with the slow pace of many hooves and the rattle of sideboards, after which Kahnsajin continued, "I mean, if they can both drink their fill at the start."

One of the wheels on the wagon I was riding in squeaked half of every rotation. I smelled a good bit of dust, telling me we were nowhere near the front of the column.

She added, "The big ones can drink a lot more, but they're heavy and wet more, too. I can see yours pees a lot more than mine."

The wagon hit plenty of bumps, but we were not racing, as we had during that wet night many weeks back when I'd had my head covered with an onion sack. Instead, a straw hat had been loosely tied over my face. When I realized I was awake, I winked up; little pricks of sunlight flickered through the gaps in the straw.

"See, he just peed agai n. I counted to near twenty in my head when he did. Mine only pees to nine or ten, and not near the splash, and he's way more than half as big."

Under me was a thick blanket. I appeared to be tied by the waist to the end of some sort of turned-down tailgate, no doubt so I wouldn't fall off. I looked over toward the front, seeing a mound of potatoes, the bulk of which was held back by a dam of weaved boards between me and the main wagon bed.

"He'll break down too, no matter how mean he is. Mine will run all day. Don't you think?"

Willow's bark! I reached for my bag, discovering that the weight at my hip was indeed my personal carry. Only one piece of willow remained. I jammed it up under the hat and into my mouth without getting up.

"Good legs. Big horses lose their legs quick. Run them with no water and their legs dry up and fall out from under a horse. That's what my mother says, and she knows everything."

The wagon hit a good-sized pothole, nearly throwing me off the back. I went with it, jolting up into a seated position.

I untied my safety line, realizing that any further rest was futile. Sitting with my legs off the back, I kept the hat well over my face. Aching, my teeth chewed dryly on the strip of soft bark.

Two horses, eight legs, were walking to either back edge of the wagon, almost like they were guarding me. One belonged to Kahnsajin, which explained the endless questions. The other had four of the best looking legs I'd ever seen on a warhorse. The warhorse was tied by a stout leader to the corner of the same wagon I'd woken up in.

Looking up a little, I saw that the horse had a face for battle, so fierce that I imagined steam coming out of his huge nose holes when he looked at me with his glassy red eyes. Of course, it was just the way he looked at me that had me imagining steam. Still, he rightly knew his enemy, as good warhorses were trained to do.

A boy sat on the animal. Loose purple and scarlet robes draped his body. His shirt appeared pale-blue silk spun so tightly that I could hardly see the threads. There were two rows of buttons on his lake-blue britches instead of one.

His stockings appeared to be pure white silk. His purple shoes seemed soft as slippers, sure to be ruined in only a few miles of real hiking. Their toes were curled up and fastened back with buttons in some strange, far-western fashion that seemed silly in our better company.

All of his carved, ivory buttons remained unfastened on his vest, helping him fight the heat of the dusty, noon march. His skin showed ribs and fat instead of muscles and it lacked hair.

At his waist was a small scabbard, minus the tiny sword. Equally, an even smaller scabbard had been emptied of its knife. Between the scabbards, the boy's hands had been bound. They rested on his pommel.

The boy was even younger than the baron who'd represented him in that field. His whole body stiffened, as if he'd not thought me alive until I'd moved. In that fashion, I met the new, young duke.

I felt at a disadvantage, for much of my hair was flying everywhere, and the rest was tied up in rats. I might have looked a hedge witch to him, which to me was a compliment, but to him probably not.

Kahnsajin nodded politely, as if nothing was amiss, but didn't stop her endless questions for even a second. All of these were directed toward the boy who also endlessly didn't reply. He pretended that it was beneath his station, I could tell, but I also saw him swallow—terrified to the bones.

Soon, I thought, the boy will learn to talk to her, lest she see it as boundless opportunity and never cease. I knew from experience that Kahnsajin had the ability to jabber in her sleep.

A horse rode up, and I found a skin of water in my hand. Angel took it back after I'd emptied most of it over my hair and finished nearly the last down my throat. I'd decided to swallow the gnawed bits of willow, hoping it would help ease the ache and head spinning a little faster.

A whole jar of water found my lap. This was given to me by Hulan. She'd ridden up to the other side of the wagon. I poured every last bit of that over my body which I found was no longer in my good fighting clothes, but was instead cleaned a little of the first layer of blood and adorned in a simple shift. The wheat-colored shift soon turned pink.

The water also made the little shift nearly transparent, but we were all women here, and it didn't matter. Well, we were not *all* women, but I felt as if most who mattered were, and that was enough to keep me from feeling immodest.

I stepped off the back of the wagon, barefoot, staying still until the horses cleared. The duke's horse made to nip at me, but I got even with him when he was almost past, poking him sharply in the hip with my elbow. The horse peed in response, but not before he was well to the backside of me.

"See, and a big horse pees more often. If you ask me. Which you should. I've counted that as well. I count all sorts of things. The Queen says it is a good way to learn."

Others were passing and coming up the road, mostly tradesmen with their families pulling or pushing carts and then some of the new recruits. The latter was only a squad, but they already marched in a ragged line and were holding sticks up above their heads with varying degrees of success. This was at the insistence of a southern squad leader. South Women had weak arm strength at first so we lost no time correcting the error.

I staggered aside and finally into the ditch where there was some shade and a little water in what might pass for a brook on a rainy day. There I planted my naked feet in ankle-deep water that smelled of rotting leaves, but was, to me, all the fresher for it because it didn't smell like human death. I decided to also sit rather than throw up.

Hulan, I suddenly recalled, had been horribly wounded! Blood stains dyed her clothing reddish brown. "For Goddess sake, woman, come sit beside me and rest," I said. "Forgive me. I'd completely forgotten your injuries."

The great swordsman looked at me curiously. "If you had, I'd not be here. Do you not remember tending me less than half a day ago?"

I thought back, and all I saw in my head was a blur of death and blood-coated bodies; a stitch here, a bone saw there . . . . "No. I do not. There were so many. Even so, your wounds are terrible. I could hardly bear to watch you return to your horse on the battlefield. Here, let me call the wagon and have them stop. You can use my bed on the bumper, or better yet, we'll leave the potatoes in the road, and have those who follow pick them up for their packs."

"Such would rock and beat me to my death, my Queen. Better a horse for resting," she said in true Debrecian fashion, for they were quite expert at sleeping while mounted.

Then she pulled her shirt down from her shoulder and showed me the arm. My stitches were plain enough, for I'd not been fancy in my haste. There were only two or three per inch, and the gash had been a foot long. Next she turned around, and only had to pull aside a great slash in the fabric to show me my crude handiwork across her back. What was most unusual was how the wounds looked white in some places and red in others, as if they'd been healing for three months.

"I will brag that the Queen herself tended these scars, and in haste because of so many wounded; as well while still on the battlefield with horses and arrows chasing all around us. These are as good as free ale for life and in any tent of my choosing. My only fear is they will heal too completely because of the magic."

Her spirit brought a smile to my face.

Angel came over with a pair of full buckets from some cleaner stream that must have been well into the woods. As well, she had a set of clothing on one shoulder, and a pair of boots laced together across the other. How she managed this was a greater miracle than the healthy scars on Hulan.

Hulan explained before the girl fully arrived, "You healed us. It wasn't Queen's magic, but shaman's. You have two gifts, and both in full. I've only heard of such healings in stories. I imagined them myths. That was before. Most of those you touched were saved. More than half of them are already riding again. Then, when you lay down with the dead, many of us thought you might even raise a few of the departed. We were worried about it, wondering if it was right to go so far. They did not, proving a wise limit to your favor with the Goddess."

I braved the light's effect on my headache and looked up into her eyes again. The woman was serious. She continued, "Our scribes will hear of this, and bards will sing into eternity."

"Ah, it was just good witchery," I told her, but her shoulder and back told me better, and Hulan knew it.

Behind her, some of Niko's men rode by. I nodded to them, but I don't think they recognized me and instead they took overly long glances at my body. One gave a call and another a hearty whistle. The rest of them found that amusing, but there was joy in their laughter and appreciation for my womanhood in their eyes. Such could not be scolded, for I loved them all, and would marry them all, were it not for Sir Daren Drake.

That, of course, reminded me of my duty. I thanked Hulan for her kind words and let her return to the road and her charges. After going into the woods, I made myself presentable with the considerable help of Angel. When I emerged a good deal later—and while still considering the state of my hair—Kahnsajin sat in the road with my horse at ready. My army had passed, save a few scouts who remained invisible.

I mounted my animal, resigned to a hard road and uncertain end. "Your counting is correct. Your horse will ride twice as long as the duke's and on only half the water."

She beamed. "Yes, as I was trying to tell him . . . ." I let her go on for a long while, liking the life in her voice. The duke glared at me with renewed hate, as if seeing me for the very first time.

* * * * *

Just to the north of the great ford is a field of ten thousand bones. Some belonged to friends—others to enemies. These mixed with the footprints of a million scavenging birds and vermin.

Our wagons and spoils from the sacking of Dorne were busy using the ferry across the Redwater. This migration was sure to occupy the ferry for several days more than convenient, requiring a visit to the south shore of the ford by my warriors. We desperately needed to secure its use.

Crossing in haste became even more apparent the day scouts came south saying that Sir Lacellor had been killed in battle.

Lacellor's castle at Norfaton remained under siege. Who commanded there remained unknown, and that didn't seem promising. We'd destroyed his logistics, but the work would not matter if he commanded the resources of a whole new land. My scouts reported that a big tent had been set up on the main Norfaton road just before the drawbridge, and our knights, bearing somber faces, had been seen entering this parlay ground.

As troubling, Sir Janis's army had made good forays toward the castle of Sir Drake. What was happening in the west, where there were four seats of the nine high lords, remained anybody's guess, but I knew the nobles out there were well outside my influence. If Sir Janis caught wind of this, and that we few in the south were the only strong groups fighting, he might be smart enough to take advantage. These same western lords had retained just enough of their knights to make it worth Sir Janis's trouble to negotiate their surrender, making these forces his own. Once this was done, he'd have endless access to the food and supplies I'd spent all my time denying him.

The good thing was, Sir Daren Drake and Sir Finley had shown the good sense to let the enemy retake the ford without suffering large losses. His harassing army periodically severed the lines between the ford and Norfaton. This also helped keep our community of warriors both a mystery and a haven situated in the far southeast corner of the kingdom.

I reasoned: Take the ford once again and the south, at least as far as the outskirts of Norfaton, will be ours. Sir Janis would be all the farther from his supply and his army would die on the limb. If we are quick enough, we might even catch Sir Janis's rear guard, causing whoever was in charge at Norfaton to reverse their negotiations and rebuff the smooth-talking Sir Janis. All hinged on these two unlikely victories.

These thoughts occupied me as I rode through the field of bones and up to the river bank.

"When do we attack them?" Kirsta asked.

Khulan, Sergeants Sasha and Niko, as well as Hulan, Hara and, of course, Angel and Kahnsajin, were also with me. Chotan, Minari, Marci and Sergeants Kreger and Hadarm were busy at the ferry and community, finishing the work of making me a second army, I hoped.

Word had been sent that Lady Finley had also returned to her old usefulness, though a scout reported that her husband had made her dress in finery. He'd also tied up two good squad leaders, making temporary maids of them over a fine and wasteful dinner that nobody had time for. If I'd been there, I'd have not abided it, for my squad leaders were precious and making maids of them was an insult. Such made mockery of them in front of their soldiers. I sent the scout back to our community, telling her to tell my leaders that Sir Finley was not to command a single one of my women, nor have any more of the resources than he needed to harass the enemy. Threatening him with arms was allowable, should he protest.

It was good to hear further reports saying the pompous lord did not stay in our camps long, and was back in the field, making better use of himself as a knight under the guidance of Sir Daren Drake. I did not doubt Sir Finley's ability to fight, once he got over himself.

As well, Sir Casar had been enticed to stay by Minari and Marci, both of whom had eyes for the big warrior. He'd been of help before and thus was quick to pick up the duties of another sergeant. I wondered if it was Minari or Marci who'd managed most of the convincing? Marci needed him the most. She had the responsibility of raising the Baron of Helfax's daughter, and was also of nearer proportions. I could imagine them lying together, their little baby plopping down on their pillow at the most inconvenient times.

"Did you hear me, Queen Abi?" Kirsta repeated.

"Oh. I was just thinking," I said.

"They have five hundred foot," the ever practical Niko said.

"And a strong contingent of over a hundred archers." Hulan was quick to notice those with bows since I'd set her above my company of northern archers.

"Bah! She will send a wind and throw their arrows back at them; just as she did against the archers of Dorne," Khulan declared.

"It was a fluke breeze," I explained for the tenth time. One did not rely upon the gods and live long.

"I think not, or at least not nature's gale. I have a hundred warriors who saw the arrows turn at the command of your shield. As for the wind, the city did not burn entirely, because of the unnatural stillness. There was no wind other than that made by our Queen."

"Ah, do not count on it, especially if I do not know how I did it, if what you say is true and I did anything at all," I advised her.

"So, when do we attack?" Kirsta remained the practical one.

"While we are crossing the ford, they will salt us with endless arrows." I bit my tongue, disparaging that prospect.

"Then at night?"

I frowned at Kirsta. "There are no clouds, and the moon is over half full. On the other side, we've no room to maneuver. It will have to be sword to sword, spear to spear, arrow to arrow. I don't like fighting our women toe to toe. They are our number, and even if we win, we are done as an army for many months. The point isn't to get across, but to do so with enough women to press Sir Janis."

Sasha groaned. "This shouldn't even be a big fight. All they have are footmen. Only a dozen knights can mount."

"And all the ground that needs crossed?" I shook my head. "The ford is high. We'll cross chest deep, like turtles. Next, we'll crawl up the far banks, dragging horses. They will be full of newly planted feathers."

Over to my right, four soldiers, an enemy outpost until the previous night, drew flies.

"Then it's to the ferry. We'll set the wagons aside, and go first. In two days, we'll be ready to attack on dry ground where their archers are next to useless." Kirsta had always been a sound thinker in battle. I appreciated her wisdom.

"Perhaps. In either case, the ford will have to be taken, lest we leave a good force in our rear." I mulled over the map in my mind. "But first, let's see if we can convince them to make a mistake. I've sent word back to our rear guard. They've been told to let the enemy messengers through. When they get here, we'll be waiting for them. In the meantime, let's get word to Sir Drake. If they don't attack us before tomorrow night, he can sweep them from the rear. If all he does is draw off their knights and kill a few archers, that will be good enough. We'll let him judge how and when to strike."

"How long can we wait, my Queen?" Kirsta asked.

"A day and two nights. By morning next, near to half the wagons will be across. The rest will have to follow us, should we need to waste two more days using the ferry.

"They'll be defenseless, should the enemy come up, or forge across the ford and find their tracks, pressing east," Niko cautioned.

We needed the wagons and all their goods, as well as their skilled labor. I nodded to Niko, letting him know it was a worry.

* * * * *

We lit fires all around the southern end of the ford, making it appear like some sort of grand duke's yard. Where the road ended next to the water, Khulan and Sergeant Sasha had the pleasure of waiting there for what we already knew to be two enemy messengers bearing down on the ford from the direction of the duke's ruined castle. It was the wee hours of night, nearer to morning than evening, but across the river, an assembly of knights watched, as did many of our women on our side, though we'd taken to the creases and woods and did most of our watching a little away from the lit grounds.

Across the river they did not know how many we were, which was always how I wished to meet my enemy. Suffice to say, they thought us many, but I was guessing a few short of our true number.

The sound of the enemy messengers' horses grew louder. Behind their hooves were ours. We gave them incentive in their last moments, driving them to the lit grounds.

The two popped over the rise, and had little choice but to ride right up to Khulan and Sasha. Each had a spear and sword, and though Sasha was only expert with the spear, it was said that Khulan had been born a master at both.

Messengers don't often bear shields, but these two had a pair of crudely made spears because of the known dangers of the north road.

Khulan rode forward first, followed by Sasha who came abreast to meet the enemy. They faked a toss before veering their horses to the sides at the last moment. This was one of our tactics against small forces. The messengers flinched down then reached with their spears, but were not expert at it. One crashed against Sasha's shield. The other thought to toss his spear at Khulan and at the same moment apparently thought better of losing his only good weapon. He dropped it between them, losing it entirely.

The messengers could see the men across the river, and even hear them cheering them on. From the sound of the roar, it was clear that the enemy thought these messengers our equals, or even better, for at first there were no jeers of frustration.

Khulan brought her horse around and chased the messenger who'd lost his spear, driving hers into his back when he had to slow before entering the water. Sasha, in the meantime, occupied the second man. He appeared to be decent with his weapon, clearly practiced. Sasha held him back, however, using her shield and spear with good defense. This allowed Khulan to return. She stuck her bloody spear into the ground and killed the distracted messenger with her sword.

Sasha had to go into the water to grab one of the horses while Khulan searched the messengers for messages and weapons. Always, they kept an eye on the far bank. On the other shore, the enemy seemed shocked into silence. It was only after my women removed the good boots and started dragging a man into the water that the enemy started yelling.

Archers snuck their way onto the shadowy portions of the far shore. They shot into the air, but Khulan ran back before the arrows fell. Once the last of the arrows landed, she ran back and kicked the dead man the rest of the way into the current. In like fashion, she taunted them. The two dragged the other man from the shallows where he'd fallen and into the deep, playing with the archers between reaching shots.

One of our other warriors came up, and took away the animals. I thought, good, another pair of warriors will be mounted.

Khulan and Sasha put some more wood on the fires and returned to their horses' backs. They turned, faced the road, and waited for another messenger, as if the men across the river didn't even exist. The bodies floated away.

We, of course, had many women waiting for the men across the river, and they knew it. This included a good squad of archers who hid in the trees and bushes well to the sides and next to the shore. Their job was to warn us, as well as to fall back, should a small group of enemy try to cross. If a big group came, well that was another matter.

We'd received word that a squad of South Women had intercepted a full score of enemy horsemen a few hours down the road. Eight men had been killed in the first skirmish. A dozen were held prisoner. This was accomplished with only ten bows. That was an amazing feat. "The men are terrified," the scout had said. "They think we are Debrecians. Some said that rumors of a haunted north road are spreading. They say, men die, but there are no bodies."

I wasn't sure if those rumors pleased me, for once again they denied us our part.

Two by two, these captive messengers were given some weapons and let go. Every hour another pair ran their winded horses across the top of the hill. Khulan and Sasha killed the first four. Near dawn, Niko and Hulan had a hand at four more.

By morning the duty had turned to Angel and me. I gave Angel a special lesson in swords as soon as we took the field, but the first man she met was good enough to deflect it entirely out of her hands. He lost his spear in turn then raced straight past her, aiming for the river. Angel tossed aside her shield and started after him. She caught up, stood on her saddle, leapt off the top of her horse and landed on the messenger, pinning him with her legs and two daggers.

They both fell into the water, and for a short time, neither came up. First the man floated to the surface then Angel. She lifted him onto her shoulder and walked him up the shore. There she tossed his body in the mud.

Everybody watched this, including the enemy archers across the river. They had retreated a little because of the growing light. I think they were too stunned to shoot, at first, probably shocked at seeing that last messenger fall. Then Angel went back in the river to get the horses. Several arrows landed around her, and both horses were slightly wounded, but the Goddess shields the insane. Angel brought back the animals, seemingly without haste or concern.

In the meantime, I'd managed well enough with my spear, tossing it when the man came within a few horse lengths. It was a clean kill, causing the man to fall from his horse just before making the bank. One of my archers popped up from a bush and grabbed the horse's tail.

We stripped the dead and pushed them in where they joined twelve others floating down the Redwater.

Every so often, we had several squads of warriors walk their horses from one side of the road to the other, showing the enemy that some unknown number of us was in attendance, and that we didn't care much if they knew it.

I thought the enemy would quickly tire of watching us and send a company or two over to clear us out. If they did, the plan was to retreat and ambush them beyond sight, which was good for the cause of confusion. Once they found that frustrating, they'd send a bigger force, I hoped. If they sent all of them, our archers would come forward and kill as many as they could while the enemy was slowed by the water. Once the first crossed, we'd hit them with everything we had and on three sides.

They were smarter than that. It wasn't until Angel and I killed our first pair of messengers that they sent a man into the water, bearing a white flag. He waited, and when we didn't send anyone forward, waved his archers back. Since I was handy, Angel and I went out to meet the man. Once we arrived, he waved again, and a knight rode his warhorse out into the water to meet us.

"Good morning to you, Ser," I smiled at the ranking knight when he arrived.

He took no time for pleasantries. "If you intend to attack us, do so with honor. We hold the ford. Remove us from it if you can. If not, leave the field or surrender, as is proper."

I was impressed that he'd come right to the point, to include respecting my army enough to offer a challenge.

"But ser, it is I who holds the ford, not you. As well, I am content, for I seem able to slay your warriors at will, and risk no losses whatsoever, finding it sport and good practice for my women. All the while, your men are surrounded and even unable to retreat to Dorne or advance to Norfaton where Sir Janis is under considerable stress, not because of too few men, but because of your inability to keep him supplied with as much as a single wagon of wheat. This pleases me beyond measure."

"We have no such problem," he lied.

"Well then, for half a score days you have seen ample traffic down the road, and Sir Drake does not dog your rear," I finished the lie for him.

He persisted: "It is I who holds the ford! Soon, the duke will send a thousand men down that road, and between us, you will suffer. I am no fool. I shall sit where I am, as ordered, and hold this ford until relief."

He was a steady man for a noble. I'd have liked to have had him on my side.

"I see. Well, I am unaware of these thousand men. If so, we are in a difficult position indeed. You are kind to have warned us. I shall have to ask the duke to verify this, though, for you might be trying to trick me."

I looked over at Angel. "Angel, would you be kind enough to go get the duke so we can ask him his intentions regarding the road back to Dorne?"

She looked hesitant to leave me, but obeyed, riding back out of the water and over the slight rise. The knight gave me all of his best impatient looks, knowing I was bluffing, and not happy that I was wasting his time, but I engaged him in small talk about the accommodations across the river. I was familiar with the builders and we'd had a hand in the layout of the defenses. This seemed to disturb him. I noticed the determination on his face to not show it.

In a short while, she came back with Hulan, Kahnsajin and the duke. Hulan guided the duke's horse into the water while Kahnsajin came as a companion. They slowed, drawing next to me. The young duke settled near my right hand. He looked at me with angry eyes, maybe a little afraid to see that he was in the middle of a river between warring hosts and under a white flag of truce. He also might have realized that it had been me who'd been sleeping in the wagon in front of his horse that first morning.

"My Lord," the knight said. The horror of recognition stood clearly painted on his face.

I looked over at the duke, seeing that his hands were better bound than they'd been on the road. I took the gag out of his mouth. "Duke, tell this man we have not done any harm to your men at Dorne, nor along the roadway."

He found the expected courage: "I shall do no such thing! You attacked and burned my city. There is also death and murder all along the road. You'll pay for that and for the knights, as well as for all those you have ambushed! My companions were friends to the King! My uncle will send a thousand men to stop you and he will send you to the hangman."

It was good to hear the boy's tongue, finally. I put the gag back over his screaming mouth and gestured for Hulan to take him back the way they'd come. The man next to the knight made a hand movement toward his knife, but Kahnsajin pulled her bow string back a little, giving him a second thought. When he eased back, she eased her draw as well, but stayed near and did not retreat with Hulan.

I said, "Now ser, you will know that I hold the ford—not you. All the way to Helfax, it seems. By doing this, my army deprives the King of good knowledge while the battle shifts in the north. My warriors have burned the fields, emptied the silos, and denied Sir Janis any other means of support along his only road, both north and as you can see, south. As well, we are burning the castles and keeps of Farstand. An army fights on reinforcements and its stomach, Sir Knight, and you alone are the reason why yours is starving."

"You met me here to gloat?" he said a little too forcefully.

"No. I came here because you called. It was courtesy. Otherwise, you interrupted my morning exercises: the sport of murdering your messengers, whom I confess we have fooled. We let them imagine that they are escaping. We find this enjoyable. I have been told that the next two are the last from their group, but there will be others along shortly. We've been long intercepting the traffic along this road and know its pace."

I nodded to Angel and Kahnsajin. We turned.

The knight said, "What is your name? I wish to know it for the King, so he will not unjustly hang some other wench."

I laughed at him. "Well, that would be new. Tell him you spoke to Abi. Tell him I have already murdered one duke, and am now tempted by another." With an eye over my shoulders, I made my way back to our shore.

As soon as our hooves met the soil, two more messengers popped over the hill. Angel pulled her knives out of her belt. Kahnsajin yanked the string back on her bow. The Debrecian girl paused, exhaled, and loosed her arrow, piercing the first man in the stomach before he came close with a spear. He dropped his weapon in shock and rode his horse over by the bushes near the edge of the river. He awaited a slow and painful death, fearing even to get off his animal. In a few moments, he gained some wit, and rode his horse into the water. We let him go, though after only a little ways into the river, he fell. This left the horse to stand about idly and too far from either line to be recovered until he decided upon a direction.

The second man only had a knife. Angel turned her horse as he rode by, and once again leapt off hers and onto the messenger's back, killing him in the water.

"This sport is a sickness," I told Kahnsajin after I watched them murder the messengers.

"I didn't want him near you," Kahnsajin said apologetically. "You are our soul."

I started to say, "I know," but paused. "Still, it has no honor. I'll not have you taking joy from it. See it for what it is, child. The only reason I'm doing this is to make the enemy angry and cause them to make a mistake. If I can't stomach it, you can imagine what they are thinking."

"You want them angry." It was not a question.

"Yes. What we do is evil. Never mistake it for honor, and it is not a good story for bragging in a stranger's tent. The only thing right about it is that we might entice them to attack us. We will do far, far better here in defense."

* * * * *

By mid-afternoon the wise knight could no longer stand the sight of Farstand men falling to our women. I imagine he'd started feeling quite alone in his wisdom over there, having to endure the complaints of all his men as their anger rose. I knew his thoughts. He worried about the duke. He grew sure I was right, that his inaction allowed the army to go unsupplied.

His view of the distant shore must have seemed filled with torment.

It was no surprise when they came. The knights had to put them into order first. They would have done better as a screaming horde, making good use of their anger and giving us less time to coordinate our repositioning.

The knights were too few to make a cavalry, and thus were used to maintain control. There were no more than two for each group of a hundred footmen. The knights rode, but the men marched across the river to the sound of their sergeants' singsong yells. Their shields came up, catching the arrows we lofted from the small rise beyond the shore. What they did not count on were several companies of our women rushing the river edge from the western extreme of the ford. They put up a storm of wood and steel rain in a crossfire that we lofted over the enemy flank. By the time the four hundred footmen crossed, only two or three hundred had not been wounded or killed.

At first, we concentrated on the out-riding knights, finding them surprisingly easy pickings for our swarms of mounted warriors. Then we raked the edges of their formations with squads. These were ten women with lances, shields and swords, followed by ten archers who stayed a little farther away from the enemy, but shot at least two arrows into them at close range before backing away. As soon as the archers passed, ten more women attacked the same flank, followed by more archers.

Once they were fully oriented on the front and left, we sent fifty women in from the right flank, slaughtering their rear. Only a couple knights remained. Sergeants worked for control. Their screamed orders became drowned in the sea of confusion. Half of the enemy pikes fell underfoot or turned, aimed to the flanks, as did half their shields, giving us good spaces through which we shot from the front, which had an advantage of height. At times they stopped to reorganize or gather their courage, which was suicide.

Once we breached in several spots, the back ranks broke for the far bank. I felt their fear. The wolf's bloodlust filled my soul. I kicked my horse, and we broke over the few who lingered, chasing the bulk of the enemy footmen who'd made our shore. They retreated into the water. Their backs were the easiest targets of all for our archers and swords. Our heaviest cavalry drove into the water. Some of our squads even carved wide spaces between the enemy ranks, giving us uncontested paths that intermingled with the retreating army.

On the opposite bank, their remaining archers killed as many of their friends as they did us, for unlike them, we'd not dropped our shields and were far faster on horses. The core of my army entered the water on their stragglers' heels. Our vanguard climbed the distant shore ahead of the few of the enemy who made it back.

On the opposite shore, the rain of arrows was a quarter of what it might have been, given that so many of their archers had gone into the attack. As soon as a few of us grew close to their embankments, even the arrows quit. The archers knew it was time to run for their lives. Other than the terrified archers, little else had been left on the far shore.

We raced through our settlement over roads of our own making. The place had been left largely undefended by soldiers, leaving only their camp followers and servants, whom we rounded up and sent directly south across the ford. This marked the third time the ford had fallen under our control.

When next I looked, the sun had nearly gone. We'd lost two hours of sunlight in a fight that I remembered as quick and simple. Bodies bled everywhere. The river teemed with them, floating to the west. As many dead littered their side of the river as did ours. Many of those on the ground were our own, including over two score dead. Twice as many had been wounded to the degree that they could not fight. In all, it proved our most costly battle to date.

From there we drove north, branching off to the east along all the good roads. Doing this, we took all the land in a box from the ford to our own community, to Sir Drake's castle, and ending at the castle of Sir Finley.

Sir Finley's castle had been taken, though only a few enemy forces held it. We did not bother with an assault, but instead cleared the towns of enemy soldiers and took all of the roads leading in and out. This left enemy in our rear, but they were few and could not come out without further weakening their defenses.

To the east, Sir Drake's castle was only under the first signs of siege. Those forces were the vanguard, so we surprised them by attacking their rear. That forced a quick surrender of some companies of footmen.

By then Sir Drake and Sir Finley had been found by scouts. They were in the east, getting ready to attack the same forces near Drake Castle. Together with three score soldiers and only thirteen knights, Sir Drake helped my women escort two hundred enemy captives to his father's castle where two knights were shown the dungeon and the peasants some plows.

I was with this northern group, leaving the eastern battles near Sir

Drake's castle to two hundred less-experienced women coming up from the community and led by Chotan and Sergeants Hadarm and Kreger.

We neared the extent of our reach. I was with the scouts who had been charged to study the battlefields south of Norfaton. The heads of many good knights stared down from a row of planted pikes. I knew some of the faces. They'd been men in the practice yard and halls of Sir Lacellor's castle.

One of the heads was Sir Lacellor himself. The great rebel's face had turned black and bloated; his eyes larger than life. Nothing of the boy remained. In place of a crown, he wore a knife that had been driven into the top of his skull.

I said to him, "So there you are, little King. I guess now you are pleased to grant me an audience." He did not answer, but his eyes were glass, overseeing us all the way past his pole. Before, I'd not really spoken to him eye to eye. Even then his gaze appeared a little above my head.

Just beyond, we found the charred bones of the knights, noted for their lack of heads. Next, we passed the bodies of a company of enemy soldiers; slaughtered by an advanced unit of my women. Less than an hour after that, we crested a hill from which I looked down into Norfaton valley. There before us sat the city, parts burned. In the midst of it Lacellor's castle appeared.

Tents were pitched along the outside edges of the castle's high walls, well within range of the rampart bows. I saw no sign of the truce tents my scouts had warned me about. That was supposed to be on the road just beyond the moat. Instead, the drawbridge was down and the gates yawning wide. Men and horses flowed freely, both in and out of the castle, obvious to all and without any sign of a struggle.

Explaining it, and from the ramparts, flew the cursed flag of the King of Farstand.

Chapter Fourteen

Lord Drake's head and eyes sagged. The tumbler of wine leaned in his fingers, spilling on the table. His wife, however, remained quite sober, continuing our negotiations.

Salonia, having only recently entered, stood before us on her wooden leg. She reported, "Two hundred South Women and half as many men hold the ford; another ten score roam the roads between our strongholds. Others are here and remain in reserve. As you know, the siege of Norfaton has ended. Some knights decided to bow and change their masters rather than trouble themselves with the hardship of siege.

"Sir Janis is probably resting before moving farther to the north and west," she continued. "He is also aware of us, and seemingly takes us seriously. The man's scouting forays increase by the hour. We are thin, so I feel that some have made it through and, I also assume, provided the enemy with good reports."

I added for the benefit of all those assembled around the war room table, "This Sir Janis has at least four thousand soldiers, possibly twice that and eight score knights, all restored to good health as a result of the stores within Lacellor's castle. I shall not call the knights of Lacellor cowards, but the word foolish suffices. Because of their hasty surrender, most of our work has gone to dust."

"Without a single stone cast from their catapults," Sir Casar said. "As for the number, it increases with every knight who bows. As well footmen; Sir Janis will rape the peasantry for footmen. I doubt he cares if we've men to reap our next harvest, and he might even see famine our due." Sir Casar was still a bear, but his fat was melting, probably because of the endless fighting.

"We shall send a letter. Sir Janis is generous . . . ."

I gave Daren's mother a murderous frown.

"Please, mother," Daren tried, though I think the woman never stopped thinking of her son as a boy and dismissed him with a wave.

Sir Lindie said, "The captured peasant soldiers might be persuaded to fight for us, particularly if we set them in the midst of our blocks." He was just trying to change the subject, I realized.

Still, I responded, "Well then, that would be what, eight hundred afoot? No, we might do better sending Lady Drake with a note, saying, please surrender. After all, Sir Janis is generous and might relent. Does he not know that he is surrounded?"

My fiancé glared at me. I had no hint that his mother or father even sensed the irony, but my knight and I were of a like mind, save in how to deal with the old woman. To be sure, my fiancé was between a wolf and a wall; these were his parents, people and lands, none of which meant pig dung if my warriors left his defense.

"I am fearful," Minari said. She'd been quiet and diplomatic, often the calming voice between our factions.

Decidedly non-diplomatically, she continued, "Sir Janis is going to win. He will send his agents to the other lords. They have no choice but to relent. We cannot even get to the western half of the northlands where nearly half of the lords sit awaiting a miracle. That means he will have eight thousand men and two hundred knights, in time."

Lady Drake said, "All sound reasons to relent and beg for mercy. These are godly men."

Minari was no longer meek when she replied, "Lord and Lady Drake, you might plea for your lands and titles, but they will not be merciful to our women, nor your son. Our women have broken all of their laws by not yielding to their men, and we have even found disfavor in your eyes for it. Did you not send knights to kill our Queen, no more than a few weeks past? If this is how you thought to deal with us, how do you imagine the King of Farstand will respond? And for you, what will be the price they ask of you to keep your titles? Will Sir Janis say, 'Bend your knee, and do this one service: Murder all the rebellious and contrite women to your south. I shall even lend you my knights and what men you feel necessary.' It doesn't take a prophet to hear it."

I saw that this argument only tempted the lady of the castle. She did not seem troubled by our demise at all. I became convinced that Lady Drake was the worst thinker in the kingdom, and so I added, "But then, having gained your knee and service, he will lead them himself, putting your men and knights to the fore. He will insist that your husband and son spearhead the first assault. They will be the first to feel our spears and arrows, and we shall surely kill them, if we must. That way he will be rid of all of his enemies, and look like a saint to the other lords who have bowed."

I saw no reaction from Lady Drake, telling me she was not listening to me.

Our fruitless discussions had gone on for some time. The maids brought more wine and looked dourly at the lord of the castle. He'd drunk four tall tumblers and was counting the ceiling frescoes. The frescos were beautiful, but the egg in the paint was also quick to flame when they came to the torch.

A sudden commotion, sounding like people wrestling, came from just beyond the closed door. Angel helped a servant drag one of the big war room doors open. I couldn't see out, but I did notice Angel draw both of her knives. A Debrecian scout, who I did not know, entered. Rain dripped from her body as she staggered into the room. Angel helped the woman over toward our long and useless table.

I stood, meeting her partway, as did Kahnsajin and four of my war leaders. The lord of the castle woke up, paying a little bit of attention. I think his wife was about to say something about the mud on her great rug, but in a moment of sheer inspiration, she apparently thought better of it when the Debrecian warrior dropped to her knees in front of me and handed me a message. Out of breath, all she could utter was, "My Queen."

"Angel, get this woman to a room and a warm fire. If she has any fellows, see to them as well. That servant and the guard at the door will help you find what you need."

The lady started to say, "I have not relieved—"

"Lady Drake. You seem to misunderstand the situation, so let me make a few things clear to you."

"Abi. You promised—" Daren started.

I shushed him with a hand. His hair blew back from some strange draft, and even more oddly, he stopped talking.

"I am not a guest at this castle," I said. "I am in command, now. Do you imagine that a half score knights and a handful of soldiers is enough to hold these lands? I have a hundred women inside your walls and seven hundred more within a day's ride. Worse, I am all that stands between you and Sir Janis. As for the stupid idea of a plea, you have gone on too long with your folly. I will not let you make a plea; it is not in my interest, and any such attempt will be considered an act of war against my people."

"Your interest!" the Lady screamed.

I threw a hushing hand up at her, and another miracle happened. Her hair flew in a whirl and dripped half of its pins. She shut her mouth.

Startled gasped arose from everyone in the room.

"These are warriors at your table, not sacrifices to be laid at the feet of Sir Janis! Even this child, Kahnsajin, has her eyes open and can see what is before her. Janis is only interested in pleas of mercy from the west. The east is past such consideration because he knows we are beaten, and he knows we deserve his wrath."

"I beg to—"

"Differ, I know."

"Please, Abi, be kind. She is my mother." Daren showed a bit of anger on his face, though he certainly had to know the truth.

"He doesn't want your knee, woman," I continued. "He wants your head! Your head, hear me! Is that clear enough? On a pike, for all the peasants to watch and admire, so they know that new lords are in charge, which to them might mean very little. One lord or the other, what does it matter to their lives?"

"God has made us who we are!" Lady Drake shouted.

"Then your god has also unmade you. Sir Janis has new lords waiting for these lands, just as he has new lords for Norfaton. We've passed whole lines of stinking heads, many of them made by some god or another. Sir Janis is pointing to this place with your own blood, woman."

"Oh, such talk!" She plopped down in her seat. A companion,

who'd been sitting beside her, took a wet towel and mopped the woman's brow. Another fanned her face.

Her drunken husband stood and shouted, "Must you be so roarin' cruel . . . to my wife . . . in my own house?"

I ignored him, his wife and even his son. Instead I broke the seal on the letter and read it to myself. It might have seemed a long pause for them because the letter was not short.

When I finished, I said, "Hara!"

"Yes, My Queen." She stepped out from the rest of the leaders.

"Our tribes are entering the war. When we are finished here, you must gather as many of your original Greyfeet as you can. Begin your return to your Queen within the hour. Take two of Sir Lindie's men, for his knights are well known among the northern lords. Queen Risha and her shaman would do well to take the castles and holdings of the two lords farthest to the northwest. This is only my strongest suggestion, for your Queen rules her own people. Yet, tell her that if her shaman hurries, she may be greeted as an ally and guest; if not, she will find the owners of these keeps allies of Farstand and looking for fresh meat north. If she sees the wisdom of my suggestion and hurries, she can slowly let it be known that we are a little more than guests to the northern lords, as you have seen by the example of Drake Castle."

"This is my castle, wench!" Lord Drake shouted. His son moved beside him, trying to keep him calm, but with a glance I could see that both men were equally angry at me.

Hara told me, "I will do as you say. And, I want you to know that I have learned much under your command and enjoyed it a good deal."

"I cannot bear to see you go. I have oft thanked the Goddess for sending you. Should I live, I hope to tell your Queen as much." That was exactly how I felt. She knew it and hugged me before she stepped back.

"You can'no be givin' no commands in my roarin' castle, woman." Lord Drake sometimes became aware enough to say something. He fell across the table when he found himself off balance because of pointing at me. His wife sobbed beside him, but then proved useful when she helped him sit back.

I turned to them. "We have had a problem from the start, Lord and Lady Drake. I think it stems from your view of my lot in life. Positions are both earned and gifts from the gods. Yes, I was born a peasant, and that is no dishonor. Many of my best warriors were even whores before lifted to warriors, before the gods put value in their lives and sent them my way. My own mother was a Queen, fallen from grace, showing that the gods see us all and care far less for birthrights than we confess."

I walked up to the table and put my finger into the face of the lord of the castle. His eyes opened fully. "Listen to me, Ser! I am the Queen of the Northern Tribes. We need no longer hide it under a bushel, now that my council has decided that they want me known to the world. I have under my command, as many as ten thousand brave and capable warriors and am no longer hesitant to use them in our defense."

"Woman," the Lord said, "get your finger out of—"

"I see no soldiers, and if these coming soldiers are women, I fail to see their worth!" Lady Drake shouted.

"That is true. You see little, and that is one good reason to stop listening to you," I said. "As we argue, my shaman comes. She is not as patient as I am, and upon one look in your direction, will call you breeder and be done talking to you. The Goddess has given her the sword of death and at the age of ten and five. She commands the wind before her path. Petition Sir Janis? I think not. Instead, I pity him. It is written that she is unleashed to war and cannot be called back until her thirst is quenched."

"You are a liar!" my future mother in law screamed.

"Quiet, breeder. Our Queen is speaking!" Kirsta had a very impatient frown on her face.

Lady Drake put her hand to her bosom and moaned while sitting back. There was nothing pleasant about Kirsta's red scowl and threatening lean.

My fiancé glared at me with a startled face.

I turned to Hulan. "Take a hundred women north to Lord and Lady Pardrill. We will have to secure their castle as well. Tell him that if the enemy arrives, make the roads as impassable as you can before locking the castle for a siege. Send scouts to our tribe. Have them tell my sister that we intend to control the northeastern lords first; as friends. If not, by force. Risha will secure the northwest. As well, we will need relief in our loose siege of the Norfaton Castle roads, which I invite her to secure all the way to Dorne; more, if it suits her. She is the shaman and will go as the Goddess leads. I intend to settle all the land and deal with Norfaton separate."

"What if Lord Pardrill doesn't allow me to enter his castle?" Hulan asked.

"Take two of Sir Esaudrin's knights with you. They will know them. If that doesn't work, attack the roads as best you can and leave the castle to its own devices." I glanced around. "With any luck, we will hold the north and east and make inroads into the west. We'll do this as well as press past the ford, well into Farstand. Let's see what two hundred knights and four thousand soldiers do with so much trouble beyond their reach. They have only two choices: Remain in Norfaton or venture out where we can kill them."

"Or they us," my fiancé said. I forced myself to nod to him politely, but otherwise ignored his comment. His words were not his best that morning, given he had to please his parents.

My women bowed slightly before turning to the door in ones and twos. They were tired, but also eager to have something to do after so much despair.

Once they departed, Daren Drake added, "Now, what am I to do, save watch you insult my mother and father, not to mention watch you take over our lands?"

I looked at him sternly. "Well, to start with, you will have to face up to your mother who has been unforgivably stupid, not to mention rude to your future wife. Once you have done that, Daren, you might choose to inform her that nothing could be more in her interest than to politely ask me if I am still willing to join her family and give it children. Tell her, as well, that I will not marry you without sufficient begging, for any good woman wishes to be wooed and appreciated by her in-laws."

The woman laughed scornfully.

"Why are you laughing, lady? The begging I referred to must come from your lips. Your son has already wooed me."

"Never!" she screamed.

I looked over all three of the Drakes. "As I see it, when you marry a queen, the son becomes a king. As well, there is a need for one. The last lost his head up on one of Sir Janis's poles. Daren, you might want to tell your mother that if she is too much of a fool to want her son to be the King of Lacellor's kingdom, then I shall be forced to appoint someone better to lord these lands, both at Drake and at Norfaton. Maybe even Sergeant Niko, who has honey on his tongue and who can't keep his eyes off me every time I pass his horse. Have I not already mentioned my respect for the gods when they have the good sense to raise a peasant?"

That made her stop both weeping and mocking, which was both fine with me and irrelevant, for I had too much to do to remain much longer in the long, insufferable and misnamed room of war.

"Better. Now that I have your attention, henceforth I shall direct my sergeants to help train your footmen. Together, with your knights, I will meet Sir Janis on the eastern fields of Norfaton, should he choose to come out and greet me. None will be left in this castle, save some servants and a few of my wounded women who will rest and guard your walls."

"Gods, you cannot take our guards!" Lord Drake yelled, though the look on his face was one of utter confusion. More precious was the look on Lady Drake's face. I think I could even see her thinking, which up to that moment had proven quite dangerous for me. Soon she might even smile when she came to understand the possibilities for her family. The notion filled me with dread.

"Daren will lead our knights, as I am sure he wishes," I said.

He looked at his mother and father. "We are far outnumbered father, but if I had a choice between riding into battle with Sir Janis's mighty army, and this little one led by Abi—"

"He's a fool in love. Let him go," his mother said. There, just for a moment, I witnessed something tender, for behind the idiocy, she showed fear for her son.

"Don't worry, mother. As I've said before, my betrothed is not just a queen; she is also friends with the gods." He kissed his mother's hand, and came around the table to join me.

As we turned to leave, Lady Drake said, "Abi. If you bring my son home alive, I shall beg you to marry him. If not, I shall see you in Hell."

I didn't even look back. "If we die, I shall show you around, for I was raised in Hell and know it well. Otherwise, when we marry, I will enjoy teaching you the Debrecian tradition, where the grandparents and fathers raise the children so the mothers may fight."

Those words echoed around the great room. With a glimpse, I saw that her face had become even whiter than before.

I was never more pleased than when that door swung shut.

* * * * *

My Queen:

I am coming south with our shaman and ten thousand warriors, needing to see my daughter. I can no longer bear knowing that she is so close to danger and has not my sword to protect her.

I have seen many new visions. I have seen endless blood. This war will not treat us kindly. By the end, many of our people will fall to the enemy's blades. I weep and fear sleep, lest I see more of this before I am doomed to live it.

Yet, I have had new dreams, and in them I have seen a little less blood. It is as if the Goddess is telling us that through good works and great courage, she honors us with less pain than might otherwise befall. While these dreams encourage me, I still wake in a bed of sweat and with a racing heart.

I have long imagined that we must have this war so my dreams may end, but such ideas I thought selfish. I told myself that I have a greater duty than my own wants.

Upon reading those words, I had to pause and reflect, for it was the greatest lesson in my life. I recalled first seeing the great Beckli Kahnsa before the duke, pleading her case for peace, and thinking for the first time in my life that something in the world was bigger than my little problems. Beckli had been looking for a queen. I had been looking for a reason to breathe.

She continued:

I asked the Goddess for a new vision; one that showed me what would become of us should we reject our Queen and go on without her. For a long time, she did not answer. Then one night I saw my daughter dying and my Queen dead beside her. I saw a thousand brown-haired women put to the sword, many hunted to the far regions of the world where they were slain like dogs.

But there came another night, not long thereafter. On that night I saw something far worse than the death of my only daughter and so many foreign women.

I saw a cabin with a roof of peat. From it walked a young woman who wore the rags and wrinkles of a prematurely aging breeder. She looked just like my own daughter, and I knew it was her. When Kahnsajin stooped to pull some carrots from the garden, a drunken man staggered out of the very same shack. He came up to the girl who was my daughter and beat her with a stick in front of a half dozen dirty and poorly fed children who wailed and hid behind the woodpile. He did not quit until he fell over from his own drunkenness. My daughter stood and did nothing. All she did was pick more carrots, which were few and scrawny.

I did not want to see any more of that, but the Goddess gave me wings. We went up into the air where I viewed thousands of cottages, all of them poorly made and surrounded by goats, pigs and struggling fields. All of these looked the same as the one my daughter had come to live in. These wretched farms were scattered all across the land, even in places that had poor soil and could grow nothing but weeds where there once had been good grass. Such had been made unfit to even graze our horses.

I knew the hills and the seams and could see where the river met a fork. The Goddess was showing me the place of my birth and the future of my children, as we flew over the spoiled lands of the once-great Debrecian tribes.

When I thought about my last vision, I understood, for the first time, why the Goddess had seen fit to lower our Queen and raise our princess among the breeders of the south.

Just as there are things greater than one's own self, there are also things worse than a field of blood. This is what you came to teach us, and we would not listen.

I told this vision and these thoughts to our council. For a long time, no one spoke. Orbai, the oldest and wisest among us, and usually the first to speak, could not stop her weeping.

Abagai, who'd been strongest against war, broke the silence, for it was not my place to put final meaning to my own visions. She said only a few words, but it was what we were all thinking.

She said, "We must bring the shaman to our tent."

Your Warrior;
Beckli Kahnsa

Chapter Fifteen

"Back when I was a member of the Guard of Lettoir, there was a man in the duke's camp who fancied himself a bard," I said. "He was old, with only one tooth and a tendency to drool, mumble, growl, and sometimes go to sleep with his mouth still open in the middle of a story. What's more, I doubt he'd ever left his own cottage for more than a trip to his village to sell his cow's butter, but he was all that we had, and if the tales were true or not, little mattered. Men listened to him for hours, often only understanding a couple words. The distraction served to ward off the pains of their wounds and the grind of their starvation."

Angel blinked and swallowed when I paused. The woman was always attentive, though silent. Instead, I heard her mind and it was fretting, which I could see by noting her shaking fingers and fidgeting feet.

"We had bards that visited the lord and lady. My lady let me listen from the kitchen," Minari said, recalling her days as Lady Lettoir's maid. She had a hand full of my hair, holding it while Marci put other parts of it up in a fashion befitting someone high-born.

I looked at the mirror, thinking my head a hive and combined with the rose water, apt to attract bees.

Kahnsajin sat across a small table from the boy duke. He sat stiffly and scowled at everyone. Occasionally he smirked at comments, as if saying our concerns were ignorant. He did not love any of us. Between them sat a game of castles and knights. Though I barely knew the game, the boy made gloating gestures, suggesting he was winning, just as he'd done the last time they'd played. At the last moment, Kahnsajin always took all of his better pieces.

The little duke never warmed to Kahnsajin, though she showered him with chatter and smiles. She continually hoped to learn something from him and was too young to understand that he thought her beneath his chambermaid. She could have taught him far more and on an infinitely greater range of subjects. This made it easy to dislike him, and I did, desperately, for he symbolized everything I loathed.

Her anxious frown told me Kahnsajin's mind was not upon the game, in spite of her victory.

"He should be nice," I said to everybody in general and in answer to the tense little looks.

"The bard? I don't understand?" Minari shoved another few strands up and around.

Marci pinned it.

"No . . . ." Surely they understood the source of my outburst without my having to look at the spoiled duke; why say it? I returned the subject back to the bard, "Well, yes, this bard. He said that there was a private tunnel into every castle; also a secret door. Usually the tunnel ends in some shallow well away from the ramparts' view where the good knights can come up and maybe even bring their horses without being seen. Usually nobody notices the old tunnel until several hundred years awaiting its need. Then the hero of the bard's story finds the hidden passage in the dungeons. The secret tunnel lingers behind some masonry with a picture painted on it. The hero tears down the wall and saves all of the good and frightened people who are by then cringing from the evil invaders just beyond the keep's last barricade."

"What fool would paint a picture in the bottom of the pits?" Minari asked.

"I should think the water would get to it," Marci added. "There's always water in the pits, I hear; sometimes a river . . . with blind fish. I knew several men who'd been chained up in a dungeon or two, though they might have been bragging just to sweet-talk me," She reflected on that, seemingly with a bit of pleasantness in the memory, judging from the way she swung her wide bottom to some tune that seemed only in her head.

Marci, my head steward, continued, "Someone brought an old painting to the whorehouse, wanting a whole night with three of us for it. Grunter tossed him out and his painting with him. The thing had gotten wet since he'd stolen it, and the paint on it had spoiled. It smelled worse than Grunter. Anything that smelled worse than Grunter was sure to see the door, save Grunter who better deserved it in most cases. Later, our Queen fixed that for us, and for a few hours the place smelled better, but then she burnt it down," Marci said, who I suppose was talking to Minari and not me, given she'd apparently forgotten my name.

We, of course, knew most of this, but I think Marci just wanted to find a way to thank us for the favor. I had to agree about Grunter. His bowels, once spilled on the floor, had smelled quite unpleasant.

"What was the painting of?" Minari asked.

"Some old woman holding a little dog and wearing a big and fancy dress like this one," Marci answered with a poke on my back.

Just then the little lady baroness woke up, started crying, and caused Marci to have to pin in the last pin so quickly that Minari had to fix it. Marci picked up the girl, who was getting bigger and who, when not sucking on goat's milk out of a skin, could say, "Ma," to Marci, "Dog," to my wolves, and, "Da," to just about anybody who wore britches, including me and half my women; who also spoiled her endlessly.

I'd had to make an order that they not feed her, for she was getting fat and wasn't skilled at walking yet. It wouldn't do to have her bend down with a big belly and topple over instead of pick up her toy sword.

"There, all fixed." Minari backed off to admire the work on my person.

The first thing I did when I stood was do some breathing. Noble dresses are insufferable, but the undergarments are known to make a person's rear go numb. I did have the good sense to dress in a noble woman's traveling clothes this time, though I think the only real difference was that the travelling varieties had a few less things embroidered on them and one of the ten or twenty petticoats appeared missing.

Outside, one of my male warriors took the duty of coach driver. Another, who'd been wounded in a recent battle, had the courage to ride beside him. His wound still seeped, though with some healing it was sure to mend.

We gave him a broken arrow to hold near the wound. He spilled a vial of blood beside that. His tendency to wince was already convincing.

I patted him on the leg before going around and getting into the carriage. Angel stood just outside the door when I shut it. Her eyebrows almost met, and she pushed her lower lip out in a particular mean-looking way. The whole middle of her face had changed to a different color from the rest of her.

"Come with the others and bring my horse. I won't be long in the castle," were my final words to her as we rode away. When I glanced back out of the tiny window, Kahnsajin had come over by Angel. My wolf ears heard her tell Angel that I'd be all right, even though the inflection in her voice demonstrated as much stress as did the scowl on Angel's face.

Over by the door of the cottage, the duke emerged. He glanced around, maybe planning an escape. Most of the warriors were looking my direction. Yellow Eyes kept an eye on him, though, from the bushes, giving me hope that the boy would run and get bit.

We rode the road west toward Norfaton, passing a pair of rotting bodies in the ruts within the first mile. The closer we came to the city and castle, the more we saw of these unattended corpses. Many weren't soldiers, but peasant women, cut down by Farstand scouts who didn't have the courage to go far enough to the east to actually find a real warrior. I thought, *good; let them think themselves winning by counting the wrong heads.*

Word of conduct such as that got around. Women increasingly crossed our lines, oft with husbands or kin. Those we could not train or trust were sent north.

We passed seven heads on Sir Janis's pikes, over the course of the last mile, none of these women.

My two outriders shouted greetings to a Farstand patrol. The patrol hailed us, but we continued past their loose roadblock. Instead, one of my outriders, splendidly bedecked in the sergeant's uniform of a Dorne guard, remained behind to explain. Marci's women had done a masterful job of cleaning and repairing the uniforms of the four men in my party. I dared not look back to see his result, but in a minute his horse galloped up and resumed its position to the front and side of my slower carriage.

We were surprised to find ourselves riding through the streets of Narfaton, without further challenge. The streets were little different from when I'd last been in the city. Even some of the soldiers were the same, having bowed to a new master and seemingly none the worse for it. The main road, all the way up to the castle, had remained untouched by the fires that had ravaged a third of the city, mostly the poorer districts.

A man in mail and a knight's helmet of steel, rode up beside us, exchanging information with our driver and sergeant. When they turned to arguing, I pushed my head out the window and yelled, "Ser! I have come long on the road north from Dorne, losing two good knights and three more from the grand duke's own guard. Can you not see that one of my men is wounded and our horses are nearly spent! I must get to Sir Rodrick in all haste. Either escort us or stand aside!"

The man backed off from leaning toward the sergeant, but continued by our side, now an escort by mistake and causing us to suffer no further distress from curious soldiers.

We trailed two horses on leaders behind the carriage, both of them bearing scars from recent battles. The horses were not apt to be much good for anything, once the wounds festered. I used them to better paint our ruse. No true soldier would come to his enemy bearing horse gifts. In this way, neither did we.

We stopped before the castle moat so quickly that one of the wounded horses bounced into the back of the carriage, nearly spilling me out. Instead of rushing, I waited for my man to come around, set down the step and open my door. My coachman bowed deeply and even offered his cape for me to stand on, once out. When I stepped down onto the cloth, I made a bother about him parking my first step on uneven ground, as well as shoved him out of the way so he fell on his face.

"Your name ser?" I asked the young escorting knight even before turning around to look up at his open faceplate.

He had been climbing off his horse, but then bowed with his heels together. "Sir Bonatos, my Lady."

I wasted no time with formalities. He was a low knight. I could plainly see that by the dullness of duty mail. He would expect dismissal by a high-born lady.

"Sir Rodrick and I share blood," I said. "I have a message for him from his wife, as well as two for the high lord: one from the duke, the other from His Majesty."

I had just met Sir Rodrick and knew he was not in the castle. He'd died in a field just off the road between Norfaton and Drake Castles. His dying words had been a request for us to tell his wife and sons that he'd died on his horse after slaying many of the enemy. I lied and said we would, though the real lie would have been honoring his request. His men had killed nobody, and he'd died on the ground with six arrows piercing his breastplate. Most of him had come to rest in a puddle of mud, the same place where he'd taken his last breath. No doubt Sir Rodrick thought we'd send a score of female sacrifices all the way to the city of Farstand to lie for him, though, for he'd died contentedly in the best armor I'd even seen on a man not also a duke. Such arrogance spoke of the highest blood, which was excellent intelligence.

I felt nothing for him or his family but hate which I collected for my stare at Sir Bonatos.

The escort knight stuttered, "I should be happy to take—"

"Stupid knight! Do you imagine the King graced my hand with his instructions, saying, 'My favorite niece, please hand this message to just any unlanded knight of low birth and at your earliest convenience.'?"

"No, of course not, Lady . . . ." He bowed again. A few other soldiers had come closer, as did two more knights, but they all stayed well out of spitting range, seeing that the young man was in considerable distress.

I did not bother giving him my name. Instead I said, "Well then. Down with the bridge, so I might find my uncle and get some rest! This miserly fiefdom is a pestilence!"

I also thought to ask for provisions for my men, but my sergeant could manage that part of our ruse on his own. He had instructed to not linger. Just as well, I'd never known a high lady to bother with common soldiers, other than Lady Lettoir. She was now Lady Finley and had never been overly high before that, but she had been overly kind and thus next to a saint in my eyes.

Several knights and two guards waved frantically, causing the low-ranking guards inside to lower the heavy wooden bridge over the watery moat. In fact, it came down quite quickly and with a bit of a crash, raising dust for a hundred yards around the gatehouse as well as above the landing.

"You! Escort me to the grand chamber, at once. I need an immediate audience with Sir Rodrick and this Janis who seems incompetent, being that he can't even get a decent message through to his king." I pointed to the cowering knight.

Regarding the others, I ordered, "The rest of you, get about your duties. Gawk at me one more second, and I'll have you all flogged."

I walked halfway across the bridge then stopped, remembering I'd forgotten my messages. After going back to extract three scrolls from the seat of the carriage, I looked up at the driver. "Are you still here? Can't you see my horses are thirsty?" I pointed my scrolls at the assistant driver. He held an arrow that poked out of a bloody spot on his tunic. "That awful man is bleeding all over my carriage!"

I slammed the carriage door and turned back under the portcullis in the gatehouse. I rejoined my escort out on the drawbridge. We were soon through the gates of Sir Lacellor's captured castle.

Behind us, the carriage wheels rolled away in haste. Several knights and soldiers laughed in the streets. Nothing is more pleasurable to them than seeing the lowborn in the midst of ample misery.

There, my escort stopped. Off in the distant portions of the lower hallways, soldiers came to attention along the walls. Word had no doubt spread of some mysterious high lady. Farther down, at a hall door, several ladies dared to glance out.

"My Lady. I regret to say that court is not in session at this time. Sir Rodrick may, in fact, not even be in attendance. His responsibilities oft take him to the field. Sir Janis, however, will surely receive you quickly. Last I heard, he was in attendance. If you will be so kind as to follow me to a good place of waiting among our highest and most honored ladies, so Sir Janis may make the best accommodations to receive you in proper—"

"Well, ser, that was a mouthful, was it not? Did they teach you all those words in knight training, or was your mother wicked with petty prose as you supped?"

"My Lady—"

"If so, it was an entire waste of time. I made my intentions clear, ser, and I take you are not deaf. You shall escort me directly to the high court, which is a proper setting for the King's words. Bring both Sir Janis and Sir Rodrick to me at once!"

"But . . . yes, of course. Follow me, my lady."

He showed the way. Two guards unfroze from rigid stances then opened the doors to the grand hall. I was escorted inside where two more guards stood at attention. One of them leaned on a fancy lance near the throne before straightening.

Sir Lacellor had made himself a throne proper for a king just before he'd died defending it. It was up on a pedestal of marble and gilded in gold. The seat had no arms, but had the back crossing in patterns of stars and golden lace. Such seemed too much for a little king of a little kingdom.

Standing halfway up the main aisle, I turned to see the young knight. Behind him, the two guards held the doors open. The guards glared and a few people passed the open doorway a little too slowly. I imagined the traffic out there more than usual.

"Leave me! And, bar that door behind you with those loitering guards. Next through the door shall be either Sir Rodrick or Sir Janis, not some other lackey! Do not make it an eternity, for my patience with you has already reached its end . . . Sir Bonatos! Hope that I do not long remember that name. No! Take those two fools with you, this one sleepy guard shall be enough annoyance for me, should I need to send a message asking why Sir Bonatos is taking entirely too long."

I could actually hear the lone guard near the throne swallow.

"Of course, my lady. I am sorry for the delay," Sir Bonatos said from the hall. The doors closed in his face. At least the door guards were in a race to do my bidding.

I looked over at the one remaining guard. He held his eyes forward. They aimed at the opposite corner of the room. The room was not overly warm, but he appeared to be melting. I knew how he felt, for I'd also once been a lackey Farstand soldier. Taking pity on him, I mouthed my spell then twirled a finger into the air, putting him to sleep. He fell with a crash of his fancy pike and pointy helm. I'm sure the guards outside heard this. I felt equally sure they had no desire to look inside and investigate the commotion.

A number of other ornate chairs braced the throne. I imagined Sir Janis sitting on one and leaving the great throne vacant, lest he insult his king. Such propriety had often been mentioned in the histories from which I'd read and learned while young and ignorant.

It seemed likely that I'd have a little while, so I pulled the pins out of my hair and let it fall. I took my nearly useless silver lady's knife out, and, after stepping out of the many useless petticoats, cut the hem from my overly ornate dress. I tied my hair up in a Debrecian fountain. It was not dyed, and thus reddish-yellow, as I'd not noticed the soldiers looking much above my bosom, on previous visits.

Looking over at the sleeping guard, I thought I might do well to take his short sword, but then thought better of it, trusting to my heart and not my training.

With a sigh, I sat down on the great throne of dead King Lacellor. The wait was not long, for I'd lit Sir Bonatos' backside.

Both of the doors opened at once. Without looking in my direction, Sir Janis walked in with an advisor on one side and a general on the other. They appeared to be discussing the many great and troubling complexities of some campaign and seemed distracted.

The knight did not look how I'd expected. He appeared elderly, portly in stature, and yet full of energy. His hair only existed on the sides, though he'd pulled a few strands across to make it look like something grew atop. He wore more of a robe than knightly apparel which I instantly recognized as closer to that worn on a priest than a fighting man. In fact, the only things knightly about his apparel were his sword, belt and a good pair of boots.

Sir Janis's attention remained fixed on his advisor. Thus he'd come into the hall with his mouth open. On one side, the general became the first to notice me sitting on the throne. He stopped midstride. The Advisor noticed next. His mouth remained open, but nothing came out.

They all stopped three or four steps into the grand room. Finally, noticing the stare from his men, Sir Janis looked my direction.

This is not to say there were not others, trailers and minor conveniences, all false splendor and thus of little worth, unless Sir Janis's discussions should touch upon an issue that needed their attention, I assumed.

I laughed, remembering the look in the eyes of that deer just before my mother and I had helped my wolves take it down with a stick and rock.

"Did not Sir Bonatos tell you?" I said. "I command more respect than an audience with a rabble and horde. These don't even have the courtesy of entering Lacellor's hall with their mouths in check. You never know who might hear your many plans, Sir Janis. The King would not be pleased to know I am so privy to his every missive."

Upon the word, missive, I tossed the three scrolls onto the floor between us. My words echoed off the vast rock walls, seemingly on some religious flight.

Sir Janis glared at me, at the soldier lying on the floor then finally at the tiny knife I still held in my hand. I put the wee thing back in the overly ornate sheath sewn to the waist of my gown.

"Do not worry about your soldier. He shall awaken shortly and be no worse for the wear. I am not a harsh mistress, save when my kindness is abused."

Some of his men made to come for me, but he called them back. "Do I have assurances of your peaceful surrender?"

I laughed again. "Sir Janis, dismiss your soldiers. Shut the door against all but your closest advisors."

He hesitated, but curiosity won. He did as I suggested, leaving only himself and the two he'd been speaking with. The chamber seemed even more of a holy echoing cave, once we were alone.

"Now, am I to consider you my prisoner?" he persisted.

"I am but one small woman in your mighty midst; call it what you will. But I ask, have the men of Farstand become such cowards that they cringe at their own threshold from the very sight of me? Need I also give assurances of surrender, lest you die from fright? Come, let us speak with a forthright heart, though I warn you, I am known for my lacking flattery in the midst of nobles."

He turned, spoke to his men, and walked forward a ways, bringing his equally armed general. I looked at them, warning the general back with a glance. As further warning, I cast a spell toward the sconces to my left and right. All six candles lit, in keeping with the flick of my fingers.

This stopped the general. Janis's next steps were alone and a bit more wary.

"Your name, witch?" The great leader slowed, now close.

"Abi, Queen of the Northern Tribe and Queen of the women of the south, soon to be appointer of the man who sits this throne. As well, if the King persists, ruler of all Farstand. The Goddess may desire it and see fit to annoy me with the unwanted burden."

"Killer of dukes, traitor to the crown, heretical witch and most of all, liar," the advisor added. He stayed well back.

"Ah yes, those little things too, I suppose, though I am not one to brag. I must retain some humility, lest my friends feel awkward," I confessed.

The councilor had no sense of humor and took several steps in my direction. I put my fingers up, and a wee wind came down the aisle, causing him to think better of it once his hair ruffled. I was sure I'd have put him on his backside with a little more will.

"Only one duke . . . so far," I said. "There is the matter of the other one. For now, I am content to watch him play with Kahnsajin, the wonderful and lovely daughter to our much-loved Beckli Kahnsa, who finds the boy amusing. Other than that, she is an intelligent young lady."

Sir Janis made to speak, but I interrupted his very first word. "I grow weary of the child's rude behavior toward her. She is far too precious to be treated badly by him. I wish to be rid of the boy. Would it bother you much if I left him in your care, Sir Janis? Otherwise, I shall need to murder him for being overly rude to this young woman."

This set him back. "You have the duke?"

"I have whomever I wish, Sir Janis. I'd have you if I wanted. A few months back I could have had the Baron of Helfax, had I not thought his baby daughter more precious. I have given her my mother's blessing and call her Mercy.

"You have little, at best," he said.

"Have you not noticed so many missing knights? Consider, for example, Sir Rodrick. He wants somebody to go home for him and lie to his wife and sons, saying he died killing many of my women. I said, 'Surely, Sir Rodrick.' Such lends truth to your advisor's words that I am a liar. I have had many opportunities to lie, overseeing many dead knights. As for the man's horse, I own that, too." I felt myself smile.

"You are rude, much as I'd expected." He spit on the stone floor.

"Ah, and I thought you a diplomat. Well, we are of a kind. I did tell you that I have no talent for speaking to nobles. You might even ask Sir Lacellor. He barred me from his castle. You have done me a favor, ridding us of him so I might return. As well, with him gone I am free of guilt over all of this death befalling us, and feel no need to worry about many things political."

Sir Janis seemed to see new possibilities. He stepped forward. "The duke might not be enough. After all, he is just a boy. We might do better making you our prisoner. The King is exceedingly eager to meet you. He might consider the boy's sacrifice a tragedy, but no more than an inconvenience. After all, he has three sons and might make better use of the lands and title if they are given to another. Much like you do not mourn the loss of Sir Lacellor; we might see advantages if the duke no longer stood in his way. After all, the boy is only a cousin."

His two advisors grinned.

"Ah, there it is! You are good. I'd been warned. You are a master negotiator, ser. There is only one problem, however. I have been a serf all of my life and know better than to trust anything you tell me. It is just as likely that the King must need his duke back in order to win the loyalty of distant lords."

"You doubt my words?" He spread his arms in a pleading gesture.

"Not in the least. In fact, I agree to the main point. I am much more the prize than the boy duke, regardless. He seems to me . . . little. As you say, it is much like this throne in a way. I used to call Lacellor the Little King, don't you know. It seems to me that much about this place is little, and it makes me want to challenge myself. Perhaps I should think larger than this little kingdom. After all, what does the King truly have to lose, bothering us every fighting season? I have not even met him, nor has his land been troubled, save for Helfax and now Dorne. We would do better toward ending this by going to the city of Farstand."

"Then you do not mind if I take you into custody so you can see his majesty's city." He took another step closer.

I stiffened. "If you touch me, I shall kill you, Sir Janis, as well as all those with you. Do you truly think I have come here alone? Do you imagine all I bring is a gift of a small boy who only believes himself above us all?"

"Show me your men."

"Not men, Sir Janis. Look. See the woman who is my shield. She is the one who has summoned me to this place." I pointed up the great grey wall to my left.

"I see naught but a poorly carved statue."

"Yes. Now tell me, Sir Janis, what is she holding?"

"Her hands cradle a sword. What does it matter? The Woman is made of wood. Even the craftsmanship is laughable," he scoffed, though he came no farther, seemingly interested in hearing me out.

"It might interest you to know that the first time she showed herself to me in this fashion, she traded her branch of peace for a hand over her heart, telling me it was time to find the love of my life. I did not appreciate it at the time, but I've grown to trust her signs. This came to pass and has beaten back all resistance to its fulfillment. Now, by your own words you confess that the Goddess comes bearing a mighty sword of deliverance. Does this not seem fitting, and does it not terrify you a little to see her resolve?"

"Such dribble means nothing, witch, save that you have an imagination. I have only seen that statue bearing that sword. It should be equally noted that our God says to pray to no graven images. I shall have it taken down when there is time."

The man was ridiculous, once one came to know him. What harm could wood do to his God? Sho was content, and didn't even seem overly troubled when speaking to the Goddess?

"It means this, Sir Janis. Leave this land. If you do not, you shall die here, as will all of your men. Once done with you, we shall not stop at the border of this little kingdom. My shaman cannot be recalled until sated, it is said, and she will not be satisfied by regaining only that which is already hers. I have come to give this warning: Give us a sign of peace, lest the Goddess comes down from her perch and you come to know something far worse than the bothersome trip home beside one annoying duke."

"No. You will yield to us, and we shall take you prisoner. In exchange for peace, you will tell your women to bow. The crown shall see your misguided women married off to my soldiers. The duke will also be returned unharmed. We want only your head, and if you are a great leader you will offer it. Once these things are set to right, the women of Farstand will be in their lawful place, as is ordained by God, and we will no longer be at war."

"I see. Well then, I am confused, for the Goddess was most emphatic that I should come and speak with you about this. None of my women agreed, but I trusted my Goddess and insisted. Now I am here. Perhaps she had some other reason for bringing me to this place? I do confess that she often confuses me, but in the end I have found there is always a purpose to her madness. I swear I shall go wherever she leads me, even if it is to my death. Now, let me have a moment, so I can ask her what she is about."

I turned my back on the men and knelt below the Goddess. As soon as I did, I felt her presence fill the vast chamber. Something like a cloud materialized, though the mist was thin. Also, a wind came up. Soon, thicker clouds swirled around the chamber walls.

At the entrance, some men started beating upon the closed doors with no success. A sound came, like lances digging at the great brass bindings.

The general drew near, but then he stopped halfway, seeing the

Goddess descending from her perch. As she came down, she brought me up. After ten or so feet, we met in the middle of the sky between the perch and floor.

There above the chamber floor, she handed me the sword. As soon as it touched my hands, it turned from stone to shining metal. Great carvings were on the parts of the wooden handle not covered by leather. The leather had been wrapped and pulled so thin over the grip that I could see the wiggling faces of many wailing women. When I gripped the handle, I felt their faces crying for vengeance and knew the sword was alive with a thirst for blood. I could not help but raise it up. The folded steel shone as if bearing a little of its own light. I could tell that the edge was perfect and not safe to touch.

Before I descended, the Goddess herself put a belt around my body and sheath across my back. Then she fell to the floor in a mighty crash. The wood exploded into a thousand pieces. Great wooden splinters violently bounced off every wall and in every direction, except for up where I hovered.

I came down, seeing the three men rising from the floor, pulling splinters out of their bodies and faces.

All around us, the cloud was swirling, carrying away chunks of wood along with twisting tapestries, breaking chairs and tinkling ornate fixtures. This went on all around the walls and nowhere else though the hair on the three men did fly a little. It became a mighty ruckus the likes of which I'd only seen in the worst storms, and yet I remained completely untouched and in a dead calm.

As well as I, the sleeping soldier, throne and six lit candles were unbothered as if there was no breeze at all. The six little flames stood straight up like guards, bleeding tiny black streams of candle smoke straight up toward the tall, domed ceiling.

All of this seemed for my pleasure; a gift to me from the Goddess's own hands. I started to laugh as I finally appreciated the beauty of it.

My mirth did not set well with the general who pulled his sword free from its sheath and came rushing in my direction. He was no small man, causing me to have to parry his first thrust with two hands gripping the wailing faces.

I stepped past, causing him to come by, and in the process brushed my sword across his leather-clad arm just below the elbow. To the gods I swear, I barely touched him, and yet half of his arm fell off. I was not one to become transfixed by an accident of swordplay, and thus, when he twisted in agony and disbelief, I pierced his side with the point of my weapon. He fell over. His own weight caused my sword to come all the way through to his back, cleaving his body nearly in two, including the bones of his back, a few ribs and half a vest of exceptionally well-made chain-mail. Never had I imagined such a sharp blade. It made butter of everything it touched.

The man fell to the floor. He braced up on an arm a little, screamed, and saw that the lower half of his body was nearly gone. It was held to the top half by only a little meat and trailing organs. One good look at that and the general eased back and died from shock in an instant pool of deep-red blood.

The advisor was also armed, but seeing this, did not draw his weapon. Instead he stood between me and Sir Janis with his bare hands, pleading. He shouted, "Are we not under the mantle of truce?"

I came forward, shouting back in order to be heard above the din of the storm, "Ah, did you gift me with wine? Did you break bread, granting me guesting privileges? Were not Sir Janis's last words meant to make me his prisoner, in spite of my good faith?"

I laughed in his face. With lightning quickness I cleaved his head from his neck. The sword flew through him like air. I turned the sword, pulled it back, and took a reverse swipe, though the instinctive move had proven entirely unnecessary. The head, catching the flat of the blade as it fell, flew across the room, spewing a stream of swirling blood. It made it far enough to get caught up with the wind, soon lending itself to the spinning clutter. His neck sprouted a fountain of its own. The body fell to the aisle with a chorus of thumps.

This left Sir Janis before me. I had to ask him, "And you, Sir Janis; how good is your silvery tongue? Can you give me a good reason to not kill you, sparing me the trouble in some later battle?"

His eyes were alight.

"You see me now, don't you, and not some little woman in a dress to be married off to some brutal peasant soldier, like was the fate of my mother. As well, you have seen my wooden god. Do you now see the power of her prophecies, once she steps beyond the sawdust?"

The man was brave, I'll give him that, for though he backed with every word, he said, "I see a demon come to life."

"Then I am through with you and grieve the blood that is on our hands. You will escort me out of the castle and give me leave to exit this city. Then I shall return the duke to Dorne. I also give ten of your men leave to use the south road, escorting him back to Farstand. Take advantage of it. The offer ends tomorrow at dawn, and it is your only chance to send messages to your King, none of which have reached him for a month. This is more than fair, for I shall meet you in a dozen days on the fields east of Norfaton. There I shall kill you all. Are these acceptable terms for you, Sir Janis?"

He hesitated, always the negotiator.

I pushed my sword up close to his robe. "Think well, for I remind you. It has been said that I am no good at long-winded speeches before nobles at court, but it is also said that no man has lived on the other end of my sword, lest I will it. Should this one as much as touch your flesh . . . ."

"You have me at a disadvantage," he confessed. "We shall meet in seven days. That will be enough, for I have you outmanned six to one and will look forward to finding your body on the battlefield."

The debris racing along the walls crashed to the floor. The doors opened on their own. A score of knights and guards, who'd been pressing at it, fell inside when the strain of the door suddenly released. They stopped when they saw the carnage and Sir Janis's hands telling them to hold. With his body pressed to my side and my sword an inch from his throat, he helped me make my way out of Norfaton. Right outside the city, Angel and Kahnsajin waited with my horse.

* * * * *

Back at our camp, I called for the duke and put him on a broken donkey. I bid Kahnsajin to whack the donkey on the ass and send him on his way. Fond of the boy for some unexplainable reason, she did not like the duty, but did as she was told.

The boy looked back once the bucking eased. I could see the hate in his eyes when he called, "Your girl is an ugly and mouthy wench. When you are caught, I'm going to strip your daughter bare, send her to the camps, and have my men rape her until she can no longer find words to bore a man."

Kahnsajin kept on watching him until he'd disappeared past a curve in the roadway. When she turned back, her face was wet with tears. She did not say a word when I came up to give her a shoulder, nor did she for an entire day thereafter.

Two days later I met with Salonia a little ways down the south road.

"Is it done?" I asked her.

She pulled her horse steady. "Yes."

"All of them?"

"Eleven," she assured me.

"Good." Surprisingly, I could not feel a single pain of guilt within my soul.

"Why? You gave your word. It is the word of a Queen. We could have let him go. He was of no real value to them; a hindrance really, should he grow and become as bad at leading as was his father."

I could not answer her. Instead I looked into her eyes and bared my soul with the sadness of my stare. I could see that she saw my heart, for the accusation on her face turned to understanding and even a spark of guilt for having troubled her Queen. Inside of her, it might have felt a little like the way I felt when I put my hand around the wailing hilt of my new sword and filled my whole arm with the misery of every slain Debrecian woman's complaint.

Then I found some words: "I struck the deal before he spoke. The boy had no right to say that to her. She gave him nothing but kindness. He was near a grown man. What kind of man is so full of hate that he can't repay many days of kindness with at least a shrug? Let someone else abide it. I will not! It seems to me that the Goddess put me here for some other reason than misplaced mercy. Next time I show mercy, it will be earned."

Salonia nodded gravely, knowing my heart and perhaps even my purpose on this earth. That was colder than some might have at first imagined. She bid me luck, and I her, as she rode away to her duties as leader of my scouts, most of whom now ranged into the lanes of Farstand that exited along the road all the way to the south of Dorne.

Chapter Sixteen

Night grew close. I followed the old witch farther into a gorge.

"It be not a proper place for a Queen. I could just go and get ya' some and be back."

I followed anyway.

She stumbled along near the top edge of a steep cliff-side trail, often stopping to lean on her cane. The path broke through heavy trees and brush. A twenty foot drop onto a quicksand bog marked the right edge.

The witch bore a basket of dry peat, I assumed for our fire. Our light faded, so she bid me to hold the lantern high. Behind, Angel carried a pair of buckets bearing more peat and a rake.

"I am not here to take all your secrets. I only wish to learn how you make your tender," I told her.

"And the price be?"

"As you said, you can see into my head and maybe catch a glimpse of the Goddess as I've seen her."

"These be old secrets up in this here canyon. But of course, the Goddess, she be a secret worth it all. It hurts though, ya' know; in here, giving up the secret to our kindle." She pointed to her head with the handle end of her stick. "I be a woman of peace. On me other hand, the King of Farstand likes us dead. We hear this from the souls of many sisters. When I hear their souls, it hurts me up here."

The witch locked eyes and lingered on me before turning back toward the trail.

I picked up the odor of the caves. Well back on the trail, the rest of my pack, Yellow Eyes and Slow Leg stopped entirely, saying in my head that they'd catch us on the way back.

Angel tapped on my shoulder, pointing to the woods. She put

down her buckets and rake, and reached up under her dress to start loosening her short britches and small clothes.

"Ah, loony girl! We be too close now. Hold on, I tell ya'," the witch said.

Angel bit her lip and picked up her buckets and rake. I knew how she felt. Just knowing I couldn't do my business had me wanting to go.

The witch stopped at the end of the pathway. She whispered some words that raised bumps on my arms and caused the leaves to rustle a little extra.

We sat down to rest there. The rank smell of the caves made my eyes water. She drank from her skin, in no hurry at all. Once she finished drinking, she handed around some hard-cake.

We took it and nibbled. Angel ate hers while hopping up and down and holding her middling parts. She didn't dare sit and didn't even drop her buckets of peat. Her rake leaned on her bouncing shoulder. I took it from her.

The old witch stood facing the end of the path. The covering limbs moved aside on their own, showing the way. We ducked through and, after a few more steps, stood in front of row after row of split wood high enough to keep a woodsman's family fat for a couple years.

A half-dozen, flat-iron pans rested over rows of fire pits. The embers under the pans had cooled and there wasn't much in the pans either, only a couple with a little whitish caked residue from whatever had been cooking down to nearly nothing.

The blonde powder in the pans was not the source of the horrible smell, however, which to me had come to almost taste like both death and the trenches in back of an army's camp. That came from the biggest cave. Down the middle of the path leading out of it, a trench leaked a trickle of brown and foul-smelling water out of the darkness, across the path and over the lip of the small cliff. The swampy foliage was missing where the water fell, replaced by an oily orange pool. A little farther out from the pool, the lilies and grasses prospered as if telling us the orange mess was too strong to live in but pretty wonderful if your roots were a little farther away.

We plunged into the black cave. It took courage to go in, given my nose was starting to sting.

"Keep that lantern up, child. There be no tellin' what the earth might do to ya' here if ya' were ta' touch fire to it. The earth be strong here, more than any other place inside the world." The witch passed several jars of dust. The jars held the same off-white powder as the residue in the pans. A little was just piled in a corner.

Farther on, mounds of chunky yellow crystals sat in more piles, flecked with black and brown particles. This had more the consistency of salt than the off-white powder. After a bit of walking, the floor appeared clean of anything but the long trough of brown and foul-smelling water.

A seam of yellow mineral wandered along a wall. I had to hold my lantern just right to see into the crack, for someone had mined it almost as far as could be reached. The seam was only a couple inches tall in most places, but I imagined the whole hill shifting down if someone wasn't careful and didn't stop scraping out the hollow to get farther in. None of what had been scraped lingered. Even its dust had been swept clear of the walls and floor.

The witch came over and pulled me away by my lantern arm.

Back a ways, a few piles of finely crushed, black powder lay beside a grinding stone. The stone was coated with dark dust. On the other side of the stone sat a stack of charcoal, laid out in neat piles of wrist-sized sticks.

A bit farther sat ten bins the size of coffins carved into the rock floor. They were heaped with debris and the source of the brown leaking water. Each of the rock depressions had a notch leading to the main trough. There was little doubt that we'd come to the source of the retched smell.

The witch turned to Angel. "That one there, the one that be the wetter of 'em all. You go and straddle, girl. Ain't right ta' make water no other place near sight of here, by rule of the cave spirits."

Angel put her buckets down and straddled the wettest pit. She glared down, probably wondering if something in the pile was going to reach up and get her. I turned around, giving her privacy. Whatever she produced wouldn't change the fact that we'd have to wash our clothes and hair in lye before we came too close to decent company.

The witch called me to one of the drier pits. She pointed. "See them there specks of yellow snow on top of that heap? Go on, take your knife and scrape off the snow. Ain't cold; won't hurt ya'. Don't bother with the night dirt. It ain't worth much but for plantin', and this here pit be near spent.

I didn't much like the scraping chore, but did as she said. I came away with a few chunks of mostly yellow mineral. She had me take it over to a pile with yellow and brown specks in it. When I pitched mine in and saw how little I'd added, I gained some appreciation for all the work the mounds of "snow" represented.

The witch told me, "We put the ash of peat in ta' start it. Any creature's water or nightshade will do, after that. It helps it along. Anything foul, we try. When the bin dries, the yellow rises. Had one with just bird and bat drippins. Did best of all, but the bats flew way, and the birds be fickle.

"Once we done, we sift and boil and sift and boil some more. Anything churnin' on top, we take aside. Then we grind the powder to dust in bowls. That's what we be after, child; near-white, like the Goddess's soul. Over here in these jars and in this pile. Look at it. It be like her way, no? Out of the dirtiest and least of us, come the pure and mighty. Taste it if ya' like, my dear, but no too much or it stop yer' heart." She leaned over the white pile of dust.

I put my lantern on a tall stone. I touched the powder and put it to my tongue. She'd just told me it had been made from dung, pee and ashes.

"Salt, only sharper."

"That it be. So, what's it good for, you may ask me."

She took me out of the cave. There, a little upwind, sat a camp. A hut had been constructed, and sitting near it on a bench was a young woman. She looked at me, maybe measuring how close I could safely get before she had to run away. The old witch came up to her and sat down on the same bench, putting a comforting hand on her leg.

"Go bring some rocks, girl, and some of those good logs, as well. Set 'em here, by the Queen, so she can see what I mean for her to see. I'm makin' a fire right in front of us."

The girl scampered away, bringing back wood and rocks to brace the fire pit. Angel helped the young witch gather more logs for beside the pit.

When she finished, the witch told her, "Get me a stick of that tender now. One that's been soaked long."

The girl came back and, at the insistent nod of the older witch, handed me a quarter-split log. It looked nearly normal, save for a few streaks of white stain, as if it had been out in the rain too long before drying.

"Now, we don't have much call for these, but we get a man ta' cart it into the cities. The merchants and lords, well, they buy it. We tell 'em it be just good wood, long held, and ripe. Some says it be demon wood and don't want it. Others, well . . . . You can see why they like it and pay us a hundred times what they pay the woodsman for common firewood; mostly the smiths pay that high." She sat the wooden stick just under the stack of wood that the young witch had configured in an upside down V.

The old woman produced a flint and stick. The flint wasn't flint at all, but some roughened slate, and the stick had something yellow painted on the end. She took the stick and scratched the stone with it. The tiny stick caught on fire. She put the burning stick onto the log she'd just jammed under the others and the wood started burning as if made of dry straw. In three breaths, the entire log burst aflame.

"Now, girl, ya' goes and brings me some charcoal. One good stick of it for the Queen."

When it came, the older witch put it over the rest of the logs. "You knows about charcoal, I will guess."

I said, "It burns hot. The smiths make it in big kilns they stack with wood. Nothing is hotter than a smith's furnace stoked with charcoal."

"Yes, so when I put me charcoal on here like this, you will be knowin' we are up for a nice hot fire to cook our potatoes. Then you can think 'bout what you saw."

So I did. And when I'd thought long enough I asked her, "What's on the stick that you so easily lit?"

"Yellow powder; gift of the cave herself. There be a seam; you seen it. Got your lantern much too close. You make a paste and coat the end of the stick. A good woman in the woods will stick with a flint, if you ask me. Flints can be getting wet, but it dries." She tossed a few potatoes into the fire.

We ate after they cooked. The time in that camp was comforting, bringing back many pretty memories of moments around the fire with my soldiers. Still, I could not rest, for a mighty battle loomed only a few days off, and I had not come up with an inspired plan, given the numbers of people who were apt to be in it; mostly on the other side.

After a while, we sat back, patting our bellies and drinking herb tea. When we'd become good and lazy, the old witch started asking me questions.

"Tell me, what do the yellow stick do?

I answered, "Brings fire in an instant."

"And the charcoal?"

"Burns hotter than anything else we know."

"Yes. So, what does the white powder born of the night do?"

"Once dried into the wood, it sets a normal log to flame with no more than a spark's touch, needing no dried moss, twigs or grass to get it started." I nodded as I spoke.

"Yes, so this is what we be noticing also. One of our men, he takes all three and grinds it to powder. Then he puts them all together and the man wraps it in some strong paper. Says he's gonna' make a better log than our Goddess can make. Tie it all up, he did, and puts bees wax into the end of it. When he be done, it look like this," she said before going into the cabin and bringing out a tiny log that on the outside looked pretty much as she'd described.

"Ah, I see." I imagined the possibilities of a log you could just scratch across a rock and get going and also have it heat like charcoal and catch in only a few seconds. A warrior could char a meal in minutes then put the log out before the smoke woke the enemy and told them where she'd camped, maybe even in the rain.

"But," I asked, "How long can a wee thing like that burn?"

"Well, this man has him an idea. He decided ta' make a whole lot of 'em and sell 'em to smiths to make their forges hotter than hellfire with no wait. He said, 'The copper can be made if the kiln's only a tiny bit hot. The iron be made if the kiln's mighty hot. We tells the smith to start his kiln with some of our charcoal. When it be hot, stoke it up with some of these here sticks.' He means to make something stronger and shinier than any metal yet."

My interest grew. "I'd like to see it work. I'll pay your tribe three coppers just to see it burn."

"Three copper, ya' say? Let me see if you have so much."

I reached into my pocket and gave her three of the four I had on hand. Marci and Minari were handling all our money by then, and they didn't give out much for foolishness.

She gave me the fancy-made stick. After smelling it, I could tell there was powder in it. "Should I just scratch it with a rock to get it going?"

"No, you gots to put some fire inside of it. Make a hole for a candle wick soaked in water steeped with the white power, so the wind won't blow her out. For now, ya' can just put it on that log on top of that fire, I suppose, seein' I don't have no wick handy." She bit her lip, as if thinking.

I did as she told me, laying it across the top of a log that had not yet caught. Then I leaned in to see how it would flare when the fire crept around the top and the little hot log took. As I watched the log under it starting to take, I asked her, "Know where I might meet this man?"

"Can't, 'fraid. He done lit one of his sticks in front of a smithy and it killed 'em both for lack of care. This one our young witch made for ya'." She pointed to the young witch who'd chosen that moment to step away. She bore a look on her face that told me she was still afraid of us. I'd thought we were beyond her distrust. All I mostly saw was her backside, though, as she turned and disappeared into the depths of the brush covering the trail.

I looked up at the old witch, bewildered to hear how the men had died and wondering what kind of mistake had caused such a calamity.

She edged up. "Best now we be steppin' over a ways."

"I can't see it if I'm way over there," I argued.

"If the Goddess be here, she be sayin' to ya', 'Do as this old witch asks ya' and go on over there.'"

I gave her a funny look. I'd paid three whole coppers, and could see that the fire was just about to get to the stick. I only stood halfway up, thinking to delay her long enough to at least see it catch.

Next, I felt the witch's hand on my tunic, pulling me to the side like some kind of mother cat pulls up her wee kitten by the neck.

The insistent witch led me away, mostly pushing, and she kept going, and kept pushing, and more and more, in a way that told me her frailty had been forgotten for the purpose of persuading me to move along. I became fairly grumpy because even with my good eyes I wasn't going to see much of the stick burning at all, even after paying three whole coppers for it.

Next I knew, my ears went deaf and a fiery wind hit me, sending me and the old witch another ten feet down the path. We sailed right over Angel and even the young witch, the latter having had the good sense to find a spot on the ground before we joined her there.

I had to stay down. Big clods of dirt, burning timbers, pea rocks and even a few new spring leaves kept raining all around us for several seconds after having been lofted skyward by the same mighty force.

When I finally grew convinced that nothing new was going to fall from the sky, I sat up.

She said, "Needs I be telling ya' the new log be no good for tender, or for lightin' the hearth or even heatin' a smith's mighty forge."

Up the trail, a few of the trees were burning on the bottom edges. The front of the cabin had shoved in, showing three of the inside walls and the scrambled wares. I couldn't see where our bench had gone. The only thing left of the fire pit was a hole that was black and streaked like a many-pointed star.

The young witch went over by a trough and handed Angel some buckets of water to toss on the forest.

I stood to help, but as I tossed water on a sapling, I asked, "Why did you think to show me this way? What good is it if it makes such a mess?"

The old witch answered, "I meant to make its magic clear ta' you. Only by seeing it in your midst can ya' know it for what it brings ta' us. Though, what good comes of it be not mine to say. On me right hand, we witches be women of peace. On me left hand, it be said that when your King of Farstand come, he be bringin' the cursed White Shirts to our home ta' kill our kin and end our ways entirely, out of not knowing us and thinking he do good work."

"I know that's true. My teacher was killed for only being a witch. Every time I meet them, I waste my time speaking of peace. They do not miss the chance to call me a witch. They find it all the excuse they need to rally their hate."

"Ah! That be rubbish. You be no proper witch. I think your teacher be no good one either. I can see by that sword on your back, what ya' are."

I had some patience with her regarding her beliefs, but I also had my own ideas about the nature of things that had been placed before my feet. "We both love the Goddess, but she has given you your peace and she has given we Debrecians our swords. You use your peace well and I love you for it, but we use our swords better and I love us just the same."

I pulled my sword out from behind my back, and used its magical edge to slice through a wrist sized branch. It fell and brought with it a flame that was threatening to spread and set the whole forest ablaze. Angel and the young witch, now better able to get to it, splashed the worst with water and stomped on the rest with their feet and some blankets.

Once the fire was extinguished, I looked at the old woman as if to tell her with my expression that my sword had proven its point.

"It only be seemin' better at the moment," was all she yielded.

I said, "There I think you are right. The problem is, old friend, the moment is upon us."

She was both sad and tired, sitting down. The young witch came up on the other side of her with a bucket of water and handed her a cup. I was worried, realizing how much the past few minutes had cost the old woman in strength and thus did not bother her rest.

"Now I be seeing the ole Goddess, as was me price for the secrets," she told me after a spell.

I slipped down beside her and let her touch my head.

I felt her inside my skull. Her touch was warm, but the spirit she moved left a cold, trailing finger. I wondered if she was stealing my memories of the things she touched and also if I'd know it. Upon finding something, she screamed and let go with her hands, as if my skin and hair were poison.

"What's the matter?" I asked her when she would not stop leaning and looking away.

"I saw her when last ya' did," the woman told me. "But the Goddess in your head be not like the one in mine."

I thought about that a moment. "How can she be? The woman is all about the business of love, spring, the good black soil and giving life to our babies. These are the duties we all love. And yet, she must often turn her face from these things when she shows herself to me, knowing the course she has set for my life."

The old woman had been scarred by what she'd seen. She still could not look my direction. Instead she asked the young witch on the other side of her, "See this magic woman of anger and war?"

The young witch nodded, perhaps afraid that I'd guess her name and steal her soul if she as much as spoke in my presence.

"Yee and your sisters be bringing all three hundred of the new sticks with the fast wicks ta' her camp. Do it by night this next day. You hear, girl? Then you get away, lest you catch the taint of these women of war."

The girl shivered. She was a woman who'd only known the seclusion of witches, yet she nodded that she'd do it.

"Ain't my chore to know what your kind be doing with the angry tender," the old witch said. "I be cleaning my left hand and my right one for days. I may still not be done with the stain. We want no coppers for it either, out of loathing. As to what it do, the gift be for your kind ta' figure out, for we cannot bear to think on the possibilities."

Chapter Seventeen

"A patrol of ten: Two knights, squires and trained guards." I handed the spyglass over to Khulan.

She took a quick look then passed the glass off to her right. There was a row of nearly thirty, mostly Debrecian leaders, lying in the grass with us on the rise.

We watched the enemy's scouts work their way through the sparse plantings of young trees. They bore spears, shields, helms, chain, but were otherwise light. Two held axes.

"Now, watch the tactics suggested by Sengelen." The woman who spoke was two over to my left, separated from me by my sister and shaman, Batya.

Our cover of trees was thin, but enough to render us invisible to those beyond the ridge. Because of cover beyond our sight, we'd not yet seen the women advancing on the men. The men did. Their whole line turned. Seven came on line while the two with axes and their squad leader fell in behind. The enemy squad did this in good order and without hesitation before their horses started to advance at a good gallop.

Five South Women came on abreast, but when within a hundred yards, stopped. From a distance of fifty yards, they lofted arrows at the soldiers. Two of the arrows sailed through the ranks, missing entirely. One hit a shield and another a tree limb. A final one struck a horse. That shaft embedded up to the feathers.

The women rode away as quickly as they'd come. They were faster than the men who were on larger horses and in some light armor. The men followed only a little farther before slowing.

They came back to the road. One dismounted and worried over the arrow embedded in his horse. Though the horse was certainly wounded beyond repair, and I guessed not likely to last the week, it remained standing.

"As you can see, there was no chance for Sengelen's spear bearers to come into play, nor could our archers shoot more than once. The enemy is intact because of their armor, shields and good instincts. They didn't take the bait and charge, preferring the defense. We have become famous for our ambushes, and good squad leaders are hesitant to fall into such obvious traps."

Some of the women on the hill gave moans of agreement. A few conversations developed as they discussed it.

Another group of five women came out of the woods to the north. Some of these woman shouted war cries, giving the men good warning, and so the men turned.

I said, "Now this is the pattern favored by Hulan and her archers. Watch how we deploy and engage instead of retreat."

The archers came on, also abreast. As well, they broke to the left, coming our way before shifting course as if turning back to form a line facing the enemy. Some of the enemy trotted their horses in the direction of the archers. After some adjustment, the enemy squad increased their pace to a rapid charge.

The archers started shooting into the line of advancing men. At the same time, ten new women rode forward and came within sight of the enemy. They also came abreast, but in a line that would pass our archers to the right.

"You see what must happen. The enemy now has archers on one flank and lances on the other. They'll be enticed to meet one or the other. If they press the archers, the lancers will come forward and hit them in the flank, killing half their force before they can turn. If they attack the lancers, our archers will shoot past the angle of their shields. As it stands, none of this matters with a small force, for our archers, having caused the enemy to raise their shields, are now shooting to kill their horses for want of better targets."

As I spoke, five more arrows were launched toward the enemy horses, two glancing past while three more hit armor and leather, though one or two sunk into the tough hides of the war animals. Two of the horses fell, giving the enemy only eight fighters. All of these continued to advance toward our women.

"Now, as our ten lances advance past the bowline, the enemy has deployed his five lances against ours. With the enemy turned, our archers have much better shots."

The enemy soldiers eagerly struck our lancers. The two men with axes broke from the group, riding straight for the archers.

Women fell, as did men. One man with an axe was hit by arrows to both his horse and thigh, falling from the leaning animal. Our archers broke left and right, shooting at the last man as he came on. He was hit three times in the breast and leg, but didn't slow even a little, cleaving the shoulder off an archer before she could get her horse to move over. One of the archers, seeing the man was apt to cause a crossfire, came up and stuck him in the back with a short sword before scooting away from his swinging axe.

As soon as the man was mortally wounded by another arrow, two of our archers fell from their horses, wanting to tend to the woman who was dying. Two had the good sense to advance and fire into the greater melee, for the other half of the battle had not yet finished.

"Do you see the confusion in the ranks of our archers? Only one woman has fallen, but for all intents and purposes, they have rendered themselves out of the fight. There, our good tactics have gone to waste at the first sign of confusion. That is to be considered in your plans. Confusion comes quickly on every battlefield, regardless of these better tactics. One of the archers who returned to the battle should have called for the other two to get back on their horses. In such cases, a common soldier outranks a sergeant. Think on these things, and make use of what you learn."

When it was done, all the men were on the ground. One of our spear bearers saw that they died without suffering. There also, three of our women lay dying. Three more had taken wounds. Sir Janis's men were good fighters.

"It is a waste." Khulan passed the spyglass back to me. I had good eyes and didn't need the glass, handing it straight over to my sister.

Batya said, "Such would not have happened, had we retreated just a little and waited before falling upon them. That would have let our archers shoot one more round. Or better yet, we might have posted a second line of archers on the other flank of our lancers."

"Possibly," I told her. "On the other hand, I don't think the enemy will be courteous enough to watch while we set both flanks. As well, if we are too many, even the most arrogant knight will not advance. This means we must be good enough to face them on more equal terms."

She passed the glass back.

I sighed. "Worse; in a larger battle, more of the fight will come in a melee. In a battle, face to face, we are at a great disadvantage."

"The answer here is a shield of two warriors, only to delay them, and only those quick on their horses," Batya said. "Put the last archers behind two spears. This will also confuse the enemy long enough for us to throw three volleys," my sister said.

"For as long as it can hold," Hulan agreed.

"And better archery, so it won't take three volleys to bring down only one or two men," Chotan advised.

"This little battle was costly for a lesson," Khulan added.

"Good that they were only South Women," Sengelen said.

I gave Batya a harsh look. She in turn passed it on to Sengelen, who was one of her leaders and should have known better.

Sengelen said nothing else that day. She was found doing penance that evening among her squad leaders, digging new latrine trenches behind the tents of Sergeant Sasha's company of South Women.

* * * * *

The battle finally developed on the plains east of Norfaton Castle. The castle was the key to our entire war. All the closer lords were bowing to Sir Janis after no more than visits from his new emissaries. I dared not wait for him to solicit their allied arms.

Once Sir Janis had three thousand footmen aligned in boxes, he seemed content to bring forward his knights on his left. The knights were set four score on each side and two score more to the rear of his footmen. Five hundred archers protected the main body of soldiers from the rear. Several rows of the blocks contained additional archers, for they knew we were both swift and had mostly archers making up the best of our army.

Up the lanes from Norfaton's walls, at least another two thousand footmen were coming, leaving only a small sum to defend the castle.

We presented a thousand mounted women, nearly all of them South Women, save for a few Debrecians who'd been with us throughout. Kirsta commanded our right where we had the greatest room to maneuver. Khulan held firm control over the rougher terrain on our left. A deep ravine hampered movement there. I'd spent a good deal of time telling all my leaders our plans. I'd also insisted that once the battle was engaged they were trusted to react as the battle presented itself.

In the middle, and staging backwards in case of withdraw, Chotan had built strong defenses for retreat and posted her artillery in logical order for withdraw. The spear-bearing Debrecian was golden when it came to matters of order at depth and range. She had brought up three catapults to counter the one that we'd failed to raid and burn on the enemy side of the battlefield. Ahead of that were ten ballistae. Farther, and nearest my position overlooking our companies, sat another fifteen ballistae, all aligned staggered back instead of abreast because of the need to keep them firmly planted on the solid lane. Women who didn't know how to fight ahorse had been first trained in the bow so they could shoot them afoot. These were also Chotans, appearing eager to offer support for the ones shooting the heavy ordnance. As well they were sacrificial rearguard for our retreat, should it come.

The heavy weapons were on carts, as were thousands of ballista arrows, each the size of a spear. We kept the cart nags staked and laden with tack, just behind them so it would take us nearly no time to pull the weapons free of the field, should the need present itself.

Just ahead were our footmen. Lord Pardrill had sent five-hundred footmen and fifteen knights south, rendering his castle defenseless, save for the Debrecians who controlled it alongside a few of Lord Pardrill's more-elderly guards. Lord Drake found nearly as many and, once combined with our captive footmen, managed a force of six hundred. We posted this thin shield of just over a thousand footmen along our front in three lines of five men deep. The three blocks were separated in depth, leaving large gaps and rendering them unable to lend support to one another. They were spaced fifty yards between them, allowing our horsemen room to maneuver left and right across the battlefield in the spaces between the three ranks of footmen. We intended to use our mounted women as mobile archers and the footmen as roadblocks.

The shields of our footmen had almost all been captured from the enemy, though painted brown, broadened and reinforced, for we meant these men to truly shield us, as opposed to carry the fight. Only the first ranks and the back ranks at the edges had long pikes. The rest relied upon short spears and swords. It was no accident that half of those in the first five rows had been our enemy only a month earlier. I knew from experience that in the heat of battle sides were more a matter of which way the pikes trying to kill you poked rather than which color was on the outside of your shield or even where you called home.

All the footmen and most of our cavalry maneuvered in front of the first line of ballistae. Our ranks extended a hundred-fifty yards to my fore. After that, another hundred yards or more separated us from the enemy.

"Sir Janis must think us poorly led. A rank of only five deep will be quickly destroyed; serving up three courses of it, not much better," Beckli Kahnsa said. She'd joined me the previous morning. It had become hard to think of her as a warrior, given she was a member of my council and the mother of my ward. And yet, there were few better with a sword, and I imagined that any team of enemy confronting the two of us would find few openings, should we be forced to fight them back to back. This was particularly true since we were cavalry.

"As well," I said for her, "they know their shields will protect them from the worst of our arrows. With so many knights on the flanks, we can't easily get around for better shots to their sides and rear. And, if they retreat just a little, their rear is protected by the battlements and moat."

"Then it is lunacy." She shook her head. "Better to yield ground and fight them in the trees."

"It's my hope that Sir Janis thinks so. Let him say, 'Tis the best they can do.' The man is eager to have at me, and so I present him with my forces for the taking."

She raised an eyebrow, glaring as if wondering if she'd made a mistake in trusting my abilities. "Is this only about you?"

"I must convince Sir Janis that it is." I signaled the drummers, causing the first beat of battle sound. It was my decision to not wait for all of Sir Janis's footmen to form up for him. If they were slow to form up, all the better.

Our catapults were laden with ceramic pots of oil set alight with torches. The first flaming shot sailed right over the entire field of battle and put the only barn on the field afire. Men fled from that.

A long delay ensued for adjustments, in the midst of which the enemy catapult tossed a rain of rocks to my left, causing several of our back ranks to open a gap where women waited on their horses. The enemy catapult did this two more times while we reset our catapults. We answered with three loads of oil that splashed fiery death across men trying to make their way into the reserve block.

I heard Chotan scream to the operators to keep firing with the two while adjusting one for a little less lift. When we hit their back ranks with two solid pots, I signaled the drums. They beat the signal to advance.

My first block walked forward at the insistence of our horses on their heels.

In response, the whole enemy force marched steadily toward us, walking out from under the aim of the two long catapults. Timely, Chotan's third catapult unleashed a loosely tied shower of rocks that fell directly in the midst of their companies. Some men scattered while others were hit. They closed ranks as if nothing had happened. Men behind shuffled to keep from stumbling over those who had fallen.

Chotan shouted for the other two to ease their spring twice as much as the first one had done. I sensed us always a little behind with this artillery.

My footmen halted, holding position, watching the gap between us and the enemy close from a hundred to under fifty yards.

A third roll of drums sounded, causing three hundred of my women to ride their horses up to twenty braziers sitting on stands three foot up from the ground and between the first and second ranks of our footmen. The second block had advanced only slightly, as planned. Those women lit their arrows then rode up close behind the last rank of the first five rows. They shot flaming arrows over the heads of the first few enemy footmen.

Shields lifted above the sea of enemy and the enemy archers answered, though they were farther back in their ranks and shot weaker bows. The range proved insufficient, hitting only a few shields of my advancing footmen.

Our readjusted catapults were next, all hitting in their ranks, killing many. Though the carnage was great, it was not enough to bother them much, particularly when they saw us stop and brace our shields and pikes.

The only thing possible for the enemy was to advance out from under the catapult hits, and so they did. The pace picked up on the heels of their battle horn sounding.

My beloved and his knights came over the hills to my right, through fields and pastures, bypassing farms and hovels alike. He had command of sixty knights, squires and a few of our women who were stout enough to wear light armor and also lift a heavy lance. Behind them, another two score of his men, led by Sergeants Niko and Kreger, and also in some light armor, lent weight to that effort. Even elderly Lord Drake had sobered up and was among the men who caused the knights on Sir Janis's left to have to break away and meet them.

Both the heavy armor and the blocks embraced in violent crashes and instant death for those who fell onto the first long pikes.

Sir Janis deployed his reserves of forty more knights to that struggle. They charged in Lord Drake's direction while the enemy knights on Sir Janis's right held, ready on the other side of the field which was poor for horses, with swamps and gullies. We had plenty of mounted women over there, ordered to delay with arrows and waylay the cumbersome maneuvers.

Our light cavalry on our right, just behind the five ranks of footmen, shifted the attention of their flaming arrows. By moving aside they avoided the advancing enemy arrows. They also had better aim toward the enemy horses. This aim was more difficult than it had been upon the footmen, but the enemy knights were unable to both fight to their left and protect against the rain of arrows meeting them from their right. Soon, the second and third ranks of their horses started going down, costing Sir Janis's forces half their weight as time went on. Sir Drake's knights were punching through, circling, and winning the little battle of armor. That was up until Sir Janis's reserves, having finally arrived from the rear, hit Sir Drake's knights in the side.

I shook in my saddle, fearing for my beloved. At one time I had to put my sword back in its hilt, having mindlessly pulled it free and imagining myself riding all the way over there and adding my weight to the carnage.

Kahnsajin and Beckli Kahnsa watched me ceaselessly, and so I held.

Kirsta pulled a hundred of her women out of the right and had them circle beyond to counter the blow. These lancers and archers worked to the far right of Sir Drake's knights and responded to the new threat by shooting arrows point blank into the side armor of the mounted new arrivals. This they did from well west and behind the extension of the enemy lines themselves. Janis had no choice but to break off a section of his foot and send them running in the direction of our South Women cavalry.

At my command, we sounded another drum. Sir Drake pulled his knights back while still fighting almost a score of the enemy knights who'd persevered.

A great exhale must have escaped me because I felt my whole body sag with relief.

Four score of our knights and light male cavalry withdrew, including nearly all of Kirsta's archers. I did some counting, realizing that we had a heavy cavalry left that was almost equal to the enemy's, though the greater of each force now sat on opposite sides of the battlefield.

Messengers were sent to find Sir Drake, requiring him to leave a handful of reserves. I needed the rest of his force to reverse behind us to the opposite flank and hopefully counter the enemy knights now close enough to threaten our footmen on our left. These knights would cause a slaughter there if they negotiated the rough ground. All I had to counter them with were some mounted archers working behind the blocks. I felt reluctant to commit many away from the desperate support of our footmen. The footmen fell far quicker than I'd hoped.

The message to Sir Drake was no small request, for the trip all the way around to our rear was sure to take a good deal of time and tire his already wounded company. Maybe if things went badly, he'd be spared entirely and be in good position to withdraw.

I saw that Sir Drake could not make the trip in time to aid the first ranks. I had the drums roll retreat. Those in the first five ranks who could, mostly in the center, turned and fled the enemy. My women did so with good order, coming to the flanks, and retreating behind their sisters, three hundred more of which sat behind the next five ranks of our men. They made it impossible for the fleeing footmen to run farther. Those who'd withdrawn were quickly forced into the back of the next ranks of five, giving us nearly seven ranks of soldiers in block two once that was completed. The maneuver wasn't finished before the enemy hit us.

Several of the braziers teetered as the enemy horde rushed by. No matter, for we had twenty more braziers of fire behind this next block. Our five hundred women lit their arrows and shot into the middle of thousands of enemy soldiers attacking our second block of footmen. Those who could not reach the braziers shot unfired arrows. Those were nearly as effective and even harder to see coming.

I looked over at Chotan who was busy seeing to lowering the tension on the catapults, but who eventually glanced my way. She acknowledged my nod. How was it possible for her to seem so calm when the blood in my veins felt ready to burst?

"Ballistae! Fire!" she screamed.

The ballista spears actually wailed as they released. Those in back shot in tall arches. Those on the closer trail shot them as flat as they could without hitting our women on horses.

Spears that hit shields went through the wood, often piercing the men behind them. Some missed the shields entirely, sometimes killing two or three of the enemy at once on the same stick. Thin rows of bloody emptiness opened up in the midst of the enemy ranks.

Nearly half our cavalry concentrated at the edges so the enemy couldn't flank our block. The bulk of this work fell to Khulan on our left. She was more masterful at the arts of deceit than the more-risk-averse Kirsta. Her brave feints toward the far left drew the attention of the enemy archers. These distracted the knights as well, keeping them out of the main battle and in the ravine.

Still, the enemy footmen were intact, having lost hundreds, but not enough to dissuade them, for each man only saw the press. Those who fell were replaced by new men joining up from the rear. Seeing the back couple of ranks of our footmen was great temptation for them because it must have given the ones in front great hope of survival. For a footman up front there is no chance of breaking clear of the carnage. There isn't even bravery. Instead, it is the sheer press of bodies at their backs and terror in their souls. I knew this from having asked those who'd survived the living hell of the front ranks in a block of footmen.

Then Sir Drake hit their left and the enemy knights found their horses leaning back and into the masses of their own footmen. Sir Casar's mighty axe seemingly didn't pause once it hit, bending back good sword arms and cleaving body parts on every pass. Beside him, the old Lord Drake butted with his shield and ran his sword under, expertly killing two squires in a row before becoming lost in the crowd. Sir Finley led five knights into the ranks of the footmen, cleaving heads and shoulders after they'd passed beyond the first layer of pikes. He started butchering in the deeper ranks that faced the wrong direction.

I'd come to know many of their knights. They were dying, leaving widows and children.

Daren's knights pressed forward, even under the rain of enemy arrows, which were effective and deadly, but also killing their own, for an arrow in the back of a Farstand knight or footman was better than one hitting our forward leaning shields.

I leaned over to Beckli Kahnsa, asking her the favor of conveying a message. She smiled, and nodded back, leaving me alone with Angel in the back and center of our forward artillery.

Soon, the company of the young Sir Drake was surrounded by

enemy knights and footmen, but seemingly in good control of the slaughter, nonetheless. Making a path where several enemy knights fell, he had to withdraw, clearly growing tired and more than likely fearing the press of so many foot and hundreds of enemy arrows.

Again, I breathed, seemingly for the first time in hours. The air came in gasps, as if I'd run miles in his armor and fought among them. How could it not be easier to do so?

I counted over three score of our knights in good health. A few others lead their horses away on foot, or limped away without their mounts. A couple score of enemy knights remained organized out of all those who'd once been under the command of Sir Janis. His knights had been equal to those of Sir Drake, but had continually been hampered in their fight by our better archers, some of whom had gotten close and shot arrows at blank range before having to withdraw because of replies from enemy archers. This resulted in more loses for him than us, giving us a temporary advantage, though both units disengaged for rest.

This did not mean that Sir Janis was not winning the battle. He had nearly three thousand men still on the field, as well as parts of another two thousand coming up. This included almost all of his archers, some of them well to the center of the block, but mostly to the rear. Who knows how many more were still coming from the city.

We had plenty of cavalry women, but only a few hundred footmen left to act as shields for our bows. I did not want to see my women in this melee. We'd established that close work in such a large mess of men was not pretty and apt to cause too many losses. I needed to retain a force capable of continuing to the next battlefield, should this one be lost. If they broke through the last of our footmen, I was ready to abandon the catapults, pull the ballistae, and retreat to a better field. Better a tactical victory than a strategic defeat, though I still hoped for both.

As it stood, it appeared as if Sir Janis's generals were happy to let their superior numbers of footmen do their work. There they had us ten to one.

I had no choice but to nod to our drums and listen to another beat of withdraw. Our men raced through our second row of braziers and then through the ranks of the last five rows, once again forced to join their back ranks. They could go no farther because of the press of nearly a thousand mounted women, most of them also having retreated to behind the last line of defense.

Upon this movement, I signaled to those handling the cart horses. They immediately worked to goad a few toward the precious ballistae. It seemed likely that we'd need to run and it would take several minutes just to position a few horses.

I counted eight rows of our footmen in the final block, more than I'd expected. I nodded again to the drummer. Upon hearing the new beat of the drums, my cavalry parted, turning both left and right, and rounding the edges. They were eager to fall upon the naked enemy flanks with raking arrow fire, and prepared themselves in new ranks at the fringes. The enemy horsemen were scattered and roaming back, engaging in a reorganization that could bring them back to a decent force. No longer were there knights close, though the footmen had good pikes along their edges and our advance was not far.

Across the battlefield several of Sir Janis's generals were pointing and sending new runners in all directions. The archers in their rear were coming up their right flank with a row of spear bearers as defense.

Our ballistae, the front row of them being at nearly point-blank range, readied new munitions, also in response to the last set of drums. Then, a hundred and twenty women came slightly forward. They grabbed the ends of forty ropes that had been buried. These led under the plowed furrows of the battlefield itself.

The hundred and twenty women yanked forty ropes, toppling the solidly planted braziers that were now in the enemy's midst.

A thousand experienced archers and lancers attacked the enemy flanks, five hundred to a side, all told to rake and not get caught up in the masses.

All of our ballistae shot spears in sparkling arches or screaming threads into the enemy footmen.

Out from behind us, Beckli Kahnsa had come with her daughter and my sister. Mother and daughter peeled off, joining me. Batya led five hundred newly arrived Debrecian women with stout shields and steel tipped lances, around our left flank. They came all the way around, engaging the back ranks of the enemy, soon murdering a company of five hundred enemy archers. These women were the most beautiful of all, for they and their horses were as one beast of death. Only a few fell.

Even the few lingering knights of Sir Janis ran from their advance. Most fell back toward the city gates.

Music to this was the sound of the new fiery wind given to me by the Goddess. Wherever the braziers fell backwards, we'd previously spilled oil and planted one of the new logs of terror. The ballistae also shot dozens of the fiery sticks into the enemy masses, all of them aiming near their center.

The noise was beyond description. Hot blood blew to the sky then rained over the battlefield. Body parts fell as far back as my horse.

The horses I'd been bringing up to pull our ballistae reared and fought their handlers. I signaled them away, least women get hurt. Messengers went forth, helping to steady them and communicate my change of plans.

In a minute, a thousand enemy footmen perished. Great holes in their companies appeared. Few of the back archers lived to lend support. Those that were in front fought on, but were no longer ignorant of the carnage within their ranks. The thunder and lightning of heaven had erupted behind them, also goading them frantically forward.

Those who broke to the rear were killed by the Debrecians. Those who broke to the flanks were slaughtered by the South Women. Those who stayed were murdered by our footmen, unmounted archers and the ballistae that had gone back to shooting simple spears. These they had to aim, for the enemy ranks were greatly depleted, consisting in places of only single men or small groups. It was just as well, for their shields were no longer aimed in any single direction. Ballista spears pierced several men at once or missed entirely because of the gaps.

I called once again for the drums. The last few ranks of our footmen backed away. Where men or women were tied up in a melee, archers worked to separate the tangles and allow our men and women to withdraw beyond spear length. It took a great deal of effort from my archers to kill those closest in combat, and thus help separate the men. Even then, spears were tossed and arrows continued to rain out from the archers who'd survived in the midst of the enemy.

We started concentrating our shots in the direction of the enemy archers who had been hidden in the middle of their ranks. The fighting stopped, save for the sounds of hooves and raw screams of pain everywhere. Several salvos from the ballistae helped to back the enemy block a few more steps.

The enemy catapult quit firing when the men around it were cut down by a charge from one of Khulan's squads.

Some of Sir Drake's knights, bloodied and tired, rested on the vacant lands between the enemy block and the idle catapult, threatening any who challenged beyond the fallen artillery. Khulan's squad had to withdraw because of their threat, though they left no skilled operators alive.

After that small success, Sir Janis's men consulted. They quit the field and made their way into the city. I felt tension drain as if through my feet.

New shouts of terror arose in the distance where Batya's soldiers continued to murder fleeing men near the outskirts. She pressed so hard toward Norfaton that Sir Janis's generals disappeared into the streets leading to the castle.

I rode forward, parting our lines of men. Angel was on my right. Having recovered from her mission, Beckli Kahnsa and her daughter, Kahnsajin, who'd been allowed up, took up stations just behind. Khulan rode up with several women known for their swordplay. She fanned them out to either side.

The ballistae stopped when I managed up through the ranks of my footmen. The enemy archers had grown timid. As well, no more ordnance fell within the enemy ranks once they'd stopped shooting. This brought a hush to the battlefield, only broken by the screams and wails of men in pain.

I took a breath, taking in the nose-stinging odor of sulfur. In a loud voice, I shouted, "Footmen and archers of Lord Janis. I am the Queen of the Northern Debrecian Tribes. We have just begun to embrace this war. When the castle falls, all of the people in the north will bow to me, including all of the lords who once swore allegiance to Sir Lacellor."

I let the words sink in. Several of the men took a step back. One or two bowed their heads slightly. Odd, I thought. The enemy still outnumbers us. Yet, it was clear to all that the wind had changed direction.

One in the back lifted his bow. I held my palm forward. When his arrow flew, a wind took it, sending it into the heavens. There it flew. As far as we know, it never came down. I glanced over at Hulan, asking her to tell her archers to spare the man. Those close to the offending archer, shrugged away. Others watched for the vanished arrow. Some fell to their knees and prayed to their gods.

"You are all dead men, no longer under the thumb of the lords who have sent you into harm's way." Some stumbled over the bodies of their brothers or slipped in their ample blood. I waited for the eyes of terror to lessen.

"But the Goddess is our mother and the bringer of life. As surely as you are dead, so too shall you rise and become whole men if you follow me. You may even enter my service, someday returning to your homes. You may keep your gods as well. The Goddess knows them too and is the kindest of all. She is not jealous. Why should she be? She lives at peace with them in the heavens."

Some of those who'd been praying looked my way as if to wonder what new thing is this?

"I was once a solder in your army. Did they feed me? No! Did they love me? No. Did they even tell me why I'd been pressed into their blocks? Not once! One day I looked around and noticed I was fighting for the worst evil I'd ever known, not my home or my people, but for idle lords who cared little for our lives. The only care I had was for the man to my side, regardless of which way we faced."

I spit onto the field.

Some of the men before me, seeing that my will was not to murder them all, even cheered when I spit. Others came to murmur words of distrust, words of escape, words of blasphemy, but also words of wonder.

"Put your weapons aside. Our wagons will bring you food and

water and sort you into a new army. In the meantime, find one in ten who can speak for you. These spokesmen will get your food and water when the wagons come, so our wagons are not rushed and the food wasted. Remember, you are soldiers still.

"The same offer is to your friends in the city as soon as the place is under my control. This will prove difficult. My sister, the vanguard of our Debrecian army, has been unleashed against them. Our shaman thirsts for blood beyond all reasonable measure. Do not taunt her when you see how young she is. The Goddess shares her horse, and her soul is ancient beyond counting."

I saw several women look at one another as if asking themselves if I was speaking of the same short woman they'd seen riding at the head of the Debrecian contingent.

But weapons fell into piles. Others joined, making new piles of weapons until only a few hostile footmen remained armed. These hardened warriors had courage, but found themselves without friends, and so they also relented. The South Women parted their lines, letting them by. A few women handed down bread and water to those who limped or fell. Such moments of compassion gained trust from the beaten men who were quick to notice any sign of it, probably imagining their survival too fortunate to be true.

It surprised me to see how many of them could still walk, for we'd gained well over two thousand footmen with just one little speech.

* * * * *

The battle was not even over before Chotan, seeing the course of the war, ordered the catapults dismantled, and the ballistae hitched. Within an hour she had all of her ordnance on the road. These weapons passed the new footmen before half had even been watered. We moved toward the castle which was two miles distant. Before her, women roamed the outskirts of the city, killing, capturing or sending into hiding all the men who'd either fled or not yet made it to the battlefield from other fiefs.

I sent riders to find Batya and tell my women to cease the slaughter in favor of spreading the word of amnesty to any man who put his weapons in the street and sat by the curb, awaiting our wagons.

Inside the city walls, word came saying that Sir Janis would not lower his drawbridge at the castle. Upon seeing his men running away from a hundred mounted Debrecians along the main road into the city, the great portcullis had fallen with a crash.

Pulling Kirsta aside, I said, "We can't trust these new men to attack their own castle and lords. Take them down the road, halfway to the ford, and set up a camp with your half of our women. Don't let them mingle, but break up their camps. You'll split their squads in half and mix them with some of our own men, forming new squads. Let the men they've elected remain as either leaders or first assistants; squad leaders being half theirs, half ours. Then we'll organize them further, putting ten of our own men over their companies as new sergeants. Find one or two of their sergeants as well. They'll see it as a sign of faith. As soon as they are in order, start teaching them how to coordinate with our cavalry and fight better. I want no untrained peasant footmen tossed into a block. Instead, give me men of arms with pride in their own squads and a new cause. You have one week with them before you march them south to the ford. I want Dorne, permanently. I am asking a good deal from you."

She said, "I'll get right to it, my Queen. I will apply fairness, with caution."

"Yes, see that they are treated well, good tents, ample mess and better weapons," I added, "but of their own making. Work with Minari and Marci on that. If you find any tradesmen among them, be sure to escort them to our men at our south camps; a good tradesman is worth twenty men afoot. You'll have some knights for captains, soon. That should serve to keep them from confronting our women."

"Would you have me coddle these breeders?" Kirsta had a limit to her ability to show kindness.

"Of course not. They are to be soldiers, not bedmates. Still, if there is cruelty, make sure it is the same kind you give to our own and make sure you listen to their complaints before you swat them on the ass with the flat of your sword. As well, think of a reason they should fight for you then let them know what it is."

"As you say, my Queen."

"Oh, and no onion sacks, Kirsta."

Once again, she bore a smile as she rode away to make her plans.

When I finished giving orders to the leaders of the South Women, I collected a good squad. Together with Angel, Beckli Kahnsa and her daughter, we rode into the tormented city of Norfaton.

Chapter Eighteen

The city was in chaos. Whole rows of houses were burning. Squads of Debrecians were forcing peasants out of the homes to assist in the fire brigades. Others still assaulted buildings full of soldiers, surrounding them with peasants bearing buckets and setting them aflame when all else failed. Still more guarded whole neighborhoods suspected of harboring enemy, or outright looted the goods in others and put them into wagons they'd confiscated for the work.

Bodies of soldiers were so thick in the streets and alleys that we had to make paths through them in places. Debrecians roamed about at will, some even alone and unafraid; in fact, searching for danger. I left them to their duties, not knowing the full extent of the battle or the nature of their orders from my sister and her captains.

I found Batya nearly within bowshot of the castle. She was giving orders to a company of women who were mounted on horses. They pranced in place as if extensions of the eagerness of their riders. Never had I seen her so busy.

I asked, "Is it possible to call in your leaders and come to some plan of reconciliation with the peasantry and the enemy footmen who are in hiding?"

"Such is not easy." Her voice was terse. I saw something ancient in her fifteen-year-old eyes when she glanced right past me and on to the next warrior. She instantly directed the warrior to send a company around the castle to hold its rear.

For the first time, I realized just what they meant by a shaman unleashed to the point where even a Queen could not easily bring her back from the terrible addiction of battle. It was one of the known curses of letting a shaman loose and one of the first things the sacred books cautioned a Queen against.

I said the only thing that had a chance of getting through to her: "The enemy footmen will be of use in fighting the enemy to the south. We have need of their pikes. Krista hopes to better train them. As for the town peasants, they have fallen under our protection, and we need their production to fashion our weapons and feed our soldiers as we advance. You are my shaman. You know the difference between a good general and a bad one is tents and food and horses."

Her eyes softened as if she'd truly seen me for the first time. "My Queen. My sister. I am sorry. Yes, of course, you are right. It will take me some time to secure our flanks though. There is fighting still, and the castle is first. We need show our forces to them, lest they see our lacking numbers. As you know, most of us have bypassed this city, and we're only five hundred warriors here. We don't have the women to round up an army, and just barely enough to kill one. I'd hoped to finish the enemy at my back in these streets within the hour. In that way we may linger at the castle gates."

I put my hand on her shoulder to steady her, for the ghost of our most ancient shaman was full and alive within her body. "Take your women from all but the castle gates and the main street to the east. I'll have the South Women do the work of rounding up the footmen and putting seals on the doors of the buildings they've set to rights. Khulan will oversee this for you; one of your better warriors, as you might recall. That will give you all five hundred of our Debrecians to deal with Sir Janis. I also have Chotan coming in on the main road. You can't help but already hear the wheels of her ballistae and catapults. We'll deal with Sir Janis together, my sister. I plan that we should personally knock on his door."

She looked over at me, and once again her eyes lit up as she saw the warrior within her sister's soul. That even got the attention of the shaman ghost, causing the old woman within her to smile.

Once I'd broken through, I saw the look on the face of Beckli Kahnsa. Her whole body sagged into her saddle as if she'd finally managed to breathe.

Kahnsajin, however, was looking up toward the gatehouse's towering rampart. "This is the very same castle we passed when we'd first come here. I remember. They'll have to let us in now. I can't wait to see inside."

* * * * *

For three days, Sir France's white flag of parlay flew, ignored, on the ramparts while we tore his portcullis out of the gatehouse and both battered and burned his drawbridge so none of his horses could make their way over the moat in a surprise attack. The gates were next. Each was shoved back in its casing until spun nearly free of the opening. We'd even dismantled much of the gatehouse with our misses. A whole mound of heavy rocks littered the front of the castle. Chotan was having a wonderful time doing nothing but this work with two catapults stationed on the main road only a hundred and fifty yards back from the castle entrance. There we'd set up just outside a bakery.

Teams of women placed bets and took turns at the catapult lever, hoping to win a golden brooch that someone had found in a dead merchant's store window. The most accurate toss into an archer's slot to the left of the gaping gates won. That tiny window had been rendered the size of a small room and so the brooch was given out and a new trinket offered for the best shot at the third window to the right.

Such sport had gone on too long for my warlord. She had ridden on to the main body of her army, the vanguard of which was nearly at the gates of Dorne. They were no doubt soon to swarm over the reoccupied shell I'd left there. Khulan and I were left in charge of a thousand Debrecians and South Women. Daren Drake and his men, now a solid hundred knights and peasant professionals, took to their swiftest horses and rode to reaches west. They'd bring in the markers of lords who'd yielded to Sir Janis out of fear of Farstand forces that had never left Norfaton.

Every so often, messengers delivered news of yet another western lord who'd been rescued or who'd found his way clear of the scouting fringes of Sir Janis's army. The last of the King's men were in full retreat south, now that the Debrecian tribes pressed them from the north and Sir Drake from our east. I had reason to believe that the retreating men of King Falstaff had learned of our control of the ford as well and thus were relearning the art of swimming across the mighty Redwater, minus mounds of armor. This meant their messengers were also finally finding ways through and to the King.

Dignitaries finally trickled in from the western lords. Some of these I sent to elderly Lord Drake's camp on the eastern fields of Norfaton where such company was more welcomed. I did not know nor did I have much patience for them.

After a lull, I said, "Angel, strike up a white flag," before retiring to my tent.

A woman woke me. "Men are swimming the moat and stringing ropes across the chasm."

I thanked her. We gathered nearer the castle moat.

A man ran up and bowed. "Sir Janis and his knights seek a word."

I motioned him away. Three knights stepped up in his place. They had braved a rope bridge.

"Why, woman, have you not honored our flag of parley for three whole days?" was the first complaint out of Lord Janis's mouth.

"Well Ser, I have patience for all things other than talking. After all, I am a woman used to waiting. I have need of your throne room, so the mother of my fiancé may enter it and beg. Lady Drake has promised to plea that I take her son's hand in marriage. I have been too long frustrated. In order to properly lose my virginity, I need for you to leave this castle rather than talk me to death. As well, all three of you might do well to bow, for I am the Queen of the Debrecians and South Women and know you have been trained to the art in your fancy world of kings and princes."

They did not bend. "Take this noble, and hang him from that window." I pointed to the man next to Sir Janis, then to the second story window of a nearby house.

A whole squad stepped up. They tackled the man and bound his hands. Sir Janis and his other man remained in place under threat of mounted women bearing spears and bows.

The house I'd picked faced the castle. All over the ramparts, men yelled at us for the breach of diplomacy, but were impotent. We were just beyond an arrow's range.

My women lowered the man out of the tallest window with a rope around his neck so his feet remained a short distance from the ground. He dangled behind us, kicking the wall for purchase that was not to be found. He gripped at the rope with his free hands, but the loop was too tight. His face grew purple and eyes bulged. After a moment, he stilled.

I had the pleasure of continuing with our conversation, seeing at least one noble on his knees before me.

"This is an uncivilized show of cowardice and barbarity," Sir Janis said.

"I am many things, but not a coward, Ser." I laughed.

He still did not bow.

I motioned to another squad then pointed to Sir Janis.

They pressed him to the ground and bound his hands.

"I am favored at court and a personal friend to the King, woman!"

"Good. He will notice." I pointed to the house.

My women led him in and shoved him out the window. There he joined his dead friend at the end of a second rope. The ropes were thick and well tied. All the worrying of his fingers on the knots did no good, though he lasted a minute longer.

I said to the last knight, "Go back into the castle and tell all the men that they have two choices, life or death. Those who bow shall live. Those who do not shall be hanged, as I have noted is your traditional means of killing women when wood is scarce. I swear by the Goddess, who is my god and my heart, if all of your men bow, all of your men shall be spared and well treated. For each day that you linger, ten men shall be added to those who are hanged, starting with those bearing noble blood.

"When you are ready to come out, leave your gold, weapons and armor. Walk across your rope. Tomorrow I bring to bear the rest of my artillery and will surely tear this castle down from around your heads."

Not until we brought up the third and largest catapult the next day did we hear the sounds of fighting inside the castle. Several men raced out of the battered gates. Only a few made it across under the hail of arrows shot from the arrow slits, most of which had been battered into the size of barn doors and thus left their archers in plain view. We responded with several shots at the archers from our ballistae, after which more men came running to the ropes. Most of them made it without arrows in their backs.

These were given food and led away under the direction of their own sergeants.

Then there came a lull, but it took only three more boulders from our catapults before another white flag was raised. Even as we loaded and shot another round, more men came across the water on the rope. This time there were no archers on the ramparts or in the windows. After a hundred men crossed, it became apparent that the castle was emptying before our eyes. We stopped the catapults and spent our efforts rounding up the prisoners.

Well before the place emptied, workmen with wagons came forward, dropped great poles over the moat, and lashed them together. We had to ward the surrendering men away from the new bridge in order to send some Debrecian cavalry over to take control of the former seat of Sir Lacellor. These women were stopped at the last gate by a handful of nobles holed up in the strong central keep, though there were not enough of them to man the arrow slits. Once we gained past the ramparts, we shot a couple of flaming arrows in through the highest keep slits. I suppose that satisfied their sense of noble resistance, for they opened the doors without further fuss.

Our women rode in. We tied up all of the nobles. Men, women and even a few of the older children were bound. The enemy had long determined that they'd already won in the North. Their first wave had come to stay, bringing all of their relatives. The babies were taken to midwives while the rest of these nobles were tossed into the same dungeons that we liberated of hostages.

The liberated included the wife and son of Sir Lacellor, though in their case it had been from a tower. The wife of the great lord immediately declared herself regent. She announced this to the Debrecian who led the squad liberating her. The young boy was too little to do much more than giggle and scream in delight at the sight of the sun on his toddler eyes.

I rode into the castle upon hearing of the keep's full surrender. There I immediately noticed Lady Lacellor. I'd seen her before, of course, standing in the rows of nobles.

She was a pretty woman of twenty and five, though in need of a bath and a cleaner gown after having been stuffed in a tower for weeks. The widow immediately started babbling to my leaders about the needs of her regency. Several of the other liberated nobles appeared equally insistent upon this.

I remained back, observing how my women handled the nobles. The highborn in northern Farstand were determined to remain relevant. I determined to allow them this fantasy for as long as it proved useful.

My war chiefs arranged for the tight security of the keep. Then I silently met the nobles while still mounted. "I am allowing a hundred domestics to cross, including your new temporary castellan, Lady Marci. I expect you to help the new castellan in any way she sees fit. Set the castle to rights by morning. Any bad report that I get from the castellan will be dealt with when I return in a few days. Then I shall see how much has been accomplished."

Several of them glanced around me and at the others in my entourage. They swept right past Kahnsajin and Angel, seeing Beckli Kahnsa who was familiar. I imagined them thinking I was her messenger. They quickly renewed their many complaints toward her.

Beckli Kahnsa said, "Send any unwanted goods into the halls for the storekeepers to gather and put away. Hot food is coming, and you shall dine in the great hall upon the ringing of a bell. Once fed, there is little time for talk. As our Queen suggests, the castle needs tending. As well, the workers will require oversight. You will help with the labor, for hands are short. When our Queen returns, the castle must be set to rights."

We retired back across the bridge where we spent a restful night in my warm and inviting tent, awaiting Lady Finley and Lady Minari. They were used to dealing with those born useless and with golden rattles in their cribs.

Suffice to say, resting peacefully was helped by my decision to not hang anyone else. We'd won. That was enough and no small blessing.

The King of Farstand had lost his last hold on the north, wasting a huge and irreplaceable army. My sister was pressing him back to his own capital city, well south where the man's armies had been so depleted by his arrogance in the north that he had only one army left. It was mighty, but it was also apparent that he'd soon see personally what war was really about if he was not careful. Where my sister's bloodlust would finally be sated is yet another story and was not my immediate concern after such a long and twisted campaign.

It was a good night. The breeze felt perfect and the stars bright, filling the sky with wonder and hope. We'd ridden from the grey days of late winter into the warm and breezy nights of summer.

After some wine and easy chatter among my friends, I laid back to get some sleep. I rested near the front edge of my tent. Kahnsajin was just outside. She was talking to some wee peasant orphans she'd taken a liking to, even going so far as to start them a camp and find some women workers as aunties.

She said, "Silly girls, you can't just run in there and say hello to the Queen! Don't you know she is always busy? Sometimes she's busy talking to the Goddess even. Big trouble, if you interrupt such.

"Sure, she lets me go in. I know when to be quiet, is why. Besides, everybody knows I am her very best friend.

"My job? Why tis bodyguard, along with Angel who is the deadliest mistress of knives you ever saw in a battle. Everybody knows that. I have a curveback, given to me by Angel who got it from the Goddess herself.

"Says I. I saw her go get it. Angel has never made a bow. This is the first anybody ever saw her hold, and you can see it's perfect. Nobody ever made a perfect curveback right off. Besides, Angel does that; goes and gets weapons out of nowhere and brings them home and gives them to people who then go and tell all their friends because it's how the South Women know they've made it into their cavalry. Angle gives them something, and they know they're in.

"That's like no wood you've ever seen before too. Comes from the Goddess's own forest . . . up there. Way up, so far you can't even see the roots.

"Well, of course we are! I get the left side while Angels gets the right side. That's why I'm sitting here outside the Queen's own tent;

it's my turn to sleep out by the door. Don't you know, even angels have to be off by themselves, sometimes.

"She doesn't talk 'cause she doesn't have to. Besides, she talks to me, and that's all that matters, being we share the same duty.

"It was me the Queen picked 'cause I declared her first, when everyone else was hesitant.

"How do I know, you ask? Cause it was warm in the tent when I first saw her. Even so, all over my arms came these tiny bumps when I peeked out and first saw her defeating our best and bravest champions. Like I do when my momma comes home, or when it's really cold, only worse, cause I even got them on my legs and back.

"What did that mean? Why it meant that the Queen had come home. And that's what I told my momma when I first saw her. I said, 'Momma, the Queen is back; momma, the Queen has returned; can't you see; didn't you feel it when you looked out at her or even when she walked by our tent!' Then, even when nobody else agreed, I told everybody I could find, saying it, cause it's true, and now they all know it and regret calling me a jabbering fool—though sometimes I have been known to talk a lot. But the Queen even taught me how to not do that when it's important to be quiet in the middle of the enemy camp, like when you're hunting and . . . ."

I found a couple of dirty shirts and put them over my ears. And though that gave me some hours of peace, I also awoke with yet another dream of yet another war, and so was the purpose of my life.

Chapter Nineteen

Three days later, I'd still not managed to inspect the castle because of the many dealings of war and training, and to an even larger measure, organization and logistics. Messengers sent by Kirsta buried me in tedious details regarding the making of another army.

That is not to say I was not informed of the many affairs going on within the castle. Marci sent back daily reports, mostly stating that work was getting done, but also that she felt more like a chief of servants than a castellan. Apparently every person of rank thought castellan was their own duty, saying so to her face. These reports sometimes came back on the lips of Lady Minari, or even Lady Finley, who were shuffling from Kirsta's camp and the castle, acting as my agents on most matters dealing with the nobility and new men. Both were continually tired, making me wonder if I might have some use for a few more nobles. That was a frightful revelation.

Immediately after one such report, and in the midst of my discussions with my southern warriors and council, Lady Lacellor's chamberlain plagued me by visiting my tent. It was an official visit full of fanfare, including pages with horns and all on horses with bells. They were so full of flourish that even Angel couldn't keep the chamberlain from barging right in.

He was the same man I'd dismissed on two other occasions when I'd barged in on the great knight Lacellor, in somewhat the same way he imposed on me. He made all sorts of sweeping bows and was escorted by two ravishingly handsome men, all in silks and colored striped britches that were both tight and showing large bulges, and no small measure of silver chain over all of that. No doubt, towing men so pretty was how he'd managed to easily pass my women, distracting even Angel and Kahnsajin.

"The regent is delighted to learn that Sir Daren Drake and Queen Abi are to be wed. She has informed me that she is sending dispatches to the west, hoping to quickly find him and bring him back to Norfaton, post-haste. My lady is sure that he will arrive no later than mid-week and has for days been busy making all of the arrangements for a wedding. These preparations include invitations to all the great lords of the north. They are encouraged to cease all activity, save hurry. All will be taken care of at Lady Lacellor's expense, to include a grand feast, our most holy men for the consecration and our grand hall full of every type of flower found within the lands of Lacellor, and a few that are not." He smiled.

"As well, Lady Lacellor has just put up Lady and Lord Drake and asks that you attend an engagement banquet in your honor this very evening. Lady and Lord Drake also request your attendance; Lady Drake especially insists that you come and delight her with your presence. She says, 'As is fitting a great Queen and the fiancé of her only son,'" the shaking man said.

I looked over at Ladies Finley and Minari. "Have Lady and Lord Drake gone to the castle?"

Instead of answering me, Lady Finley told the chamberlain, "Sir, we are delighted to hear of your efforts in our Queen's behalf. She shall, of course, be delighted to attend. Now, hurry along Ser, and tell Ladies Lacellor and Drake that we will make every effort to give a pleasing appearance. Being women, we are losing time needed to make ourselves presentable, so yes, yes, hurry along, good man."

He smiled, genuinely for the first time, bowed and departed. Several in my council let their eyes linger on the backsides of his two escorts before the tent flaps shut them out.

"I would as soon kill the man as entreat him politely," I told Beckli Kahnsa. She smiled, by then having gotten used to my ironic comments; which were not all that ironic, but the point is, she knew I would not harm an innocent.

"We should be careful to husband some of our thoughts on these matters, Abi," Lady Finley said.

Minari agreed, though only by shaking her head. I owed the former maid apologies, given she'd done so much work as my ambassador and gotten so little results in exchange. I had no head for it and tended to spoil all of her good work.

Beckli Kahnsa also agreed, "These nobles are unlike our people, and yet their traditions mean a great deal to them. We can't hope to rule alone here. Without their help, we may even have trouble doing much good at all; not unless we intend to spend all our time ending the chaos that is likely to replace their skills in order."

"I do not much like their orderliness."

Lady Finley said, "You would if there was naught but chaos."

Even a few of the Debrecians in the tent were looking at me as if pleading for reason. They'd seen the streets of Norfaton and a few other cities as well. They'd also seen the passing of refugees north, where there was little, and back south where there was less. The migration south had started even before the roads had been secured.

With so many dead, the lands of northern Farstand were in disorder and largely unruled. It did not help that many of them saw us Debrecians as next to demons from Hell. Their elders told tales of ancient raids, breeding mistrust whenever we neared.

"I confess too little patience with the nobility and too much love for the peasants. And my soldiers, whom I love the most, for I am close to their hearts."

"That is how it should be for a Queen," Beckli Kahnsa said. "A Queen should expect better things from those who have risen in rank around her. She should open her most forgiving heart to her people. Still, this is why she has those around her whom she might call nobles, knights, council or just friends of confidence. Otherwise, she has to go out and bless every one of her people, one by one; a chore that has no end and no hope of success."

Lady Finley also said, "You once were a soldier in my guard. Could I have done all of the good work of all of my men, even in such a small fiefdom? You did more by your presence than you did by your sword. And, did not the people look up at you as if a lord?"

"We were as gods once," I confessed, not bothering to tell her that the higher I rose the smaller I felt because I didn't feel as if I could change things nearly as easily as I had with a sword and a fast galloping horse. Nothing I knew was more free and closer to the gods than that. The world did not swirl around me then, but I through it. The duke had died nearly at my whim, and the rude little other one had died with no more than a word. The Baron of Helfax had seemed so large and come to nothing. I'd parted streets of angry peasants with a look and ran with the wolves in the rain. Yet, I should never forget poor Bullor. He had so innocently embraced his sins that I often begged the Goddess's forgiveness for his little murder.

"We will go to Lady Lacellor, and I shall wed the handsome knight, Sir Daren Drake, so the land might be tamed."

* * * * *

Judging from the look on the faces of the old gatehouse guards, one might think I'd come to invade the castle again. I had a whole company of South Women inside, so that was unlikely. A runner vanished to warn the nobles. I spit into the moat only once. The invitation proved some steps forward for me, given I'd never actually been asked to visit the insides of the castle before. That's not to say I'd not found my way in on occasion, disguised or abided or otherwise swinging a sword.

What truly startled the guards was when they saw the wagons ride up in my wake. Beckli Kahnsa was left to do the intense negotiations over the numbers. The guard captain pretended that he had some decision to make about accommodations, even while the first wagon started across. Next came twenty more wagons and several score women on horses until three hundred warriors and servants pressed the inside walls.

We in my leadership group assembled then walked into the grand hall. There, a great table had been positioned in front of a score of the heaviest throne-room chairs. Along the sides, six perpendicular rows of tables had been spaced, looming all the way from front to back of the extensive room.

Off to the left sat the women and off to the right the men. They all stood when some man in a fancy and multi-striped uniform blew a horn. The guard on the other side of him nodded to me.

Then the chamberlain yelled, "Our Lady Abi, Queen of the Northern Tribes and South Women, fiancé to Sir Daren Drake who is heir to Lord Drake. Welcome, our honored guest!"

I did not miss what he'd left out, but smiled to him nonetheless, as was advised by Beckli Kahnsa. She'd caught up, and smiled to him as well. This seemed to please the chamberlain who dutifully backed away, sweeping his hand forward.

Lady Lacellor stood from where she'd been waiting off to the side. She greeted me with both hands upon my own and a wide smile. She'd cleaned up well. When I later commented upon her obvious beauty, saying that she was by far the fairest maiden in the land, it surprised me to see rolling eyes, for nothing could have been more apparent.

"I am so delighted to finally meet you formally, as opposed to in the midst of so much trouble and strife. It is wonderful that the war has ended," she said. I thought she might kiss my hand, but the woman fell just short of it, which gladdened me some.

Still, I had to tell her, "Lady Lacellor, while I find your greeting lovely, and it is no small effort on your part, I must tell you that my very own sister now rides in Farstand. She is with an army of eight thousand warriors. The King made the same mistake of imagining the strife non-existent simply because it was in some distant land and out of sight of his banquet table. We will not."

She put her hand to her mouth and said, "Oh, I am terribly sorry. I did not mean to offend."

Beckli Kahnsa's fingers were on my shoulder, both as comfort and reminder.

"You have not offended me, but instead graced me with a great welcome. I will not be an ungracious guest, for I am truly pleased. It is I who have offended you, but I cannot help at least commenting about so many warriors still fighting because of my decisions. I am constantly reminded of the blood and death that brought me here. I must never forget it, lest soldiers die from some mistake on my part. It is a grave burden to be the maker of nations, is it not?"

I saw that I'd struck a nerve deep inside her, for she showed me the most honest face she'd shown me so far. I had to add, "Well, of course you know this; your dear husband . . . ."

She pulled a cloth from the pretty ribbon around her waist and touched her eyes.

I felt remorse. "We did not often see eye to eye, but we fought the same fight, and I confess that no man ever stood as strong against the might of Farstand. I can say this because I have read all of the histories and can foresee his place there, firmly, but graciously written by the scribes."

"You are most kind." She took a moment to compose herself. "Let us go sit at the honored table. There you'll find all eight of the remaining mighty lords, for none of our great men could be kept away from the occasion of your engagement feast, Lady Abi."

"I say it is a victory feast!" Lord Pardrill yelled. I'd had many good discussions with him since the battle. He, more than any, had stood firmly in our camp. He had not even taken offense to so many of my warriors near his castle. As a result, fewer of them remained. I loved the man already, for he confirmed my belief that one good man was worth a company of fools.

Sir Finley was also there, having survived, even through the deadly ordeal of proving his worth in the battle for the road. He countered, "I overrule!" He lifted his cup of wine and yelled, "It is the engagement feast of my wife's best friend, Lady Abi. As well, the betrothal of Sir Daren Drake, my great friend and my brother in arms, as well as a man who I regret is still returning from the west, but for whom I must speak in his absence!"

"She is the grandest prize any man could hope for," seconded the elderly Lord Drake himself. "Clearly it is a victory banquet, but more a dinner in anticipation of the great victory abed." He was only weaving a little, but the evening remained young.

Some of the women put their hands to their mouths, but I gave a little chuckle as I walked forward, causing them to drop their fingers.

I looked over to the side tables and noticed Lady Drake. She was not scowling as expected, but instead she'd dropped her hand from her mouth and smiled sweetly, as if she was my very best friend. I was good at reading deception on faces, and was genuinely surprised to note how honestly she wore her expression of pleasure for me. Truly, Beckli Kahnsa had been right when she'd told me that the nobility was special, for there was no doubt that Lady Drake was now highly pleased that I'd soon become her daughter. I was sure my smile was not nearly as genuine, as hard as I tried.

A western lord raised his cup next, as we approached. I did not know him, but from reports, had grown to dislike him. He'd yielded to Sir Janis days before Norfaton castle had fallen, suffering nothing throughout the war, save a few knights he'd been compelled to lend to Sir Lacellor in the early goings.

He said, "I am Lord Paulis of Westroos. I ask if this can be the mighty warrior who defeated the greatest army Falstaff has ever mustered? How can it be that the most beautiful woman on earth can be so courageous and capable, rescuing us from their grip?"

"I as well, am dumbfounded. This I did not expect; both a beauty and a beast. Sir Drake is the most blessed man alive," another smooth-talking western lord said. I noticed he took only a sip of his toast. I thought, those two are dangerous, even more so than the third, western lord who'd said nothing, didn't get up, and only belatedly nodded. I could deal with an honest man, and I resolved to spend some time confiding with him in the future, regarding the west.

This left the two northern lords, both of them now guesting hundreds of Greyfeet on their lands. They would both plot for a non-Debrecian influence upon their King, as well as fear the discovery of the plots because we held their lands so firmly. I imagined they'd had to ask Queen Risha for the right to even make the trip south. Even I'd have to ask her what she'd take in exchange for leaving the men alone, should I find the idea appealing, which at the moment I did not. As far as I was concerned, the good Queen could keep their castles forever, assuming she could stomach the walls. I doubted that too.

Those two stood, said something meaninglessly nice, and sat down as if hoping to hide.

I laughed.

Beckli Kahnsa's grip on my shoulder told me I'd found them amusing at an inappropriate time.

"I am delighted to finally meet the eight great lords. As well, I assume, our Lady Lacellor speaks for the ninth?"

I introduced my entourage to the lords. Queen Risha's, Hara, had rejoined us. "The Goddess has already found her worthy of a shaman's test. This is for her Queen to see, as well as her council. The Greyfeet are blessed." Hara blushed, but stood straighter.

All of these women were dressed in newly tailored short skirts and half britches of our warriors, to include wool shirts, brown leather vests and their hard-earned necklaces, showing coins of worthiness, the value of which might well have been lost in the eyes of the nobles, but not by me.

Following them, I gave honor to Jamukho who represented our men, taking time to lavish him with honor and words of love, telling the assembly of their tireless work and place of honor in our tribes. Jamukho, who'd had a hard time picking from all the captured noble clothing given to him by three warriors, appeared striking and in his glory. Not a soul in the house was better adorned. No doubt, all by himself he totally destroyed the myth that Debrecian women were hard on their men.

Sergeant Hadarm was honored with words, though he still toiled at the community and would not leave it. He would not allow me to raise him to captain either, though I paid him twice as much as one and not a person alive was given the right to overstep him, lest they find themselves before my tent. This, of course, included me, given that I was still a recruit in his eyes, which apparently was how he saw everybody; thus his worth.

The rest of my better war leaders were mostly south, assisting my sister in the war. This included Hulan, Sengelen, our head of scouts, Salonia, and of course soon to join up, the great leader Kirsta, with her new army of several thousand footmen. Last of the missing, the name of my sister fell from my lips as benediction to the little prayer I laid before the assembly.

I made mention of Angel, my bodyguard; Captains Sasha, Niko and Kreger; as well as both Minari and Marci, both of whom they knew. They all seemed rightly impressed that we had men of rank, though they did not seem nearly as impressed with my bodyguard, nor the two women I'd so often leaned upon for the necessary work of logistics and husbandry. Without them, we would have all failed miserably. I said, "We have not deserved their humble service," meaning every word of it.

Yet, they could not mistake the nobility of Beckli Kahnsa and the second council member, Abagai, who'd recently arrived. I claimed them two of the north's great lords, "as high as any of the nine."

Lady Finley had come earlier, sitting with the women, seemingly content. I nodded. "And my good friend whom you all know and have come to love."

When this was done, I had Kahnsajin come forward from where she'd been left peeking into the room from the grand doorway. She beamed when I called her forward, introducing her as, "Lady Kahnsajin, both the heart and future of our tribe. She is our soul and who every Debrecian looks to before a fight, lending them her courage."

She came forward, finally standing between me and her mother. The girl had temporarily fallen speechless.

Done with the introductions, we of highest rank went around and sat at the great table, including of course Kahnsajin who I personally invited to a seat. She sat between a western lord and the son of Lady Lacellor, instantly engaging them with questions and battle stories.

Each of us at the high table sat between men, apparently a means of getting us all to talk, or better yet, forcing us to listen. I, on the other hand, sat to the left of Lady Lacellor.

On the other side of her sat her son, a toddler, though he was old enough to talk some and had been taught to sit straight and act stiff like a king. Kahnsajin had captured every ounce of his attention. He wavered between listening and giggling while wearing a little brooch, and a little cape, and if they thought they could get away with it, might have placed a wee crown of gold and jewels about his head. No doubt they'd tucked it away for an occasion, afraid that it might too soon divulge their resolve.

The first order of business was for Lady Lacellor to have the guesting cup brought forward. Once set in place, it was filled with the finest wine from the cellar.

I thanked Lady Lacellor, putting the cup to my lips. I leaned it back. Once I'd wetted my lips, I used my cuff to wipe my mouth then put it down before Lady Lacellor.

I said, "It is custom in the North to offer the guesting cup second to all the highest lords who have offered it." Beckli Kahnsa and Abagai both looked at me curiously. I smiled back at them.

The beautiful and gay Lady Lacellor said, "I have not heard of this custom, but it seems a generous gesture." She immediately raised my cup to her lips. Just before she swallowed, I hit her soundly on the back. The sound echoed through the hall. Guards jerked, but did not advance.

She spilled the mouthful and nearly dropped the ornate cup on the table. I had to take it from her and set it gently down, lest it spill too much of the vintage.

"Oh, I am so sorry." I helped her clean her dress before the wine stained it mercilessly.

"I was overly enthusiastic, Lady Lacellor," I said. "I shall buy you a new dress if this one is stained. Sometimes I forget my own strength. Besides, I forgot that another part of the custom is to find the most needful person to share the second swallow. My mistake. Obviously we were hasty in giving the second drink to you. Now, for that I shall have to go around front so I can see into the eyes and soul of every noble in your assembly. There I shall surely find the one most deserving."

I stood. Many in the room had started conversations, and as I'd noted, most had been drinking, but seeing the commotion, all of the voices stopped and every eye rested upon me. I went around, picked up the cup, and looked into the eyes of Lord Drake. Then I went to the side tables, finding his wife. Neither was the one I was looking for, and in fact they appeared eager to win my love by drinking from my cup.

Finally I came to the western lord next to Kahnsajin. I had the eyes of a wolf, but more importantly, I had the nose of a wolf. I'd smelled the poison even before they'd filled the cup with wine. Looking at the western lord, I now smelled something else that wolves were good at smelling: Fear.

"Kahnsajin, dear. I wonder if it would trouble you much to go see about the food we have brought as our feasting gift. It is a great honor."

Looking over at Lady Lacellor, I added, "I hope you don't mind that we thought to share some of our delicacies with you, even as we partake of the feast I am sure your cooks are preparing. This way I can bring some of my warriors to the empty seats and reward them for their service because of the extra portions. I was a soldier once and know what it means to them."

"Oh, surely." Lady Lacellor clapped her hands excitedly.

Kahnsajin left her seat, causing me to add, "Take young Sir Lacellor with you, child. He seems to have taken to you and being so young, might enjoy stretching his legs before dinner."

Her eyes lit up even brighter. She pushed his chair back energetically, saying, "Come along. I'll show you my horse. I have a bow too, but you have to be careful with it." And then they were off.

Once the children departed, I set the cup in front of Lord Paulis, the boisterous lord of Westroos.

Angel, sensing something amiss, stepped behind his seat. I couldn't see her hands. That meant trouble for the stoutly built man seated before her.

Gone was the formality of my smile. The polite silence of the room turned to something thicker.

The man laughed into the vacuum then reached for the cup, but appeared to accidentally knock it over.

My hand was lightning as I grabbed the guesting cup before all of the wine spilled. Several swallows were still in the bottom, as was most of the poison, I knew. The cup reeked of it, to my good nose. Too bad the man had not solicited the services of a good witch. One would have at least lent some disguising scent. Ah, but such as him no doubt did not believe in good witches, nor was his nose able to smell the abomination.

A serving wench came over with the rest of the wine, offering to refill the cup, but I held my hand over it and waved her away.

I picked up and held the cup before him.

He said, "I appear to have already had too much to drink, spilling my share, Lady Abi. I thank you for the honor, but because of the need for sobriety on this grand occasion, I must pass and make my next cup water."

Khulan came up to his right. I set the cup in front of her. She put her fist around the cup, protectively, allowing me to step back from the table.

I'd worn a pretty dress, but insisted that it be loose and that it only burden me with one thin petticoat. That way I wouldn't be uncomfortable with my sword over my back and my knife in the pretty cloth belt. Turned so as to see the whole crowd, I pulled my sword out of its sheath.

The crowd inhaled.

"Last I was in this room, Sir Janis thought to test the Goddess," I said. "Two of his greatest nobles lost their heads to this sword. Even then he was not convinced of her certain will." I swung the sword before me. The swish sounded fast and of unmistakable confidence. I did it again.

I put two hands on the hilt and buried the point of my sword into the stone floor. The enchanted blade didn't stop until it sank a foot deep. The room swelled with a second sound of gasping nobles. I looked over at Beckli Kahnsa. She remained silent.

"The gods have spoken. As I see it, the great lords have voted eight to nothing to give good lands to Lady Lacellor and her kin." I paused, but none dared speak. "I was at first mistaken, thinking Lady Lacellor disloyal for seeking *this* seat of power, but there is nothing wrong with wanting the best for her son. That is a sentiment we all can share. Even the lowest peasants want good things for their children. As well, good service should be rewarded. That is why I have decided to give her the rich lands of Westroos. There she can prosper and her son will become a great lord. May he serve the people well and learn the contagion of contentment."

"What is this, my lady!" Lord Paulis of Westroos came to his feet.

"You, ser, shall either drink the last of that cup or come and take my sword. However! Before you think it easier to slay me, think first of the ladies in attendance and their pretty dresses. We should spare them the splattered blood on this grand occasion of celebration. Think also of your kin, regarding whose future I am uncertain. Is it not better that our good Lady Lacellor should find small holdings for them, than a Debrecian Queen whom you have every reason to distrust?"

Several women on the women's side of the room wailed. One

voice, of course, was surely his wife's.

Yet, the man came around the table and forward. I backed away from my sword, letting him put his hands on the hilt. He struggled, but couldn't move it. Then he stepped back, seeing my hand near the knife in my belt.

Beckli Kahnsa unsheathed her sword, and tossed it on the floor behind him with a great clatter. She said, "If you are wise, you shall leave what I have offered and drink from the cup." Ah, I thought, always the master of diplomacy. Now none would fault me his murder, given that he could easily arm himself, and my own sword was solidly stuck.

He stepped back, reached down, and groped for the exquisite sword of the great prophetess.

"Think of your sons," Beckli Kahnsa said.

I stepped forward and pulled mine from the stone without the least bit of efforts.

He staggered back farther, not believing his eyes. Then he had a stroke of genius, threw Beckli Kahnsa's sword down, and grabbed the cup, drinking it to the last. Once he'd returned to his seat, I put the sword back into the crease in the stone floor as a reminder to everyone of the power of the Goddess.

The man lasted ten long minutes, most of it sitting in his seat where he sweated, groaned, coughed, sank, and strangled for every breath. In the end, he could not even hold up his own head. His wife came to the table, comforting him and pleading for someone to cure the great lord and take him to a bed. She found nobody willing, or at least none who were both willing and capable of healing him, for all who had such skills were solidly aligned to my way of thinking.

I reminded Lady Lacellor that the man had seemed content to watch her drink from the cup that had killed him. She was also pleased when I had the guards close the door, not allowing Kahnsajin and the boy back to the high table too soon, for fear of the impression his dying might make upon the children. Little did she know what Kahnsajin had seen during the war, and I chose not to tell her, for we had unpleasantness enough.

Surprisingly, Lady Lacellor was full of apologies while we

awaited the death. She surprised me even more by thanking me for the boon of good lands, for Westroos was the north's most prosperous domain.

I told her, "Sir Daren Drake shall be your King of the north, and I shall impress upon him the need for your friendship. May my son and your own ride into battle together as if kin, and may your son be king enough in his own land, bearing forth peace and prosperity to even the lowest of his people."

Cheers arose, loudest from the Debrecians at our lower tables. Even the nobles from the north, where the Greyfeet were still settling their tents, appeared less worried that their troubles could not be overcome, perhaps even without treachery.

On the heels of the dead man's removal, our contribution to the food came. It was brought in at Marci's guidance. She'd left the great table to make sure of the order. The first of it was borne in by a pair of warriors, each owning only one good arm, thankfully opposites. This was a great kettle of warrior's stew, still steaming. I knew that it had many wild leaves, onions and roots, gifts from the witches. These were mixed with a hundred different meats from small birds. It was the ginger that made this all work together, and though it was made in the spirit of a stew patched together on the march, it was far better than most road stews, which often had only two or three of whatever was at hand.

Behind the stew came a hundred warriors on crutches and some carried in on litters. These each held two or three empty bowls. In twos, they came forward, filling the bowls and bringing them to the tables where they found seats that had been laid near the feet of the nobles. On the heels of this, Marci lead twenty warriors with platters full of frog legs, all battered in dough and fried with good lard. Another four women carried in platters of crayfish patties seasoned with onions and peppers. They set these platters on the tables then found seats as well.

Some of the nobles squirmed uncomfortably with so many commoners seated in their midst, women among women, women among men. A wiser few made up for those who did not see the meaning and significance of my bringing so many afflicted women, a few who were still in considerable pain and attended by the others.

I rose and asked the servant for a fill of my fresh cup. "These are the delicacies of an army on the march. As well, these are some of the women who have suffered injury for the north. Some were too sick to make it and be honored by this feast. Still others, peasants and warriors alike, have paid for this war and are now lying dead across the kingdom. It is for all of my warriors that I raise my cup and ask the blessings of whatever gods each of us worships. To the health of those who live and to the memory of all the others. It is our duty to see that those injured are cared for.

"Lord Pardrill has proclaimed this a victory celebration. Well said. Let us remember the dead, and let us look upon the injured with love as we eat our warrior's stew."

Some of the nobles had looked upon the stew as if it was an insult, but then, after the toast, they sat with considered faces and not a one refused the meal. I didn't have the heart to tell them I'd redirected most of their lovely meal of roast ox, succulent pig and vegetable pies to two hundred of my warriors and the castle guards, all feasting in the yard.

Still, it didn't take them long to realize that the stew we'd made for them was not just odd, but also delicious. Some took a frog leg or a crawfish cake—demon food, should they ever be told what they were eating. Each gave a nibble, and all who did went back for more. A few were slow to catch on, only getting one or two before the platters at their tables were empty. Marci let this shortage settle for a few moments then waved in a few new platters. Ale and wine made good rounds, and the eating soon became in earnest.

"This is delightful, Lady Abi. What is it?" Lady Lacellor asked as she nibbled a cake. Sir Drake was pleased as well, raking a couple handfuls of the frog legs out of the platter, as if afraid he'd run out before he'd drunk enough ale to pass out.

"Ah, if I told you all of a warrior's secrets, you'd have no more use for me and nobody would join my army. As well, I must save the recipes to make sure I'm never short on visitors."

Just then, two wolves came scampering into the door with a pair of guards on their heels. Lady Lacellor gave a start. Several of the women shrieked. From the men's side of the tables, several brandished eating knives and started across the platters.

Kahnsajin, who'd come back with the boy, laughed and jumped up from her seat because of her easy attraction to anything resembling excitement.

My women also laughed when one of the guards tumbled over a wounded woman's litter. A few started bashing the second guard with crutches, causing him to retreat. Every woman in our army had seen my wolves.

"Yellow Eyes! Slow Leg! What have you been up to?"

Then I noticed Slow Leg's belly and had to also tell Yellow Eyes, "Well, congratulations, my friend. Seems you still have it in you."

He walked up to my table, sat right in front of us, and smiled with his tongue out, more pleased than I'd ever seen him before. His smug and contented look was delightful, gaining the attention and thrill of all the people in the room.

Then he asked me for some frog legs. That's the way it was with him; a few seconds of hello and a half day of wanting to know what new food I had in store.

I tossed him a crawfish cake, which he didn't bother chewing, catching it with his throat. Lord Drake put his hands over his plate and looked at the wolf sternly. Seeing this, the wolf went searching for more willing handouts.

He and his bitch trotted from table to table, jumped on a few, and looked at the people with hunger in their eyes. Our women gave handouts to bring them near. Most of the nobles tossed leavings to keep them away.

Kahnsajin brought young Lord Lacellor down to the floor where she gleefully showed him her bravery by patting my wolf on the head and biting him gently on the ear. The boy squealed with laughter when Yellow Eyes possessively bit her leg in response, sending the laughing girl tumbling with a couple of bloody tooth-marks on her ankle. Such a wound, I was sure, she'd show to everybody, once she left the castle.

This playing lasted only a few seconds, for the wolves quickly returned to the chore of begging at the tables. I don't think they chewed anything. Thus, after so many handouts, it only took a minute for both to fill. They curled up, entwined, and took a nap on the edge of the aisle.

A couple of Lady Lacellor's minstrels came in, trying to top the opening act, which they did admirably by taking good notice of the varied stations within their crowd and keeping their songs common. This raised voices from nobles and warriors alike. After every song, the servants came around with a little of the beef and bread. Wine or ale poured ceaselessly, causing me to ask for some tea from a midwife among my warriors. Lord Drake was more often snoring than singing, though his wife seemed to be having a gay time, telling all her friends about how good a match I was for her son while tossing coins at the lute player and even a couple at the closest wounded women lying on cots. The injured warriors looked a little mortified, seeing that they were being treated like street beggars, but they put the coins in their pocket, nonetheless.

I stood, inspiring quiet. "Let us swear that any wounded soldier who can no longer ride or march into battle, be given night watch duty in our castles, or positions in our stables and kitchens, such that they need only sit or do as they are capable, but otherwise earn their keep. North Farstand should have few beggars in the streets, as is so common after a war."

"An excellent idea!" Sir Esaudrin yelled. He'd just arrived. He came marching in while still wearing some of his battle armor. Next I recognized Sir Lindie and Sir Carling, arm in arm, as if champions. Sir Casar ran in while laughing. Champions they were too, for their charges upon the enemy knights at Norfaton had been masterful and crushing to Sir Janis's forces. Now we all could tell that the banquet was sure to go well into the night, full of tales of adventures in the west, as I felt sure we'd swept the country of lingering Farstand forces.

"Hey, Chamberlain! You might want to stand by the door and do some serious announcing," the jubilant Sir Esaudrin declared. Sir Lindie patted the chamberlain on the back, sending him in the right direction, though while coughing from the blow.

The man returned to the door just in time. "May I present, the great lord and knight, Sir Daren Drake!"

Just like that, the man stood before me. He'd taken off the top half of his mighty armor. Both legs were encased in shining metal though, and he was yanking on the last mesh glove, showing some haste. It fell to the floor in a clatter. His under-tunic appeared plain, course and stained, suggesting long days in the saddle. Also, it suggested his mighty muscles.

I came around the table.

He saw me, stopped, then took a few steps as well.

Every man and woman in the place fell silent, including a minstrel who had been in the midst of a particularly beautiful ballad.

Once we came close, I stopped and fell on one knee to the first man I'd bowed to since murdering the first Duke of Dorne. As well, all the nobles within the halls of Norfaton knew that I'd never bowed to Lord Lacellor and had made a point of my rudeness on several occasions.

He too knelt. While looking at me without ceasing. We had conquered each other in equal measure, I suppose.

So, there, with the mighty and magical sword of the Goddess beside us, I prayed thanks for the dowry my father could never imagine.

Gary is the author of several short stories and the novel *Zombies in Our Hometown*. He is one of the founding members of the Ohio Writers and North Columbus Fantasy/Sci-Fi writer's groups and is a longstanding member of the prestigious Columbus Writing Workshop. Gary has a BFA from the Columbus College of Art and Design, teaching certification from Otterbein College, an MBA from the Ohio State University.

VISIT THE LOCONEAL BLOG AT

www.loconeal.com

Breaking News
Forthcoming Releases
Links to Author Sites
Loconeal Events

www.ingramcontent.com/pod-product-compliance
Lightning Source LLC
Chambersburg PA
CBHW032025240626
47154CB00003B/789